A PLUNDER OF SOULS

ETHAN KAILLE NOVELS BY D. B. JACKSON
FROM TOR BOOKS

Thieftaker
Thieves' Quarry
A Plunder of Souls

A PLUNDER OF SOULS

D. B. Jackson

A TOM DOHERTY ASSOCIATES BOOK

NEW YORK

A PLUNDER OF SOULS

Map reproduction courtesy of the Norman B. Leventhal Map Center
at the Boston Public Library

Designed by Heather Saunders

A Tor Book
Published by Tom Doherty Associates, LLC
175 Fifth Avenue
New York, NY 10010

www.tor-forge.com

Tor® is a registered trademark of Tom Doherty Associates, LLC.

The Library of Congress Cataloging-in-Publication Data
is available upon request.

ISBN 978-0-7653-3818-1 (hardcover)
ISBN 978-1-4668-4078-2 (e-book)

Tor books may be purchased for educational, business, or promotional use.
For information on bulk purchases, please contact Macmillan Corporate
and Premium Sales Department at 1-800-221-7945, extension 5442,
or write specialmarkets@macmillan.com.

First Edition: July 2014

Printed in the United States of America

0 9 8 7 6 5 4 3 2 1

For Faith Hunter and Misty Massey
Colleagues, friends, kindred spirits

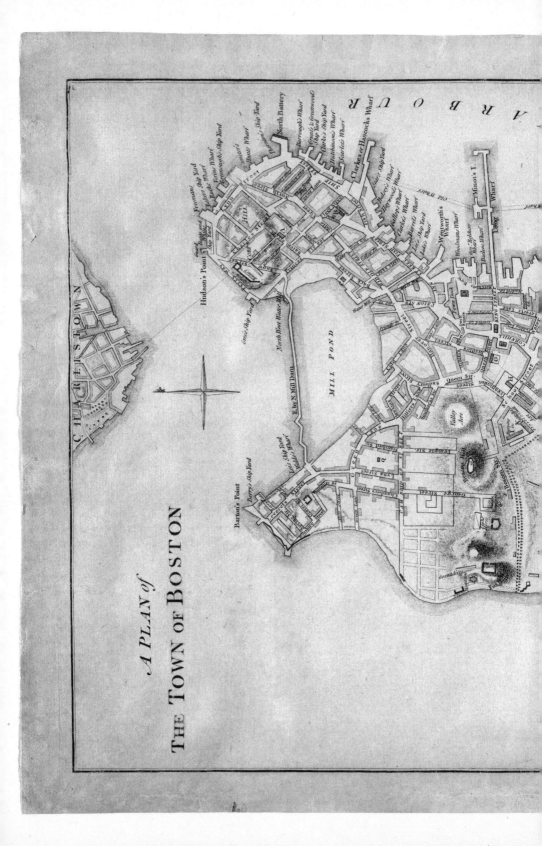

A PLAN of
THE TOWN OF BOSTON

CHARLESTOWN

HARBOUR

MILL POND

Barton's Point

Hudson's Point

North Battery

Clarke's or Hancock's Wharf

Long Wharf

Minot's T.

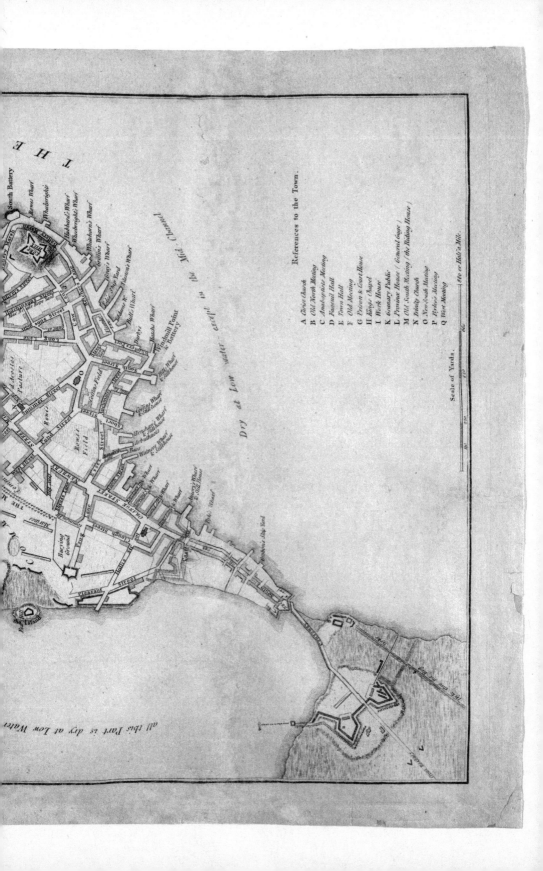

References to the Town.

A First Church
B Old North Meeting
C Anabaptist Meeting
D Faneuil Hall
E Town Hall
F Old Meeting
G Prison & Court House
H Kings Chapel
I Work House
K Granary Public
L Province House (General Gage)
M Old South Meeting (the Riding House)
N Trinity Church
O New-South Meeting
P Hollis's Meeting
Q West Meeting

Scale of Yards.

440 220 110

660

80 or Half a Mile.

A PLUNDER OF SOULS

Chapter
ONE

Boston, Province of Massachusetts Bay,
July 13, 1769

*E*than Kaille knew that he was followed. Like a fox running before hounds, he sensed Sephira Pryce's toughs bearing down on him, snarling like curs, determined to rob him of spoils he had claimed as his own.

Even as the men closed on him, he himself pursued a thief who had stolen a pair of ivory-handled dueling pistols from a wealthy attorney in the South End. His quarry, Peter Salter, led him out along Boston's Neck, the narrow strip of land that connected the city to the causeway across Roxbury Flats. British regulars had established a guard post at the town gate, and so before reaching the end of the Neck the young thief turned off of Orange Street to cut across the barren leas that fronted the flats. Ethan could see the pup ahead of him, wading through the grasses.

The western horizon still glowed with the dying light of another sweltering summer day, and a thin haze shrouded the quarter moon and obscured all but the brightest stars in a darkening sky. Not a breath of wind stirred the humid air, heavy with the sour stink of tidal mud; even with the sun down, the heat remained unabated. The city itself seemed to be in the throes of ague.

Ethan's sweat-soaked linen shirt clung to his skin, and his waistcoat, also darkened with sweat, felt leaden. His usual limp grew more pronounced with each step he took, the pain radiating up his leg into his groin. He hoped that the sound of his uneven gait wouldn't alert Salter to his pursuit, or allow Sephira's men to locate him too soon.

If not for the concealment spell Ethan had cast, making himself invisible to all, Sephira's toughs might have spotted him from a distance, and Salter would have needed only to glance back to see him. Still, Pryce's men dogged him, whether directed by his tracks or by Sephira's uncanny knowledge of all that he did, Ethan could not say.

Ahead, the young thief slowed, then halted. He surveyed the ground before him, turning a slow circle. After a few seconds of this he let out a soft cry and strode forward with greater certainty, taking three or four steps before stopping again and dropping to his knees.

Ethan crept after him, placing his feet with the care of a deer hunter, and drawing his blade with a whisper of steel against leather. He could barely see Salter, who was hunched over, no doubt digging up the goods he had stolen. The pup was of average height and build—much like Ethan—but he had a reputation as an accomplished street fighter. If Ethan could avoid a fight he would. He knew, though, that the chances of this were slim.

He continued to ease toward the man, but as he drew within a few yards, his bad foot caught on a clump of grass and he stumbled. He managed not to fall, but at the sound Salter leapt to his feet.

"Who's there?" he called, brandishing a flintlock pistol.

Ethan cursed under his breath. Since the beginning of the city's occupation by British troops the previous autumn, it seemed that every man in Boston had taken to carrying a firearm. Every man but him. He scanned the ground at his feet and thought he could see a rock or clump of dirt just in front of him. He squatted, wrapped his fist around what turned out to be a stone, and tossed it a few feet to his left.

It rustled the grass and landed with a low *thump*. Salter pivoted with lightning speed and fired off a blind shot. The report of the pistol echoed across the Neck.

Seeing no one there, the pup blinked once and let the hand holding his weapon drop to his side. Before the thief could do more, Ethan launched himself at him, covering the distance between them in three quick strides and driving his shoulder into Salter's gut. As they toppled to the ground, the pup flailed at him, using the butt of his pistol as a cudgel against Ethan's back. But Ethan had the advantage. With Salter pinned to the ground beneath him, he hammered his fist into the man's jaw once, and a second time. A third blow left the pup addled and unable to fight back.

Ethan rolled off of him and flexed his right hand. His knuckles ached. He took Salter's pistol, which lay on the ground beside them, and tossed it beyond the lad's reach. The weapon would have to be reloaded before it could be fired a second time, but Ethan didn't wish to be hit with it again. He picked up his tricorn hat, brushed a bit of dirt off of it, and set it back on his head. Seeing that a thin trickle of blood ran from Salter's mouth over his chin, Ethan whispered a spell.

"Fini velamentum ex cruore evocatum." End concealment, conjured from blood.

His spell thrummed in the ground beneath him, deep and resonant, and the air around them sang with power. A ghost appeared beside him, like a flame suddenly igniting atop a candle. The spirit, which glowed with the deep russet hue of a newly risen moon, was the shade of an old warrior. He was dressed in chain mail, his tabard emblazoned with the leopards of the ancient Plantagenet kings, his expression as hard and cold as a sword blade. Ethan called the ghost Uncle Reg, after his mother's waspish brother, though he didn't know for certain where in his family tree the man would have been located when he lived. So far as Ethan knew, his name wasn't actually Reg, either.

The ghost was a guardian of the power-laden realm between the world of the living and the domain of the dead. Without him, Ethan could not conjure. Reg regarded Ethan with bright, gleaming eyes, appearing annoyed at having been disturbed from whatever it was he did when Ethan did not conjure. Seconds later, he faded from view.

As the concealment spell Ethan had cast wore off, Salter stirred. He squeezed his eyes shut, opened them again. After a few seconds he tried to push himself up, but Ethan laid the edge of his blade against the pup's throat. Salter stiffened, his eyes going wide.

"Easy, lad. You wouldn't want my hand to slip."

"Who are you?" the pup asked, staring up at him.

"My name is Ethan Kaille. I was hired by Andrew Ellis to retrieve the dueling pistols you pinched from his home."

"I didn't—"

Ethan pressed the knife against Salter's neck and shook his head. "Don't lie to me, lad. I haven't much time, and I've even less patience."

Salter swallowed.

"You've buried the pistols here, isn't that right?"

The pup hesitated before nodding.

"You intended to sell them tonight? At the Crow's Nest, perhaps?"

"How did you—?"

"It's not exactly a new approach to thieving."

Salter scowled. "Well, it works for me."

"You mean it has worked, up until now."

The scowl remained on the pup's face, but he said nothing.

"You're in a bit of trouble, Peter."

"From you?" Salter asked, sounding incredulous despite the knife at his throat.

"Aye, from me. And also from Sephira Pryce. She and her men are on their way here now."

At that, the thief tried to sit up once more. Ethan pushed him back down and tapped the edge of his blade against Salter's throat.

"For now at least," he said, "you still have more to fear from me than from her."

"But if she finds me, she'll kill me."

"She might. I can protect you, but I'll need some help in return."

Salter laughed, high and desperate. "How can you protect me from Pryce? I've yet to meet anyone who's a match for her and her men."

"You'd be surprised," Ethan said. "I've dealt with Sephira for many years, and she hasn't killed me yet." He didn't bother to mention that several years earlier she had killed one thief Ethan tried to protect, or that just the previous fall one of her men had slit the throat of another, though Ethan managed to save this second man's life. "Now, listen to me. If we work together, you'll survive the night, and I'll be paid what I'm owed by Mister Ellis."

"And what about the pistols I pinched?" Salter asked.

"Those have been forfeit from the moment I learned your name."

The pup's mouth twisted sourly. "So, you're a thieftaker, too?"

"Aye."

Salter narrowed his eyes. "Where did you come from, Kaille? To-night, I mean. I didn't see you before; not until I came to."

Ethan glanced toward the spot where Salter had been digging. "What are the pistols in?" he asked. "A box?"

Salter continued to stare at him. "I've heard of your kind," he said, his voice hushed. "You're a witch, aren't you? That's how you crept up on me, and how you managed to knock me down without getting yourself shot."

Conjurers didn't think of themselves as witches. Witchcraft was the stuff of myth and nightmare, a term used by those who possessed no spellmaking abilities to explain powers they didn't understand. Conjuring, on the other hand, was real. Nevertheless, the better part of a century after the tragic executions of twenty men and women in nearby Salem, so-called witches were still put to death in the Province of Massachusetts Bay. Ethan had hoped to finish this encounter without having to admit to Salter that he was a conjurer—a speller, as his kind were known in the streets of Boston.

"What are the pistols in, Peter?" he asked, hoping to change the subject. He should have known that wouldn't work.

"I'd wager Miss Pryce would be interested to know that about you. It might be worth some money . . ." He trailed off, his newfound confidence wilting at the sound of Ethan's laughter.

"She knows, lad. How do you think I've survived as her rival all these years? How do you think you're going to survive the night?" He paused, allowing the words to sink in. "Now, the pistols?"

Salter didn't respond at first, and Ethan had to bite down on his tongue to keep from hurrying him. A year ago he wouldn't have feared a confrontation with Sephira. Yes, she was deadly, not to mention brilliant and beautiful. But he was far from defenseless. He could cut his arm to draw blood for conjurings, or he could use the grass growing around them to fuel spell after spell. Sephira's men were as dangerous with their fists as they were with blades and pistols, but Ethan's spellmaking was more than a match for them.

In the past year, however, Sephira had added a conjurer to her retinue of toughs. The man, a Portuguese spellmaker named Gaspar Mariz, had claimed Ethan as a friend after Ethan saved his life. But he still worked for Sephira, and Ethan had no doubt that he would follow any orders she gave him. With a conjurer in Sephira's employ, Ethan's one advantage over the Empress of the South End was gone.

Ethan heard voices coming from the direction of Orange Street. He gazed into the darkness for a second before facing Salter again. "Now, Peter. The pistols."

"They're in a sack," the thief finally said. "Burlap."

Ethan nodded. "Good. Quickly then, here's what we have to do."

He explained his plan, making every effort to be succinct.

For several moments after he had finished, Salter gaped at him. "That might be the most idiotic thing I've ever heard," the lad said.

"Aye, but it will work."

"All right," Salter said. "Let me up and I'll retrieve the pistols."

Ethan read a different intent in the pup's eyes and tone of voice.

"You do that, lad. And remember as you dig that with my . . . my witchery, I can turn you into a human torch with no more than a thought."

Salter licked his lips and nodded, the defiance Ethan had seen in his eyes vanishing as quickly as it had come.

Ethan removed his knife from the lad's throat and watched, wary and alert, as Salter resumed his digging and retrieved the burlap sack.

Sooner than Ethan would have thought possible, Sephira and her men emerged from the gloaming. She led them, and notwithstanding the dim light, Ethan could see that she looked as lovely as ever. Black curls cascaded down her back and framed a face that was as flawless as it was deceitful. She wore her usual attire: black breeches, a white silk shirt opened at the neck, and a waistcoat that hugged her curves like a zealous lover. Behind her strode Nigel, yellow-haired with a long, horselike face; Nap, dark-eyed, lithe, watchful; Gordon, hulking, ginger-haired, and homely; and Afton, as huge and ugly as Gordon. Mariz brought up the rear, appearing tiny beside the others, a knife poised over his bared forearm should he need to cut himself for a conjuring.

Nigel and Nap held pistols and kept them aimed at Ethan.

"Whatever you're doing, stop it," Sephira said, a note of command in her throaty voice.

Salter darted a nervous gaze Ethan's way.

Sephira halted a few paces short of the hole Salter had managed to dig. "So good to see you again, Ethan."

"I wish I could say the same."

She pouted. "I would have thought you were expecting me. You know how I feel about you working for men as wealthy as Ellis."

"Aye, and you know how little I care."

Her expression hardened and she turned to Salter. "I take it this is our thief?"

The pup said nothing.

"Peter Salter," Ethan said. "He was just digging up the pistols for me."

Sephira's smile was dazzling. "I think you mean to say he was digging them up for me."

Ethan glared at her. "Ellis hired me, Sephira. That may nettle, but it's the truth."

"Yes, and you know as well as I how little that truth is worth. When I return the pistols to him, he won't care who he hired. He'll pay me the balance of your fee—no doubt less than my services would have commanded, but I'm sure a substantial amount nevertheless—and he won't give you a second thought." She reached out her hand toward Salter and nodded toward the mud-stained sack he held. "Give me that."

Salter looked at Ethan again.

Ethan grabbed the sack from him. "These are mine to give to Ellis. And that payment will be mine as well."

"I don't think so," Sephira said, her tone glacial. "Nigel."

Nigel and Nap turned their weapons on Salter. The thief stumbled back a step.

"Give me the pistols, Ethan, or he dies."

Ethan drew his knife once more. Mariz shook his head, his own blade still hovering over his arm.

"Do not try it, Kaille," the conjurer said, the words thick with his accent.

Sephira smiled again. "You see, Ethan? Even your witchery isn't enough to save you anymore." Her expression turned stony. "My patience has limits. Give them to me."

Reluctantly, Ethan stepped forward and handed her the sack, her cool hand brushing his.

"Very good," she purred.

"There's enough grass around us for me to kill every one of you,

Sephira," Ethan said, his voice tight. "You've got what you wanted. Now leave."

"Salter—"

Ethan shook his head. "You're not to touch him."

"Ellis won't be happy."

"I don't give a damn."

She smirked. "You're too tenderhearted for your own good. You know that, don't you?"

"Just go," he said.

She continued to eye him, and Ethan wondered if she would make an attempt on the pup's life, or on Ethan's. But at last she nodded once to her men, and started to lead them away.

"My thanks, Ethan," she said, holding up the burlap sack, but not bothering to look back at him. "It's always a pleasure to do business with you."

Ethan didn't deign to answer. He and Salter watched as she and the toughs receded into the darkness. Only when they were beyond hearing did Ethan say, "That was well done, lad."

"What do we do now?" Salter asked. "Before long, she'll look in that sack and realize what you've done."

Ethan retrieved Mr. Ellis's dueling pistols from where they lay in the hole, brushing off the dirt and grass with which he and Salter had covered them in their haste. As an afterthought, he also retrieved Salter's weapon.

"That's mine," the pup said.

"It was." Ethan glanced back to make certain Sephira hadn't decided to come back and kill them both after all. "Sephira is my problem, Peter. You're to leave Boston, never to return."

"But Boston is—"

"Your home," Ethan finished for him. He had heard similar protests from thieves in the past. He preferred to let them go free when he could. He had spent too many years as a convict to take lightly the notion of sending a young man to prison over a few baubles. "Aye, I'm sure it is," he said. "But you forfeited your right to remain here when you decided to do your thieving in the home of a wealthy man. Either you leave, or I'll place you in the custody of Sheriff Greenleaf. He's likely to be far less gentle with you than I've been. Or, if you like, I can leave you to Sephira and her men. As you say, it won't be long before she realizes that she's carrying your dirt-filled shoes instead of these ivory-handled pistols."

"Can I go back to my room and gather my things?" the pup asked. "Can I try to find another pair of shoes?"

"You can. But I assure you, Sephira knows where you live."

"How? Why? She doesn't know anything about me, at least she didn't before tonight."

Ethan sympathized with the pup. How many times had Sephira bested him by somehow knowing his every movement, his constant whereabouts? "Believe me, I understand. But she knows now who you are, and your room will be the first place she looks for you."

Salter's expression curdled. "So, I'm supposed to walk out of the city and across the causeway wearing nothing on my feet?"

Ethan grinned. "Be glad I caught you in July rather than January."

The pup didn't appear to find much humor in this. He nodded toward the pistols. "How much is he paying you to retrieve those?"

"Three pounds," Ethan said.

"I could have sold them for twice as much. Maybe more."

"Aye," Ethan said. "I'm sure you could have." After a moment's consideration, he tossed Salter's pistol to the lad before turning away and starting the long walk back to the home of Andrew Ellis. "But," he called over his shoulder, "they're not yours to sell."

Chapter
Two

*U*nfortunately for Ethan, Andrew Ellis's estate on Winter Street stood almost within sight of Sephira's mansion, which was located at the south end of Summer Street. Ethan had known since the day he took on this inquiry that it would be even harder than usual to keep Sephira from interfering with his search for the pistols, simply by dint of how close she lived to the client. But still—whether out of bravery or foolishness he couldn't say for sure—he had accepted the job anyway.

He made his way from the Neck along the unpaved lane that fronted Boston's Common, rather than following Orange Street back toward the South End. This allowed him to approach Ellis's house from the west, rather than the east. If Sephira and her toughs were searching for him, he would see them coming.

As he walked he felt the power of a spell hum in the road. At first he wondered if it was Mariz, perhaps casting a finding spell in an attempt to locate him. But in the next instant he realized the spell had come from farther off. If he had to guess, he would have said it came from the South End waterfront. He wondered if old Gavin Black, a sea captain and conjurer who had lived in the city for years, was casting spells. Or if perhaps there was a new conjurer in Boston. His eyes trained eastward, he walked on.

The Ellis house, an imposing brick structure with a semicircular white portico in front, and a sloping lawn bounded by rich gardens, stood on the north side of Winter, halfway between the Common and Marlborough Street. Candlelight glowed in the windows; a warm breeze rustled the leaves of large elms growing in the yard, and whip-poor-wills sang overhead. Ethan followed a flagstone path to the door, glancing toward the street, and listening for Sephira and her men. Upon reaching the door, he rapped once with the brass lion's-head knocker. After a short wait, the door opened to reveal an African servant wearing a white silk shirt and cravat, pale blue breeches, and a matching waist-coat.

The man regarded him with an expression that bespoke, in equal parts, indifference and disapproval. It occurred to Ethan that his clothes must look rumpled and filthy from his struggle with Salter, although as usual, the thought came to him too late to rectify the matter.

"Ethan Kaille to see Mister Ellis," he said, hoping he sounded more dignified than he appeared.

The servant looked him up and down once more. "A moment please." He started to walk away, but stopped and glanced at Ethan again, seeming concerned that Ethan might enter the house. Or rob it. "Wait here," he said, and shut the door.

Ethan did not have to wait long. The door opened a second time, revealing the bulky figure of Andrew Ellis. He was dressed in a green silk suit with matching coat, breeches, and waistcoat—a ditto suit, as such sets were known. A pair of spectacles sat perched on his crooked nose. His hair was powdered and pulled back in a plait, accentuating his steep forehead and dark, wide-set eyes.

"Mister Kaille," he said, sounding surprised to see him. "To what do I—?"

Ethan held up the dueling pistols, one in each hand.

A smile split the attorney's face. "You've found them!"

"Aye, sir."

Ellis took the weapons from him and started to walk back into the house, examining the pistols as he did. "Come in, come in," he said over his shoulder, almost as an afterthought.

Ethan removed his hat, closed the door, and followed his client through the foyer and a large sitting room into a smaller study, the walls of which were lined with bookshelves. The house smelled of bayberry—no spermaceti candles for a man of Ellis's means—and some kind of savory stew. The aroma made Ethan's stomach rumble.

Ellis stopped in front of a writing desk on which burned an oil lamp, and eyed his weapons more closely. He brushed a small clump of dirt from one of the barrels, but then straightened and nodded.

"Well, these seem to have come through their ordeal relatively well." Facing Ethan once more, he asked, "What can you tell me about the thief?"

"His name is Peter Salter, sir."

"Salter," Ellis repeated. "I've never heard of him."

"I would have been surprised if you had, sir. He's a street tough, a pup with little sense and even less ambition. But he won't trouble you again."

He hoped this would satisfy Ellis. He assumed that, like most of the men who hired him, the attorney would want to see the thief dealt with harshly. Ethan felt certain that Salter would leave Boston rather than risk Sephira's wrath or Sheriff Greenleaf's hard justice. He was less sure that the pup would manage to stay out of trouble in whatever town he inhabited next, but that was not his concern. He had endured nearly fourteen years as a convict, and he had seen what Sephira did to the thieves who crossed her path. Salter was a fool and a ruffian; he was often in the streets on Pope's Day, brawling with the North End gangs. But Ethan couldn't bring himself to destroy the pup's life over a pair of dueling pistols. He hoped Salter wouldn't be so careless as to allow Sephira and her men to find him.

"Very well," Ellis said. He pulled a small pouch from a drawer in his desk. "I paid you fifteen shillings when I hired you. I believe that leaves me owing you two pounds and five."

Ethan nodded. "Aye, that's my recollection as well."

The attorney counted out the coins, piling them carefully on the desk. When he finished, rather than picking up the coins and handing them to Ethan, he backed away from the desk, said, "There you are, Mister Kaille," and gestured for Ethan to take them himself.

Ethan thought this odd, to say the least. But after a moment's hesitation, he crossed to the desk. "Thank you, sir," he said, taking his payment and pocketing the money without bothering to count it.

"I hope that I will not require the services of a thieftaker in the future," Ellis said, facing Ethan. "Once was quite enough." A hint of amusement flickered in his features. "But if ever I should, I will not hesitate to engage you again."

"I'm grateful to you, sir."

Ellis led him from the study, back toward the front foyer. "Of course. If the opportunity arises, I'll recommend you to my friends and colleagues as well."

They reached the door, and Ellis pulled it open. Ethan proffered a hand, but the attorney looked down at it, wrinkling his nose. "I think not, Mister Kaille. Forgive me. But with the smallpox broken out in the city, I feel it best that we part with but a civil word."

Ethan dropped his hand. "I understand, sir. In that case I'll wish you a good evening and be on my way."

He replaced his hat and started down the path back toward Winter Street.

"You think me overly cautious," Ellis called to him.

Ethan stopped, turned. "No, sir. But I fear that even such precautions as these won't save us from infection if this outbreak is anything like those of sixty-one or sixty-four."

Ellis walked out onto the portico, eyes wide with alarm. "Do you think it will be as bad as that?"

"I don't know," Ethan said.

"I pray it won't."

"We all do, sir. Good night." Ethan started away again.

"Good night, Mister Kaille."

He walked some distance with his head down, his eyes fixed on the street. The only light came from the moon and stars overhead, and from candles burning inside the homes that lined the lane.

So, had it not been for the soft scrape of a boot on cobblestone, Ethan would have had no warning at all. As it was, he barely had time to grab for his blade and push up his sleeve before hearing several sets of footsteps converging on him. *Sephira's men,* he had time to think. *Mariz will be with them.*

He had but an instant to decide whether he was in greater danger from the conjurer or from Nigel, Nap, and the other toughs. He slashed at his arm.

"*Tegimen ex cruore evocatum,*" he said under his breath. Warding, conjured from blood. The conjuring rumbled in the cobblestones; his feet tingled with it. Uncle Reg winked into view next to him, his bright eyes avid, his brow furrowed.

Rough, powerful hands took hold of him, pinning his arms to his sides. One of Sephira's men tore his blade from his grasp. He struggled to break free and retrieve it, but to no avail. Nigel loomed before him, huge, teeth bared in a harsh grin. The tough hit him in the jaw, his fist as solid and heavy as a brick. Ethan tasted blood; his vision blurred.

Ignis ex cruore evocatus! Fire, conjured from blood! He recited the conjuring in his mind, using the blood in his mouth to fuel the spell. Power pulsed a second time.

Nigel staggered back, as did Gordon and Afton, who had been holding his arms and now lost their grip on him. But no flames appeared.

"They are warded, Kaille," Mariz said from the darkness. "We all are."

"What do you want, Sephira?" Ethan asked, ignoring the other conjurer.

"I want those pistols," she said. "I wasn't amused by your little deception."

"Ellis has his pistols."

"In which case, you have his money. I'll take that, instead."

Ethan shook his head. "I don't think you will."

In spite of himself, Ethan had always enjoyed the sound of Sephira's laughter. It was throaty, like her voice, and unrestrained. Too often, though, it was directed at him. As it was now.

"How do you propose to stop us?" Sephira asked. "Mariz has rendered your magick harmless. Do you honestly believe you can fight off all of my men?"

She had a point.

"So much effort for two pounds," Ethan said, stalling now, racking his brain for some way to escape with his nose unbroken and his hard-earned coin still in his pocket. "One would think you have one foot in the Almshouse."

"The money is of no concern. Surely you understand that, Ethan. But I don't want you thinking that you can get away with such antics in the future. Shoes for pistols? You should know better."

Ethan opened his mouth to respond, but as he did, he saw something flash in front of him and off a bit to the right. It took him a second to realize that it was one of the lenses of Mariz's spectacles catching the candle glow from a nearby house.

An idea came to him.

"Are you listening to me?" Sephira asked, sounding angry.

"Of course I am. What was it you said?"

He bit down hard on his cheek, drawing blood again.

Velamentum ex cruore evocatum, he recited silently. Concealment, conjured from blood.

The spell thrummed, like the string of a harp. Reg grinned at Ethan.

"What did you do, Kaille?" asked Mariz, who, as the lone conjurer among Sephira's men, was the one person other than Ethan who could have felt the spell.

But by the time the words crossed Mariz's lips, Ethan was already moving. He stooped, grabbed his blade, and while still in a crouch, ran forward past Nigel and straight toward the other conjurer. He kept his shoulder lowered and barreled into the man, knocking him off his feet. Mariz grunted as he sprawled onto the street; his knife clattered across the cobblestones.

Ethan stumbled, but righted himself, a hand holding his hat in place, and ran on. He veered left and right, knowing that his spell would keep Sephira's men from seeing him, but that his footsteps would give them some idea of where he was.

A shot rang out, echoing across the lane. A bullet whistled past, too close for comfort. Reaching Marlborough Street, Ethan turned left. He could hear Sephira's men pursuing him, and already his limp was growing more pronounced, his bad leg screaming. Still he ran, turning off of Marlborough at the next narrow lane and cutting down across Bishop's Alley and into d'Acosta's Pasture, a broad expanse of grazing land. Cows eyed him as he passed, his footfalls now muffled by the grass.

He emerged from the lea onto Joliffe's Lane, and from there followed back streets through the Cornhill section of the city. By the time he drew near to the Dowsing Rod, the tavern on Sudbury Street that he frequented, he felt reasonably sure Sephira and her toughs had broken off their pursuit. Even Sephira would think twice before stepping into a crowded tavern and hauling Ethan off for a beating. He wasn't so foolish as to think that his escape would settle matters in any way; Sephira had a good memory and held tight to her grudges. But for tonight, at least, he was safe.

He grinned in the darkness. Victories over Sephira were about as rare as audiences with His Majesty the King; he wanted to savor this one. He had money in his pocket, and his spirits were so high that not even the sight of British regulars patrolling the streets of the city was enough to dampen them.

Nevertheless, as he passed the regulars, still concealed by his conjuring, he slowed, so as not to give himself away with a false step or the jangling of the coins in his pocket. He turned a corner and halted, the scene before him like cold water on his mood.

A torch burned in a sconce mounted on one of the houses near the intersection of Hanover and Treamount streets, next door to the Orange Tree tavern and just a stone's throw from the Dowsing Rod. And beside the torch, a red flag rose and fell lazily in the soft breeze blowing in off Boston Harbor. A man stood outside the house, leaning against one of the iron posts that lined the street.

The red uniforms of the soldiers hadn't darkened Ethan's mood, but this red flag was a different matter. Smallpox. That was what it signified. The distemper had come to this residence, and those inside had chosen to remain in their home rather than be removed to the hospital in New Boston.

The flag was a warning, a symbol of infection, of quarantine. *Within this house dwells pestilence,* it said. *Fever, scarring, perhaps even death. These reside here now. Enter at your own risk.* And if the red cloth wasn't warning enough, the guard out front was there to keep away the concerned and the curious. No one could enter or leave, save a physician.

The flag had been up for several days now, but it still made Ethan's blood turn cold each time he saw it. He feared for Kannice Lester, who owned the Dowsing Rod, and who had been his lover for more than five years. He feared for those who frequented her tavern and who worked for her. And yes, he feared for himself. Smallpox was no trifle. The outbreak of 1764 had killed well over a hundred people, and those who were sickened but survived bore terrible scars on their faces and bodies. The practice of inoculating people against the distemper had proved somewhat effective, but it was an expensive process, one that few other than Boston's wealthiest families could afford. And many remained leery of the science cited by physicians; using the disease to fight the disease seemed to make little sense. Despite advances in controlling the distemper, every person in the city lived in fear of another epidemic. Many fled to the countryside at the first report of an outbreak. He had known people to refuse newspapers, food, and other goods, out of fear that they carried infection. Andrew Ellis's unwillingness to shake his hand, or even place coins in his palm, was more typical than he cared to admit. If more red flags appeared in the city, panic would set in.

Sobered, Ethan continued on to the tavern. Kannice, he knew, would be careful. But what if one or more of her patrons was less vigilant? If he had known a spell to ward Kannice and himself against the distemper, he would have cast it, but he wasn't sure such conjurings even existed.

Reaching the Dowser, he slipped into a narrow alley between two buildings. There he cut himself again and removed the concealment spell. Once he could be seen, he returned to the main avenue and entered the tavern.

Upon stepping inside, he was greeted by the familiar din of laughter and conversations, and a melange of aromas: musty ale and savory stew, pipe smoke and freshly baked bread, and underlying it all, the faint, pungent smell of dozens of spermaceti candles. In spite of the apprehension that had gripped him upon seeing the red flag, he smiled, only to wince at the pain in his jaw from where Nigel had hit him. In his desperation to get away from Sephira, he had forgotten to heal himself. He considered retreating to the alley to cast another spell, but even as the thought came to him, the Dowsing Rod's massive barkeep, Kelf Fingarin, caught his eye, grinned, and held up an empty tankard, a question in his eyes.

He would heal himself later. He nodded and crossed to the bar.

"Good evenin', Ethan," said Kelf, speaking so quickly that his words ran together into what would sound to most like an incomprehensible jumble.

"Well met, Kelf." Ethan placed a half shilling on the bar as the barman set the tankard—now full—in front of him.

"That's the Kent pale."

"My thanks."

"Diver's in his usual spot," Kelf said. He gestured toward the kitchen. "And Kannice is in back, workin' on another batch of the chowder."

Ethan sipped his ale. "I'll be with Diver. She'll find me eventually. She always does."

Kelf winked, already grabbing a tankard for another patron.

Ethan wended his way to the back of the great room, slipping past knots of wharfmen and laborers, and tables crowded with men drinking Madeira wine and eating oysters. A few people looked up as he went by; fewer still met his glance or offered any sort of greeting.

More than twenty years ago, he had been convicted of taking part in the *Ruby Blade* mutiny and sent to the island of Barbados to toil on a sugar plantation. The conditions had been brutal: unbearable heat, food that was barely edible, sleeping quarters that were little more than jail cells crowded with vermin-infested pallets. A stray blow from another prisoner's cane knife wounded his left foot; the resulting infection nearly killed him. The plantation surgeons removed three of his toes, and thus saved his life. But that was the least of what he lost during his fourteen years as a convict. His pride, his first and greatest love, the future he once had imagined for himself: all of this and more he left in the cane fields.

After enduring those conditions for fourteen years, he earned his freedom, returning to Boston in the spring of 1760. He soon established himself as a thieftaker of some minor renown here in the city. But those who remembered the *Ruby Blade* affair and Ethan's role in it still regarded him with suspicion. Others who were too young to know anything of the *Blade* took their cues from those around them. And still others, who cared not a whit about Ethan's past as a mutineer, might have heard rumors of his conjuring talents, and so shunned him because he was a "witch."

Whatever the reason, Ethan had few friends here in the Dowser, and not many more beyond its walls. On the other hand, those he did consider his friends, he trusted with his life.

Among them, Diver—Devren Jervis—was the one who had known him longest. Diver was younger than Ethan by several years and though he was now in his early thirties, he still looked as youthful as he had nine years before, when Ethan returned to Boston from the Caribbean and almost immediately ran into Diver on Long Wharf.

At first, Ethan hadn't recognized his young friend; Diver had been but a boy when Ethan was convicted. But Diver recognized him right off, and greeted him as he might a blood brother. For Ethan, it was one of the few bright moments in an otherwise difficult transition back to life as a free man.

With his unruly dark hair, his dark eyes, and a roguish smile, Diver was seldom without a girl on his arm. For years it had seemed to Ethan that it was a different girl every fortnight. But for many months now, since the previous autumn, Diver had been with the same woman: Deborah Crane, an attractive redhead who lived in Cornhill, near Diver's room on Pudding Lane. The two of them sat together at a small table near the back wall of the Dowser. Seeing them engrossed in conversation, their eyes locked, their heads close together, her hand in his, Ethan faltered.

He found another empty table, also at the rear of the room, and sat with his back to the wall, looking out over the tavern and sipping his ale. A short while later, Kelf walked back into the kitchen and emerged again with Kannice, an enormous tureen of fish stew, or chowder, as Boston's residents had taken to calling it, held between them. Ethan saw Kelf whisper something to Kannice. She looked up, searching the room. After a few seconds, she spotted him and they shared a smile. Just as quickly, her attention was back on her patrons and their empty bowls. She began to ladle out the chowder, saying something that made the men around her laugh.

Kannice was younger than Ethan by some ten years: a willowy beauty with auburn hair and periwinkle blue eyes. She once had been married, to a man who died of smallpox during the outbreak of 1761. She inherited the Dowsing Rod from him, and though barely more than a girl, managed to transform the tavern from a shabby, run-down haven for petty criminals and whores into a respectable publick house that turned a tidy profit. She had a simple set of rules: Anyone was welcome in the tavern, so long as they refrained from fighting, whoring, or discussing matters that were likely to lead to a brawl. With Kelf behind the bar, implacable, as immense as a mountain, she had little trouble enforcing her decrees, though in truth, Ethan had met few men who would dare defy her and thus earn one of her legendary tongue-lashings. Kannice was as savvy as any merchant in the city, and as clever as Samuel Adams and his fellow Whigs. She also had a sharp wit and could tell stories that would make the most hardened sailor blush to the tips of his ears.

She loved Ethan, and had suggested with ever greater frequency that perhaps the time had come for him to join her in running the Dowser.

"You could live with me," she had said, the last time they discussed the matter, a few nights before. "We would share in the work and the profits, and you wouldn't have to worry anymore about Sephira Pryce and her ruffians."

It was never easy to say no to Kannice, and it was particularly difficult when she was resting on top of him, her smooth skin against his, her silken hair shining with candlelight.

"That's a generous offer," Ethan had said, taking care with his choice of words.

She smiled down at him. "But you're going to refuse it anyway."

"I'm a thieftaker, Kannice. It's what I do."

"Maybe. But you can't do it forever," she said. "Sephira can hire new toughs when the ones she has now grow too old. You're on your own."

"You're saying I'm old?"

She ran her fingers through the hair at his temples, which had long since turned gray. "You're seasoned."

Ethan laughed. "And you have a silver tongue."

"Think about it?" she said, a plea in the words. "For me?"

He kissed her. "I will. For you."

They both knew that he would have done just about anything for her, except he would not marry her—after losing his betrothed when he was imprisoned, he had vowed never to wed—and he could not yet bring himself to give up his work as a thieftaker. Of course he hated contending with Sephira at every turn, and looking over his shoulder for Nigel and her other toughs each time he ventured out into the streets. And it was true: He couldn't do this forever. He would be forty-three in October, and there were mornings when he felt every year in his bones and aching muscles. Odd as it seemed, though, he enjoyed thieftaking. The challenge of each new inquiry, the pursuit of those who had done wrong, even the danger—he found all of it intoxicating. In his heart, he knew that any other profession would bore him.

Kannice glanced up from the bowl she was filling and saw that he still watched her. Her cheeks colored, even as her lips curved upward again. After a moment though, her brow creased and she reached a hand to her jaw. She had noticed the bruising on his face. Ethan mirrored the gesture and gave a small shrug. Kannice shook her head, though with a touch of humor in her eyes.

"Are you trying to avoid us?" Diver's voice.

Ethan turned. Diver and Deborah had halted a pace or two shy of where he sat.

"Not at all," Ethan said. He stood and indicated the empty chairs at his table with an open hand. "Sit. Please."

Deborah took the chair to Ethan's left. Once she was seated, Ethan and Diver sat across from each other.

"I didn't wish to disturb you," Ethan said. "You appeared to be deep in conversation."

She cast a look Diver's way. Diver's face turned red.

"That was kind of you," Deborah said.

And at the same time, Diver said, "We weren't talking about anything important."

They looked at each other. Diver smiled; Deborah didn't.

"You didn't think it was important?" she asked.

Diver's face fell. "I meant it wasn't so important that he couldn't have joined us. Of course it was imp—"

"You tell me if you think this is important, Mister Kaille. Derrey is thinking of asking the selectmen to appoint him as watch on one of the infected houses."

"Pat Daily is doing it," Diver added quickly. "He's working just down the street at the Tyler's place. And Ed Baker is doing it, too. They're making good money at it. Three shillings and four for each of them. That's per day," he said, glancing at Deborah. "I was making less than half that at the wharf. And with these nonimportation agreements in place, a cove can't even make that much."

"Maybe," Deborah said. "But at the wharf you don't run the risk of being infected with smallpox." She faced Ethan, looking very young and very pretty. "Don't you agree, Mister Kaille?"

"It's Ethan," he told her, as he had several times before. "And I'm afraid I can't agree with you entirely. Diver risks infection each time he leaves his room. All of us do."

"But surely he would be in far greater peril were he to stand watch outside a house that had been visited with the distemper. Won't you even agree with that?"

Ethan chanced a brief look at his friend, who sat with his hands folded and resting on the table, his eyes downcast.

"I'm not sure I want to answer, Deborah," he said, meeting her gaze once more. "This is a matter for you and Diver to decide. I've no part in it."

Her expression turned cold. "I see." She cast a glance Diver's way, her lips pressed thin. "In that case, I don't have more to say to either of you. You should do as you please, Derrey. I believe you intended to anyway."

She pushed back from the table and stood. Ethan and Diver both jumped to their feet, but she didn't appear to notice. She walked to the tavern door without a backward glance and strode out into the night.

Diver stared after her, his mouth open in a small *o*. Once the door had closed behind Deborah, he turned to Ethan. "What should I do?"

"You should probably go after her."

"And should I tell her I won't take the job?"

"That's for you to decide. I can't help you."

"I need the money, Ethan. There's little work to be had on the water-front right now."

"I know."

Diver stared at the door, a pained expression on his face. "I'm not very good at this."

Ethan schooled his features. A year ago, this would have been the moment when Diver threw up his hands in frustration and moved on to the next girl. Deborah had changed him, and Ethan was glad. It seemed his friend was finally becoming an adult.

"You're better at it than you think," Ethan said. "Go on. If you don't catch up with her soon, she'll really be angry."

A weak smile flickered across the younger man's face. "Right. Good night."

"Good luck."

Ethan sat again, caught Kelf's eye, and held up a finger. The barman nodded and reached for another tankard.

Long after Kelf brought him the second ale, Ethan continued to sit and gaze out over the throng of customers. The Dowser was more crowded than usual this night, which was surprising with word of the distemper spreading through the city. But at last, as the hour grew late, the crowd began to thin.

Kannice made her way to Ethan's table, her cheeks flushed, wisps of loose hair falling over her forehead. Reaching him, she stooped and kissed him lightly on the lips. Her breath smelled of Irish whiskey, as it often did after a long night in the tavern, and her hair smelled of lavender.

"I see you've managed again to hit someone's fist with your jaw," she said, taking Deborah's seat. She grinned to soften the gibe.

"Aye," Ethan said, smiling as well. "I gave his knuckles quite a beating."

"And who was this unfortunate soul?" Before Ethan could reply, she held up a hand. "No, wait. Let me guess. The yellow-haired one."

"Nigel. Very good."

She scrutinized the bruise, grimacing as she did. "Can I do anything?"

"I'll heal it later."

Kannice took his hand in both of hers. "You know, I was here all night, working. So was Kelf. And neither of us was hit even once."

"Well, obviously you weren't doing it right."

Kannice laughed, throwing her head back.

Ethan dug into his pocket, pulled out the coins Ellis had given him, and placed them on the table in front of her.

Her eyebrows went up.

"My jaw will be fine by morning," Ethan said. "And meanwhile I have this to show for my labors. And my bruises."

"It could have been worse."

"I passed the Tyler house on the way here. The flag is still out, and a man is standing watch on the street—a friend of Diver's, I think. I don't need Sephira and her brutes to make things worse."

"I know that but—"

"Let it be, Kannice."

She nodded, her gaze fixed on their intertwined fingers. "Deborah looked unhappy when she left."

"Aye. Diver wants to ask the selectmen to put him on the watch."

"To guard a quarantined house?" Kannice asked.

"Aye. And she doesn't like the idea."

"I can't say that I blame her."

"It pays well," Ethan said. "And every job carries some risk." She started to object, but he raised a finger, stopping her. "Even running a tavern. There are fewer regulars in the city now, but remember how worried you were when the occupation began. If General Gage had chosen to billet his men in Boston's publick houses, it might have put you out of business."

He saw that she wanted to argue. They both knew, though, that he was right.

"It's not quite the same," she said after a brief silence.

"No, but a man has to make a living."

"I know." She pushed herself up out of her chair. "I've a bit more to do in the kitchen." She canted her head to the side, candlelight in her eyes. "You're staying the night?"

"You don't mind sharing your bed with a bruised old man?"

"Not any more than I did last night."

He grinned. "In that case, I'll stay."

"Good." She started back toward the bar before facing him again. "If you find yourself without anything to do, you can join us in back. There are a few dozen bowls that need cleaning."

He lifted his tankard. "I'll be working on this, I think."

"Aye, I'm sure you will."

Chapter
THREE

*E*than slept fitfully, awakened several times by what he thought were pulses of conjuring power shuddering in the walls of Kannice's tavern. He couldn't tell if the spells were real or if he had dreamed them, but imagined or not, they troubled his sleep. He woke for good early the next day. He had expected to slumber through much of the morning—it had been late when he and Kannice finally went to sleep, and he was exhausted from his recent inquiry. But though he did not feel refreshed when he woke, he could not fall asleep again. He lay still, not wishing to wake Kannice. And his thoughts churned.

For all of his certainty about not wanting to give up thieftaking, he also knew that jobs were harder to come by now than they had been as recently as a year before. The arrival of British troops in the city had frightened away some of Boston's less desirable citizens. And, of course, Sephira had used every tool at her disposal to take the lioness's share of those clients who still required the services of a thieftaker. Despite Ethan's success the previous evening, he knew that his prospects were not good. Before Ellis hired him, he had gone two months without conducting an inquiry. Now that this one was finished, he wondered when he would be hired again.

He could live for some time on the coin Ellis had paid him, but he owed a month's rent to Henry Dall, the cooper from whom he let a room, and would owe him again come the middle of July. He didn't dare express his concerns to Kannice, lest she take this confidence as a sign that he was thinking of leaving Henry's shop to come live and work with her in the Dowser.

It occurred to him that he, too, could earn some coin watching a quarantined house. He couldn't ward himself against smallpox, but if Pat Daily and Ed Baker managed to take on these duties without being afflicted, so could he. Were it not for Diver's determination to secure one of the appointments, Ethan might have tried. But there weren't many watch postings available, and Diver needed the money more than Ethan did. For now, at least.

Work will come, he told himself. *It always does.* The king's army had not driven away every thief in Boston, and Ethan was not willing to concede every client to Sephira. He needed only to remain patient.

On this thought, he swung himself out of bed, taking care to make no noise. He dressed, let himself out of Kannice's room, and descended the stairs to the tavern's great room.

There, he walked back into the kitchen and took some bread and butter from Kannice's larder. He dropped a few pence in the bar till, and took a seat at the nearest table. He was just finishing his piece of bread when Kannice descended the stairs, dressed, her face still puffy with sleep.

"I'm sorry," Ethan said. "I tried to be quiet."

"You were. I just can tell when you're gone. Are you all right?"

"I'm fine. Restless."

She nodded. "I can make you something. There's bacon, or a bit of last night's chowder."

He shook his head. "My thanks, but no."

Kannice narrowed her eyes. "You paid for that, didn't you?"

"Of course."

"Ethan—"

Before she could say more—no doubt about how she didn't like to take his money—there came a knock on the tavern door.

They shared a look.

"Kelf?" Ethan asked.

"It's too early for Kelf."

He thought back on his encounter with Sephira Pryce the night before. It wasn't like her to knock, but again, she was never one to limit herself to doing what was expected. He drew his knife and pushed up his shirt sleeve.

He nodded once to Kannice, and followed as she walked to the door.

"Who's there?" she called.

"Um, Robert, ma'am," came the reply. The voice was that of a boy.

The tension drained from Kannice's face. Ethan kept his knife poised over his forearm, but when she reached for the key, a question in her eyes, he nodded again.

She unlocked the door and pulled it open, revealing a boy in torn breeches and a white linen shirt that was far too small for him. He was alone, and he clutched a piece of folded parchment in one hand.

"I gots a message for Ethan Kaille," the boy said.

Ethan sheathed his blade and pushed down his sleeve before advancing into the daylight.

"I'm Kaille."

"In that case, this is for you, I guess."

Ethan glanced at Kannice and took the parchment. Unfolding it, he saw written in a neat hand,

> *Please come to King's Chapel at your earliest convenience.*
> *—T. Pell*

"It's from Mister Pell," he told Kannice.

"Aye," the boy said, eager. "That's who gave it to me. The minister at the chapel; the young one. He said you'd give me a bit of coin for my trouble."

Kannice looked away, her eyes dancing.

"Did he?" Ethan asked. "Was this before or after he paid you?"

"Oh, aft—" The boy clamped his mouth shut, his face coloring.

"It's all right, lad," Ethan said, laughing now. He fished in his pocket for tuppence. "Here you are."

"My thanks," the boy said, beaming as he pocketed the coin. He started to turn away.

"Wait, boy. Did Mister Pell say anything more?"

"No, sir."

"All right. On your way then."

The boy hurried away.

Ethan pulled the door closed once more.

"I should go without delay. Pell wouldn't send for me if he hadn't need."

"Of course," Kannice said. "Come back later?"

"Gladly." He kissed her cheek and left the tavern.

King's Chapel stood a short distance south of the Dowser, on School Street, just off of Treamount. In order to reach it, Ethan had to walk back past the Orange Tree tavern and the Tyler house with its bright red flag. Daily was out front again, standing watch and looking glum, but unmarked by the distemper. Perhaps Deborah would be reassured.

Though King's Chapel was home to one of the oldest and most influential congregations in Boston, it might well have been the city's least attractive church, at least from without. It had been rebuilt some fifteen years before, its graceful wooden sanctuary enclosed within a new granite exterior. The stone façade was proof against fires, and Boston had seen many in the years since the new exterior was constructed, including the devastating blaze of 1760, which swept through the Cornhill section of the city, destroying hundreds of structures. But the chapel now had a ponderous look that set it apart from the soaring spires and elegant lines of Boston's other churches. Worse, it remained incomplete, with no spire of its own to lessen the severity of its appearance.

Ethan entered the churchyard through a gate near the corner of Treamount and School streets, followed a short path to a set of low stone steps, and walked into the chapel through a pair of thick oaken doors, removing his hat as he did. Inside, in marked contrast to the austere stone exterior, the church was as welcoming and handsome as any in the city. Columns, painted in shades of brown and tan, their crowns intricately carved, supported a high vaulted ceiling. Sunlight streamed into the sanctuary through banks of windows two stories high, reflecting off the polished wood of the boxed pews and the wooden floorboards of the central aisle.

Three men stood in the rounded chancel beyond the church's altar.

One of them was tall and narrow-shouldered, with a sallow complexion and an expression to match. The second was shorter and rounder, with a far more pleasant aspect. Both of these men, Henry Caner, the stouter of the two, who was rector of the chapel, and John Troutbeck, the curate, wore black robes and the stiff white cravats that marked them as ministers. The third man, whom Ethan did not know, was taller than Troutbeck and more rotund than Caner. He wore red breeches and a matching waistcoat, and had bone-white hair that he wore in a long plait.

Neither of the ministers harbored much affection for Ethan. Both viewed him as a servant of Satan, a witch whose use of magick was offensive to God and themselves. Ethan thought they would have been pleased to see him burned at the stake for his sins. Given the opportunity, they might even have thrust the first torches into his pyre. He expected that their large friend would feel much the same way.

Ethan's sister, Bett, and her husband, Geoffrey Brower, an agent of the Customs Board, were members of the King's Chapel congregation. They were no more fond of Ethan than were Caner and Troutbeck. Though the same conjuring blood that flowed through Ethan's veins also flowed through Bett's, long ago she had eschewed spellmaking in favor of piety. She made every effort to conceal her family history, and to deny that she had a brother here in Boston.

The one friend Ethan had in King's Chapel, Trevor Pell, the young minister whose missive had summoned him here, was nowhere to be seen. Ethan wondered if he had been foolish to come, and he thought about leaving the chapel before Caner or Troutbeck noticed him.

"Is that Mister Kaille?"

Would that he had thought to leave a minute earlier.

Mister Caner, who had spoken, was already striding up the aisle in Ethan's direction. Ethan had no choice but to fix a smile on his lips and walk forward to meet the rector.

"Well met, reverend sir," he said.

"And you, Mister Kaille." Caner's mien remained somber, but he had not yet ordered Ethan out of his chapel, which Ethan took as a small victory. He looked back at the altar. "Mister Troutbeck, would you please find Trevor and tell him that Mister Kaille has arrived?"

Troutbeck scowled, but said, "Yes, reverend sir," and descended the marble stairway that led to the chapel's crypts, where Ethan had spent entirely too much time over the past few years. At the same time, the third man walked toward Ethan and the rector with a rolling, lumbering gait.

"Mister Pell will join us in a moment," the rector said, facing Ethan once more. "It was his idea to invite you here, so I prefer to wait for him before we speak of these matters."

Ethan wasn't sure what "matters" Reverend Caner referred to, but for the moment he kept his questions to himself.

"In the meantime," Mister Caner went on, "I would like you to meet Doctor Silvester Gardiner, who is rector's warden here at King's Chapel. Doctor Gardiner, this is Ethan Kaille."

Gardiner stared hard at Ethan, his expression so stern beneath his prominent brow that Ethan felt like a schoolboy caught in the glare of a displeased catechist.

They shook hands, Gardiner's massive paw seeming to swallow Ethan's.

"A pleasure to meet you, Doctor Gardiner."

"I'm grateful to you for coming," the man said, his voice far softer and more mild than Ethan had expected.

"As you might imagine," Caner said, "Doctor Gardiner takes more than a passing interest in these events."

Ethan frowned. "I'm sorry, reverend sir. I'm afraid I don't understand."

"Didn't Mister Pell tell you?"

"No. His message requested that I come here at my earliest convenience. It said nothing more."

Caner clicked his tongue and glanced at the warden. "I see. Well, I think I would prefer that he was with us for this conversation."

"All right," Ethan said, perplexed.

They did not have to wait long. The young minister emerged from the crypts with Troutbeck behind him, struggling to keep pace.

Trevor Pell had not changed at all in the four years Ethan had known him. He was slight, with straight brown hair, bright blue eyes, and a face so youthful that he would have looked more like an altar boy than a minister if not for the robes and cravat that he also wore.

He walked with grim purpose, his expression uncharacteristically somber. "Mister Kaille," he said, stepping past Caner and Gardiner to shake Ethan's hand. "Thank you for heeding my summons so quickly."

"It's good to see you again, Mister Pell."

"Mister Pell," Caner said, "I thought you intended to tell Mister Kaille what has happened. He knows nothing right now."

"Yes, reverend sir," Pell said. "You impressed upon me the need for discretion. I thought you would prefer that the note I sent to Mister Kaille be as vague as possible."

Caner considered this. "I suppose you're right." To Ethan he said, "You'll have to forgive me, Mister Kaille. I have little experience with affairs of this sort. But Mister Pell believes that you can help us, and despite our past differences, I am hopeful that he is correct."

"What's happened?" Ethan asked, eyeing the men.

The warden answered. "This church and its congregation have been the victims of a foul crime."

"More than one, actually," Pell said. "Over the past several nights, the sanctity of the King's Chapel Burying Ground has been violated."

"Resurrectionists?" Ethan asked.

Pell nodded. "I'm afraid so."

The practice of stealing cadavers from graves had been common in England for some time. Schools of medicine and private physicians alike needed bodies with which to study anatomy and practice dissections. At the same time, most churches prohibited any desecration of the dead, even if done in the name of science. As a result, a rather profitable market in corpses, particularly bones, had established itself outside the bounds of the law. In recent years, so-called resurrectionists—grave robbers who spirited away the bodies of the dead—had brought their grisly work to the American colonies. And with schools of medicine having been recently established in Philadelphia and New York, and likely to be founded in other cities as well, the demand for cadavers would only increase.

Ethan had heard as well of conjurers using bones for spells the way he used blood. Bones were said to be every bit as effective, and they eliminated the need for a spellmaker to cut himself. He also knew that Tarijanna Windcatcher, a conjurer who owned a tavern on Boston's Neck, sold ground bone in her tavern, along with oils, herbs, and minerals that were said to enhance the power of conjurings. Most of the bone Janna sold came from animals rather than people, but he wouldn't have been surprised to learn that she had vials of both. And there were those who trafficked in gruesome goods regardless of whether they could cast spells. A market for bone had thrived for years in this city, and thieves looked for profit where they could, caring not a whit for the sensibilities of others, even in matters of death and the sanctity of a grave.

"Members of our congregation deserve to know that their loved ones can lie undisturbed in their graves," Caner said. "They should not have to fear that the poor souls will be profaned by rogues and craven thieves."

"Of course, reverend sir. I understand completely."

"We wish to engage your services, Mister Kaille. We want you to find the villains who have been desecrating these graves. You will, of course, have our full cooperation. Whatever you need, Doctor Gardiner and Mister Pell will see to it. You have my word on that. In return, we are prepared to pay you five pounds. As I understand it, we would pay you some of that now, and—"

"No," Ethan said. "I'll do what I can to help you, but I won't take your money."

Pell shook his head. "Ethan—"

"I'll not take payment from a house of God. Besides, if all you say is true, this is a dark business; no one should profit from it."

Mister Caner blinked, but said nothing.

Pell glanced sidelong at the rector before saying, "Thank you."

Ethan faced Caner again. "I'll do my best to find those responsible, reverend sir." A small grin tugged at his lips. "And in deference to you, I'll also do my best to . . ." His eyes flicked toward Gardiner. "To use conventional means to the extent possible."

That, of all things, brought a smile to Reverend Caner's face. "You're most kind, Mister Kaille. I was reluctant to hire you, as you might imagine. But Trevor insisted you were the right person for this task. I see now that he was right. When can you begin?"

"Immediately. If one of you would be so kind as to show me the disturbed graves."

The rector nodded. "Yes, of course. Silvester? Trevor?"

Gardiner gestured toward the chapel entrance. Ethan bid good day to Caner and Troutbeck, and allowed the warden and the young minister to lead him out into the sunshine.

It had been cool when Ethan left the Dowsing Rod a short while before, and dew had lain heavy on the lawns along Treamount Street. But the sun now hung higher in the morning sky, and already the air was turning uncomfortably warm. This promised to be another sweltering day.

Gardiner led Pell and Ethan around the side of the chapel to the old burying ground at the north end of the churchyard. As they approached the jumble of tombstones, Ethan spotted a man squatting in the shade over what appeared to be a disturbed gravesite.

"That's James Thomson," Gardiner said before Ethan could ask. "He's our sexton."

Marking their approach, Thomson straightened, and Ethan realized that he, like Gardiner, was uncommonly tall; he was also spear thin. Everything about him appeared stretched out, as if he had somehow survived years of torture on the rack. His limbs were spiderlike, his neck overlong and thrust forward at an odd angle. His steel-gray hair was tied back in a plait, and his face was weathered and lined. He wore a dark blue waistcoat over a white linen shirt that was stained dark with sweat under the arms.

Despite his awkward appearance, he came to greet them with long, loping strides that were almost graceful.

"Good day, Mister Pell," he said, in a rough voice. "Doctor Gardiner."

"Good morning, James," Pell said.

"This our witch?" the sexton asked, turning to Ethan.

Ethan glanced at Pell, who stared at the ground, his lips pursed. Ethan had the feeling the young minister was doing everything in his power to keep from laughing. Gardiner glowered at them all.

"Aye," Ethan said, proffering a hand. "I'm your witch."

Thomson gripped his hand firmly and nodded, oblivious of having given offense. "Glad you're here," he said, and returned to the disturbed site. He squatted once more and pointed down into the grave. "It's grim work they did," he said. "Not seen anything like it in all my years here."

As soon as Ethan, Pell, and Gardiner joined him graveside, they were assailed by the smell of decay. Pell gave a soft grunt and turned away, covering his nose and mouth with an open hand. Gardiner retreated in haste, a look of disgust on his fleshy features. Ethan pulled a handkerchief from his pocket and held it over his face.

"They weren't gentle about it," Gardiner said, from a few paces away. "Seemed in a bit of a hurry, if you ask me."

Ethan had to agree with the warden. Dirt had been hastily shoveled aside, and the coffin had been splintered, most likely by an axe. Through the broken wood, Ethan could see that the linen burial cloth had been cut open and pulled away from the corpse, exposing clothing and part of the neck and chest.

"They didn't steal the entire body?" Ethan asked of the sexton, who seemed unaffected by the stench.

"No. They took the head, and the right hand off of each. It's strange, isn't it?"

"Aye," Ethan said.

"Not only that, but they also took an article of clothing from each grave, or at least a piece of something." He pointed down into the grave. "This one was wearing a cravat, and that's gone."

"Have you ever heard of other resurrectionists doing that?" Ethan asked.

The sexton shook his head. "No, but then again, I've not heard much of anything about their kind. And I would have been content to keep it that way."

"I don't doubt it," Ethan said. "I gather that the family has already been here."

"No, why would you think that?"

"Well," Ethan said, "I didn't expect that you could remember so clearly what the man was wearing when he was buried."

"He only went in the ground nine or ten days ago." Thomson swept his arm in a wide arc, encompassing more than half a dozen graves, all of which appeared to have been desecrated. "Every one of these sites was dug in the last four months or so."

"Do you mean to say that every grave that's been robbed is a new one?"

"Aye. And that's not all."

Thomson climbed down into the grave and unbuttoned the soiled linen shirt in which the corpse had been buried. On the left side of the dead man's chest, carved into the rotting skin over his heart was an odd symbol: a triangle, its apex pointing toward the man's chin, with three straight lines cutting across the shape from the left edge to converge at the bottom right corner.

"What is that?" Ethan whispered.

"I was hoping you would know," the sexton said. "Come with me."

He covered up the chest of the cadaver and nimbly climbed out of the grave. He straightened and strode to another grave, which lay perhaps twenty yards from the first. Ethan followed, noting as he reached this second site that the gravestone was somewhat thicker than others nearby, and had more ornate carvings around the edges. The family name Rowan was engraved on the stone. Below etched in smaller letters, were the words "Abigail, Devoted Wife and Loving Mother, b. 23 September 1701, d. 28 May 1769."

"Abigail Rowan," Ethan whispered. "I remember hearing of her death. Her husband is a man of some repute."

"Aye," Thomson said, keeping his voice low, and looking back at Pell and Gardiner, who lingered near the first grave. "Rich men usually are." He lowered himself into this grave, as well.

Ethan squatted beside the site and peered down at the broken coffin. Again, the wood had been shattered, and the body of poor Abigail Rowan uncovered. As with the last, it seemed the burial cloth had been slit open with a blade. He could see that her body was badly decomposed.

"They took her head and right hand, just like with the last one," Thomson said. "And they took a shred of clothing, too."

"What shred?" Ethan asked.

"They cut a square from her dress. That's not important." He uncovered her chest. The symbol carved into her leathered skin was similar to the other one. Similar, but not identical. The lines within the triangle were curved, rather than straight—like waves.

"Do you think that was intentional?" Ethan asked.

"I'm sure of it. Because every dead man who was dug up has the other mark, and every dead woman has this one. So tell me, thieftaker, what do you suppose that means?"

Ethan had no answer. "How many graves have been disturbed?" he asked instead.

"Nine of them, all told."

"And you say all of them were newly dug?"

"Aye."

"And over how many nights have the desecrations taken place?"

"Three nights. The first graves were dug up on Sunday last. The thieves came back on Tuesday, and again last night."

"Can you show me more of them?"

Thomson stood again, and set out in the direction of the nearest open grave. He had started to favor his right leg. "You can see all of them for all I care. There's not much difference among them."

He pointed down into this third site. Ethan could see what he meant. The damage to the coffin was much the same; once again the burial cloth had been sliced open. The head was gone, as was the right hand. And the decaying skin over the woman's heart had been scored just the way Abigail Rowan's had been.

"Then maybe there's no need for me to look at the rest," Ethan said.

"Oh, I think there is," the sexton said. "I expect you'll be thinking of them differently once you've seen them all."

"What do you mean?"

Thomson regarded Ethan through narrowed eyes. "Why don't you walk with me for a time, and look at each grave, and after you can tell me what *you* think I mean."

"All right," Ethan said.

For the next quarter hour, Ethan and Thomson walked from gravesite to gravesite, examining the exposed bodies, comparing the marks on their skin and taking stock of what clothing had been taken. Pell and the warden trailed behind them, both of them keeping silent. Pell still grimaced at what he saw in the broken coffins, but like Ethan, he seemed to have become inured to the smell. Gardiner had pulled out a handkerchief of his own, and he held it firmly over his mouth and nose.

After looking at all of the desecrated graves, Ethan circled back to take second looks at a couple of them. At last he halted near the first grave Thomson had shown them. He stared at the ground, trying to make sense of what he had seen.

"I was wrong before," he said at length. "The warden and I both were. These men weren't careless. They had a specific purpose in mind. I don't know what it was, but they made their marks, they took the head and hand from each body, and they took the scrap of clothing as well."

"Can you think of any reason why someone might do that?"

Ethan turned. Mister Pell stood a short distance off, his skin flushed, a sheen of sweat on his cheeks and brow. He spared not even a glance for the sexton. He had asked his question of Ethan alone, and Ethan could tell that he was asking him to respond not as a thieftaker, but as a conjurer. He thought once more of the spells that had awakened him during the night. Perhaps he hadn't dreamed them after all. This last, though, he kept to himself.

"I can't," Ethan said. "Not yet. But there must be a reason, and a meaning to those symbols." He thought once more of Janna. If anyone could tell him how a conjurer might use what had been taken from the dead, it was her. "I can speak to some people. One person in particular, who knows more about this sort of thing than I do."

Pell nodded.

"But you should know, Mister Pell, that there is a chance nothing will come of these conversations. Sometimes—most times, really—a theft is just what it seems to be." He gestured back at the open graves. "The skull and the bones of the human hand would be of great interest to physicians, and therefore could be quite valuable. The rest . . ." He shrugged. "It could all be nothing more or less than superstition. I don't pretend to understand the workings of a resurrectionist's mind."

They all fell silent. Pell shifted his gaze to the sexton, who still stood beside Ethan. Gardiner had come closer as well, and it was he who spoke first.

"You haven't yet told him?" the warden asked, eyeing Thomson.

"No. I wanted him to see what there was to be seen. And I wanted to know first what he thought. As he says, it might all mean nothing."

"What are you talking about?" Ethan asked the sexton. "What haven't you told me? Was something else taken?"

"Yes," Trevor said, his expression pained. He faltered; he appeared not to know how to say what was on his mind. "Ethan," he went on at last, "every corpse in every one of those desecrated graves has had three toes removed from his or her left foot."

is first response, which an instant later struck him as comical, was to think, *That's interesting: I'm missing three toes on my left foot, too.* But of course Pell knew this. Ethan could see from the look in the young minister's eyes that he was all too aware of the implications of what had been done to these bodies. Questions swarmed through his mind. Had this been done to mock him? Or to make it seem that he was responsible? Who knew about the injury he had suffered as a prisoner? Could there be a deeper, darker purpose to this particular indignity done to the cadavers? Could a conjurer use this body part to harm Ethan or bind him to the spellmaker's will?

Or was he allowing his imagination to get the better of him? Why would the people responsible for these thefts single him out in this way?

To which a voice in his mind responded, *I don't know, but they have.*

For how else could he explain what had been done to the corpses? Already these events struck him as bizarre and unsettling. Yet there was also a certain logic to them. Thinking as might a physician or one who aspired to the profession, he could see the value in stealing or buying a skull and a hand. But what possible value could there be in three toes from a left foot? Why would anyone take just part of a foot not from a single cadaver, but from nine of them?

He understood now why Mister Pell had summoned him, and why

Reverend Caner had been willing to overlook his abhorrence of Ethan's conjuring powers.

"Ethan?" Pell said, concern etched on his face.

"I need to see them again," Ethan said, starting back toward the first gravesite. Thomson fell in step with him, but Pell and Gardiner hesitated.

Pell took a step toward him. "Perhaps you should—"

"It's all right, Mister Pell," Ethan said, his tone crisp, despite the roiled state of his emotions. "I'll meet you back inside the chapel."

If anything, this served to make the minister appear more worried. Pell, though, was the least of Ethan's concerns.

He and the sexton moved with grim efficiency from grave to grave. Thomson climbed down into each site and held up the profaned foot for Ethan to see, before leading Ethan to the next one.

Ethan soon realized that every foot looked much the same. The three smallest toes had been removed perhaps half an inch below the joints; the cuts were clean, precise. If the resurrectionists had hoped to mimic his own old injury, they had been both too exact and not exact enough. His wound was not as straight or neat as these cuts; it had been made by plantation physicians who hardly knew what they were doing. Ethan had often remarked to himself and to others that it was a miracle their butchery hadn't cost him his entire leg. Also, his ordeal had left him with somewhat less of his foot than the cadavers now had.

Still, seeing what had been done to the corpses reaffirmed what he had already deduced: The people who did this knew him and wanted Ethan to understood that.

"What kind of witchery uses bones?" Thomson asked, breaking a silence that had stretched on for many minutes. Ethan wondered if he was trying to make conversation.

"Dark," Ethan said.

"Isn't it all dark?" the sexton asked, surprising Ethan with a conspiratorial grin.

Ethan smiled. "No, not all." He turned a slow circle, his expression growing grim as he surveyed the burying ground. "This is, though. I don't understand it, but I'm certain there's some dark purpose here." He proffered a hand to Thomson. "You have my thanks for showing me all of this. I should speak with Mister Pell before I go."

"Of course," the sexton said, shaking his hand.

"If I have more questions—"

"Mister Pell knows where to find me. So do Doctor Gardiner and Reverend Caner."

Ethan nodded before walking back toward the front of the chapel, more aware than ever of his limp.

"Thieftaker!"

He stopped and turned.

"I have friends who are sextons at other churches, with other burying grounds. I don't know if it's the same everywhere, but King's Chapel isn't the only place where these robberies are happening."

Ethan felt the hairs on the back of his neck stand on end. He raised a hand, acknowledging what Thomson had told him. Turning away, he hurried into the sanctuary.

Pell, Gardiner, and Caner were waiting for him just inside the door.

"James showed you?" Caner asked.

"Aye," Ethan said. "I'm wondering if there is anything more that links the mutilated corpses beyond their membership in your congregation, and the fact that they all died within the past several months."

Caner pondered this, his brow knitting. Pell and Gardiner wore similar expressions.

"Some among them share certain traits," the rector said at last, "just as you would expect. Abigail Rowan and Bertram Flagg were neighbors, and also had in common considerable wealth. John Newell and George Wright both practiced law, but they were the only attorneys among those whose graves were robbed. I can go on, but you see my point. Many of them had certain attributes in common, but I can't think of anything—beyond the factors you mentioned—that links all of them." He faced Gardiner and Pell. "Can either of you?"

Both men shook their heads.

"I assumed as much," Ethan said. "I should be on my way."

"Where?" Pell asked.

"To start, I need to speak with a friend." He turned and pulled open the door. "I'll keep you apprised of what I learn."

He hadn't made it two steps down the path leading back to the street before he heard the door open again. He knew without looking who had followed him.

"Ethan, wait."

"You needn't be concerned about me, Mister Pell," he said, facing the man.

"I'm not sure I believe you."

Ethan's amusement was fleeting. "Will you accept that, while unnerved, I am all the more resolved to complete my inquiry?"

"Aye. I just hope that you'll exercise some caution. More than you usually do."

"I'm always cautious," Ethan said, frowning.

"If that's so, why is it that every time you conduct an inquiry, you wind up beaten, or thrown in gaol, or at the wrong end of a pistol or blade?"

"I wouldn't say that happens every time."

Pell raised an eyebrow.

"I'll have a care," Ethan said.

"Good. If you require help of any sort, let me know."

Ethan gripped the minister's shoulder briefly and left him there.

He walked to Marlborough Street, and turned southward to journey back out to the Neck. He could admit to himself that he shared Pell's concerns. But he wasn't about to hide in his room on Cooper's Alley, or in the back of Kannice's tavern. The best thing he could do was find the resurrectionists, whoever they were. And the truth was, intentionally or not, they had helped him narrow his list of suspects to those who knew him, or at least of him.

Speaking to Pell, he had referred to Janna as a friend; the truth was he had never been certain that she thought of him that way. Or anyone else, for that matter. Janna could be generous and kind, she could be as witty as anyone he knew. But most of the time, she was cantankerous to the point of rudeness.

She was also defiantly proud of her conjuring abilities, and acted as though she had never given a thought to the possibility that church leaders or representatives of the Crown might decide someday to hang her for a witch. She had long ago proclaimed herself a "marriage smith." Indeed, the sign on her tavern read "T. Windcatcher, Marriage Smith.

Love is Magick." Short of writing "I am a conjurer" across her brow, she could not have been less subtle about her talents.

Reaching her tavern, the Fat Spider, Ethan knocked on the door. Early as it was, he couldn't be certain that Janna would be awake. But at his knock, he heard a voice call for him to enter. Ethan opened the door and walked inside, hat in hand.

It took his eyes a moment to adjust to the darkness. Before he could see properly, he heard Janna say, "Kaille," drawing out his name as if it were a curse. "I shoulda known it would be you. No one else bothers me before noon."

"Good morning, Janna," Ethan said, walking to where she sat.

It was cooler in the tavern than it had been on the street, but it was still warm in the building. Nevertheless, Janna sat with a shawl wrapped around her bony shoulders, a cup of what was probably watered Madeira wine resting on the table beside her. Janna claimed to come from somewhere in the Indies, and it seemed to Ethan that she had never adjusted to life away from the tropical clime. She was always cold, even on the hottest days of the Boston summer.

He had heard some say that she was an escaped slave, and she herself admitted that it was possible she had been born to servitude. But she was orphaned at sea as a young girl, and rescued by the crew of a ship out of Newport. To this day, Ethan wasn't sure how she had managed to avoid being sold into slavery, but according to one account a wealthy man took her in and over time a romance developed between them. She chose the name Windcatcher for herself, having no recollection of her family name. Windcatcher had no particular meaning; she once told Ethan that she simply liked the sound of it.

Whatever the truth of her past, today Janna was one of the few free Africans in Boston. Her skin was a deep, rich nut brown, and her hair was white and shorn so short that one could see her scalp peeking through the tight curls. She was thin, almost frail, with a wizened face. But her dark eyes were fierce like a hawk's.

"What do you want?" she asked, as Ethan took the seat across from hers. "As if I don't already know."

Ethan often came to Janna for information, because she knew more about spellmaking than anyone else he had met. More often than not, she helped him, though only after complaining that he never paid her for anything. Today, he thought to surprise her.

"I need to make a purchase or two."

Janna sat forward, the expression on her face conveying such surprise that Ethan nearly laughed out loud. "You came to buy somethin'?" she said.

"Yes. I'm out of mullein, and I always prefer to have some on hand."

"You should," she said, nodding with enthusiasm. "You should. There ain't a better herb for protection spells. And I have some in fresh, as good as you'll find in Boston. How much do you want?"

"How much will three shillings buy me?"

Janna considered this briefly before holding up her fist. "A pouch 'bout like this, packed full."

"All right." He pulled out three shillings and handed them to her.

She eyed the money, pocketed it, and stood. "I'll be right back."

"I'll take a cup of Madeira, too," Ethan said, following her to the bar. She went around the bar and disappeared into a room in back, adjacent to her kitchen.

"You steal somebody's coin purse, or somethin'?" she called.

Ethan laughed. "No. But I got paid yesterday, and I managed to dupe Sephira Pryce long enough to keep her from stealing the money from me."

He heard Janna cackle. "Good for you, Kaille."

In all of Boston, Janna might have been the one person who disliked Sephira more than Ethan did. To this day, he wasn't certain why. Janna remained closemouthed about whatever had passed between her and the Empress of the South End. When asked, she said only that Sephira had once cost her a good deal of coin.

Janna emerged from the back room bearing a small leather pouch that was filled near to overflowing with leaves. She handed it to Ethan.

He drew it open and held it to his nose. Right away, the air around him was redolent of the pungent, subtly bitter fragrance of fresh mullein.

"Don't that smell good?" Janna asked.

"It does," he said, as he slipped the pouch into his pocket. "My thanks." He placed a half shilling on the bar.

Janna took it and poured him a cup of Madeira. "Watered?" she asked.

"Just a little, thank you."

Janna watered her own Madeira so much that it had little flavor. Given how much of it she drank, this was wise; if she drank it undiluted she would have put herself out of business, and been too drunk to notice.

She added some water to his wine—more than he would have put in, but less than she added to her own—and slid the cup to him.

"Were you conjuring last night?" he asked her.

"When?"

"Late."

"I was sleepin' last night, late. Why?"

He shook his head. "It's not important." He took a sip of wine. "Do you have any bone to sell, Janna?"

Her expression grew guarded. "Since when do you conjure with bone?"

"I don't," Ethan said. "But you have some, don't you?"

"O' course. I always have some. But I don't like sellin' it. Don't like where it comes from."

"And where is that?"

She stared at him briefly before motioning with her head toward the table at which she had been sitting when he came in. Ethan picked up his wine and followed her.

She lowered herself into her chair and gathered her shawl around her shoulders once more. Ethan sat opposite her.

"Why are you sudd'nly so interested in bone?"

"Work," Ethan said. "I need some information."

"Yeah, I figured as much." Her expression had soured, but her voice remained mild. "You come in here throwin' money around like that, an' I knew you'd want knowledge from me. You always do."

Ethan said nothing, but watched her, awaiting some sign that he could ask his questions.

"Well, go on!" she said. "You spent your coin. Might as well make the most of it."

He smiled. "Thank you, Janna."

She scowled and waved away his gratitude.

"What did you mean before, when you said that you didn't like selling bone because of where it comes from?"

"What do you think I meant? I can make money sellin' bone. People pay a lot for it. But I don't like thinkin' 'bout graves bein' dug up, and dead people bein' riled." She shook her head. "Wrathful dead ain't good for any of us."

"Are there resurrectionists here in Boston?"

"O' course there are. Have been for as long as I can remember. We didn' always call them that. For a while they was just grave robbers, like the rest. But, yeah, they're here."

"Can you tell me who they are?"

Janna shook her head. "I may not like what they do, but I've still got to do business with them. I can' risk makin' them angry."

"I understand. Tell me this: Are certain bones more powerful than others?"

"You mean for spells?"

Ethan nodded.

Janna sipped her wine. "I suppose. Skulls are the most powerful. No doubt about that. Ribs are said to be powerful, too. I'm not sure I believe it. Most of what I sell is ground anyway, and there's no tellin' what's in that. I know it's human," she added, anticipating his next question, "because if it wasn' the spells wouldn' be as strong."

"What about a foot?" Ethan asked.

"A foot?" Janna repeated. She shook her head. "No, there ain't nothin' particularly strong about the bone from people's feet." She regarded him, her eyes shining in the lamp light. "What's this about, Kaille?"

"I'm not sure yet. There have been a series a grave robberies at King's Chapel. Skulls and hands taken from all of them. And a few other parts as well."

"Like feet," she said, her expression shrewd.

"That's right. And from what you're telling me, I gather that any bone can be used for conjuring." He regretted mentioning the feet. He didn't want every conjurer in Boston to know that the dead were being mutilated to look more like him.

"Yeah," she said. "Animal bone will work, too. Not as well, o' course.

Human is better, and skulls is best. After that, a foot is probably as good a source for a livin' spell as anythin' else. Thing is, though, if it was conjurers stealin' bone to sell, they'd take everything. Takin' parts is a lot of trouble for not much goods, if you know what I mean."

Ethan gazed down into his cup, mulling what she had said. Conjurers spoke of three types of spells. Elemental spells, the simplest of all conjurings, drew upon one of the elements—earth, water, air, or fire—as the source of "fuel," for lack of a better word, for the spell. These tended to be weak conjurings, illusions mostly; visions conjured to mislead the unsuspecting. Living spells, those Janna had just mentioned, were more powerful, and therefore demanded more substantive sources. Such castings drew upon blood or bone or flesh, leaves like mullein, the stems of plants, or the bark or wood of a living tree. The resulting conjurings could change the shape of matter. They could break wood or metal, set objects afire, heal wounds, or slice through flesh and shatter bones. Most of the conjurers Ethan knew relied on elemental or living conjurings. These two groupings accounted for every spell Ethan had ever cast save one.

That one spell had been what was called a killing spell. Killing spells were far and away the most powerful conjurings a spellmaker could cast. They could be used to murder at will, to control the minds and actions of others, to wreak havoc and destruction on a scale most people who knew nothing of conjuring could scarcely fathom. They were, to Ethan's mind, inherently dark, but he knew that some conjurers would argue the point.

He could perceive spells cast by others, just as he did his own. They felt like the thrumming of a bowstring, or the deep rumble of distant thunder. And he liked to think he would have known if within the past few days someone had cast a killing spell here in Boston. But he couldn't be certain, and once more he thought back to the conjurings that had disturbed his sleep the previous night.

The raiding of the King's Chapel graves and the mutilation of the corpses struck him as too odd, too sinister, to be nothing more than the work of a thief with odd predilections. And yet Janna raised a legitimate question. With other sources for living spells available, why would a conjurer go to such great lengths to steal bone? Perhaps he hadn't needed to come to Janna after all.

"You don't think that these thefts were committed by a sorcerer," he said.

She shook her head. "I never said that."

Ethan's apprehension had begun to abate. Now it returned in a rush.

"I can't imagine anyone who wasn't a conjurer stealin' specific body parts like that," she said. "But it wasn't done to sell the bone."

He reached for his wine, but thought better of drinking it. "There's more," he said. He didn't want to tell her, but Janna was the one person who might help him judge what sort of threat he faced. "I said that the robbers took feet. That's not quite right. They took part of the left foot on each body. And that part corresponds to the part I lost when I was a prisoner."

Janna gaped at him and pulled her shawl tighter. "I don't like the sound of that, Kaille. Not one bit."

"Also, there was a symbol carved into the chest of each corpse. Do you have something I can use to write?"

Usually Janna would have told him where he could find a quill, ink, and parchment. Not this time. She got up herself, walked behind the bar, and came back seconds later with what he needed.

"This was cut into the men," he said, drawing the triangle with straight lines within. "And this was cut into the women." He drew the second symbol. "Do those mean anything to you?"

She shook her head, her jaw muscles tightening.

"Do you have any idea what kind of conjuring the people behind this might have it in mind to do?"

"No. I don't know for sure that it's for spells. But I don't like it. It just seems . . . wrong."

Ethan couldn't argue. He stood.

"My thanks, Janna."

"For what? I didn't tell you anythin'."

His smile was rueful. "No. But you confirmed everything that I was already thinking. There's something wicked at work here."

"Yeah," she said. "And it's aimed at you."

"I'd prefer that we keep this conversation between us."

"All right."

Ethan crossed to the door.

"Who are you workin' for?" she asked, as he reached for the door handle.

"King's Chapel," Ethan said. "But I'm working for free."

She nodded her approval. "You use that mullein, all right? It won't protect you from everythin' but it'll keep you safer than just a regular wardin'."

"I will. Again, thank you."

He stepped out of the tavern into blinding daylight and oppressive heat. Remembering what the King's Chapel sexton had said—that King's Chapel wasn't the only place where this was happening—he retraced the path he had taken the night before. Rather than following Orange Street back to the South End and Cornhill, he cut up to the unpaved road that ran along the edge of Boston's Common.

Children played tips on the grass, laughing and shouting taunts at one another. A pair of women walked toward him, each carrying an infant. Swallows and swifts swooped and darted overhead, chattering, and high above them a lone hawk circled lazily in the hazy sky. It felt much like any summer day in Boston, save for the shadow that hung over him.

There weren't many other conjurers in Boston other than Ethan and Janna, and none of those of whom Ethan was aware would have resorted to robbing graves for spells. Which meant that someone new had come to the city, someone with unholy purpose.

Before long, Ethan arrived at the Common Burying Ground, the newest of Boston's cemeteries, and also the largest. Although it had been established just thirteen years before, it was already crowded with gravestones. Ethan entered the grounds and walked a short distance before halting and looking around. Unlike the King's Chapel Burying Ground, this expanse was not affiliated with any church. Ethan wasn't certain where to begin his search for someone he could ask about any possible desecrations.

He resumed his wandering, and for what seemed like an hour he walked up one row of graves and down the next, seeing no sign of disturbed earth. The burying ground was vast, but eventually Ethan realized he had covered all of it without finding any desecrated graves. He should have been relieved; perhaps the sexton had been mistaken, and these incidents were limited to the King's Chapel Burying Ground. Try as he might, though, he could not convince himself of this.

His trepidation growing, he left the Common Buying Ground and continued along the edge of the Common to the old Granary Burying Ground, one of the oldest cemeteries in the city; only the grounds at King's Chapel and at Copp's Hill, in the North End, were older. Here were buried several men of note, including Peter Faneuil, for whom the marketplace in Cornhill had been named, and Samuel Sewall, the judge who had presided over the witch trials in Salem in 1690, and who had seen the sentence of death carried out for the convicted.

Ethan followed a narrow stone path into the burying ground and once more searched for a caretaker or gravedigger. There was no church in this burying ground either. The granary located in the middle of the expanse was just that: a building constructed long ago that housed the town's supply of grain.

He began to walk the perimeter of the grounds, the sun beating down on him. A few years before, elms had been planted along the road, but they were too small to offer much shade, and the property was otherwise devoid of trees. Still walking, Ethan removed his waistcoat and draped it over his arm, all the while sweeping his gaze over the graves before him, searching for signs of disturbed earth.

Before long, he found what he sought: a single grave had been dug up much as those at King's Chapel had been. He faltered in midstep, both relieved that he had managed to find what he sought, and troubled at the thought of more desecrations. Forcing himself into motion once more, he approached the site, but faltered a second time when the stink hit him.

"Damn," he muttered.

Pledging to himself that he would never again take on an inquiry that required him to look into grave robberies, he closed the remaining distance between himself and the grave. He looked around the grounds again. Seeing no one—and hoping no one could see him—he lowered himself into the grave and examined the damage done to the coffin. As with those at King's Chapel, the wood appeared to have been shattered with an axe. The burial cloth had been cut open, and the corpse—that of a woman, judging from the clothing—had been beheaded. The right hand was missing as well, and it appeared that a piece of cloth had been torn from her dress.

Steeling himself, he pulled down the front of the dress until he could see the rotting flesh over her breastbone. The symbol he had seen on the dead women at King's Chapel had been carved into this corpse, too. Finally, he worked her left foot free. Or what was left of it.

"Damn," he said again.

He covered up the corpse as well as he could, climbed out of the grave, and resumed his search, now walking with greater urgency. He did not immediately find another desecrated site, but he did spot a man working on a grave, a shovel in his hands. Ethan strode toward him, wiping sweat from his face.

"Well met, sir!" he called.

The man glanced up from his work, but said nothing, and soon turned his attention back to the grave at his feet. He looked to be about Ethan's age. He was short, powerfully built, with small dark eyes and black hair. He wore torn brown breeches and a stained blue linen shirt that was soaked through with sweat.

"Can I speak to you for a moment?" Ethan asked, stopping a few steps from the man.

"I suppose," the laborer said without pausing.

"Is this a new grave, or one you've had to cover up again because of a robbery?"

At that, the man ceased his labors and turned. "Who are you?"

"My name is Ethan Kaille. I've been asked by the Reverend Henry Caner to inquire into a series of desecrations at the King's Chapel Burying Ground. I spoke this morning with Mister Thomson, the sexton there."

"You know James?" the man said, squinting against the sun.

"Aye." Ethan extended a hand. "You are?"

The man stared at Ethan, his mouth twisting. At last, he wiped his hand on his breeches and gripped Ethan's for just a second. "Robert Helms." The name tumbled out of his mouth in a jumble.

"It's a pleasure to meet you, Robert." Ethan surveyed the burying ground. "Have resurrectionists struck here, too?"

"Aye," the man said. "Graves have been disturbed each of the last three nights. Six in all."

"What was taken?"

Robert shook his head. "It's a gruesome business."

"I realize that. But I need to know what they took."

"Heads off of each one," he said. "And a hand, too. Damn surgeons and their dissections. I'll have nothing to do with any of them."

"Was that all?" Ethan asked, keeping his voice level. "Just the heads and hands?"

"I think so. Why? Isn' that enough?"

Ethan didn't answer. "Would it be all right if I took a look at the graves that have been disturbed?"

"Aye. I can take you around, show you where they are. They're scattered about, and it's a large burying ground."

"I'd appreciate it."

"This was the first one right here," Robert said, gesturing with his shovel at the grave he had been working on when Ethan found him. "We can' bury him again until that coffin is repaired. I've been clearing away as much dirt as I can so that we can bury him proper a second time."

Ethan bent to look at the gravestone, which read, "Emmett Peter George, b. 5 November 1728, d. 26 February 1769." Glancing down into the grave, Ethan saw a grisly and now-familiar sight: a broken coffin and a burial cloth slit to reveal a decayed corpse, headless, a hand missing.

He didn't want to have Robert with him as he examined the corpses to see if each one had been marked and had its left foot mutilated. He felt ghastly enough climbing down into the graves and handling the dead. Having an audience would make it that much worse. But he couldn't imagine how he might ask the man to keep his distance.

"Forgive me, Robert, but I need to look at Mister George's corpse."

"What d'you mean? Look at it how?"

"I need to see his chest, and his left foot."

The caretaker's eyes glinted dangerously in the sunlight. Ethan could see that he had tightened his grip on the shovel. "Why?" he asked.

Ethan sensed it would be a mistake to mention that he had already looked at one corpse here in the Granary Burying Ground. "Because every corpse in every disturbed gravesite at King's Chapel has been . . . marred in the same ways."

Robert paled. "Marred?"

"Aye. I expect you'll want to stay right here, so that you can make certain I do nothing to harm this grave or the body therein. But, with your permission, I need to look."

The man wet his lips and nodded, his head jerking up and down. "All right."

Ethan eased himself down into the grave and reached into the coffin to unbutton Emmett George's shirt. When he exposed the cadaver's chest, Robert gave a small gasp.

"Lord have mercy!"

"Aye," Ethan said, the word coming out like a sigh. "I'm not done yet." He pulled the man's foot free, drawing another sharp breath from the caretaker.

"They did that to all of them?" Robert asked.

"So far."

Ethan tucked the corpse's leg back in place and climbed out of the grave. "Was he wearing a cravat when you buried him?"

"I don't remember. Why?"

Ethan shook his head. "It doesn't matter. Shall we check the others?"

The caretaker nodded, but didn't move. "Why would someone do those things?"

"You're not the first to ask me," Ethan said. "I don't know the answer yet, but I'm going to find out."

"I bet it's witchery," Robert said, still gazing down into the grave. "Word is there's witches all through this city, workin' their mischief, tryin' to lure regular folk to their devilish ways." He looked at Ethan. "You should have a care. You spend enough time in a buryin' ground, you're bound to run into one of them."

"I'm sure that's true," Ethan said. On another day he might have found some humor in the turn their conversation had taken. But with all he had seen this morning, he could not. Henry Caner had allowed Trevor to summon him because he believed these robberies to be the work of witches. Robert had already reached a similar conclusion, and others would do the same. It wouldn't be long before Sheriff Stephen Greenleaf, and perhaps even Thomas Hutchinson, who in less than a month would assume duties as the acting governor of the Province of Massachusetts Bay, heard of these incidents. They, too, would blame "witchery," and since Ethan was the "witch" they knew best, their suspicions would fall on him.

"There's more of them than you think," the caretaker said, nodding. "Witches, I mean. You mark my word."

"Why don't you show me the rest of the desecrated graves, Robert. And then you can get back to your work."

"Right."

Robert led Ethan around the burying ground to the other five disturbed graves, including the one Ethan had examined previously. Ethan made a show of looking at the body once more. The caretaker's horror grew at every stop: Every one of the corpses had been marked on the chest and was missing part of the left foot, as well as the head and right hand. Ethan, of course, was not surprised in the least.

The clothing on several of the corpses, although not all, had been torn. Ethan assumed that those without tears in their clothes had been wearing cravats, or had been buried with kerchiefs. When they had finished with the last of the graves, Robert led Ethan back to the burying ground entrance. He said not a word as they walked, but halting next to the gate, he looked Ethan in the eye.

"Who was it you said you was workin' for?"

"Reverend Caner of King's Chapel."

"Does that mean you'll only be guardin' the buryin' ground there?"

"I'll be looking for whoever did this," Ethan said. "I don't care if I find the fiend at King's Chapel, or Copp's Hill, or here." He paused for the span of a breath. "But I can't be in two places at one time, Robert. And I need to know if the people who did this come back here."

"Oh, I'll be watchin' for them," the caretaker said. "You can count on that."

"Thank you. If you need to find me for any reason, you can leave a message for me at the Dowsing Rod on Sudbury Street, or at Dall's cooperage on Cooper's Alley."

"All right. Kaille was it?"

"Aye. Ethan Kaille."

They shook hands again, and Ethan left him, intent on making his way to the Copp's Hill Burying Ground. He knew what he would find there, but he could not ignore the possibility that someone at the cemetery might aid his inquiry.

Copp's Hill was the resting place of many men of note, including Cotton Mather, who had played so central a role in the trials at Salem; who had devoted so many of his sermons to diatribes against the dark evils of witchcraft; and who was also the first and greatest advocate for inoculation against smallpox, which had proven in recent years to be a powerful defense for some against epidemics of the distemper.

He made his way to the North End as quickly as the old injury to his foot would allow; by the time he reached Copp's Hill, his limp had grown more pronounced and his leg was aching. Entering the grounds, he saw a cluster of men and women gathered around a gravesite, including a parson, who was administering rites.

Ethan began yet another search for disturbed graves, making sure to give the mourners a wide berth. Even so, when he found sites that had been desecrated, as he had known he would, he did nothing more than give a cursory examination of the damage done to the coffins. He didn't dare touch the corpses. Nor did he have to.

What he saw in these sites resembled in almost every way what he had seen at King's Chapel and in the Granary Burying Ground. The disturbed graves—seven in all—were the final resting places for men and women, old and young, even a child. According to their grave markers, all had died since the beginning of the year. Each one had been robbed of its head and right hand. Ethan had no doubt that if he had climbed down into the graves he would have found the same odd symbols carved into each corpse's chest and each left foot mutilated to resemble his own. Again some, though not all, had rents in their clothing.

He made note of the names on the gravestones, just as he had at the Granary. At last, weary, sweating, he left the burying ground and trudged back toward the Dowser.

Halfway there, on the edge of Middle Street, he stopped and stood blinking in the midday glare, swaying like a drunkard. How foolish he had been. Ignoring the pain in his leg, he hastened back to King's Chapel.

e had walked past the graves of both Cotton Mather and Samuel Sewall, sparing little more than a glance for either. But now it occurred to him that perhaps the Common Burying Ground had been spared for a reason. Or more precisely, maybe the grave robbers had chosen to strike at Boston's three oldest burying grounds because of something specific in their history.

He strode into the courtyard at King's Chapel and entered the sanctuary. Mr. Troutbeck stood at the pulpit, reading from a large Bible set on a carved wooden stand. As an afterthought, Ethan grabbed his hat off his head.

Troutbeck looked up at the sound of Ethan's footsteps. "Mister Kaille—"

"Who is buried here?" Ethan asked.

"Excuse me?"

"In your burying ground. Samuel Sewall is in the Granary Burying Ground. Cotton Mather is at Copp's Hill. Who is here?"

"This is the oldest burying ground in Boston. I assure you, we have no shortage of great men interred on our grounds. And several women of note, as well."

"I don't doubt it, reverend sir. But I need to know who. Are there any who were present at the trials in Salem?"

Troutbeck stiffened. "I don't know about that. John Cotton is buried here, but he died in the 1650s, I believe."

"Cotton," Ethan repeated. "He was——"

"The father of Maria Cotton, who married Increase Mather."

"So, he was Cotton Mather's grandfather."

"Yes."

"Who else?" Ethan asked.

"John Davenport was a minister as well. I believe . . ." Troutbeck
hesitated, licked his lips. "I believe he played a role in the witch trials at
Huntingdon in the middle of the last century."

Ethan nodded slowly.

"Why?" the minister asked. "What does all this mean?"

"I'm not really certain." Ethan stood thus for another moment before
looking at Troutbeck again. "Thank you." He turned to leave.

"Mister Kaille! What is this about?"

"I'll be back when I know more," Ethan said, and walked out of the
chapel.

He started down the path toward the street, but after a few steps
veered off and walked back to the burying ground. The sexton was
nowhere to be seen, which came as a relief in light of what Ethan needed
to do.

With each new bit of information, he felt more certain that a conjurer had robbed the graves and disfigured the corpses. And he guessed—
though he had no real evidence to support this theory—that the speller
in question had chosen these three burying grounds because of the men
buried in each. Thinking this, a memory stirred deep in the recesses of
his mind—a name from his past. He dismissed the notion as quickly as
it had come. Sephira Pryce was the likeliest suspect for these foul deeds,
especially since she now had a conjurer in her employ. He didn't need to
compound his problems by imagining enemies in every shadow.

He had assured Reverend Caner that he would try to cast as few
spells as possible on the congregation's behalf, but already he could tell
he would be conjuring far more than the rector would like. He needed to
know if the thieves had used conjurings to locate the graves they wished
to rob. If they had, he wanted to see the color of the power they wielded.

He chose the grave James Thomson had shown him, which was

farthest from the chapel, in a corner of the burying grounds shaded by maples and elms. It belonged to a woman named Mary Clark, who had died at the age of twenty-two. Ethan knelt by the open grave, and making certain no one could see him, drew his knife and pushed up his sleeve. But he paused with the blade over his forearm, wondering if blood was the proper choice. He sheathed the weapon and instead pulled out the pouch of mullein Janna had sold him.

Different spells demanded different sources. Ethan was not always as careful as he should have been in choosing what to use as fuel for his conjurings, which was one of the reasons he was not yet as accomplished a spellmaker as he wanted to be. Most of the time he still used whatever was at hand; more often than not, this meant blood. He was learning, though. He now used mullein for most of his wardings. A revealing spell, which was what he intended to try here, didn't need any special source to be effective. But though he was not a religious man, he didn't like the idea of using blood for a spell on the grounds of a church. He knew Caner would have liked it even less.

Pulling three leaves from the pouch, Ethan held them in his palm and said, *"Revela potestatem ex verbasco evocatam."* Reveal power, conjured from mullein.

The leaves vanished. Ethan felt the conjuring hum in the ground and saw Uncle Reg appear beside him, ethereal in the dappled light. But nothing else happened. No glow appeared on the corpse or coffin, or even on the earth that had covered the grave. He sat back on his heels, frowning.

The conjuring should have revealed the glowing residue of any spells cast on the gravesite. Every conjuring left some residue, and the power of every spellmaker glowed with a unique color. In the past, Ethan had used the *revela potestatem* spell to learn the identities of conjurers who had committed crimes of various sorts.

"The spell worked, didn't it?" he asked the ghost. "I felt it."

Reg opened his hands to indicate that he didn't know.

Ethan walked to another of the disturbed graves, watching for signs of the ministers or the sexton. Seeing no one, he tried the same spell on this site. Again he felt the spell and so assumed his conjuring would have worked had there been any residue of power to reveal.

Whatever the intent of those who had robbed the graves, no spell had been directed at the grounds or the corpses themselves. Another idea stuck Ethan, and he pulled out three more leaves. *"Reperi evocationem ex verbasco evocatam."* Locate conjuring, conjured from mullein.

This second spell should have found the residue of any power used anywhere in the vicinity of the burying grounds. But again, nothing happened, beyond the thrum of his conjuring in the earth beneath him.

"Were any of the people in these desecrated graves conjurers?" Ethan asked Reg.

The ghost shook his head.

"What about at the other burying grounds?"

Reg shrugged, his eyes burning in the midday light.

"Right," Ethan said. "I needed to ask you when we were there."

A nod.

It wasn't worth the effort to walk back to both burying grounds. If there were conjurers among the dead victimized by the grave robbers, Ethan thought it would have been coincidence. These sites were chosen because of how recently those buried within them had died. He felt certain of it.

He knew where he wanted to go next, but before he could leave the burying ground, he spotted a group of people walking toward King's Chapel. They were led by Reverend Caner and a well-dressed man who appeared to be speaking to the minister. Silvester Gardiner walked alone at the rear of the small company. The well-dressed man with Caner gesticulated animatedly as they walked, and his voice was raised so that even at a distance, Ethan could make out a word or two of what he said. He guessed whose family this was well before they entered the churchyard.

Ethan stepped out of the shadows and placed himself where Caner could not fail to see him. For the first time in the course of their long and contentious interaction, the minister seemed pleased to see Ethan. He said something to the well-dressed man, and led him and the others to where Ethan stood.

The man speaking with Caner was tall, lean, and severe in aspect. He wore a black tricorn hat and a powdered wig, although Ethan could see wisps of his white hair sticking out from beneath. The black silk ditto suit he wore over a white shirt must have been oppressive in this heat, but he appeared not to notice. He had spoken once more to the minister before they halted, but now he stood, both hands resting on the gold handle of his walking cane, his imperious gaze raking over Ethan from unpowdered head to worn, mud-stained boot.

"Mister Kaille," Caner said. "I'm glad you're here." He indicated the man with an open hand and a tight smile. "This is Mister Alexander Rowan, widower of Missus Abigail Rowan. Mister Rowan, this is Ethan Kaille. He is a thiefta—"

"I know who he is," Rowan said in a deep baritone, as he appraised Ethan. He proffered a hand. "Abner Berson is a friend. You did a great service to him and Catherine after the death of their daughter."

It was a kinder greeting than Ethan had expected. "Thank you, sir. You and your family have my deepest condolences on your loss."

Rowan turned to look back at the cluster of people who had followed him and Caner to the burying ground. "Thank you," he said, his tone brusque. "That is my son, Alex, his wife, Eliza, my daughter, Jane, her husband, Jonathan, my other daughter, Margaret, and her husband, Joseph."

They were all well-dressed and somber, and Ethan wasn't sure he could have assigned a name to any of them, expect perhaps for Rowan's son, who was as lean and grim as his father. But he raised a hand in greeting, and the men nodded in acknowledgment.

"I've just told Mister Rowan that the chapel has engaged your services to inquire into these foul desecrations."

"Yes, reverend sir," Ethan said. To Rowan he said, "I've only just begun to look into this matter, but you have my assurance—"

"I don't want assurances," Rowan said, rapping the butt of his cane on the ground. "I want Abigail made whole again! We buried her here with the expectation that the rector, his warden, and the sexton would see to it that she could rest in peace."

He half turned in Caner's direction as he said this last.

"Can you think of anyone who would wish to disturb your wife's grave, sir?" Ethan asked, drawing Rowan's gaze once more.

"Of course not. And I was given to understand that it wasn't just her grave that was desecrated. There were others, weren't there?"

"Yes, sir. But surely Missus Rowan was the most renowned of those who were disturbed, and—forgive me for being blunt—everyone in Boston knows you to be a man of substantial resources. I don't know what the thieves thought to accomplish, but it may be that they hope to ransom these . . . things they have taken. It is possible that the other sites were desecrated as an afterthought, and that your wife's grave was foremost in the designs of the fiends who did this."

"I see your point," Rowan said. "But surely you don't think I am likely to consort with anyone who would commit such crimes."

"No, sir. Of course not. Can you tell me," Ethan continued after a moment's pause, "have you noticed anything unusual at your home or at your place of business in recent days?"

The other members of the Rowan family had been speaking in low voices among themselves during Ethan's exchange with Mister Rowan. But at this question they fell silent. All of them looked at Ethan before facing the family patron.

"I don't believe I know what you mean," Rowan said. He sounded far less sure of himself than he had seconds before, and it seemed to Ethan that his hands trembled, though he gripped the cane so tightly his knuckles had gone white.

"I don't mean anything in particular, sir. Have you noticed anyone loitering outside your home, or near your warehouses on Long Wharf?"

"No, nothing like that."

"Something else then?" Ethan asked. They had seen something, or someone. Rowan's demeanor and the silence of his family made that much clear.

"No, there's nothing," Rowan said, sounding more frightened than commanding. "There is just the matter of Abigail. Nothing else matters. *I want her whole again!* You're a thieftaker, aren't you? That's your job: to retrieve what was lost." Rowan turned to Caner, dismissing Ethan with a simple pivot. "Take me to her grave, Henry. I want to see what was done to her, and I want to know how you intend to make certain it doesn't happen again."

Reverend Caner's gaze flicked toward Ethan. Ethan thought he saw an apology in the man's eyes, and perhaps gratitude as well. Caner and Rowan started toward the grave, followed by the rest of the Rowan family.

Or most of them; one of Rowan's daughters lingered, waiting until her father was beyond hearing. Ethan didn't remember if this was Margaret or Jane.

"I apologize for my father's rudeness," she said. "This ordeal has taken its toll on us all."

"I don't doubt it, ma'am. Again, my sympathies to all of you."

"Yes, well, that was all I wished to say." She offered a thin smile. "Good day."

"I sensed that perhaps your father hadn't told me everything," Ethan said, as she began to walk away.

She halted but didn't face him. "No," she said. "I don't believe that to be the case."

"So, you've seen nothing strange at your father's estate? He hasn't said anything to you about people he might have seen?"

At this she did turn, the smile still frozen on her lips. "There's nothing, Mister Kaille. Whatever it is you're looking for, you'll not find it with my father or with any of us."

"Of course," Ethan said. "Again, thank you."

He watched her leave, more convinced than before that all was not right with the Rowan family. But he didn't believe this was the time or place to pursue the matter too aggressively.

Gardiner had remained a short distance removed from the others throughout Ethan's conversations with Mr. Rowan and the merchant's daughter. Now, though, he strolled to where Ethan stood, stopping beside him.

"I don't envy the rector having to mollify Mister Rowan," the warden said.

"Nor do I. Will he tell them of all that was done to Missus Rowan's corpse?"

Gardiner shook his head. "Not unless he has to. They know that her skull was taken, of course, and the hand as well. The rest, though, is . . . well, it's all rather gruesome, isn't it?"

"Some might say that he has an obligation to inform the families of everything."

"He has struggled with that, Mister Kaille, I assure you. Secrecy does not come easily to him. But in this case he has been forced to consider whether the truth might be so . . . unsettling to the families that a small omission is the greater balm."

Perhaps the warden had a point. It wasn't a choice Ethan would have wanted to make.

"I know it's been but a few hours, but have you learned anything yet?" Gardiner asked.

"Yes. I know now that your sexton was right: Yours is not the lone burying ground to have been violated." He nodded once to the man and limped toward the School Street gate. "I'll send word when I know more."

Gardiner offered no response. When Ethan reached the street, the warden was still standing just as he had been, gazing after Caner and the others.

Ethan was already considering how he might contrive to speak once more with Mister Rowan, perhaps at the family estate. There was more to their tale than either the father or daughter had let on, and he believed that before he finished this inquiry he would need to learn what it was. For the time being, though, he had other avenues to explore.

He followed Queen Street past the courthouse and the Old Meeting House, before continuing onto King Street, which took him by the Town Hall. At Merchant's Row, he turned north. As he threaded his way through the crowds walking to and from Faneuil Hall, however, he caught sight of an all-too-familiar shock of yellow hair. Nigel. Nap, Gordon, and Mariz couldn't have been far away. Ethan kept his head down, as he followed the edge of the lane closest to Wentworth's Wharf, hoping Sephira's toughs wouldn't see him. This once, luck was on his side. He reached Ann Street without incident and crossed Mill Creek into the North End.

The first street after the creek was a narrow byway called Paddy's Alley. And at the southern corner of the lane, a stone's throw from the wharves and shipyards, stood a run-down tavern called the Crow's Nest.

If the resurrectionists intended to sell the body parts they had stolen, it was possible they would eventually find their way here.

The Crow's Nest was about as different from the Dowsing Rod as a publick house could be. Where Kannice maintained a strict prohibition against illegal activities, Joseph Duncan, the current proprietor of the

Crow's Nest, could not have remained in business were it not for the illicit trades—whoring, smuggling, and the buying and selling of pilfered goods—that went on under his roof.

Reaching the tavern, Ethan pushed through the door into a dimly lit great room that smelled of stale ale and tobacco. A dozen or so men sat at tables, speaking in low tones, and several more stood at the bar, trying hard to look like they were just there for a drink. All of them turned toward the door as Ethan walked in, but few spared him more than a perfunctory glance.

One who did was a small, dark-haired man by the bar, who held a pipe clenched between yellowed teeth. His cheeks were pitted and scarred from a bout of smallpox. He marked Ethan's approach the way a sparrow might watch a feral cat.

"Good day, Dunc," Ethan said, joining the man at the bar.

"Kaille," Duncan said, sounding even less welcoming than Janna usually did. "What do you want?"

He spoke with a Scottish brogue, and with the pipe in his mouth his accent was nigh impenetrable.

"I just have a few questions, and I'll be on my way."

"Every time you come to me with questions, I seem to end up with with a broken nose or a blackened eye. I think I'll pass this time."

Ethan nodded. "I can understand that."

"Well, good," Dunc said, sounding surprised. "It's not that—"

"Of course," Ethan went on, dropping his voice, "if you won't help me out, I'll have no choice but to tell every fence and cloyer in Boston that you *did*. Starting with Sephira."

Dunc stared back at him, puffing so hard on his pipe that the leaf in his bowl glowed like a brand, and pale smoke billowed around his head. "I don't think you will," he said. "You're no nose. That's something herself might do, but you've never been as mean you make yourself out to be."

"That might be the nicest thing you've ever said to me."

"Aye. Don't think too much of it. I still haven't forgiven you for almost burning down my place."

Ethan grinned, but quickly turned serious again. "I really do need to ask you some questions, Dunc," he whispered, "and while I might not be a nose, I am still a speller. And my conjuring can cause all kinds of mischief."

Dunc eyed him still, looking like he'd just sucked on a lemon. At last he gave a single curt nod.

"My thanks," Ethan said, keeping his voice low. He slid a threepenny bit onto the bar. "An ale," he said to the barkeep, a lanky man with over-large eyes and a crooked nose. Ethan had never learned his name.

The barkeep filled a tankard for him.

Ethan sipped it, and nearly spit it out. After forcing down this one mouthful, he said to Dunc, "This is swill. You should serve the Kent pale that Kannice gets."

"People don't come in here for the food or drink," Dunc said with a glare. "Now what is it you want?"

"I'm sorry. I thought you'd want me to buy a drink, linger a bit, make it look like I'm doing something other than wringing informa-tion out of you."

Dunc paled. After a moment, he signaled for an ale as well.

"Have you heard anyone in here mention that they've taken to strip-ping graves in the last week or two?"

"What?" Dunc asked, making no effort to keep his voice down.

"Resurrectionists," Ethan said in a whisper. "Grave robbers."

Dunc pulled the pipe from his mouth. "No," he said, his cheeks turning red. "I've heard nothing. And if I had, I would have told them to take it out in the streets. You might not think much of me, Kaille, but you should know I don't tolerate that sort of thing in here! Not from anyone, not even Miss Pryce!"

Ethan didn't ask how he would manage to tell Sephira to take her business outside without getting himself beaten to a bloody mess. Dunc sounded as serious as Ethan had ever heard him; he wondered if the Scot's outrage was real.

"Calm down, Dunc," he said. "I apologize. I didn't know you felt so strongly about it."

Dunc replaced his pipe with a click of his teeth on clay. "There have been robberies?" he asked, speaking around the pipe stem.

Ethan nodded. "Nearly two dozen. At King's Chapel, Copp's Hill, and the Granary."

"What did they take?"

He shrugged. "Heads, hands. Just the sort of things a young man fancying himself a surgeon might need to educate himself." He didn't say anything about the feet or the mutilation of the cadavers' chests. Even if Dunc truly had been offended by the suggestion that he would traffic in body parts, he was bound to mention the robberies to someone. Despite all his protestations to the contrary, Dunc was not Boston's most discreet proprietor. That was fine with Ethan: let word get around that graves had been robbed, and let those who were responsible believe that Ethan thought the desecrations nothing more or less than the work of resurrectionists interested in making a few pounds.

"Well," Dunc said, "if anyone shows up here trying to sell anything gruesome, I'll order them out. And I'll get word to you."

"Yes, I'm sure. If you don't inform me, I'll hear of it sooner or later. You understand that, don't you?"

"I was serious before, Kaille. I tolerate a lot in here; maybe more than I should. But my da's grave was stripped back in Dundee. I've never forgotten it."

Ethan met the man's gaze. "In that case, you have my apologies a second time." He took another sip of his ale, but couldn't stomach more. It was time he returned to the Dowser and had a proper drink and some food. He patted Dunc on the back and left the Crow's Nest.

He walked to the Dowsing Rod the way he always had when coming from the North End, forgetting until it was too late that since the beginning of the occupation, his usual route took him just past Murray's Barracks, where the Twenty-ninth Regiment was billeted. By the time he realized what he had done, he was nearing the corner of Brattle and Hillier's streets. British soldiers, resplendent in red and white, were everywhere. Most ignored him as he strode past, but a few eyed him, their faces like stone.

He had served in His Majesty's navy, and though he soon chose to leave the service and pursue his fortune, he long clung to the belief that the Crown and Parliament were the best arbiters of how the American colonies ought to be governed. He had been a Tory for many years. No longer; the occupation had changed his mind. He could not abide the presence of soldiers in his city, and though he was not yet ready to join

Samuel Adams and the Sons of Liberty in agitating against the King's laws, he no longer found fault with their ambitions. Indeed, he could imagine a day when he might join their cause, and that, in itself, marked a startling change from just a year ago at this time.

More, since the day the troops first landed at Long Wharf and paraded into Boston, he had been convinced that eventually the occupation would lead to bloodshed. Over the past year, several altercations between soldiers and citizens had resulted in injuries, some of them serious. As of yet, though, no one had died. Ethan wondered how much longer their good fortune could hold.

As if magicked into being by the thought, a group of young men—their clothing torn and stained, their voices loud and boisterous—turned the corner onto Hillier's from Dock Square. These were just the sort of reckless pups who for months had been harassing uniformed regulars with taunts and insults.

"There are the bloody lobsters now," said one of the huffs, pitching his voice so that everyone on the street could hear.

Ethan slowed, then halted, eyeing the gang of young men. He was caught in between. Ahead of him, several soldiers had gathered in a tight cluster, their rifles held ready at waist level, their bayonets gleaming in the sun.

"What are ya goin' to do, ya thievin' dogs?" the huff called. "Ya goin' to shoot us?"

Ethan saw no officers on the street. A pair of soldiers ran off toward the barracks; he hoped they would return with someone who could take command of the situation without making matters worse. And he hoped they would do so with haste.

"You Yankees had best move on," a soldier called back. He sounded young, and his voice quavered slightly. "You don't want to get hurt."

"Now we're Yankees," the mouthy youth said, drawing laughter from his mates.

The soldier and his comrades began to sing "Yankee Doodle," a song with which the British had mocked colonial militia during the war with the French, and with which they had goaded colonists in the years since. They sang off-key, and in weak voices, as if their hearts were not really in it.

But their singing wiped the smiles off the faces of the young men. One of the pups picked up a stone off the street and threw it at the soldiers. The rest followed his example. Most of the stones missed their targets by good distances, but one whizzed past the head of a regular, and another hit a man in the shoulder.

The soldiers ceased their singing. Passersby had stopped to watch the confrontation, and now an eerie silence settled over the street. Several of the regulars raised their weapons to their shoulders.

"Throw another," one of them growled. "I dare ya."

Ethan saw no sign of the two men who had run off toward the barracks. And so he did the one thing he knew he could.

"*Imago ex aqua evocata,*" he whispered under his breath. Illusion, conjured from water.

They were near enough to the Town Dock that he thought he could cast a spell sourced in water. And as Uncle Reg appeared next to him once more, insubstantial in the afternoon sunlight, he felt the spell thrum in the street.

But the image he had hoped to summon—that of a British officer—did not appear.

"I must be too far from the harbor," he muttered, glancing at Reg.

The ghost merely stared back at him.

The soldiers began to advance on the pups, brandishing their weapons, their expressions grim. For their part, the youths picked up more stones. Ethan started to chant the spell again, intending this time to use the air around them as his source.

But at that moment, at last, the two soldiers sprinted back into view, with an older man—an officer by the look of him—following close behind.

"You men, fall back!" the officer shouted.

The soldiers halted, looking toward their commander.

The pups, however, showed no sign of backing down. Ethan hurried toward them.

"That's enough," he said, approaching their leader. "Leave here, before you get yourselves or someone else shot."

"And if we don't?" the mouth demanded.

Ethan bared his teeth in a grin. "Then I'll break your nose."

D. B. JACKSON

The pup blinked, and took a step back. He recovered quickly, though. "You're a damned lobster lover."

"And you have the brains of an oyster. Are you trying to get yourself killed?" Ethan looked at the others one at a time. "Are you? And you?"

None of them answered.

"Go home. We have enough to worry about in this town without oafs like you starting fights they can't finish."

Ethan didn't wait for their reply, but turned away and headed up the street past the soldiers. His hands were shaking.

He could hardly fathom the idiocy of those lads. Eventually one of this lot, or some other fool just like them, was going to push the soldiers too far, with tragic results.

He walked on, his heart pounding. He was wary now, eager to get off the street. But as he put more distance between himself and the barracks, it occurred to him to wonder why his illusion spell had failed. Yes, he had been far from the water, but he had felt the spell, and Uncle Reg had appeared. The conjuring should have worked.

He considered attempting another illusion spell, but by then he had reached the Dowsing Rod, and this stretch of Sudbury Street was crowded with people heading to their homes. Vowing to try a spell later, he pulled the door open and stepped inside.

The tavern's great room was relatively empty, and Kannice was nowhere to be seen. Kelf, though, shouted a greeting and waved him to the bar.

"Good day, Kelf."

"Kannice is at the market," the barkeep said, running the words together. "She'll be back soon enough. But in the meantime, you've been in demand."

"What do you mean?"

"There was a couple in here earlier, lookin' for ya. I think they want to hire ya."

Usually, Ethan limited himself to one client at a time, but since he had refused payment from the King's Chapel congregation, he felt justified in taking on a second job.

"Did they say more than that?" Ethan asked.

"Aye, but they was talkin' to Kannice, so you'll have to wait for her. In the meantime, what can I get ya?"

Ethan ordered an ale—a real ale this time—and a plate of oysters. Kelf filled a tankard for him before retreating into the kitchen and emerging again a few minutes later carrying a plate that was piled high with oysters.

Ethan sipped his ale, allowing the Kent pale to wash away the lingering taste of Dunc's swill. Then he set to work on the oysters. As he shucked and ate, he considered what he might do next to find those who had desecrated the graves. It was possible that Dunc would send word, that the stolen goods would wind up at the Crow's Nest and Dunc's antipathy toward grave robbing would lead him to keep his promise. But Ethan thought it unlikely.

It wasn't Dunc he doubted—much to his own surprise—but rather the robbers themselves. Even without finding any trace of conjuring power in the burying grounds, he remained convinced that the robberies were tied in some way to spellers. Several of the graves had contained items that might have been worth something: hair combs, a cane with a brass tip and ivory handle; Abigail Rowan had been buried wearing a small brooch. Why would ordinary thieves work so hard to dig up graves but then leave behind these sellable items? And who, other than a conjurer intent on dark spellmaking, would mark every corpse?

But while he thought it possible that a spellmaker had robbed the graves, he couldn't imagine who this person might be. He knew Janna wasn't involved, and he doubted that Gavin Black, who lived near Murray's Barracks, would be party to such horrors either. Gaspar Mariz, on the other hand, might very well have committed such a ghastly crime on Sephira's behalf. Before long, Ethan would need to speak with him, although first he would have to figure out how to arrange a conversation without also involving Nigel, Nap, and Gordon.

"There you are!"

He turned. Kannice was crossing to the bar bearing two canvas sacks filled with fowl, vegetables, and fish. Her cheeks were flushed, and he could see corded muscle beneath the skin of her slender arms. She kissed him lightly on the lips and heaved the bags onto the bar.

"Kelf!" she called.

The barman emerged from the back.

"There's flour and cream waiting at the market. It's paid for, but I couldn't carry it."

"Course you couldn't," Kelf said. He glanced at Ethan and shook his head. "Wisp of a thing like her—I don't know how she carries anythin'." He lumbered to the door. "I'll be back."

Kannice carried one of the sacks into the kitchen.

"Do you need help?" Ethan asked.

"Don't you start, too!" she called.

"All right." He waited until she came back for the second sack. "Kelf mentioned that someone came in looking for me."

"That's right. A young couple, Darcy and Ruth Walters. Darcy said you knew his mother."

Ethan felt an involuntary shudder run through his body. "Aye," he whispered.

Kannice's brow creased. "Are you all right?"

"What else did he say?" Ethan asked.

"Just that they needed your help."

"I'm sure they do." He drained his ale and headed for the door.

"Who are they? Who was his mother?"

"A conjurer," Ethan said over his shoulder. "She died a fortnight ago."

atience Walters was a spellmaker of modest abilities who lived in New Boston until succumbing to pneumonia in mid-June. Ethan had gotten to know her only in the last year or two of her life, but he enjoyed her company. She was a diminutive woman with bright green eyes, a quick smile, and a soft, almost demure laugh. She liked to talk about conjuring—something Ethan didn't get to do very often—and though she did not cast many spells in the last years of her life, she seemed to take great pleasure in asking Ethan questions about his spellmaking. He downplayed his own talent, often telling her that he knew of several spellers, including Janna, who could tell her far more about conjuring than he could, but each time she would wave off his protestations and ask him for another story.

Darcy had not inherited his mother's abilities, but he and Ruth welcomed Ethan into their home, and often sat with him and Patience as they talked. Ruth had recently given birth to a son, Benjamin, whom they named for Darcy's deceased father.

With all that he had seen this day, Ethan had little doubt as to why they wished to engage his services. Still, he was puzzled. Patience had been buried only a fortnight before in the Common Burying Ground, and Ethan had seen no disturbed graves there. He even convinced himself that because no one who had been involved in the old witch trials was buried there, the burying ground had been spared. He had attended

Patience's funeral, and so knew exactly where on the grounds she had been buried. Yet today he had been too distracted to think of seeking out her grave in particular. She had died so recently; if any graves at the burying ground had been robbed, hers would have been one of them. He berated himself for his carelessness.

The Walters house was a small brick structure on Lynde Street, near the West Meeting House, and only a short walk from the Dowser. Ethan covered the distance in as little time as his bad leg would allow, and knocked on the door rather more forcefully than necessary.

He had to wait but a moment before the door opened.

"Ethan!" Darcy said. "We didn't expect you so soon."

"I came as quickly as I could," he said.

Darcy waved him into the house, and shut the door behind him. He was taller than his mother, although not by much. In other ways—the vivid green eyes, the oval face, the easy, open manner—he resembled her a good deal. He wore his dark hair in a plait and was dressed plainly in a white linen shirt and brown breeches.

Ruth sat by the window holding Benjamin in her arms, her long, wheaten hair reaching nearly to the floor, her round face pale and a bit pinched. Ethan hoped that she was well.

"Good day, Ruth."

"Good day, Ethan," she said, managing a smile that brought a hint of color to her cheeks.

"Kannice told me you were engaged in another inquiry," Darcy said. "I'm sorry to take you away from that."

"I'm not sure you are taking me away from it. Indeed, I think I know just why you sought me out."

Darcy frowned. "You do?"

"Aye. I fear so." Ethan hesitated. Darcy and Ruth might not know yet of the mutilations; he would want to present those tidings to them as gently as possible. Once more he wondered how Patience's grave could have been disturbed; he had walked every path in the burying ground, and though he had failed to look for her headstone in particular, he had not noticed any disturbed graves. Perhaps whoever was responsible for the robberies was as brazen as he was cruel, and had struck in the middle of the day, in the hours since Ethan's visit to the burying ground. This was the only explanation that made any sense to him. "Did someone come to tell you what had happened," he asked, "or did you go out to the burying ground yourselves?"

Darcy regarded him the way he might a babbling lunatic. "The burying ground? Ethan, what are you talking about?"

"Your mother, of course, and the desecration of her grave."

"What?" Darcy and Ruth said simultaneously, her voice so sharp that Benjamin began to fuss.

"Something's been done to her grave?" Darcy asked.

"Isn't that why you came to the Dowser?"

Darcy shook his head. "No. But if something's happened—"

"Perhaps it hasn't," Ethan said. He should have been relieved, but instead he felt his apprehension increase. "Forgive me. Tell me what it is you want me to do."

Darcy and Ruth shared a look. She had paled again.

"It *is* about Mother," Darcy said. "She's been dead and buried for two weeks now. But . . . but her shade is still here."

Ethan gave an involuntary shiver. "Her shade?"

"Aye. In her bedroom."

"And has it been here since the day of her death?"

Darcy glanced at Ruth again.

"I don't think so," she said. "I first noticed her three days ago. I thought . . . I was afraid that I had imagined it, so it wasn't until yester-day that I told Darcy."

"Ruth is awake late at night more than I am. Because of Benjamin. And she wanders the house."

Ethan nodded. He had encountered ghosts too many times to count. He saw Reg most every day. Shades did not usually frighten him. But this . . . A trickle of sweat ran down his temple. "Have you tried to speak with her? Do you have any idea why she's come back?"

"None. My father wasn't a speller so I don't know . . . Is this normal?"

"No, it's not. Your mother would have communed with a spectral guide who allowed her to access power for her spells."

"Aye. She said it was her great-grandfather. But that was different, wasn't it?"

"I'm afraid so. Can I see her room?" Ethan asked.

"Of course," Darcy said. "This way."

He started to lead Ethan to the back of the house, but before they left the common room, Ruth said, "She won't be there."

Ethan and Darcy turned. Ethan shivered a second time. The woman sounded terrified.

"She comes at night. I've . . . I've looked for her at other times, but she's never there. Only at night."

"Still, we should check," Darcy said, his tone so gentle it made Ethan's heart ache. "If you need us, call out."

He led Ethan back toward Patience's room. Once they were out of the common room, he whispered, "This has been a terrible ordeal for Ruth. She was afraid she was going mad, and even now that I've seen Mother—or rather, her ghost—she's still frightened. I think she fears for Ben."

The small bedroom at the back of the house was sparsely furnished. The bed in the far corner had been covered with a colorful quilt, and a simple chest of drawers stood nearer to the door, its top bare save for a single white candle in a pewter holder.

"Her personal effects?"

"She never had much. There's some clothing left in the drawers. Her wedding ring is in a small box in my wardrobe. There wasn't much else."

"You said you had seen her, too. What can you tell me about her appearance?"

Darcy knitted his brow. "What do you want to know?"

"Did she look . . . whole?"

The young man shrugged, then nodded. "Aye."

"Was she solid or more like her spectral guide?"

"More like him," Darcy said. "Not solid at all. And she glowed like he used to."

"With the same color?"

"No," Darcy said, his tone giving the impression that he had just realized this for the first time. "Great-Grandfather was a bright yellow, quite a lovely color really. Mother looked more like a sickly green." He looked stricken. "I should have noticed that earlier. Do you think it means something?"

"I don't know," Ethan told him. "You also said that you tried to speak with her. What happened?"

"Very little. She didn't answer, but I didn't expect she would."

"Did she know you were there? Did she seem to know where she was?"

Darcy weighed this for several seconds, chewing his lip and staring down at the floor. "She looked at us," he said. "I think she could tell we were here. And she definitely knew where she was. She walked around her bed rather than through it or over it. But she didn't seem well."

"Explain. Please."

"She was agitated, frightened even." He raised his gaze to Ethan's. "I believe she understands she shouldn't be here, but I don't think she knows how to leave."

Ethan rubbed a hand over his face. "I don't know what I can do, Darcy, but I'll help you in any way I can. I was fond of your mother. This is a cruel fate for one as kind as she."

"Thank you. We haven't a lot of money, but we can pay you something."

"We can talk about that another time. As I said, I'm not even sure I can help."

"Again, you have our thanks."

"Can I come back here tonight?" Ethan asked. "I want to see her myself."

"I think that having you here tonight would come as a great relief to both Ruth and me."

Ethan offered what he hoped would be a reassuring smile. "Good. I'll be back sometime after dark."

He turned, intending to leave Patience's bedroom.

"Just a moment, Ethan," Darcy said, lowering his voice. "You thought I had called you here for another reason. You thought something had been done to Mother's grave. Should I go out to the burying ground?"

"No," Ethan said. "I don't think that's necessary."

"Can you tell me what's happened?"

"A small number of graves have been desecrated, probably by resurrectionists." Ethan didn't dare say more.

"Dear Lord! Do you think that's why Mother—?"

"No. I was in the Common Burying Ground today. I searched it thoroughly and didn't notice any damage to your mother's grave. I doubt that it's been violated in the hours since."

Darcy let out a long breath. "Thank God. Ruth has been through too much already. I don't think she could endure another shock, particularly one so gruesome. To be honest, I'm not certain that I could, either."

They walked back out to the common room, where Darcy informed Ruth of Ethan's intent to return that evening. Ruth still looked pale, but her face brightened at these tidings, and she thanked Ethan several times before he managed to excuse himself and leave.

Only when he was no longer with the young couple did he give in to the trepidation that had gripped him upon hearing of Patience's ghost. As a thieftaker, he didn't believe in coincidence; as a conjurer he understood that even seemingly disparate events and phenomena could be related to one another. He refused to believe the grave robberies had nothing to do with the appearance of Patience Walters's ghost.

But how were the two connected?

The sun had started its long descent through the western sky, and the streets of Boston had begun to empty. It would be light for several hours more, but already Ethan could smell cooking fires and the aromas of roasting fowl and fish. It seemed that this day had lasted forever, and with the promise he had made to Ruth and Darcy, it was far from over. But a half plate of oysters and some ale had done little to take the edge off his hunger.

He headed back to the Dowser, his thoughts racing in a hundred different directions. Fear for himself had given way to cold anger at the thought of a conjurer somehow using him to harm his friends. Patience had never done a cruel deed in her life; she deserved peace.

Ethan heard a commotion ahead of him, and looked up in time to see a small cluster of people walking toward him, two of them carrying someone in a sedan, with a black cloth covering. A young man, tall, well-dressed in a black coat and breeches, walked several yards ahead. He had short powdered hair and dark, expressive eyes. Ethan thought that he had seen him before, though he couldn't recall where.

"Please stand aside, sir," the man called, as he drew near. "We are bearing this child to the Province Hospital."

Ethan stepped off the road, taking care to stand on the upwind side. Province Hospital, which was located on the remote western edge of New Boston, was also called the Pest House. It was where those unfortunates who fell ill with the most contagious of distempers were sent to recover. Or not. Ethan had little doubt that the person in the oncoming sedan had been taken with smallpox. Which meant that this gentleman before him . . .

"Might you be Doctor Warren?" Ethan asked him.

"Yes, I am," the man said, his manner sober, his voice strong. "Doctor Joseph Warren, at your service. Have we met, sir?"

"No. I know you by reputation. But those who speak of you do so with admiration. It's my pleasure to make your acquaintance."

"And you are?"

"Forgive me. Ethan Kaille. I'm—"

"A thieftaker. Yes, I know. Yours is a name one hears with some frequency as well."

"Followed by an imprecation, no doubt," Ethan said, and smiled.

For the first time, the man grinned, and it seemed that ten years fell away from his features. "Not at all. Some instruments were stolen from my office a year or so ago. An associate mentioned you, thinking I might wish to engage your services."

"Mister Adams, perhaps?"

"Yes, that's right," Warren said, with obvious surprise.

"But you went to someone else?" Ethan asked, thinking of Sephira.

"Actually, no. I recovered them myself, from a patient who was less than pleased with services I had provided."

"I believe, Doctor, that you might be in the wrong line of work."

Warren's grin flashed again, though it faded as he watched the sedan holding his patient—a boy of perhaps twelve years—pass by, followed by a man and woman Ethan assumed were the stricken lad's parents.

"Smallpox?" Ethan asked, gazing after them.

"Aye."

"In that case, I won't keep you. It was a pleasure meeting you, Doctor Warren."

"And you, Mister Kaille." He glanced down the road. "Avoid crowds if you can. And give any house bearing a red flag a wide berth."

"I will. Thank you."

He tipped his hat to the man, and they went their separate ways. It occurred to Ethan that if he was interested in robbing graves, and wanted to find corpses that hadn't been dead for long, he would come to a city like Boston in the middle of the summer, when disease was prevalent. The bodies might be infected for a few days after the poor souls died, perhaps even for a week. But after that, the resurrectionists could begin their grim harvest.

He usually arrived at the Dowser later in the evening, after the dinner hour, when Kannice's regular clientele crowded around tables and the bar. This early in the day, there were fewer patrons in the great room, and many of those present were dressed in red and white uniforms.

Over the past several years, Kannice had become ever more vocal in her opposition to the taxes and tariffs imposed on the colonies by Parliament and enforced by the Crown. The arrival of occupying troops, and their expectation that they could eat in publick houses without having to pay for their food, had convinced her that Britain could no longer lay claim to the loyalty of her American subjects.

There were perhaps twenty-five regulars in the tavern, all of them crowded around five tables in the center of the great room. They were speaking in loud voices, laughing lustily at one joke or another.

Kannice stood behind the bar, a dishcloth slung over her shoulder. The look in her bright blue eyes could have melted steel. Kelf hovered beside her, though whether because he feared for her safety or the safety of the soldiers Ethan couldn't say. So intent was she on the regulars that she didn't notice that Ethan had come in until he planted himself in front of her.

She started, but then a smile crossed her lips. "I didn't see you," she said.

"You had your mind on other things."

Her pleasure at seeing him gave way to a scowl. "They've already spilled four ales," she whispered. "It's not enough that they take my food and drink without offering to pay so much as a penny, but then they slosh it about like it's naught more than water. And who do you think gets to clean it up?"

"Kelf?" Ethan asked, feigning innocence.

The barkeep snorted. Kannice glared at them.

"It's not funny."

"I know," Ethan said. "I'm sorry."

"Where's the rum-dell?" one of the soldiers called, holding an empty tankard over his head.

"Rum-dell am I now?" Kannice said through clenched teeth. She tried to push Kelf out of her way so that she could step out from behind the bar. Ethan thought it likely that she intended to shove the tankard into the soldier's ear, or perhaps elsewhere.

"I'll go," Kelf said. "No sense gettin' us shut down."

He filled a tankard, pasted a smile on his face, and walked out into the great room. "Here ya go, sir," he said, his voice pitched to carry. "Never been called a rum-dell before; I think I like it."

The soldiers laughed uproariously. Kannice seethed.

"Kelf's right, you know. They're not worth getting angry over, or doing something you'll regret."

"Something stupid, you mean?"

Ethan didn't reply, and a grin crept across her lovely face.

"Afraid to answer?" she asked.

"Very."

She laughed. "What would you like to eat, Mister Kaille?"

"Whatever they're having. What's good enough for the king's men is good enough for me." He leaned forward and winked at her. "Just don't spit in mine," he whispered.

She laughed again and walked back into the kitchen, returning moments later with a bowl of fish chowder and a round of bread. Ethan fished in his pocket.

"Don't you dare," Kannice said, growling the words.

Despite her warning, he pulled out a half shilling. "You're having to give away too much food tonight. Let me pay for this."

She glowered at him, but when he didn't shrink from her gaze, she took the coin. "Tonight," she said. Her smile returned, deepened. "Speaking of tonight, will you be here?"

"I'm not sure yet."

"That's not the answer I was looking for."

"I know. But I have a previous engagement with a ghost."

She sobered in an instant. "Tell me."

He glanced back at the soldiers.

"In here," she said, gesturing toward the back rooms behind the bar.

Ethan walked around the bar and joined her in the kitchen, where a large pot of chowder simmered over a cooking fire. He related to her what he had seen at King's Chapel and the other burying grounds, as well as what Darcy and Ruth Walters had wanted of him. The lone detail he omitted was the mutilation of the cadavers' feet. She would have worried, and he remained so perplexed as to what it might mean that he wouldn't have been able to ease her mind.

As it was, by the time he had finished, her forehead was creased and her lips pressed thin. "Where would you even begin to look for the people who did this?"

"That's a fine question. If they're conjurers, they'll cast eventually, and I'll feel their spell."

Her expression hardened. "Didn't you tell me that Sephira Pryce has a conjurer working for her now?"

"I've considered that," Ethan said. "This doesn't feel like something with which Sephira would involve herself. Too much effort, not enough profit."

She started to say more, but Ethan stopped her with a raised hand. "I plan to speak with Mariz anyway. Even if he isn't involved, he might have some ideas as to who is."

"And you expect him to help you? Sephira's man?" She laid the back of her hand on his brow. "You must have taken a fever."

Ethan grinned.

"Come on. Your chowder is getting cold." She took his hand and pulled him back out to the bar.

Ethan ate and sipped his ale. As he did, though, he thought about what he had said to Kannice. Speaking to Mariz was not as odd an idea as Kannice thought. If this actually was Sephira's doing, she would be relying on the bespectacled man's conjuring abilities. And if she had nothing to do with the grave desecrations, Mariz might well prove a valuable source of information.

A year before, Sephira's man was grievously wounded in a confrontation with other conjurers. Drawn to the site of the encounter by the thrumming of the spells, Ethan found Mariz, healed him as best he could, and summoned Sephira's other toughs so that they could take the man back to her estate. Mariz remained unconscious for days, and when at last he woke he named himself Ethan's friend, without Sephira's knowledge, and swore to come to Ethan's aid should Ethan have need.

"I still work for Miss Pryce, and I will follow what orders she gives me," the man said at the time. "But when I am not acting on her behalf, I am free to honor whatever friendships I choose. And like it or not, Kaille, you and I are now friends."

Janna hadn't known what to make of the robberies and the symbols carved into the corpses. Maybe Mariz would.

After some time, the regulars sauntered out of the Dowsing Rod. No more than a minute later, as if they had been watching the tavern door, several of Kannice's usual patrons filed in. Ethan finished a second bowl of chowder, and lingered over a second ale until at last night fell.

He waited until Kannice and Kelf had carried another tureen of chowder from the kitchen—to the cheers of Kannice's hungry customers—before picking up his tricorn from the bar and catching Kannice's eye. She was speaking to Tom Langer, one of her usual crowd. Ethan saw her falter, her grin slipping. He nodded once to her. She forced a small, thin smile in return.

He wended his way through the crowd to the tavern door, and slipped out into the warm air. It was another hazy night; the gibbous moon cast dull shadows across the lanes. A freshening breeze out of the west carried the suggestion of rain, and perhaps a respite from the heat. But thus far this had been a summer of empty thunder and deceptive zephyrs.

The streets of New Boston were largely deserted, and because this part of the city was sparsely populated, they were dark as well. Faint candlelight from a few windows spilled out onto the cobblestone lanes, but Ethan had to place his feet with care on the uneven pavement.

The Walters house was more brightly lit than most; its windows beckoned to him with a welcoming glow. No one passing by would have guessed that the family within had been haunted by a shade, which perhaps was the point.

Ethan approached the house and knocked once on the door. After several moments, it opened. Ruth stood before him, holding Benjamin, who was crying.

"She's here," the woman said, and walked back into the common room.

He removed his hat and entered, shutting the door behind him.

Darcy stood at the mouth of the corridor that led to Patience's bedroom. His face was careworn, his upper lip beaded with sweat.

"Thank you for coming back, Ethan," he said over the sound of his son's fussing.

"She's back there?" Ethan asked.

Darcy nodded, swallowed.

"Let's go see her," he said, trying to infuse the words with a confidence he didn't feel.

Darcy faced Ruth. "Do you want to—?"

"We'll wait out here," she said, her voice tight.

He nodded and led Ethan to the back room.

The shade of Patience Walters made no effort to conceal herself. When Darcy and Ethan entered the room, she was by the window, gazing outside. Perhaps she could hear them, for she turned as they stopped in the center of the room. She looked first at her son before turning to stare at Ethan, and while she offered nothing by way of greeting—no gesture, no change in her countenance—she kept her eyes fixed on his.

She looked much as Ethan remembered her; through the murky green glow that clung to her like silver mist on blades of grass, he could see the lines around her mouth and eyes, the smooth brow and high cheekbones, her upturned nose. She was dressed in a simple gown and petticoats; a kerchief covered her head.

Her eyes shone so brightly that at first Ethan didn't realize Patience was the sole source of light in the bedroom. Darcy had not lit the candle on her chest of drawers.

"Try speaking to her," Ethan said.

Darcy glanced his way, looking nervous. But he gave a nod and faced his mother again. "Can you hear me, Mother?"

The shade fixed her gleaming eyes on him and, after several moments, nodded slowly.

"My God," Darcy whispered. "Are you all right? Has something happened to bring you back to us?"

She didn't reply in any way. After staring at Darcy for a few seconds more, she turned back to Ethan. Her movements were slow, graceful; she almost appeared to be underwater. She reached with her right hand to her left arm, and began to push up the sleeve of her gown.

"What is she doing?" Darcy asked.

"Did she use blood to conjure?"

"Yes, sometimes, but—" Darcy raised a hand to his mouth, reminding Ethan of Patience. "You're right. That's just what she's doing. Can she—?"

"No," Ethan said. "But I can. I think that's what she wants."

He pulled out his knife and held it up for the shade to see. The bobbing of her head was achingly slow, but for the first time a smile touched her lips.

Ethan didn't cut himself; he didn't have to for what he needed to do. "*Veni ad me,*" he said in Latin. Come to me.

Uncle Reg materialized beside him, his russet glow adding to the light in the room. He didn't spare Ethan so much as a glance, but stared hard at the shade before them. She turned her gaze on him, her eyes widening.

"Can you communicate with her?" Ethan asked.

Reg nodded, still not looking at him.

"Ask her—"

Reg rounded on him, eyes blazing.

"Right," Ethan said. "You know what to ask her."

Ethan's ghost faced Patience once more, and for a long time the two shades remained motionless, gazes locked.

"What are they doing?" Darcy finally asked.

"My spectral guide is finding out what he can from your mother's ghost."

"To what end?"

"I'm hoping he'll be able to tell us why she's here."

"Can he speak? Great-Grandfather never could."

"He can't, either," Ethan said. "But he can be quite expressive in his own way."

For several minutes more, the shades regarded each other, communing silently. At last they broke eye contact, and Reg turned to Ethan. He appeared troubled, his eyebrows bunched, his habitual scowl more pronounced than usual.

"She's not here by choice, is she?" Ethan asked.

Reg shook his head.

"Is she being held here?"

The ghost hesitated before nodding.

"What does that mean?" Darcy asked. "How can she be held here?"

Reg's gaze flicked to the younger man, but immediately fixed on Ethan again.

"He didn't like the way I phrased the question," Ethan said. "I'm not sure yet what he means." He chewed his lip, eyeing Reg. "It's not that she's being held here. Rather, something is preventing her from moving on. Is that right?"

This time Reg didn't hesitate at all when he nodded.

"A conjuring?"

Another nod, emphatic.

"Is this related to what we saw at the burying grounds today?"

Reg answered with a small shrug.

"We have work to do, you and I."

A fierce grin split the old ghost's face.

"Is she . . . is she well?" Darcy asked. "I feel foolish asking that about a spirit. But is she . . . suffering in any way?"

Ethan looked to Reg, who shook his head, though he appeared troubled once more. "I don't think she's suffering," Ethan said. "But this isn't right. She doesn't belong here, and until she can move on to the realm of the dead, she won't be content."

"Is there anything I can do to help her?"

"Don't be afraid of her," Ethan said, watching Reg. "Let her see you. Let her see her grandson."

Reg nodded. Patience, who had been watching Ethan's exchange with his ghost, turned her glowing eyes to her son and smiled.

Darcy smiled in turn. "We can do that."

Ethan turned back to Uncle Reg. *"Dimit—"*

Reg threw up a hand, forcing Ethan to stop. He had been about to say *Dimitto te,* Latin for "I release you."

"There's more?" he asked.

Reg nodded. He pointed to Patience, and to himself. He held up two fingers. Then a third, a fourth, and a fifth. He held up his other hand, and opened his fist one finger at a time.

"God help us," Ethan said, breathing the words.

"What is it?" Darcy asked. "What is he trying to say?"

Ethan let out a long shuddering breath. "There are more shades like your mother," he said. "They can't leave either, and there are a lot of them."

Chapter
SEVEN

fter delivering these last tidings, Uncle Reg agreed
to be released. Ethan and Darcy joined Ruth in the common
room, where they offered her assurance that as unsettling as
it might be to have a shade in her home, the ghost of Patience Walters
posed no danger to her child or to her. Soon after, Ethan departed their
home and, hesitating but for an instant, left New Boston for the opu-
lent mansions of the North End.

This time he made certain to avoid Brattle Street and the barracks
of the Twenty-ninth Regiment. Still, he saw many regulars on the streets,
including four soldiers who were being taunted by yet another group of
reckless young men. "Bloody-backed scoundrels!" the pups shouted.
"Lobsters!" One called, "Damn the king! Damn his soldiers!" This drew
laughs from his companions. These regulars, like the others Ethan had
seen earlier in the day, held their rifles waist high, their bayonets fixed.
Ethan half expected them to open fire.

He gave the regulars and the pups taunting them a wide berth, and
crossed into the North End by way of Hanover. He then followed Back
and Salem streets, making his way past the North Meeting House,
with its soaring spire and clock tower, to Ellis Street and the impressive
mansion of Alexander Rowan.

It was late to arrive at anyone's home uninvited and unannounced. It
was especially so for one as wealthy and influential as Mr. Rowan. Ethan
didn't care.

The entire Rowan family had behaved strangely in the King's Chapel Burying Ground, and after his encounter with the shade of Patience Walters, Ethan thought he knew why.

Like the Walters house, the Rowan mansion was constructed of brick. The resemblance ended there. Alexander Rowan's home stood three stories tall, and had banks of windows across the façade and marble columns on either side of the entrance. The door itself was oak, with a polished brass lion's-head knocker. Candlelight still glowed in several of the windows on the first and second floors, but not all. Ethan wondered if some in the family were already abed.

He followed the stone path to the door and rapped with the knocker. At first there was no response, and Ethan knocked a second time.

At last the door opened, revealing not a servant, as he had expected, but Mr. Rowan's son. He was in shirtsleeves, and kept one arm hidden behind his back.

"Yes, what is it?" the young man demanded, sounding cross.

Ethan moved forward a half step, so that the light from within fell upon his face. Rowan the younger retreated a step and produced a pistol, which he held in the hand that had been hidden. Ethan raised his hands to show that he carried no weapon.

"I'm unarmed, Mister Rowan."

"Who are you?" Rowan asked, though Ethan saw a flicker of recognition in the man's eyes.

"I'm Ethan Kaille, sir. Reverend Caner has engaged my services to inquire into the unfortunate incidents in the King's Chapel Burying Ground."

Rowan lowered the pistol, looking much relieved. "Of course, Mister Kaille. I remember you now." He frowned. "Are you in the habit of disturbing people in their homes at such a late hour?"

"No, sir, I'm not. I wouldn't have come without good reason."

"Well, I'm sorry to say that my father has already retired for the night. If you wish to speak with him, you'll have to come back in the morning."

"I believe you can help me, sir."

If anything, this prompted a deepening of Rowan's frown. After a brief hesitation, however, he beckoned Ethan into the house and closed the door after him.

"I wonder, sir—"

"Not here," Rowan said. He walked away, leaving Ethan little choice but to follow.

They crossed through a large parlor, followed a dim corridor toward the back of the house, and entered a well-lit study. An open book rested pages-down on a wooden side table beside a plush chair. When he had shut the door, Rowan faced Ethan, looking like he intended to say something. Instead, he glanced down at the pistol he still held and crossed to a writing desk along the far wall of the study. After placing the weapon in a drawer, he turned to Ethan again.

"Now, what is it you want?"

"Today, at the burying ground, I asked your father if he had noticed anything odd, either here or at your family's warehouses."

"Yes, I remember. And he told you that he hadn't."

"Aye, he did. But you and I both know that wasn't true."

"Now see here, Kaille—!"

"Do you truly expect the ghost to leave of its own accord?" Ethan asked, his voice echoing in the small room.

Rowan gaped at him, looking frightened and young. "I don't know what you mean."

"Of course you do, sir," Ethan said, speaking in softer tones. "When did your mother's shade first appear?"

Rowan shook his head, saying nothing. After a lengthy silence, he dropped into the nearest chair and asked, "How did you know?"

"Yours is not the only family in Boston being haunted. How long has it been?"

"She appeared three nights past. My wife noticed her first. We've been living here since Mother died. Father has not been himself since he lost her, and Esther and I felt that he shouldn't be alone in a house of this size. The servants are all quite competent, of course, but . . . well, you understand."

"Aye."

"On Tuesday night, Esther went into Father and Mother's room to make certain that his bedclothes had been laid out properly. And when she entered, she saw the . . . you called it a shade. That's as good a word as any. It's a foul, horrible thing. I shudder to think of the fright Esther took."

"Wait," Ethan said, his eyes narrowing. "The shade doesn't look like your mother?"

"Heavens, no. It's—" He shook his head again. "I suppose there is really no delicate way to say this: It looks like a ghoul in Mother's clothes."

Ethan considered this, staring down at his tricorn, which he held in his hands. He had assumed that this ghost would resemble Mrs. Rowan, just as Patience's shade resembled her.

"I'm sorry, sir," he said at length. "Please go on with your tale."

"There isn't much more to tell," Rowan said. "Esther screamed, and the rest of us hurried to the room. The apparition didn't flee, as one might expect. It merely stood at the window, gazing out into the night."

"Did it make any sound? Did it seem to recognize any of you, or make an attempt to communicate?"

"We didn't give it the chance," Rowan said, sounding appalled at the very idea. "We removed my father's personal effects the following morning, and have not been back in the room since. For the past several nights he's been sleeping in the room that used to belong to Margaret."

"So, you don't even know if it's come back," Ethan said.

Rowan took a long breath. "We do, actually. Late at night, when the candles in the corridor have been extinguished, I can see the fiend's glow seeping out from beneath the door."

"Have you seen it tonight?"

"I haven't yet looked."

"I realize that this is an imposition, Mister Rowan, but I would like to see this shade."

"You mean now?"

"Aye." When Rowan didn't answer, Ethan said, "I can come back another night, of course. But it would be every bit as much an imposition then. And perhaps it's best that we do this tonight, while your father is sleeping, rather than trouble him some other evening."

Rowan didn't move. "You said that you're a thieftaker. What do you think you can accomplish here?"

"I believe the appearance of your mother's ghost may be tied in some way to what was done to her grave. I believe that seeing her might help me determine how it is she's come to be here."

"Do you mean to tell me that you have experience with . . . beings of this sort?"

He couldn't very well deny it. "Aye, sir. As I've said, yours is not the only household to be so afflicted. I believe I can help you. But I need to see her."

Rowan wiped sweat from his upper lip with a shaking hand. At length he nodded and stood. "Yes, all right. But I beg of you: Please try to remain quiet as we make our way to the room. I don't wish to wake my father, or Esther for that matter."

"I understand, sir. Lead the way; I'll make as little noise as possible."

Rowan nodded, and led Ethan from the study, back through the parlor, to a broad curving stairway with a polished wood banister and white balusters. The wood of the steps matched that of the banister. A portrait of Mr. and Mrs. Rowan, he in a black suit, she in a pale blue dress, hung on the wall over the stairs. Several of the steps squeaked as they trod on them. Ethan winced each time it happened, but Rowan did not appear to be too alarmed.

At last, with Ethan lagging behind, the young man turned and whispered, "My father is not so light a sleeper, Mister Kaille. I'm more concerned with any noise you might make in his and Mother's room, or in the corridor upstairs."

Reaching the top of the stairway, they turned left and made their way down a dark corridor past several closed doors. At this point, Rowan began to walk more slowly, and with greater care. Ethan did the same.

Halfway down the corridor, Rowan stopped in front of a closed door and looked back at Ethan.

"In here," he mouthed.

Ethan stepped past the man and pressed on the door latch until he felt it give. He cast one quick glance at Rowan before pushing the door open and slipping into the room. Rowan made no effort to follow, which suited Ethan. He didn't want to explain what he was doing with a pouch of mullein or a bloody cut on his forearm.

As soon as he was in the bedroom, he saw the shade of Abigail Rowan. She sat on the edge of the bed, her hands folded in her lap.

Or what was left of her hands, in what had once had been her lap.

Rowan had prepared him, but still Ethan shuddered at the sight of her. She wore a dark dress; Ethan thought it must be the gown in which she had been buried. Her face was like something out of a child's nightmare. Her cheeks were sunken, her lips dried up and pulled back to reveal her teeth and the bone that would have been covered by her gums in life. Her nose was gone; all that remained was the split cavity where it had been. No doubt her eyes would have been equally appalling, but they glowed so brightly that Ethan could not see the horror beneath the glare.

Her hands had darkened and were now covered by what looked like a thin layer of hard, leathery skin. Ethan could see the contours of the bones beneath.

She glowed purest white, like starlight, or the color of a winter moon. She had not been a conjurer in life, and so, it seemed, she did not show a conjurer's hue in death. Or so he thought. Staring at her intently, Ethan realized that he could discern some faint hint of color in her face. But she was insubstantial, translucent, and he couldn't be sure that what he saw wasn't pigment from objects behind her.

When she perceived that he was there, she stood and backed away from him.

"Don't be frightened," Ethan said, raising his hands in a placating gesture, as he had a short while before upon being greeted at the door by her son and his pistol. "I won't harm you." *Not that I would even know how.* "I met your husband and children today. I'm trying to find out what has happened to you."

She didn't back away farther, but she watched him warily, like a bird poised for flight.

"Do you know why you're here?" Ethan asked.

She stared back at him, giving no indication that she understood, or that she had even heard him.

"*Veni ad me,*" Ethan said, watching the woman, hoping she wouldn't vanish when Reg appeared. Come to me.

She took another step back as the ghost winked into view beside Ethan. For his part, Reg just stared at the shade, his eyes burning like torches.

"She's being kept here the same way Patience is, isn't she?"

Reg turned to him and shook his head.

Ethan blinked. "She's not? Then how—?"

Reg held up his hand right in front of Ethan's face, and pointed at Abigail's shade.

Ethan looked at the shade once more, and realized that her right hand did look different from the rest of her. Its glow was darker, and it did have some color: a bluish tinge, or maybe sea-green. It reminded him of a hue he had seen, though he couldn't place it. Scrutinizing her face once more, he realized that he had not imagined that hint of color a moment before. Her head and her hand both glowed with it.

"So she's being held here," Ethan said. "That's why the heads and hands were removed from the corpses."

Reg nodded.

"Ask her if she knows why she's here," he said. "Please."

The old ghost stared at the shade for several seconds, before turning to Ethan again and shaking his head.

"Is she in pain? Is she suffering?"

Reg grimaced at the question, but didn't nod or shake his head.

"You have no easy answer for that, do you?" He eyed Abigail, mulling his own question. "How long has she been here?" he asked, wondering if Abigail would have a different answer than had her son.

But Reg held up three fingers. *Three days.*

"So, she was at peace already," Ethan said, the horror of what had been done to her dawning on him. "She was in the realm of the dead, and she was pulled back."

The old ghost nodded, Ethan's fury mirrored on his features.

"How?" Ethan asked. "How could they do that? It couldn't be enough just to take her hand and skull, or even that piece of cloth. It would have to be—" He felt cold radiating from his gut through the rest of his body. "The symbol," he said in a whisper. "That's how they're doing it. Am I right?" he asked the ghost.

There were times when Reg appeared to delight in leaving Ethan uncertain and uninformed. He was a splenetic old fool, and the power binding him to Ethan had spawned a relationship that was complicated to say the least. But his shrug this time conveyed such sadness that Ethan knew he took no pleasure in his inability to answer.

"Before, when we saw Patience, you said that there were more ghosts here in Boston. Are the others more like Patience, or more like this one?"

Reg pointed to the shade of Abigail Rowan.

"I was afraid of that," Ethan said. "Would that there was some way she could tell us who's done this to her."

"Or that she could speak to her husband."

Ethan spun. Alexander Rowan stood in the doorway, his son behind him. The father was dressed in a sleeping gown and he held a single burning candle.

"I don't know who you're talking to, Mister Kaille, but I trust you've found a way to communicate with my wife."

"Sir, I—"

"It's all right, Mister Kaille. I've heard people speak of witches. For a time I didn't believe in them. And after that I convinced myself they had to be evil. But there stands the ghost of my wife, looking like a monster, and acting like she's afraid of us all. Who am I to decide what is evil and what is Godly?"

"Aye, sir," Ethan said, surprised by the man for the second time that day. He faced Reg again. The ghost, who could be seen only by conjurers and those with conjuring blood in their veins, held out a hand to the shade.

Appearing reluctant, almost shy, she came forward to stand before her husband and son.

"I don't know what she would say to you if she could, sir," Ethan said. "My powers don't run that deep. But I also don't believe you have anything to fear from her. I think that she has been denied her eternal rest by those who desecrated her grave. If I can find them, perhaps I can restore her to where she ought to be."

"You would be doing a great service to all of us, Mister Kaille."

"Yes, sir."

Rowan turned to him. "I lied to you today. You have my apology for doing so. I'd like to hire you, as King's Chapel has done."

"Save your money, sir. I'm working on behalf of your congregation. When my work for the chapel is done, so will be any work I might have done for you."

"All right. Then how about this: When you've finished your work for the chapel, come by here. Provided this shade is gone, I'll have a small reward for you."

"Thank you, sir. That's most generous of you."

Mr. Rowan the elder returned to the bed in his daughter's room, while his son led Ethan back to the front door.

"I'm sorry that I woke your father," Ethan said.

Rowan waved the apology away. "You didn't. I did while lurking outside the room you were in. In the end, I think you did him a great service tonight. You have my thanks, Mister Kaille."

"Yes, sir. With your permission, I might return here as my inquiry progresses. It may be that your mother can provide me with more information."

Rowan crossed his arms over his chest, as if suddenly cold. "And how is it you might get that information? My father said something about witches."

"It's enough to say that I have access to the realm in which your mother now dwells," Ethan said.

The young man huffed a breath, obviously dissatisfied with that response. Before he could ask anything more, Ethan bade him good night, and walked back out to Ellis Street. He had yet to dismiss Reg, and the ghost glided beside him, watching him.

"I have more questions for you," Ethan said, his voice low. "That's why I haven't yet let you go."

It was too late for him to knock on more doors, but he was eager to visit with the families of those dead whose graves had been disturbed. He headed back to King's Chapel so that he could find out where some of the other families lived. He kept to side streets and narrow lanes. He was determined to avoid the occupying soldiers, to say nothing of Sephira Pryce's men, and he wished to make sure that he was not overheard speaking to Uncle Reg.

"Are there spells that can summon the dead back into the world of the living?" he asked. "Even if they've been dead for months? Janna would tell me that a conjurer can do anything with the right spell and enough spellmaking ability. But can a conjurer do even this?"

Reg nodded.

"Do you know how to do it?" Ethan asked, feeling resentful of the ghost's certainty. "Am I strong enough to do it?"

The old warrior pointed to Ethan's head and nodded. He then pointed to his chest and shook his head.

Ethan glowered at him. "You believe I have the ability to do it, but I lack the courage. Isn't that so?"

He was angry enough that he almost sent the ghost away. But Reg thrust a glowing hand in front of Ethan, clearly intending to stop him.

Ethan heaved a sigh, halted, and turned to face the ghost. Again, Reg pointed to his head and nodded. He placed his hand on Ethan's chest, and holding Ethan's gaze with his brilliant glowing eyes, he shook his head slowly.

And Ethan understood.

A year before, as British naval vessels carrying troops for the occupation lay anchored in Boston Harbor, a powerful conjuring struck one of the ships, HMS *Graystone* out of Bristol, killing every man aboard, close to a hundred in all. Agents of the Customs Board hired Ethan to learn what had happened to the ship. In the course of his inquiry, Ethan demanded that Reg help him summon the shade of a conjurer who had been among the dead. Ethan needed to communicate with the dead conjurer to ask what kind of spell had killed him and his shipmates. Or he thought he needed to. Reg had disapproved from the start, and Ethan soon realized why: Summoning the spirit from the realm of the dead had been wrong; it had been a violation of the living man's humanity. He wound up releasing the poor soul after asking just a few questions.

What the grave robbers who struck at King's Chapel, Copp's Hill, and the Granary had done was worse by far than Ethan's transgression. Ethan knew this, and so did Reg.

The old ghost wasn't questioning Ethan's courage; he was saying that while Ethan had the ability to cast such spells, his heart would not allow it. It might well have been the greatest kindness Reg had ever shown him.

"Aye," Ethan said. "I see now. My thanks."

A rare smile crossed the old warrior's lips.

Ethan resumed walking. "Have you ever seen that symbol before?" he asked the ghost. "The one carved into the corpses?"

Another shake of the head.

"I hadn't either. But what bothers me most, is that I've yet to feel a spell, at least one that I know for certain was cast for this dark purpose."

Again Reg stopped him. This time, the old ghost squatted and laid his hand on the cobblestones of the street on which they stood. His gaze never strayed from Ethan's face.

Ethan shook his head. "I'm sorry. I don't—"

Reg slapped his hand on the street three times, though of course this made not a sound.

Ethan's mouth dropped open. He lowered himself to the ground to rest his hand on the stone. And doing so, he felt a low hum in the stone, a soft tickle of vibration. Power. A conjuring.

"Good lord," Ethan said. "They're conjuring right now?"

The ghost nodded.

"And they have been all this time, haven't they?"

Reg nodded again.

"Can you tell where it's coming from?"

No.

Ethan drew his knife and cut his arm. "*Locus magi ex cruore evocatus.*" Location of conjurer, conjured from blood.

His finding spell pulsed in the street, dwarfing the touch of that other conjuring. But though he felt his power radiate out from where they stood, the spell had no effect.

"He's masked himself?" Ethan asked.

Reg shrugged.

Ethan cursed under his breath. He walked the rest of the way to the chapel in silence. When he and Reg reached the gate to the churchyard, he dismissed the ghost.

"I don't think Reverend Caner would want you here," Ethan said.

The ghost smirked; an instant later, he vanished.

He walked into the sanctuary, aware of how late it was and expecting that he would have to search for Caner or Pell. But Trevor Pell sat in one of the pews, a few rows down the central aisle from the door.

"You appear to be waiting for someone, Mister Pell."

The young minister stood. "And he's just arrived."

"You're waiting for me?" Ethan said, halting. "Why? How did you know I'd be coming back?"

"I would tell the rector that it was merely intuition."

Ethan raised an eyebrow. "What would you tell me?"

"That a voice in my mind wouldn't let me retire for the evening. What have you learned?"

Ethan regarded Pell closely, thinking that Caner wouldn't have been pleased at all to hear what the young minister had just said. He kept this to himself, however.

"I'd rather speak of this outside," he said.

Pell nodded, and they went out into the darkness and struck out across the yard. Once they had put some distance between themselves and the chapel, Ethan told the minister about the ghosts he had encountered at the Walters home and the Rowan estate.

"I believe both families would prefer that no one else hear of this," Ethan said. "But I need to see if other families are being haunted as well. That's why I came back. I was hoping you could direct me to the homes of the others whose graves were desecrated."

"Of course. But they might be reluctant to speak with you."

"I'm sure they will be. Mister Rowan's son was, until I convinced him that I could help return his mother's spirit to where it belongs."

"And do you truly believe you can?" Pell asked.

"I hope so."

"All right," Pell said. "Wait here. I'll be just a few moments."

He walked back to the chapel, leaving Ethan alone in the churchyard. Ethan soon discovered, though, that the grounds weren't as deserted as he had thought. As he waited for Pell to return, he spotted a faint orange glow near the burying ground. He pulled his knife, pushed up his sleeve, and started in that direction, wary, making little sound.

When he had covered half the distance, he heard a familiar voice say, "It's all right, thieftaker. You can put your knife away."

James Thomson, the sexton.

He sheathed his blade. "You're watching for them?"

Thomson puffed on his pipe and blew a great cloud of smoke into the warm air. "Aye. But they must know I'm here. Aside from you and

Mister Pell, I've seen no one. Thought you might be one of them when you first arrived, but once you went inside the chapel, I knew better."

"I'm sorry if I gave you a fright."

Thomson held up a hunting rifle, which had been resting beside him. "Wasn't frightened at all," he said, and patted the weapon.

Ethan wasn't convinced that a rifle would help him against the conjurer who was responsible for the desecrations, but he nodded and said nothing. They remained thus for a few minutes, neither of them speaking, until at last Pell emerged from the chapel once more.

"Well, good night, Mister Thomson," Ethan said, eager to be away.

"Good night," the sexton said, his tone mild.

"Who was that?" Pell asked, when Ethan reached him.

"Your sexton. He's sitting watch over the burying ground."

"Bless him," Pell said. "It's not a duty I would want."

"Nor I."

Pell handed him a piece of folded parchment. "Those are the names, along with their addresses."

"My thanks, Mister Pell."

"Am I to understand that you can see the ghosts only after nightfall?"

"Aye. But still, I can visit the families. They may be less afraid to speak with me when the sun is shining."

"Perhaps," Pell said, but Ethan heard skepticism in his voice. "Good luck, Ethan."

"Sleep well, Mister Pell."

Ethan left the churchyard and headed back to the South End. Kannice would still be awake, and would have welcomed him, but he had not stayed in his room above Dall's Cooperage in several nights, and Henry, the cooper who let him his room, grew concerned if he went for too long without seeing Ethan.

But as he crossed Cornhill onto Water Street, he felt the thrum of a spell in the street. He recognized the conjuring straight away: a finding spell. It seemed to come from the south, which probably meant it had been cast by Mariz. Sephira's men were looking for him.

The conjuring swept through the city, as relentless as a tide, and though Ethan drew his knife and cut his arm, the conjuring reached him before he could speak a masking spell of his own. It touched his feet and swirled about his legs, an invisible wave of power.

Mariz and the others were coming for him.

"*Tegimen ex cruore evocatum,*" he said. Warding, conjured from blood. His power pulsed as had the finding spell. Mariz would know with even more certainty where Ethan was, but at least Ethan was now protected from an attack spell. Reg had reappeared and was watching him.

"They're close," Ethan said.

The ghost nodded.

He hesitated, then cut himself again, deciding that a concealment spell might enable him to avoid Sephira's men. "*Velamentum ex cruore evocatum.*" Concealment, conjured from blood.

Once more he felt the hum of power. The blood disappeared from his arm. But, he felt nothing more after that, and he saw Reg's eyes widen.

"Nothing happened!" he said, gaping at the ghost.

He heard footsteps in the distance, approaching fast.

e cut himself once more. *"Velamentum ex cruore evocatum."* Concealment, conjured from blood.

He felt the rumble of the spell and watched to make certain that the blood vanished from his arm. And at last, he felt the cold sprinkling of power settle over him like a spring mist. The conjuring had worked. This time. But what in heaven's could have happened with his previous effort? Had the same thing happened earlier, when he tried to cast the illusion spell near Murray's Barracks?

Before he could think on it more, he heard voices. Even with the concealment spell in place, he took the added precaution of retreating into the inky shadows of a cramped byway.

"You said he was near here," someone said. It sounded like Nigel.

"Yes, I did." Mariz's voice, his accent even more pronounced than usual. "I sensed him with a conjuring of my own, and I also felt him cast a spell. He has not gone far."

He saw a bulky figure stop at the mouth of the alley, saw as well the glint of a gun barrel.

"Where are ya, Kaille?" Nigel called, sounding far too sure of himself. "We know you're around here. Might as well show yourself."

Ethan pressed himself against the stone wall of one of the buildings. There was a way through to the next lane if he could slip farther down the byway. But they would be listening for a footfall, and he didn't think he could take a step without giving himself away.

"Miss Pryce wants a word, Kaille! She don't like it when you meddle in her affairs."

He would have liked to remind the fool that she was the one who stole gems and watches and dueling pistols from him, and who kept Ethan from completing his jobs. She had tried to interfere with his attempt to retrieve Ellis's property, not the other way around. But he didn't expect that any of them would listen to reason.

"I think he's down here," Nigel said, still lingering in front of the alley. "He's hiding in the shadows. I can hear him breathin'."

Another of the toughs joined him, a man almost as big as Nigel. Gordon, or maybe Afton. It was hard to tell in the darkness. "I don't hear nothin'," the second man said.

"That's cuz *you* breathe like an ox."

"He could be anywhere by now," Mariz said. He joined the others, so that Ethan could see all of them. "He has used a concealment spell. He could be standing next to you and you would not know it."

"So try that findin' spell again," Nigel said.

"Yes, I will. You keep searching for him. I will cast the spell and let you know what I learn."

"Yeah, all right," Nigel said, growling the words.

He and the other big man walked out of view, heading west. Seconds later, a third man, smaller than the others, stepped past Mariz heading in the same direction. Nap. At the same time, Mariz drew his knife and pushed up his sleeve to cut himself. But though he held the blade to his skin, he did nothing more. Instead he stared after the others.

After a few seconds he said in a loud whisper, "It is all right now. They have gone."

Ethan's jaw dropped. He didn't respond. He didn't so much as draw breath.

The other conjurer took a step toward him. "Kaille, they are gone. But we have not much time."

Ethan cut himself. "*Fini velamentum ex cruore evocatum.*" End concealment, conjured from blood.

Mariz glanced at Uncle Reg when he appeared, and he kept his knife over his arm, but he didn't cut himself.

Ethan held his blade ready as well. "What is this about, Mariz? What are you doing?"

"We need to speak, you and I."

"About what?"

"Let us begin with the spells you have cast this evening. You responded to my finding spell with three conjurings. I would hazard a guess that the first was a warding, and the last was the concealment spell you just removed. But what was the middle one?"

"What does it matter?" Ethan asked.

"It matters a great deal, and you know it."

Ethan said nothing.

"All right," Mariz said. "Let me tell you about a spell I cast earlier today. It was to be what my father used to call an unlocking spell."

"Does Sephira have you gutting houses now, Mariz?"

The other man flashed a quick smile. "That is not important." His expression turned grim. "What does matter is that the first time I tried the spell, it failed. I felt my conjuring as I always do. My guide appeared, and indicated when I asked that I had performed the spell correctly. But it did not work." He paused, eyeing Ethan. "Just as I believe your first attempt at a concealment spell failed a short time ago."

"Had this happened to you before today?" Ethan asked, an admission in the question.

"Not since I was first learning to conjure."

"It was the same for me, although I will admit that this may have been the second time today one of my spells failed. I didn't realize it until now."

"Do you know why this is happening?"

Ethan started to say that he didn't but stopped himself. "Before I answer, let me ask you a question. Have you and Sephira been robbing graves?"

"Graves!" Mariz repeated, his voice rising. "Never, Kaille! I would not do such a thing, and I do not believe Miss Pryce would either."

He didn't share Mariz's confidence in Sephira's scruples, but this, too, he thought it best to keep to himself. "Forgive me for asking," he said. "There have been a series of grave desecrations in the city over the past several days. And I know of at least two families being haunted by shades."

"Shades?"

"Ghosts."

Mariz frowned. "And you believe that this has something to do with our conjurings?"

"I do. I have no proof, but I trust my instincts, and that's what they're telling me."

"Mariz!"

They both turned to look back at the mouth of the alley.

"That is Nigel. You should go, Kaille."

"Sephira won't be happy with you."

"Sephira will not know, will she?" He grinned and so did Ethan.

"We'll speak of this again."

"Yes," Mariz said, "we will."

Ethan eased toward the far end of the byway. "Sorry for knocking you over the other night."

"We will speak of that again, as well."

Ethan smiled and slipped out of the alley. He knew better than to think that Mariz would have let him go had he not been concerned about the failure of his spell earlier that day, just as he knew not to expect such kindness when next they met. But he had to admit that he liked the man.

More, he was deeply alarmed by their conversation. He had to resist an urge to start visiting the names on Pell's list this very night—propriety be damned. He knew, though, that angering the families of the dead would do him no good.

He cast another concealment spell and, accompanied by Uncle Reg, walked with speed and stealth to Cooper's Alley, only to find that Nap and Gordon had planted themselves in front of Henry's cooperage.

He thought about putting them to sleep with a spell, and getting past them that way. But such a conjuring would not last long, and he didn't want them trying to break into his room as he slept, or worse, breaking into Henry's room and threatening the cooper.

After a few seconds' consideration, an idea came to him, one that promised not only an escape, but also some amusement. *Interested in a bit of sport?* he asked within his mind.

Reg nodded, eager as a hunting dog.

What he intended could have been done with an elemental spell, but Ethan wanted to make it convincing. He pulled up a tuft of grass growing beside the road.

"*Imago ex gramine evocata,*" he said under his breath. Illusion, conjured from grass.

His spell worked on the first attempt. The image of himself that appeared between him and Reg looked quite convincing. This second Ethan was dressed in the same clothes, and even had the faint, yellowed remnants of a bruise on his jaw, from where Nigel had hit him two nights before.

Ethan, still concealed by his previous conjuring, scraped the sole of his boot on the cobbled street and made a small sound, like a gasp of surprise.

Nap and Gordon spun around.

"There he is!" Nap said.

Ethan sent his illusion running back up Cooper's Alley toward Water Street. The two toughs followed, passing so close to Ethan that he could feel the brush of air on his skin.

Because he had used grass rather than air, or the thin mist hanging in the air over the city, he could maintain the illusion for some time and at a considerable distance. That insubstantial Ethan would lead them all the way back to Cornhill before he vanished. Sephira's men would be searching the streets for hours.

He smiled at Reg. "My thanks. Good night."

The ghost faded from view, still staring after the toughs, still pleased. Ethan made his way up to his room, making little noise, and eschewing the use of candles. He locked and warded his door, removed the concealment spell, undressed, and climbed into his bed. He was asleep in moments.

Despite being exhausted, he slept poorly, driven from his slumber again and again by odd, elusive dreams. Most of them slid by without leaving any impression, but one was more vivid than the rest.

He was back in the street, walking through the same narrow alley in which he had hidden from Nigel and the others. There was little light, but he soon realized that there were corpses strewn throughout the byway. All of them were naked, headless, handless, marked on the chest with the odd symbols he had seen in the burying grounds. All of them were missing three toes from their left feet. He should have stopped to examine them, but he was stalking someone, or something. At first he thought it must be Sephira, but eventually he saw her, leaning against one of the walls, looking as beautiful and alluring as ever.

"It's that way," she said to him, nodding in the direction he was already walking.

He had his knife out, and she glanced down at it before looking him in the eye again. "He has one of those, too."

He said nothing to her, but kept moving. By now the alley had stretched into a long, narrow road that he didn't recognize. At the far end, he thought he saw a flame, inconstant and dim. The color wasn't right—it wasn't a normal fire—but it struck him as familiar somehow. He couldn't say why. He looked back and saw that Sephira was following him, a pistol in her hand. He started to ask what she was doing there, but even as he opened his mouth to speak the flame in front of them flared with such brilliance Ethan had to shield his eyes. Someone screamed. Ethan felt the heat from the fire slam into him like a fist. He turned, saw that Sephira was gone. He wanted to run, but before he could take a step, he felt a hand close around the ankle of his bad leg, vise-strong. He drew breath to cry out.

And woke to an emphatic knock on his door.

He was sweating, breathing hard. His bed linens were tangled around the ankle of his bad leg. Morning light streamed through his window. He extricated his foot with a mirthless laugh and rolled out of bed.

His visitor, whoever it was, knocked again. Ethan pulled on his trousers and drew his knife.

"Who's there?" he called.

"A friend."

He didn't recognize the voice. "I'll be the judge of that. Give me a name."

"I bear a message from certain gentlemen who keep company with a dragon."

Alone in his room, Ethan grinned. *Gentlemen who keep company with a dragon.* Samuel Adams and his fellow Sons of Liberty had for several years used a tavern called the Green Dragon as a meeting place. Still gripping his knife, Ethan unlocked and opened his door. The man on the landing wore the clothes of a craftsman: a linen shirt, worn breeches and waistcoat, a tricorn hat. He looked respectable if not well-off. He was closer to Diver's age than to Ethan's, with dark brown eyes, red hair, and a freckled face.

He handed Ethan a folded piece of parchment and turned to leave.

"Did Adams himself send you?" Ethan asked.

The man started down the stairs without looking back. "All you need to know is in the message."

Ethan watched the messenger leave before unfolding the parchment.

> *Mr. Kaille,*
> *We would very much like to speak with you regarding a*
> *matter of mutual interest and benefit. Please meet us at the*
> *sign of the Green Dragon at your earliest convenience.*
> *S. Adams*

He had last spoken with Mr. Adams the previous fall, as the occupation of Boston began. And they'd had dealings several years before, at the time of the Stamp Act riots, during Ethan's inquiry into the Berson murder. He couldn't imagine what he had done this time to earn the man's attention. His curiosity piqued, he washed himself with the tepid water that had been sitting in his washbasin and dressed.

As he did, he considered the dream from which he had awakened. Most nights, he didn't put much stock in such visions; even conjurers could dismiss as nonsense most of the images that disturbed their sleep. But something about this one troubled him, something more than just the mutilated cadavers. Why had the color of that fire looked so familiar? What had Sephira been doing there, and why had she seemed to be working with him?

Upon leaving his room, he heard Henry hammering at a barrel in the cooperage below. As he had business with the cooper that couldn't wait, he went first to the workshop.

Dall's cooperage had been built in 1712 by Henry's grandfather, and had withstood more than fifty years of storms and fires. A sign over the door read "Dall's Barrels and Crates," and another beside the door said "Open Entr." Before Ethan could heed this second sign, a gray and white dog bounded up to him, tail wagging, tongue lolling. She ran a tight circle around him and yipped happily before allowing Ethan to scratch her head.

"Well met, Shelly," he said.

She licked his hand.

Shelly had been a constant companion to Henry for several years now. She once had a mate: Pitch, a black dog who was as sweet as she and as protective of both Ethan and Henry. But several years before Ethan had been attacked by a conjurer who threatened his life as well as that of Holin, the son of the woman who once had been Ethan's betrothed. The conjurer was far more powerful than Ethan, and had been on the verge of killing him when Pitch appeared. With no other hope of surviving the night and saving Holin, Ethan cast a spell, sourced in the life of the poor dog. The conjuring incapacitated his enemy and allowed Ethan and the boy to escape. It also killed Pitch. To this day, despite knowing with certainty that he'd had no choice, he considered it the darkest deed he had ever committed, the one he regretted above all others, including those that had earned him his conviction. Every time he saw Shelly, he felt he ought to apologize to her.

He patted her head one last time and let himself into Henry's shop.

The cooper sat on a low bench, his face damp with sweat, his shirt soaked through. But he smiled at Ethan, exposing a gap where his front teeth should have been.

"All right, Ethan?" he said, before taking a sip of water from a metal cup.

"I'm well, Henry. And you?"

The cooper shrugged. "All right, I gueth," he said, lisping the word as he always did. "Saw Sephira's men out in the street last night. They wasn't givin' you trouble, was they?"

"Not really," Ethan said. He crossed to the bench, fishing in his pocket for the coins he had gotten from Andrew Ellis. He counted out a pound and handed the coins to Henry. "That should pay for my room through the end of September."

Henry closed his hand over the coins, a look of concentration on his face. At last he nodded. "That's how I figure it as well." He put the money in his pocket. "My thanks, Ethan."

"Well, you have my thanks for letting me pay you late for June."

Henry waved away the words. "You pay me in advance more often than you pay me late. It was no matter." He stood and picked up the cloth-covered mallet he used to hammer hoops in place on his barrels. "You working on something these days?"

"I'm staying busy," Ethan said, not wishing to say more. Henry didn't know that Ethan was a conjurer, and when he didn't see Ethan around the shop for too long, he worried as a father would for his own son. Hearing of the grave desecrations and the ghosts haunting Boston's families might have scared the man.

"Well, good. Be careful."

"I will. Thank you, Henry."

He left the shop, and turned north on Cooper's Alley toward Water Street, the ring of Henry's hammer fading as he walked away.

The Green Dragon stood near the corner of Union and Hanover streets in what Ethan imagined must have been for Samuel Adams and his allies uncomfortable proximity to the barracks of the Twenty-ninth Regiment. It was a nondescript building, notable only for the cast-iron dragon perched over its main entrance. The tavern itself was located in the basement, down a steep, dimly lit flight of stairs.

So early in the day, most publick houses in Boston would have been nigh to empty. Not the Dragon. The great room was filled with artisans and men of means, many of them gathered at the bar, others crowded around tables. Overlapping conversations blended into an incomprehensible din; Ethan wasn't sure that he could have made himself heard even to ask one of the men where he might find Samuel Adams.

Fortunately, he didn't have to. As he stood in the doorway, surveying the crowd, a man near the bar detached himself from a cluster of patrons and approached him. Adams had changed little since their encounter the previous year. His face might have been a bit more careworn; the palsy that had afflicted him all his life might have been somewhat more noticeable. His hair had long since turned gray, though he was but a few years older than Ethan, but his brow remained smooth, his dark blue eyes as clear and keen as Ethan remembered.

"Mister Kaille," he said, proffering a hand and smiling broadly.

Ethan gripped his hand. "Mister Adams, sir. It's a pleasure to see you again."

"And you. Can I buy you an ale?"

"Thank you, no."

"Very well. If you'll follow me, we can join the others and speak without fear of interruption."

Ethan didn't know what others he referred to, but he followed Adams through the throng to a small chamber off the rear of the great room. There they found four other men, including Dr. Warren, whom Ethan had encountered just the night before. Adams shut the door against the clamor, before taking his place at the table where the others were already seated.

The four men had fallen silent upon Ethan and Adams's arrival, and were watching Ethan, who lingered near the door, though there was an empty chair at the table. Eyeing the men, he realized that he recognized all of them; Adams had invited him to an august gathering.

In addition to Warren, Adams's companions included James Otis, a masterly orator and a man who was nearly as famous for his unpredictable mood changes as for his activities on behalf of the Sons of Liberty; Dr. Benjamin Church, who several years before attended to Ethan's injuries after a particularly harrowing encounter with Sephira and her men; and Paul Revere, the silversmith, whom Ethan had never met, but knew by reputation.

"Please sit with us, Mister Kaille," Adams said, indicating the vacant chair with an open hand.

Ethan crossed to the table and took his seat, conscious of the gazes upon him.

"You remember James Otis," Adams said. "May I also introduce—"

"Doctors Church and Warren I've met," Ethan said. "I'm pleased to see both of you again. And this would be Mister Revere," he went on, facing the silversmith. "I'm honored to make your acquaintance, sir."

Revere replied with a solemn nod.

Adams appeared pleased. Otis, on the other hand, eyed Ethan with unconcealed suspicion, his protuberant dark eyes and untamed hair making him look somewhat mad. He and Ethan had clashed when last they met; clearly he remembered.

"Well," Adams began again, "if introductions are unnecessary, I'll move on to the business at hand. We wish to thank you, Mister Kaille, and to welcome you at long last to the cause of liberty. We're hopeful that this marks the beginning of a long and fruitful partnership."

Ethan stared at him, his forehead furrowing. "Forgive me, Mister Adams, but I'm not sure I know what you're referring to."

"Come now, Mister Kaille. There is no need for modesty. We're all friends here. James and I have long been aware of your . . . extraordinary talents, and we have taken the liberty of explaining to our colleagues what it is you've done."

"For my part, I've known for some time of your magicking abilities," Church said. "If you recall, you came to me having already mended several of your injuries."

Ethan said nothing to the doctor, but instead fixed Adams with a hard glare. "You told them I'm a conjurer?" he said. "You had no right."

"Your secret is safe, Mister Kaille. You have my word."

"My secret was not yours to share, sir."

"But surely if we're going to be allies—"

"We're not. I have no idea what this is about, but I assure you I have done nothing on behalf of your cause that would warrant a discussion of my 'talents,' as you put it."

"Do you mean to say that you were not responsible for—"

Revere laid a hand on Adams's arm, silencing him. "You truly have no idea what this is about?" the silversmith asked, his voice a mild baritone.

"None at all."

He shared a glance with Adams, and then with Warren.

After a lengthy silence, Adams said, "I fear we may have wasted your time, Mister Kaille." His face had paled; he appeared shaken.

"What's happened?" Ethan asked. "What is it you thought I had done?"

Warren caught Adams's eye and gave a small shake of his head.

"I believe discretion dictates that we not answer," Adams said.

Ethan smiled thinly. "Of course it does." He stood. "Gentlemen."

He started toward the door.

"You haven't used your magicking to do anything that might draw our interest?" Adams called after him.

"Not that can think of. Not that I did intentionally."

He stepped back into the warmth and the noise of the tavern's great room, wended his way through the crowd, and ascended the stairs back to the street. He was breathing hard, and he had his fists balled. How dare Adams speak to others of his conjuring abilities! He had presumed too much, and might well have put Ethan's life in danger. Janna and Gavin were more open about their conjuring abilities, but Ethan could not be. Not in his line of work, not when he made new enemies every day.

But even as he seethed, Ethan wondered again what it was the Sons of Liberty thought he had done. Was the conjurer who had desecrated the graves acting on behalf of those who sought to resist the Crown and Parliament? Was he trying to make it seem that Ethan was party to whatever actions had drawn the notice of Boston's Whigs? Or was it mere coincidence that he heard from Adams now, as his inquiry into the grave robberies deepened?

Whatever the answer, he needed to find this new conjurer before men less forgiving of his spellmaking tried to blame him for conjurings he had not cast.

He struck out toward the North End, intending to visit the first of the families whose names Pell had given him the night before. As he walked, though, he felt a conjuring and knew it right away for a finding spell. It seemed that Sephira remained eager to speak with him.

The spell reached him in mere moments, twining about his legs like a vine. It had come from a distance—probably from Sephira's home on Summer Street—so Ethan knew that he had some time before Mariz, Nigel, and the rest would reach him.

Still he needed to ward himself and he was on a crowded lane, surrounded by people.

He took out his pouch of mullein and removed three leaves. Already he had used a good portion of the leaves Janna had sold him. At this rate he would have to buy more in a matter of days.

Holding the leaves in the curl of his fingers as he continued to walk, he whispered to himself, *"Tegimen ex verbasco evocatum."* Warding, conjured from mullein.

He felt his own power hum in the street, an answer to Mariz's finding, and saw Reg gliding beside him. Something in the ghost's expression made him falter in midstride.

Did the spell work? he asked.

Reg shrugged, his cheeks looking more drawn than usual.

"You don't know?"

A woman passing in the other direction stared at him. Only then did it occur to Ethan that he had spoken aloud. *You don't know?* he asked again. *You can't tell if the conjurings are doing what they're supposed to?*

The old warrior shook his head.

Ethan considered ducking into an alley to cut himself and try a concealment spell, but at this hour the street was crowded enough to make him reluctant to do so. While he was still pondering what to do next, he heard someone call his name.

Looking up, he spotted an older man walking in his direction, a hitch in his step.

Gavin Black lived not far from here in a small house on Hillier's Lane, which was not to be confused with Hillier's Street, where Murray's men were billeted. After Janna, Ethan, and now Mariz, Black might well have been the most accomplished conjurer living in Boston. He had once captained a merchant ship, and had often used his spells to navigate through the worst of the weather he encountered. He knew conjurings to raise and diminish winds, to calm rough waters, and to heal a breached hull—things Ethan had never learned to do, even during his years as a sailor. But from conversations they'd had since the old captain ceased his voyaging and settled in the city, Ethan gathered that Gavin cast spells infrequently now.

He had white hair and a ruddy, open face that usually bore a grin. His eyes were pale blue, and, as usual, he was dressed plainly in tan breeches, a white linen shirt, and a worn, faded blue coat that might well have accompanied him on every voyage he sailed.

Ethan smiled at the sight of the old man, but Black appeared deadly serious as he halted in front of him.

"You've been conjuring," Black said, keeping his voice low. "Just now, I mean."

"Aye," Ethan said. "A warding. Sephira's men are looking for me, and one of them used a finding spell. It's only a matter of time before they get here."

Black pressed his lips together and gave a small shake of his head. He wouldn't meet Ethan's gaze.

"I cast fairly often, Gavin. You know this. Why would it trouble you today?"

"Your spells didn't bother me at all," the old man said. "It's just—" He broke off, shaking his head again and muttering something under his breath. "It matters not. I'm sorry to have kept you." He turned to leave.

Ethan put a hand on his arm. "Gavin, wait. Tell me what's happened."

Black looked around them and exhaled heavily. "Do your spells still work, Ethan?"

Ethan felt the blood drain from his cheeks. "The finding spell cast by Sephira's man worked. I know it did. I have to hope that my warding did as well. Yours . . . ?"

"They don't do a thing. None of them. I don't know if I'm getting too old, or if I'm doing them wrong, but they don't work at all."

"I thought you didn't cast anymore."

"I do on occasion. To light a cooking fire, or heal a wound. Sometimes I just do it to see if I still can." A wistful smile touched the old man's lips. "I miss it sometimes." He held up his hand. He had cut his thumb just below the knuckle. "I tried to heal this last night, but I couldn't. When that spell didn't work, I tried to do other things. And—" His voice had started to rise and he paused now and licked his lips. He leaned in closer to Ethan, and when next he spoke it was in a whisper once more. "And I can't conjure anymore."

"It's not just you. Nor is it because you're getting too old. I cast a spell last night that didn't work, at least not the first time. And . . . another conjurer I know mentioned that the same had happened to him."

Gavin closed his eyes and let out another breath. "Thank you, Ethan. That comes as a great relief." Despite the words, concern still furrowed his brow. "Do you know what's causing this?"

Ethan shook his head. "I don't, but I'm trying to find out. Perhaps you can help me in that regard." He steered the old man to the edge of the lane and described for him as quickly as he could what he had seen at the burying grounds the day before. "Does any of that mean something to you? Do you know why grave robbers would take hands and skulls?"

"Other than to sell them, you mean?"

"Aye," Ethan said.

"There are conjurers in the islands of the Caribbean, who claim that they can bring back the dead using parts of the body."

It seemed to Ethan that a cloud passed in front of the sun, though the light didn't change and a warm wind still blew in off the harbor.

"Did they need anything else to do this, other than the body parts?"

"Aye," Black said. "Now, keep in mind, this was just what they told me. I never saw them do it, nor did I wish to. But they claimed that they also needed something of this world: a possession, something that could be used to bring them back."

Of course. "A piece of clothing perhaps?" Ethan asked, his voice flat.

"Aye, that would work."

"Kaille," he heard from behind him. Nigel's voice.

He cast a quick glance at Sephira's men. Mariz stood next to Yellow-hair, looking like no more than a child beside the man. He had his knife in hand. Nigel held no weapon, but Ethan was certain that he had a pistol at the ready. Nap and Gordon had positioned themselves behind the other two.

Ethan nodded to them. "I'll come with you," he said to Nigel. "Just allow me another minute to speak with my friend."

"And why should I do that?" Nigel asked, with a smug smile.

"Because he's a conjurer, too," Ethan said, not bothering to raise his voice. "And because even with Mariz standing there beside you, the two of us can snap your neck if we choose to."

Nigel's face fell. Ethan turned back to Gavin before the tough could say more.

"Was there more to the conjurings? Specific words that had to be included in the incantation, or maybe some sort of symbol?"

Black shook his head, his gaze flicking past Ethan toward Nigel. "Honestly, Ethan, I don't know. I'm sorry."

"You needn't apologize, Gavin. I'm grateful to you. And I'll do what I can to help with your problem."

The old man appeared more frightened by the moment. Ethan assumed that Nigel had produced his firearm.

"Do you need me to . . . do you need help?" he asked.

Ethan grinned. "I'll be fine." He turned to face Sephira's toughs. Nigel did indeed have his pistol in hand. "I'm ready when you are, gentlemen. We shouldn't keep herself waiting any longer."

Chapter
NINE

hey marched him through the streets of the South
End as they would a prisoner, Gordon and Nap in front of him,
Nigel and Mariz behind. Most people ignored them as they
went past, although a few—perhaps those who recognized Sephira's
men—halted and stared. None of the toughs spoke a word, not even
when Ethan chanced a quick look back at Nigel and said, "It's not like
her to hold a grudge for this long, especially over something as insig-
nificant as dueling pistols."

Yellow-hair stared past him, his expression unreadable.

"I was paid all of three pounds. Has business gotten so bad for her?"

Still nothing.

Ethan held his tongue as they covered the rest of the distance to
Sephira's mansion on Summer Street.

The Pryce house was an impressive structure built of white marble
and fronted by an expansive lawn and carefully tended gardens. He had
long considered it a far nicer home than she deserved; then again, if he
had lived here and she in the shabby room he rented, he still would
have thought her quarters too good for her.

Mariz and Nigel led him up a low set of steps onto the front veranda. There they stopped, just in front of a broad oak door.

"Your knife," Mariz said, holding out a slender hand.

Ethan had expected this; it was a precaution Sephira always took
with him, despite knowing that he could still draw blood by biting the

inside of his cheek, or scratching his arm, as he once had done in her house. Even if it didn't make her any safer, she seemed to like lording over him whatever advantages she could gain. He removed the blade from its sheath and handed it to Mariz.

"And your mullein."

Ethan frowned, but handed over his pouch containing the herb.

Mariz faced Nigel and nodded once. Yellow-hair led them through the door.

Within, the house was decorated with tapestries and other works of art; Ethan had been here several times before and so knew what to expect. But he still found it jarring to be reminded that Sephira, whom he thought of as little more than a glorified brigand, possessed such refined taste.

They crossed through the small front foyer, and through a vast common room, to a dining room that was nearly as spacious as the parlor. Sephira sat at the far end of a long table, a goblet of Madeira and a plate of cheeses and fruits set before her. She was reading a newspaper when they walked in; she looked up from it, her sharp gaze finding Ethan straightaway before shifting to Nigel.

The subtle lift of her eyebrow was all the warning Ethan had.

Nigel swung around, leading with his fist, which caught Ethan high on his cheek, just below the eye. He staggered back—into Gordon's grasp, as it turned out. The big man pinned Ethan's arms to his side, rendering him defenseless. Ethan lashed out with a kick, which Nigel deftly avoided. Yellow-hair dug a fist into Ethan's side, making him gasp. He hit Ethan again, full in the jaw. After that, Ethan was too addled to keep track of every blow Nigel and the others landed.

It seemed that they hit him several times more before Sephira finally said, "Enough."

They broke off their assault, and Gordon released him. Ethan collapsed to the floor, coughing, gasping for breath. Blood ran from his nose and his split lip, choking him. He spat a mouthful onto the floor, hoping he managed to stain Sephira's rug.

He heard the click of a boot on wood, but only realized when she started speaking that Sephira had gotten up from the table and was standing over him.

"You've gone too far this time, Ethan. I'm tempted to kill you where you lie and have them dump your body on the Common, or in the mud-flats. You should know better, but of course, I'm continually amazed by your foolishness."

He could barely reply. "All this trouble . . . for a pair of . . . of dueling pistols?"

For several seconds, she said nothing. Then, "You just don't learn, do you?"

He felt himself lifted again, knew the beating was about to resume. "Sephira, wait!"

"Are you going to stop this nonsense?" she asked, her tone mild.

"I truly don't know what this is about. I thought it was the pistols. I was wrong. But I'm at a loss as to what else it could be."

She stared at him, shaking her head. "You brought this on yourself," she said. To Nigel, she said, "Kill him."

Ignis ex cruore evocatus! he said within his mind. Fire, conjured from blood!

The blood vanished from his face, and Nigel's coat burst into flames.

Gordon and the others rushed to smother the fire. Ethan stood his ground, making no attempt to flee. Mariz remained beside him.

The toughs extinguished the flames in mere seconds. Nigel scrambled to his feet, his clothes still smoking, and pressed the barrel of his pistol against Ethan's chest so forcefully that Ethan stumbled back a step.

"You bloody bastard!"

Ethan ignored him, keeping his gaze fixed on Sephira. "I don't know what this is about," he said. "If you're really going to let him kill me, the least you can do is first tell me why."

"You insist on playing these games with me."

"This is not a game, Sephira; this is my life. And I swear to you on the life of Kannice Lester, I don't know what this is about."

"It's about me killin' you!" Nigel said with a snarl. "Finally, after all these years!"

But he didn't pull the trigger. Rather, he looked back at Sephira, awaiting her orders. And it seemed that Ethan's oath reached her.

"Not yet," she said.

Nigel sulked like an overgrown boy denied his favorite toy. He lowered the pistol. A second later, seemingly as an afterthought, he smacked Ethan's head with an open hand. Ethan reeled; he would have fallen had Mariz not held him up.

"That's for ruinin' my coat," Yellow-hair growled.

"You don't know why I brought you here?" Sephira asked.

"That's what I've been telling you. I thought you were still angry with me for giving you Salter's old shoes instead of the dueling pistols."

"I am still angry with you for that," she said. "But you're here for a far more serious transgression."

"And I'm telling you that I can't think of anything else I might have done."

Even as he said the words, he heard in his mind the echo of his conversation with Adams and the others. Were the two encounters related?

"You mean to tell me that you haven't been to the warehouses of Alexander Rowan or Sebastian Wise?"

"Rowan?" Ethan said. "You're working for Alexander Rowan?"

"So, you do know him?"

"Yes. I was at his house last night."

Sephira's smile could have frozen the harbor solid. "I know you were. Why do you think you're here now?"

"I didn't know that you were working for him."

"So if you had, you wouldn't have taken his money?" she asked, her voice spiraling upward. "You wouldn't have interfered in my business? You wouldn't have made him think that I had—?" She clamped her mouth shut, and looked at Nigel. Ethan expected to hear her repeat the order to kill him.

"He didn't give me any money—not a penny—and I'm not working for him," Ethan said, keeping his voice level. "I'm working for the congregation of King's Chapel, of which he is a member. I'm inquiring into a series of grave desecrations and robberies that include the burial site of his wife."

"Grave robberies," she said, sounding doubtful.

"That's right. Resurrectionists, most likely, since they took the head and right hand of each corpse."

She returned to her seat at the table and took a long drink of wine. When she spoke again, she sounded more composed.

"And what about his warehouse? When did you go there?"

"I haven't been. Not once."

"You see, Ethan, that's where you disappoint me. You take so much care in crafting a wild story about resurrectionists, and then you tell a lie that no one could possibly believe."

"You've known me for a long time, Sephira. And while you might think me a fool, you must know that I'm not so stupid as to lie to you in your house, surrounded by your men, with a pistol aimed at my head. So maybe you should tell me what's happened. If this involves Mister Rowan, it's possible that we can help each other." He chanced a grin, though it hurt his jaw and lip. "You can always kill me later."

She looked away, chuckling. "Sit," she said, gesturing at the chair to her right. "Get him a glass of wine," she said to Mariz.

Ethan sat, and Mariz placed a goblet of Madeira in front of him. He took a long drink, managing to dribble just a bit of it over his swollen lip. Sephira frowned at him.

"Can't you heal that?" she asked.

"I will later. Tell me what this is about."

"I've been hired by Rowan, Wise, and a few of their friends, to protect their warehouses. I have men there now."

"Their warehouses," Ethan said, more to himself than to her. "Why would . . . ?" It dawned on him. "They're not honoring the non-importation agreements, are they?"

"No," she said. "They're not. And they have been threatened repeatedly. Last night, not long before you arrived at the Rowan house, the warehouses of Rowan and Wise were attacked. Most of their goods were destroyed."

Ethan had heard of similar actions being taken against other merchants who had Tory leanings. Many merchants in Boston, and throughout the rest of the American colonies, had expressed their dissatisfaction with Parliament's policies by refusing to import goods from England. Many, but not all. And those who violated the non-importation agreements not only weakened the boycott of English goods, but also profited at the expense of those who honored it. They were among the most reviled men in the city. Even someone like Rowan, who was wealthy and otherwise well-respected, could not escape the wrath of Whig sympathizers.

"I can understand why you're angry," Ethan said. "I'm sure Rowan won't be pleased when he finds out. But why would you think that I had a hand in the destruction of his goods? What possible reason—?"

"Isn't it obvious?" she asked. "To discredit me. To make me look incompetent, so that he'll turn to you for protection."

"Sephira, I—"

"The goods were destroyed with magick!" she said, spitting the words at him. "You can deny it all you like, but Mariz here is certain that it was witchery that did all the damage."

Of course. This was the reason the Sons of Liberty had summoned him. Sephira and Adams both thought that he was responsible for the damage done to the merchants' warehouses. The difference was, Adams and his allies wished to congratulate him and enlist him in their cause; Sephira wanted to murder him.

Ethan turned to the other conjurer.

"What the *senhora* is telling you is true," Mariz said. "The damage was done with conjurings."

"Did you use a *revela potestatem* spell?" Ethan asked.

Mariz shook his head. "No. The *senhora* thought there was no need. She has believed all along that you are responsible."

"What are the two of you babbling about? What is that . . . that magicking you asked about?"

"A *revela potestatem* spell," Ethan said.

"Yes, that. What does it do?"

"It's a conjuring that allows us to see the residue of power from a spell that's already been cast. Every conjurer's power looks different—each has a unique color. This spell reveals that color." He paused. "You've actually seen me cast such a spell. Last year, after Mariz was attacked, I used it to determine who had hurt him."

Sephira nodded, looking far less certain of herself than she usually did. "I remember."

"We can cast the same spell on Rowan's damaged property. That would at least prove to you that I had nothing to do with it."

"Do you know this spell?" Sephira asked Mariz. She gestured at Ethan. "I don't trust him to do it."

"I know the spell, *Senhora*."

Still, she appeared uncertain. Ethan couldn't imagine that she liked having to rely on conjurings for anything, and he was sure she didn't wish to entertain the possibility that she had been wrong about him. But she was a thieftaker before all else.

"All right," she said. She looked at Nap and Gordon. "You two, get my carriage ready. Nigel, Mariz, bring Ethan out front." She glanced at Nigel. "Gently. I'll join you in a moment."

Yellow-hair and the conjurer escorted Ethan out to the veranda. A few minutes later, a large bay pulled Sephira's black carriage around to the front of the house. Nap sat on the box in front, steering. At the same time, Sephira emerged from the house. She had put on her indigo waistcoat, and she carried a pistol.

"Nap will drive," she said, starting down the path toward the carriage. "Nigel, Mariz, and Ethan will ride with me."

Gainsaying her would have been unthinkable. Ethan climbed into the carriage; Mariz and Nigel sat across from him, Nigel holding his pistol loosely in his hand. The acrid smell of his burned coat filled the carriage. Sephira climbed in, glanced at her men, and sat beside Ethan. Nigel reached a hand out over the door and tapped once on the roof. Ethan heard the snap of the reins, and the carriage lurched forward, beginning the slow, jarring journey to the waterfront.

For a long time, no one spoke. Sephira gazed at the street. Ethan kept his eyes downcast, although he was conscious of Nigel watching him, his trigger finger no doubt itching.

It was Nigel who broke the silence.

"I thought you used your witchery to protect us," he said to Mariz.

"I thought I had as well."

"Then how did he light my coat on fire?"

Mariz's gaze flicked toward Ethan. "Sometimes spells do not work as we wish them to. I am sorry."

Nigel glowered.

"That old man you were speaking to when we found you," Mariz said to Ethan. The man's spectacles reflected the light from the carriage openings so that they appeared opaque. "Is he truly a conjurer?"

"Aye. His name is Gavin Black. He doesn't cast much anymore, but he was a sea captain once, and an accomplished spellmaker."

"How many of us are there in this city?"

"Too many," Nigel muttered.

"I don't know," Ethan said. "Twenty? Thirty?"

Nigel stared out at the street. "Like I said, too many."

"How many of them are strong enough to attack Rowan's warehouse and destroy his goods?" Sephira asked.

Ethan shook his head. "I can't know until I see the damage. But even if there are fifty conjurers in the city, no more than a dozen or so are accomplished spellers." He thought of his sister Bett, who could have conjured if she wanted to, but had forsworn spells years ago, believing her powers to be evil. "Even fewer can cast as Mariz and I do."

"Is that true?" she asked Mariz.

"I would think so."

They lapsed back into silence. The scent of brine in the air had grown stronger, and the strident cries of gulls echoed all around them. They were nearing the harbor.

The carriage slowed to a stop, and there came a tap on the roof.

Nigel opened the carriage door, climbed out and held it as Sephira followed him. Mariz gestured for Ethan to go next. Once outside, Sephira led them out onto Long Wharf, which was crowded with wharfmen, sailors, and laborers. They walked past hulking warehouses and moored ships, until at last they came to a building with a sign mounted over the door that read "Christian Rowan & Sons."

The door was open, and laborers worked within, sorting through goods that had been shattered and burned. Ethan spotted the younger Mr. Rowan, standing off the to the side, grim-faced, his arms crossed over his chest as he surveyed the damage. He wore a dark silk suit and looked as out of place in the warehouse as Ethan would have at one of the elder Rowan's notorious fetes. Ethan glanced at Sephira and pointed toward the man. She nodded and strode in the young merchant's direction, tossing "Wait here" over her shoulder.

The rest of them watched as Sephira greeted Mr. Rowan with a disarming smile and spoke to him for several minutes, occasionally gesturing at one part of the warehouse or another. Soon, she was walking back toward the front door, while the merchant gathered his workers and spoke to them.

"They'll be vacating the premises shortly," she said, as she rejoined them by the door.

"What did you tell him?" Ethan asked.

"Just that I needed to examine the damage for a short while before his men finished clearing it away."

The laborers began to file out a second door at the back of the warehouse. Rowan, however, crossed to where Sephira, Ethan, and the others were waiting. As he neared them, he recognized Ethan, his eyes widening at the sight of him.

"Mister Kaille," he said. "What ever happened to your face?"

Ethan reached a hand up to his split lip. "An encounter with a gang of ruffians," he said, keeping his tone light. "It's a common hazard in my line of work. There's no avoiding the rabble."

He heard Nigel rumble beside him.

"Well, you should really have a physician take at look at you."

"Thank you for your concern, sir."

"I must say that I'm perplexed by all this mischief and violence directed at our warehouse. My father and I make a point of trading only in North American goods, but somehow these agitators and the riffraff who follow them have got it in their heads that we are selling proscribed items, which I assure you is not the case."

"Yes, sir."

Rowan glanced at Sephira. "I didn't know that you were helping Miss Pryce with her inquiry."

"He's not," she said before Ethan could respond. "Ethan is still somewhat new to the thieftaking trade, and he's . . . observing so that he might learn something of the craft for future inquiries."

Ethan wasn't sure whether to be angry or to laugh at her audacity. In the end, he just mumbled something about being happy to help in any way he could, and left it at that.

Sephira assured Mr. Rowan that he and his laborers would be able to resume their work in short order, and tried to send him on his way.

"I'm still not entirely certain why it is you need us out of here," the merchant said.

Sephira cast a look Ethan's way, but he refused to meet her gaze. She had essentially declared him her apprentice; it wasn't his place to answer a question directed at her.

"You can be," she said at last, her smile as dazzling as ever. "But I assure you that we will finish far sooner if we're allowed to work without interruption or distraction. I assume that you wish to put this unfortunate incident behind you as soon as possible."

"Well, yes, naturally."

"I thought so. That being the case, I would urge you to let us conduct our business and be done with it."

"Of course," he said, sounding rueful. "Even now, I delay you. Forgive me, Miss Pryce."

"There is nothing to forgive, Mister Rowan."

He walked away. Ethan and the others followed Sephira into the warehouse. Nap closed and locked the door and planted himself there. The rest of them approached the piles of rubble. The Rowans, it seemed, specialized in imports of furniture. Ethan saw tables, chairs, bureaus, and desks that had been splintered or burned or both.

"That was well done with Rowan," he said to Sephira. "Perhaps I *can* learn a thing or two from you."

She smirked before turning her attention back to the damaged items. She surveyed the destruction, hands on her hips, a look of disgust on her features. "If it turns out that you did this, I really will have them kill you."

Ethan said nothing.

"All right," she said, facing Ethan first and then Mariz. "How do we do this?"

"We'll need Nigel," Ethan said.

"Me?" Yellow-hair said. "I'm no conjurer."

But Mariz was already nodding. "Yes, he is right."

"What can Nigel do?" Sephira asked.

Ethan grinned. "He can't do a thing. But I lit his coat on fire with a spell, which means that there is a residue of my power on him. A conjuring will reveal the color of it, which you can compare to the color of the spells used on the furniture."

Sephira's gaze shifted to Mariz. "Is that what you were going to say?"

"It is."

"Fine," she said. "Do your witchery. Him," she said for Ethan's benefit, pointing at Mariz. "If you so much as look at your knife, I'll give Nigel leave to do with you whatever he wishes."

Ethan offered no response, but he was thinking about the night before, when Mariz had let him escape after the two of them shared their concerns about failed spells.

Mariz drew his knife and cut his arm.

"What am I supposed to do?" Nigel asked of no one in particular.

"Stand there and look addled," Ethan said. "Oh, my apologies. You were already doing that."

Sephira actually laughed. "Cast your spell," she said to Mariz.

Mariz spoke the spell under his breath, so that Ethan could barely make out the Latin. But there could be no mistaking the thrum of power that echoed in the walls and floor of the warehouse. A ghost appeared at Mariz's shoulder: a young man who looked much like the conjurer, wearing clothes more appropriate to Renaissance Portugal than contemporary Boston, and glowing with a warm beige color that Ethan recalled from his first encounter with the conjurer a year ago.

None of the others noticed either the rumble of the spell or Mariz's spectral guide. They were all staring at Nigel, whose coat was now covered with a glow of its own. It was a rich russet, the color of a full moon balanced on the horizon; the color of Uncle Reg.

"That's Ethan's magick?" Sephira asked.

"Aye," Ethan said. "It is."

"I have seen his *fantasma*," Mariz said. "His spirit. It is the same color."

"Yes, very well." She waved a hand at Rowan's broken furniture. "Get on with it."

"What about me?" Nigel said, as the rest of them approached the piles of debris. "How do you make this go away?"

Sephira ignored him, so Ethan did the same. It warmed his heart to think that for just a short while Yellow-hair believed the glow of Ethan's power would remain on him forever.

Mariz had cut himself again, and now he cast a second *revela potestatem* spell. Ethan felt this conjuring as well. He caught Mariz's eye and nodded. For right now at least, the conjurings were working as they were supposed to.

Ethan heard a small intake of breath from Sephira and knew that the spells had convinced her of his innocence. He turned to look at her, feeling just a bit smug. But when he saw the glow that clung to the broken furniture, all thoughts of gloating fled his mind, to be replaced by a cold foreboding.

"Are you sure you did that correctly?" he heard Sephira ask.

"Yes, *Senhora*. These items were destroyed by a different conjurer."

A boot scraped; Sephira turning to look at him. "I suppose that means I don't get to kill you today," she said.

But Ethan couldn't bring himself to speak. He stared at the broken table legs, the split chair backs, the charred remains of chests and desks, and he couldn't even bring himself to blink. That color—deep aqua, like the ocean on a calm summer morning—he had seen it before, and its presence here made his heart labor.

"Do you know who that color belongs to?" Sephira's voice.

"No, *Senhora*. I do not."

"I do," Ethan said. He turned at last to face Sephira and Mariz. "This is far, far worse than I thought."

Chapter
TEN

orse for whom?" Sephira asked.

Ethan glanced at Mariz again. He desperately wanted to speak with the conjurer alone, away from Sephira and her toughs. But that conversation would have to wait.

"For all of us," he said. "That color belongs to a man named Nate Ramsey."

She shook her head, unmoved. "That means nothing to me."

"It will," Ethan said. "I encountered Ramsey nigh unto six years ago. His father was captain of the merchant ship *Muirenn*, just as Nate is now. And he was also a conjurer, as is the son. Captain Ramsey the elder had dealings with a pair of merchants—Isaac Keller and Deron Forrs."

"Keller and Forrs?" Sephira said. "They're both long dead."

"Aye. I'm telling you how they died."

Her cheeks might have paled. She nodded for him to continue.

"Keller and Forrs knew that the older Ramsey was, as they put it, a witch. And they used that knowledge to cow the man into doing their bidding. He smuggled on their behalf, running molasses up from Martinique, and they paid him barely enough to cover his expenses. When he informed them of his intention to end the arrangement, they threatened to have both him and his son hanged as witches."

"What does this—?"

"Patience, Sephira. In the end, the old man saw only one way to escape them. He had lost his wife years ago, and his son was old enough to take care of himself and captain the family's vessel. So Captain Ramsey hanged himself from the main yard of the *Muirenn*.

"The son took command of the ship, and refused to do business with Keller and Forrs. Instead, he vowed revenge. He swore that the merchants would suffer for what they had done to his father."

He gazed at the aqua glow again. Six years later, the memory of his failure still tasted bitter. "The merchants came to me," he said. "Actually, Sheriff Greenleaf brought them to me. He has long suspected that I'm a conjurer, though he hasn't been able to prove it. But in this case, rather than wanting to see me hanged for a witch, he thought to make some coin off of my 'dark talents.' He introduced us, and Keller and Forrs hired me to protect them from Ramsey.

"Of course, they told me their side of the conflict and nothing more: The father was mad, they said; he had accused them without cause of stealing money from them, and now the son was making threats. I went to speak with Ramsey, and it was from him that I heard what the merchants had done to his father. But by then, of course, I was working for Keller and Forrs. And the rest you know."

"He killed them," Sephira said.

"Aye. I saw him kill Keller. He and I battled and I managed to hurt him, but he was relentless, bent on revenge. He would gladly have traded his life for theirs; in the end there was nothing I could do to stop him. He had burns on his face and hands. He had a broken leg thanks to a spell I cast. And still he got away from me and killed Forrs, too."

"Then what?"

"Then he sailed away from Boston. I thought at the time that he had left for good."

"It seems you were wrong," Sephira said. "So, help me to understand. Is this Ramsey character more powerful than you are?"

Ethan shook his head. "No. But he's no weaker, either. He's cunning, and I'm afraid he's a bit mad. If I'm remembering the color of his power correctly, and if he has come back to Boston, he has a reason."

"Do you know what that reason is?"

"I wish I did," he told her.

Mariz stared hard at him, and Ethan knew why. The night before he had told the man of the grave robberies; they had spoken of the odd troubles they were having with their conjurings. Ethan had no doubt that these things were connected in some way to Ramsey's return. Mariz suspected as much as well. But the conjurer couldn't bring this to Sephira's attention without revealing that he and Ethan had spoken without her knowledge, or that he had helped Ethan evade Nigel, Nap, and Gordon.

The truth was, Ethan didn't know anything for certain, and he wasn't yet ready to tell Sephira more about the desecrations or to share with her his vague suspicions about Ramsey. He avoided meeting Mariz's intense gaze, knowing that the conjurer could do nothing more than glare.

"Well, Ethan, it sounds like this is your fault after all. You let this Ramsey character escape from you six years ago, and now he's back. So, I'm going to leave it to you to deal with him."

"I'm going to need to speak with Rowan," Ethan said.

"About *my* inquiry?" she demanded, indignant.

"Ramsey was here," Ethan said. "It may be that he has some history with the Rowan family. Perhaps the elder Rowan worked with Keller and Forrs. I can't 'deal with him,' as you put it, without speaking to both the son and the father."

Sephira's glare left little doubt as to how she felt about this. But she said, "Fine. Speak with them both. Just make it clear that you're doing it for me, that this is still my job."

"Of course. What kind of thieftaker would try to steal a job from a rival?"

If she recognized herself in his question, she didn't give him the satisfaction of showing it.

"Get him out of here," she said to Mariz.

"I need my knife and my mullein."

He thought she might refuse, but after a moment's hesitation, she nodded to Nigel.

The big man handed Ethan the blade and the pouch. "One day she's goin' to let me do as I want with you, an' then, the beatin' you took today will seem like a stroll on the Common."

Ethan turned and walked away, Mariz trailing behind him. Once they were outside, the conjurer said, "You should have told her."

"I should have told her what? That I think Ramsey might be robbing graves, and that whatever he's doing is making my conjurings less reliable? I don't want Sephira to know that."

"I could tell her."

"Yes, you could. But you know how smart she is. It wouldn't take her long to understand that if my power is weakening, yours is, too. She already knows that the warding you put on Nigel today didn't work. Do you really want her to question your usefulness?"

Mariz didn't answer. He escorted Ethan to where young Mr. Rowan was waiting. But just before they reached the merchant, he said in a low voice, "You are afraid of this Ramsey, are you not?"

"Aye," Ethan said. "As I said to Sephira, he's not any more powerful than you and I are. But he would do anything, kill anyone, to achieve his ends, whatever they may be."

"So, I will help you fight him."

"Sephira might have something to say about that."

"If Miss Pryce feels that he is a threat to her clients, she will want me to kill him, and it sounds as though in a battle with this man, I might require your aid."

Ethan wasn't sure how to reply. "Perhaps it won't come to a battle," he finally said.

Mariz quirked an eyebrow, but said nothing.

The younger Rowan marked their approach and closed the remaining distance in a few quick strides. "Can my men get back to work now?"

"Yes, sir," Ethan said. "But I wonder if I might have a word with you before you join them inside."

"What about?" He cast a quick look at Mariz.

"I will return to Miss Pryce," the conjurer said. To Ethan, he added, "We will speak again soon."

"Aye," Ethan said. "I look forward to it."

Once Ethan and Mr. Rowan were alone, the merchant asked, "Did you wish to speak of . . . ?" He wet his lips. "Of what you saw at our home last night?"

"Not directly, sir, though it may be that last night's encounter and what happened here at the warehouse are connected."

"That is a most remarkable assertion, Mister Kaille. How is that possible?"

"I have few answers right now, sir, and a great many questions."

"Yes, of course. Proceed."

"Thank you. Have you or your father had dealings with a merchant captain named Nathaniel Ramsey?"

"Ramsey," Mister Rowan repeated. "The name is familiar, although I can't remember exactly why. I've not had dealings with him, but it's possible that my father has."

"Would you mind if I approached him about this?"

"Not at all. Do you believe that this Ramsey fellow is responsible for the damage done to our warehouse?"

"I should have been more precise with my question. There were two Nathaniel Ramseys. One, whom your father might have known, died seven years ago. The second is his son, who I believe may recently have returned to Boston. I believe it's possible that he was responsible for the damage inflicted on your goods."

Rowan glanced around and asked in a whisper, "And how might this be connected to the appearance of my mother's ghost?"

"That is a more difficult question, sir. I believe it's possible that the younger Ramsey, Nate, might have been connected to the desecrations at King's Chapel Burying Ground. And I believe that those desecrations might have . . . unsettled the dead."

"Had I not seen my mother's shade with my own eyes, I would say that you were mad. But of course I have seen it, and it seems that my entire world has been turned on its head."

"Yes, sir."

"Why would Ramsey do these things? What is it he wants from me?"

"I don't yet know the answer to that, sir. I once had dealings with him, and I found him to be clever, but unbalanced, and utterly ruthless. Whatever his purpose, I don't believe you and your father are his only targets. A good many graves have been disturbed, and from what I hear from Se—that is, from Miss Pryce, yours was one of several warehouses to have been abused in this way."

"That is my understanding as well." Rowan took a breath and pulled himself to his full height. "All right. I have tasks to which to attend, and you have an inquiry to conduct. My father is at home today; you can find him there. I would like you to report back to me when you can."

"Yes, sir," Ethan said. It pained him to speak his next words, but he had made a promise to Sephira, and a pointed one at that. "Miss Pryce is conducting the inquiry that pertains to your warehouse. I'll leave it to her to speak to you of those matters. But I promise to keep you informed with respect to my inquiry on behalf of your congregation."

"Very good. Thank you."

Ethan left Long Wharf, pausing once he reached King Street. He wanted to speak with Mr. Rowan the elder, but he also wished to approach Sebastian Wise, who had warehouses on Burrel's Wharf. He had a list of more than a dozen names from Pell: the recently deceased whose graves had been violated. He wished to speak with their families as well. He wanted more information from Janna, and from Gavin Black. And a part of him wanted to search Boston's entire waterfront for the *Muirenn*. If he could find Ramsey, he might not need to speak with any of the others. He had little doubt that the captain was behind all the mischief that had been visited upon the city in the past several days.

He dismissed this last idea as rash; Ramsey was not a foe with whom he could trifle. Before he confronted the man, he needed to know more about what he had already done, and where his scheming might lead.

He made his decision and headed up Merchant's Row toward the North End. Sephira would not be pleased with him when she learned that he had gone to speak with Mr. Wise without her permission. He could not have cared less.

Burrel's Wharf was a broad pier off of Fish Street. It jutted out into the harbor between Clarke's Wharf and Lee's Shipyard, where Diver once worked. Sebastian Wise's warehouse stood closest to the street. Upon entering it, Ethan was presented with a scene similar to that which he had seen on Long Wharf. Laborers sorted through the ruin of spoiled foodstuffs and shattered plates and glasses, while a man in a green silk ditto suit looked on, rage and disgust etched in his features.

This man appeared to be a few years older than Ethan himself. His black hair was salted generously with white, but his mien was youthful, and he was hale and stood straight-backed.

Ethan intended to approach him, but almost as soon as he entered the warehouse, he was accosted by a brawny laborer brandishing a wooden cudgel.

"Who are you?" he said, more growl than question.

"I'm here to see Mister Wise."

"That's not what I asked, is it?"

Ethan allowed himself a smile, his eyes holding those of the brute. "My name is Ethan Kaille. I'm a thieftaker, and I would like very much to speak with your employer."

"He's a bit busy right now, and as far as I know, he ain't had nothin' pinched." He took hold of Ethan's arm. "So I think it's time you was leavin'."

Ethan didn't budge, nor did he allow his smile to slip. "I understand that you're doing your job, and I know as well that you wouldn't guess it from looking at me, but you're taking a bit of a risk right now. So, let go of me before I shatter every bone in your arm, and tell Mister Wise that Ethan Kaille is here to see him."

The brute blinked, his mouth hanging open.

"Who is this, Robert?"

Ethan and the brute turned. The well-dressed man had ventured a few steps closer.

"My name is Ethan Kaille, sir. I'm a thieftaker and an associate of Sephira Pryce. Are you Sebastian Wise?"

"I am."

"I wonder if I might speak with you, sir. I won't take up much of your time."

"Yes, of course." He beckoned Ethan over.

Ethan patted the brute's shoulder as he stepped past him. "My thanks, Robert."

"You say that you're a friend of Miss Pryce?" Wise asked as Ethan joined him.

"I believe 'associate' is the better word. I'm gathering a bit of information on her behalf. Your business arrangement is with her, of course. But I'm conducting an inquiry that I believe is related to hers."

"I see. And you said your name is Kaille?"

"Aye."

"The same Kaille who took part in the *Ruby Blade* mutiny?"

Ethan felt his cheeks burn. But he refused to look away. He had labored fourteen years for his crime, suffering indignities and injuries that would remain with him for the rest of his life. He refused to be shamed by this man or any other.

"One and the same, sir," he said.

"I remember reading of the incident," Wise said, "although many of the particulars escape me now. I was a young man at the time."

"So was I."

"A fair point," Wise said. "What can I do for you, Mister Kaille?"

"I just have a few questions for you, sir. I'm wondering if you have had dealings with Captain Nathaniel Ramsey?"

"The elder or the younger?"

"Either."

"I haven't personally, no. But my father did, before he died. He was Sebastian Wise as well, and he did business with the elder Ramsey, until the captain's death."

"Have you ever met the younger Ramsey?"

"Not that I remember, though I suppose it's possible I have."

You would remember, Ethan wanted to say. But he kept that thought to himself. "Can you tell me anything about the business your father conducted with Captain Ramsey?"

Wise shrugged, marking the progress of his workmen with his dark eyes. "I don't believe there was anything unusual about it. My father was a merchant, as am I. Captain Ramsey transported items, which my father bought from him and sold at a profit."

"Yes, sir. Can you tell me if your father also had dealings with Isaac Keller and Deron Forrs?"

"I believe so, yes. But they both died years ago, not long after Ramsey died, if I'm correct. What do they have to do with all of this?"

"To be honest, sir, I'm not sure yet. I have one last question, and I'll leave you to your work here. And I hope you'll forgive me for the indelicacy of this. But have you recently lost a loved one?"

Wise recoiled. Clearly this had been the last thing he expected Ethan would ask. "No, I haven't."

Ethan had been so sure. "No one?" he asked. "Not in the past half year or so?"

"Not in the past four years. My father died back in sixty-five, but since then, thank the Lord, we have been quite fortunate."

Ethan nodded. He knew that he looked troubled by what should have been glad tidings, but for a moment his confusion allowed him no other response. At last he managed to say, "Yes, sir. I'm glad to hear that."

"But you were expecting me to say something else."

"I was," Ethan admitted.

"Can you tell me why?"

Ethan rubbed a hand over his face. "It would take me some time to explain it all, sir, and you have more pressing matters to which to attend. Suffice it to say that I thought that your connection with Ramsey might be one of several things you would have in common with others I've spoken to in the past few days. I was wrong."

"I'm not sure I understand," Wise said. "But as you say, I have other matters to occupy my time."

"Yes, sir. I'll be going. Thank you for answering my questions."

Ethan left the warehouse, tipping his hat to Robert as he walked past.

From Burrel's Wharf, it was but a short distance back to the Rowan mansion on Ellis Street. For the second time in less than a day, Ethan knocked on the door and was admitted to the great house. Before long, he stood in Alexander Rowan's study, shaking hands with the old man.

When Ethan asked him about the elder Captain Ramsey, Rowan indicated that Ethan should sit in an armchair set before the empty hearth. He took the chair beside Ethan's.

"I remember Nathaniel well. I was shocked when I learned of his death. He was a decent man, and a fine sailor from what I understand."

"Did you and he have extensive dealings?"

"For a time, yes. But at the risk of being too candid, he turned to smuggling in the final years of his life, and I wanted no part of that. I told him so, and we stopped doing business."

Ethan hadn't expected this, either. "Did you know Isaac Keller and Deron Forrs?"

Rowan's expression turned shrewd. "You know more about this than you let on, Mister Kaille. Forrs and Keller were among those who bought smuggled goods from the man."

"Yes, sir. And did you do business with them as well?"

The old man laughed. "With Isaac and Deron? No. They disliked me and I felt the same way about them."

Ethan started to ask another question, but was interrupted by the thrum of a distant spell, one so powerful that he could feel it vibrating in his chest. He closed his eyes, trying to gauge how far the pulse had traveled, where it was headed. He couldn't tell what sort of spell it was, but he had an inkling of who had cast it. He needed to leave—there was too much he didn't understand. But first . . .

"Mister Kaille? Are you well?"

He opened his eyes once more. "Aye, I'm fine. Thank you, sir. Tell me, do you feel about Sebastian Wise the same way you felt about Keller and Forrs?"

"Sebastian the younger, you mean?"

Ethan nodded. In his impatience to be moving, he had started to drum his fingers on the arm of his chair. He willed himself to stop.

Rowan did not seem to have noticed. He was gazing up at the ceiling. "No," he said at last. "I didn't care much for his father, but the son is a different matter. He can be abrasive, but I trust him; I wouldn't hesitate to do business with him."

"Did his father engage in smuggling as well?"

"I think I'd rather not answer that, Mister Kaille. I do have dealings with the son on a regular basis." A grin curved his lips. "I suppose that tells you what you need to know, doesn't it?"

"Mister Wise will hear nothing of this conversation from me, sir," Ethan said, getting to his feet.

Rowan smiled as he stood. "Thank you, Mister Kaille."

Ethan walked out of the house a short time later. He couldn't say with certainty where the spell he felt had come from, but given its might, the distance it seemed to have traveled, and the direction the power seemed to flow, he thought that it had come from somewhere out on the harbor. Casting on water magnified the strength of a conjuring, something Ethan was sure Nate Ramsey knew. He halted along Ellis Street and gazed out over the harbor, searching in vain for Ramsey's ship. There was little about the *Muirenn* to distinguish it from other merchant vessels; he knew this, and yet he searched anyway, as if hoping that the man would be flying a black flag on his mainmast to let Ethan know where he was.

He could almost hear Ramsey laughing at him. *No, Kaille. I'm not going to make it that easy for you.*

Ethan walked to the Dowsing Rod, avoiding the barracks along the way and thus coming to the tavern from the north end of Sudbury Street. It was the middle of the day; the tavern was usually quiet at this hour. But upon entering, Ethan was struck by the somber quality of the silence that greeted him. Kannice was behind the bar with Kelf, but as soon as she saw him, she came out, and rushed into his arms.

"What's the matter?" he asked, his breath stirring her hair. "What's happened?"

"It's Missus Tyler," she said, her voice low.

It took him a moment to place the name. "The house down the street," he said. "The one that's been quarantined."

"Aye." She pulled away to look him in the eye. "She died this morning."

ho did you hear it from?" Ethan asked.

"Diver, actually," Kannice said. "He was looking for you. He had it from Pat Daily."

"Aye. The one who's been posted at the house."

She nodded, her cheeks colorless, fear in her bright blue eyes. "We should leave, Ethan," she said in an urgent whisper. "Now, before it gets bad."

"Kannice—"

"Please. It's not just the Tyler woman. There are more outbreaks in New Boston. It's getting worse."

He gathered her in his arms and held her close. He could tell she was crying, and wondered if she was thinking of Rafe, her husband, who had died of the distemper eight years ago.

"I don't know where we would go," he said after some time, speaking the words into her auburn hair.

"We could stay with my sister," Kannice said, whispering into his chest. "I don't think there's been any illness out in Dorchester."

"I'm not sure your sister would welcome me into her home."

Kannice looked up at that. "She would if I asked. She would if it meant saving your life."

"But what if it seems to her that I'm endangering hers, or the lives of her children? For years, she's been after you to sell the tavern. And she knows that my work takes me into the streets. Would she want us in her home? Or would she think we were bringing small-pox to her?"

"Well, if not Dorchester, we can go somewhere else."

Ethan gazed unseeing over the top of her head. Despite her pleas, he didn't want to leave. Mrs. Tyler had died, which meant that her ghost might well be here, and her grave might be the next one desecrated by those who had violated the burying grounds. Was he afraid? Yes, though more for Kannice than for himself. He considered telling her that she should close down the Dowser and leave without him until this outbreak had passed. But he knew she would be hurt by the suggestion. Probably, she would refuse.

"I can't leave, Kannice," he said. His eyes met hers. "I know why you're frightened; I am, too. But I can't leave."

She was strong and pragmatic, and as smart as anyone he had ever known. She wiped the tears from her eyes, and she didn't argue. "The work you're doing for Pell?" she asked.

"Aye. And for Darcy and Ruth Walters. We haven't had a chance to talk about any of it, but the fact is that Missus Tyler's death might be of importance. It might . . ." He faltered, but then pressed on. "It might even be of some help to me."

She grimaced. "How?" Before he could answer, she shook her head. "No. Don't tell me."

"It's better that way," Ethan said. "This is a dark business, even more so than usual." He hesitated again, feeling self-conscious. "Do you know what's to be done with her, and more important, when they'll take her?"

"According to Diver, they'll bury her tonight sometime after mid-night." A haunted look came into her eyes. "I'm sure they'll take all the usual precautions," she said, her voice flat.

Ethan nodded, feeling selfish. This had to be terribly difficult for her. Perhaps he should take her to Dorchester, his inquiries be damned. He could get her settled there and be back in the city before midnight. He was about to say as much when he heard Kelf clear his throat. They both turned to see the barman, red-faced and as diffident as a school-boy, holding a cask of wine on his massive shoulder.

"This was just delivered in back," he said, his voice rough. "I was wonderin'—I'm sorry to interrupt—but I didn't know where you wanted it."

Kannice glanced at Ethan, a smile on her lips. "Come on then, Kelf. I'll show you."

Left alone, Ethan turned his thoughts back to the death of Mrs. Tyler. The "usual precautions" Kannice mentioned included wrapping the corpse in a sheet treated with tar, placing it in a coffin, and having pallbearers carry it over a specified route, to wherever she was to be buried. The town selectmen had probably mandated that the burial take place in the middle of the night so that there would be as few people as possible abroad in the streets when the body was carried from the Tyler house to the burying ground. As an added precaution, a man would walk ahead of the corpse to clear the lanes of any who might still be about.

The house itself would be cleansed several times, and smoked with brimstone and frankincense. Mrs. Tyler's bedding would be taken to the Pest House at Rainsford Island for smoking and airing. And Patrick Daily would be relieved of his guard duty in perhaps a week's time, when the selectmen were convinced that the danger of infection within the house had passed.

Somehow, Ethan needed to get inside the house before that week passed. He couldn't wait so long, and he couldn't miss the opportunity to communicate with Mrs. Tyler's shade. The question was, how could he enter the house without endangering his own life and the lives of Kannice, Diver, Henry, and everyone else with whom he had contact?

Kannice came back out of the kitchen a few minutes later and walked around the bar to where he stood.

"I'm sorry," she said, draping her arms around his neck. She kissed him. "I'm not supposed to be the sort who gets hysterical over trifles."

"This is hardly a trifle."

She gave a little shrug. "Still. You can't just up and leave Boston. I know that. To be honest, I can't either." A weak smile touched her lips. "Where would Tom Langer get his ale if not here?"

"Now, that is a fair question."

She kissed him a second time and broke away, heading to the bar. "Anyway, I won't mention it again."

"I had thought of saying that you should go to your sister's. I was going to offer to take you there myself. Once you were settled I would come back to continue my work. But I was afraid you'd be angry with me."

She walked back to where he stood. "Not angry, really. It's a kind offer, though I believe I can find my way on my own."

"Would you consider going?" he asked. "I'd rest easier if I knew you were out of harm's way."

Kannice shook her head. "I've already lost one man to smallpox, and I'll be damned if I'm going to leave you here to face this epidemic on your own. I'd rather be sick with you, than far away wondering if you're all right."

He frowned. "I'm not sure that's completely reasonable."

Kannice arched an eyebrow. "But?"

"But I appreciate it nevertheless. And I have no intention of letting either of us get sick."

Her eyes went wide. "Can you . . . ? I mean, does your . . . ?"

For all their time together, Kannice had never felt comfortable speaking of his spellmaking.

"My powers don't work that way," he said. But even as he answered her, he found himself thinking back on a conversation he'd had with Janna the year before. He had gone to ask her, as he often did, if it was possible for a conjurer to do something that he assumed was impossible.

To which Janna had replied, reproach in her voice, "All the time you ask me if spells can do this or spells can do that. Haven't you learned yet? Spells can do anythin' if the conjurer castin' them is strong enough."

So why couldn't he do this? Or if he wasn't strong enough, why couldn't Janna? He didn't expect that she could guard them against the distemper indefinitely, but he also couldn't remember hearing of a conjurer dying from smallpox in Boston, or even one being taken with the disease.

"What are you thinking?" Kannice asked him.

"That maybe I was too quick to say no." He turned and started toward the door.

"You just got here," she called after him. "Where are you going now?"

"To speak with Janna."

"Don't you want to eat first?"

"I'll buy food from her. She tells me more when I do." He smiled.

So did she. "You'll be back later?"

"I promise."

He walked to the Fat Spider heedless of his limp and the growing ache in his bad leg. As soon as Janna saw him enter, she raised a finger to warn him off of asking her questions. Ethan silenced her by holding up a shilling.

"Can I have some food and perhaps a bit to drink?" he asked, removing his hat, and taking a seat at a table near the bar. The tavern was mostly empty, but it smelled of fresh bread and one of Janna's dark, spicy stews.

"You think you can come in here an' buy my food an' get all sorts of information out of me. Well, I'm tellin' you, Kaille: I've got other things—"

"Which would you prefer, Janna? That I buy your food and get information from you, or get my information from someone else, and spend no money here at all?"

She glowered at him, her mouth twisting. But without another word she retreated into her kitchen to get him his meal. She emerged again moments later and placed a bowl and a round of bread in front of him.

"Ale?" she asked.

"Please."

She filled a tankard and set that on the table as well. For a few seconds she stood over him. Then, with a huffed breath that signaled her surrender, she sat. "Go ahead an' ask."

"This stew is excellent," he said, and meant it.

"I know that."

Ethan took another bite and laid his spoon aside. "You've told me in the past that any spell is possible if the conjurer casting it is strong enough."

"That's right."

"Are you afraid of smallpox, Janna?"

A smile crept over her face. "You're gettin' smarter and smarter, aren't you?"

He felt his pulse quicken. "So, you do know how to protect yourself from it?"

"It's not just a spell," she said.

"An herb as well."

She nodded, coy now. "A lot of them. I have a recipe I use."

"Mullein?" Ethan asked.

"That's one. There's wood sorrel in it, too. And larkspur, windflower—the blossoms, not just the leaves—Saint-John's-wort, sassafras, and . . ." She grinned again. "Well, a few others. I gather them all in a sachet and sell those. Each is good for one spell."

"I need to buy some from you."

"This just for you or for your woman, too?"

"Does it matter?"

She grew serious. "It matters how you use the sachet and how you word the spell. This is high magick, Kaille. Harder than most of your ordinary conjurin'."

"But if it protects against—"

"It guards you from the pox, but it's a matter of how long it lasts. An' if there be two of you . . ."

"I need to go into the house of someone who just died of smallpox. And I might not be able to wait until it's been thoroughly cleaned and smoked."

She scowled. "That's what I mean. That kind of foolishness will take a whole sachet by itself. These are not made to protect you from bein' stupid, an' they ain't cheap."

"How much?"

"Three crowns each."

Ethan stared back at her before reaching for his ale. "Three crowns?"

"They take time to put together, an' the windflower blossoms alone are worth almost half that."

"If I didn't go into the house, if I just used them to stay well during this outbreak, how long would a sachet last?"

Janna shrugged her bony shoulders, her gaze sliding away. "I can promise a fortnight. After that . . ." She shrugged again.

"Do these really work, Janna?"

She sat forward quickly, her expression so fierce that Ethan almost dropped his tankard. "You're damn right they work!"

"I apologize," he said. "I shouldn't have asked."

"No, you shouldn't have! You know me longer an' better than just about anyone in this town. An' you ask me if somethin' I'm sellin' is gonna work?" She shook her head. "You should know better."

"You're right. I'm sorry." He reached into his pocket. "I'd like to buy one, but one is all that I can afford right now."

She nodded, her lips pursed. She wouldn't look at him. "What are you goin' to do with it?"

He didn't answer right away. The truth was, a fortnight of protection for either him or Kannice was worth little. This outbreak would surely last longer than that; epidemics always did. But if this concoction of Janna's, along with whatever spell she taught him, could keep him safe while inside the Tyler house, that might well be worth the money he would have to spend. If Mrs. Tyler's ghost was there and could communicate with Reg.

"I don't have a choice."

"Goin' in that house is crazy. You know that. This is meant to protect you from getting' sick when you're goin' about your business. But what you're talkin' about . . ."

"Will it protect me?"

She sucked at her teeth, nodded. "I think so."

"All right." He counted out the money and handed it to her.

She took it, dropped it in her pocket without bothering to count it herself, and walked behind her bar to the room in which she stored her herbs.

When she came out again, she carried a small bundle wrapped in paper. Even before she handed it to him, Ethan he could smell the sorrel and mullein.

"The spell ain't easy," she said. "It has more than one part, an' it has to be spoke just so." She recited the conjuring to him in Latin a few words at a time, pausing between each section and inserting a word in English, so as to avoid actually casting the spell at that moment. Ethan repeated it back to her in the same way, and soon had it memorized.

When they had finished, Ethan reached for his hat and stood.

"You sure about this, Kaille?"

"Aye. I trust your herbs, and your spell."

"But still, goin' into that house might not be so smart."

"When have I ever let that stop me?"

They both grinned.

"I really am sorry, Janna. About before."

"I know. You be careful. Come back an' buy more of my food."

"I will."

He let himself out of the tavern. The wind off the harbor had strengthened, but it did little more than stir the hot, sour air that had settled over the city. Ethan began the long walk back to the South End and Cornhill, where several of the people on Pell's list had lived. He hadn't gotten far, though, when he felt another spell rumble in the street beneath his feet.

He knew immediately that it was a finding spell. But rather than originating at Sephira's house, like the finding spells Mariz had cast, this one came from farther off, though from a similar direction: the waterfront, to the south of the Battery, near Adams' Wharf.

The spell rushed toward him, like a breaker sweeping over a beach. And when it reached him, it was nothing like the finding spells Mariz had cast: it was far more aggressive. This was no twining vine; rather it felt like hands reaching up out of the earth to grab at his legs. Just like in his dream. A heartbeat later, it was gone.

With Mariz's spells Ethan knew what to expect. Usually the conjurer showed up within minutes of locating him. Sometimes Mariz was alone; other times he had the rest of Sephira's toughs with him. But one way or another, when Ethan felt one of Mariz's finding spells, he knew to expect a run-in with the Empress of the South End.

This spell promised another sort of confrontation. His previous encounters with Nate Ramsey had taken place in but a single day. Still, Ethan knew what Ramsey was capable of doing, and how he conducted his affairs. He didn't think the captain would leave his ship to track Ethan through the city lanes. That spell had been a summons, and also a challenge.

Ethan's good sense warred with his curiosity. He didn't want to face Ramsey until he knew more about the spells the captain had cast and his purpose in returning to Boston. But for better or worse, Ramsey wanted to speak with him, and Ethan wished to know why. In the end, his curiosity prevailed. He followed Orange Street to Essex Street, turned eastward, and walked to the southern extreme of the South End waterfront. Upon reaching Windmill Point, Ethan halted and scanned the wharves and shipyards that projected into the harbor between the point and the South Battery to the northeast.

He wasn't sure that he would recognize the *Muirenn* if he saw it moored beside other similar vessels. But he should have known that Ramsey wouldn't waste Ethan's time, or his own, by making him try.

Another spell pulsed, weaker than the previous one: an elemental spell, sourced in water or air. Ethan spotted an eagle wheeling above Tileston's Wharf, the longest of the piers before him. It flew in lazy circles, its great wings held steady, its tail twisting in the wind. And then it faded from view: an illusion, conjured for his benefit. He followed the narrow harborfront lanes to the wharf and walked out onto the pier, eyeing each ship he passed.

Halfway to the end, he spotted a lone man standing on the deck of a pink. The man, whom Ethan recognized as Ramsey, marked his approach before disappearing from view. Ethan had checked his stride at the sight of him, but now he continued toward the ship. She was a small vessel, but clean and obviously well tended. She was tied between a pair of bollards, and sat light in the water. Whatever cargo she might have carried had already been off-loaded. Now that he saw her again, Ethan recognized the *Muirenn*. He wondered where Ramsey had gone, and went so far as to pull out the pouch of mullein he had bought from Janna. Warding himself would have been the prudent course of action. But the captain would feel the conjuring and would assume that Ethan had come looking for a fight. He put the mullein back into his pocket.

The ship's gangplank was down, but Ethan paused at her prow, and called, "Ahoy, the *Muirenn*!"

"Ahoy!" came the reply. A moment later Ramsey appeared again. He stood at the rails amidships, holding a flask of what was probably Madeira and two cups. "You came."

"I did. Permission to come aboard?"

"Granted."

Ethan walked up the plank and hopped onto the deck just in front of the captain, who watched him with a faint, sardonic smile on his face.

The years had not touched Ramsey at all; he looked just as Ethan remembered. Tall, spear-thin, he had a long face and a dark, unruly beard. His eyes were pale and his grin exposed yellow, crooked teeth. He wore a white silk shirt and tan breeches, as he had the last time he and Ethan met.

Ethan proffered a hand, which Ramsey seized in a firm grip. An instant later he pulled Ethan into a rough embrace and thumped him on the back.

"It's good to see you again, Kaille," he said, the words colored with a faint Scottish burr.

Ramsey released him and Ethan took a step back. He couldn't keep a smile from touching his lips even as his brow furrowed in puzzlement.

"Is it?" he asked.

"Of course! Men like us—we don't have many friends. We have to enjoy those we do have."

"Forgive me, Captain, but the last time we met—the only time we met—we fought. We came close to killing each other. And you murdered two men I had been engaged to protect."

"Aye, I remember. I also recall that you were not as keen on keeping those men alive after you heard my reasons for wantin' them dead. And we were well matched, you and I. It's not often that I find a conjurer who's as skilled as I am."

"That may be, but—"

"Leave it, Kaille. Friends, enemies. There aren't that many people in this world who inspire passion in me one way or another. So stop arguin' and drink with me." He walked to a pair of barrels and sat, gesturing with the hand that held the two cups for Ethan to follow.

Ethan stared after the man, laughing to himself. He strolled to where Ramsey had perched himself and seated himself on the other barrel.

The captain filled one cup with wine and handed it to Ethan. After filling his own, he raised it. "What shall we drink to?"

"I believe we drank to your father last time," Ethan said. "We should again."

The look in Ramsey's eyes hardened, but he nodded once and said, "Thank you," as Ethan tapped the rim of his cup to Ramsey's. They both drank.

"You look old, thieftaker. The years haven't been kind to you."

"I was thinking that you hadn't changed at all."

"Sure, I have," Ramsey said. "I'm smarter now. Stronger, as well."

"Is that a warning?"

"It's a fact."

"What brings you back to Boston?"

Ramsey let out a soft laugh. "That was direct."

"It was a simple question."

"I think we both know better." He drank, nearly draining his cup. "I'm not ready to answer you. There's more that I have to do, and I think you already know more than you're lettin' on."

"Have you hired men to rob graves here in the city?"

"I just docked today." Ramsey finished his wine and poured himself more. He held the flask out to Ethan.

Ethan shook his head. His cup was still nearly full.

"You didn't answer my question."

Ramsey drank, his eyes dancing with mischief.

"Do you know much about resurrectionists?" Ethan asked.

"I've read a bit. I know they steal cadavers."

"Or body parts. They do it for profit—they sell the dead to surgeons and those who aspire to the trade. That's what most people here think lies at the heart of this latest spate of desecrations. Greed."

"Most people," Ramsey said. "But, I take it, not the great Ethan Kaille."

"I make no claims to greatness. But I do know better than to think that this is about money."

"And that's supposed to impress me?" Ramsey laughed. "I don't imagine it was too hard to figure out. The gap between what these others think and what you know is more a product of their stupidity than any cleverness on your part."

"As I said: I make no claims to greatness."

"And yet," Ramsey said, his voice silken, "you intend to match your wits against mine, your power against mine. You may not claim to be great, but you're still reachin' higher than you have any right to. You should be careful, thieftaker: stretch your arm out too far and you might overbalance. Or you might simply lose a limb."

Ethan's laughter sounded harsh to his own ears. "Is this how you speak to all your friends?"

"Why did you come here, Kaille? What did you expect to find? What did you think I'd tell you?"

"I came here because you as much as asked me to," Ethan said. "It was your finding spell that drew me, your illusion spell that told me where the *Muirenn* was moored. She remains a fine ship, by the way. You should ask yourself if you wouldn't be better off putting back out to sea. It's safer for you out there."

Ramsey drained his cup again and set it down smartly on the rail. There was no trace of mirth left on his face. "You should go."

Ethan sipped his wine, making no move to leave. "I think you brought me here because you're torn. You say that you're not ready to reveal your purpose in being here. But you're just bursting at the seams, wanting to tell me everything. You're so enamored of your plans that keeping them secret hurts."

"Is that so?" Ramsey asked, his voice tight.

"Aye. So, go ahead and tell me. I'm going to find out soon enough. Think of how much more satisfying it will feel to tell me to my face, to see my reaction."

For the span of a heartbeat, it seemed to Ethan that Ramsey was tempted. He could see the eagerness in the captain's eyes, the boyish excitement in the smile that tried to break through his stolid mien. But the moment passed and he shook his head.

"I think I won't. But I give you credit for makin' the attempt." He did smile then, but it was cold and clearly forced. "I'm goin' to enjoy these next few days."

Ethan finished his wine and stood. He tipped his hat to the captain and crossed to the gangplank.

But as he started to walk back down to the wharf, Ramsey called his name, stopping him.

"Your foot," he said, nodding toward Ethan's bad leg. "Did we have that right?"

Ethan had let down his guard, thinking that their interview was over. He felt his cheeks go white, and could think of nothing to say.

Ramsey threw back his head and laughed. He picked up his flask and cup, and went belowdecks.

Chapter
TWELVE

s Ethan stepped off the gangplank onto the wharf, his hands shook. Rage, frustration, yes, even a touch of fear: a storm of emotions raged in his mind. He had very nearly gotten the better of Ramsey; he was certain that the man was on the verge of telling him everything. And in a moment of weakness, he allowed the captain to turn their encounter to his advantage.

He was desperate to know what Ramsey was planning, to understand what role he himself played in the man's scheme.

"Yes, well, he's not going to tell you," Ethan muttered to himself, drawing a disapproving look from a passing wharfman.

The sun hung low in the west, still obscured by the haze that had settled over the city days before. The breeze had died, leaving the air hot and stagnant. It would be another hour at least until darkness fell and the shades Ramsey had released from their slumber appeared once more.

Ethan set out again for the North End. Bertram Flagg, another of the dead in the King's Chapel Burying Ground who were mutilated by Ramsey's men, had lived a short distance from the Rowan family. Ethan chose to begin his search for other ghosts at his home.

Mr. Flagg had been a shipbuilder whose yard was located in the North End, near the Charlestown ferry. He was no less wealthy or influential than Alexander Rowan. His home might have been more modest than the Rowan mansion, but only just. It was a two-story brick house with black shutters and a white colonnade at the entrance. It stood at the corner of Hull and Salem streets, at the base of Copp's Hill and within sight—and smell—of the foul waters of Mill Pond.

Ethan approached the door only to have it open before he reached it. A young man walked out of the house and halted upon seeing him.

"Who are you?" he asked. He was a few inches shorter than Ethan and slight of build, with a soft, almost feminine face. He couldn't have been more than sixteen or seventeen years old.

Ethan thought he might retreat into the house at the first word he uttered.

"My name is Ethan Kaille," he said. "I'm a thieftaker hired by Reverend Caner to find those who desecrated the burying ground at King's Chapel."

The lad gazed back at him, seemingly waiting for Ethan to say more. At last he stepped forward and stuck out a hand, which Ethan shook. "I'm Charles Flagg," he said, not quite looking Ethan in the eye.

"I'm sorry about the passing of your father," Ethan said.

Charles shrugged, looked down at his feet. "Thank you." They fell into a brief, strained silence. "I have to go," the lad finally said. "I have . . . I just have to go." There was something in his manner . . .

"I take it you have a meeting to attend."

The lad's eyes widened, with fright at first, but when Ethan offered a faint conspiratorial smile, he nodded, and even chanced a grin of his own. "You won't say anything, will you?" he asked, dropping his voice to a whisper. "My father had nothing but contempt for the Sons of Liberty, and I don't want to get in trouble."

"I won't say a word. Is your mother inside?"

"My stepmother is. My mother died when I was seven."

Ethan grimaced in sympathy, thinking that in this respect at least, Charles had already lived a more difficult life than many men twice his age. "Again, I'm sorry. What is your stepmother's name?"

"Edith."

"Thank you, Charles."

The boy nodded. "You're welcome," he said, and strode away, looking much like a boy trying to act older than his years.

Ethan went to the door, which Charles had left open. He rapped with the brass knocker and called, "Missus Flagg?"

"Yes?" came a voice. A few seconds later a woman walked into view. She looked to be but a few years older than Charles. She was pretty but careworn, with wheaten hair and green eyes. She carried a babe in her arms, and was trailed by a second child, a girl who might have been five years old.

Ethan introduced himself again, and as he did, a single crease formed in the middle of the woman's brow.

"Why would you come here?" she asked. "Shouldn't you be looking for answers in the burying ground?"

"I believe there might be answers here, ma'am."

She looked away. "I don't know anything about what happened to Bertram's grave, except that it was gruesome and foul."

"Who is that, Mama?" the girl asked, staring at Ethan with large round eyes the same shade as her mother's.

"He's just a man who works for the church, dear. And he won't be staying."

"This must be very frightening for all of you," Ethan said. "Not being able to feel safe in your own home. I believe I can help you."

Edith's face had gone white.

"You're not the only ones, you know," he went on, pretending not to notice. "Families all across the city have had shades in their homes. You needn't be embarrassed."

"What's he talking about, Mama?"

Edith bent and cupped her daughter's face in a gentle hand. "It's nothing you need to worry about." She straightened and called, "Cecille!"

An African servant came to the foyer. "Yes, ma'am."

Edith handed the infant to Cecille. "Can you take Alice and her brother into the parlor? Perhaps you and Alice can sing him to sleep again, as you did yesterday. Can you do that?" she asked the little girl.

Alice beamed and followed the servant as she carried the babe into another room. Edith stared after them.

"I'm sorry about that," Ethan said.

The woman shook her head. When she faced him again there were tears on her cheeks. "She's going to find out sooner or later. It's been here every night this week. I know that it's not my husband. Not really. But it wears his clothes, and all through the night it wanders around his study or lingers in our room. I can't sleep in there anymore."

"Yes, ma'am. Would you mind if I were to wait for him with you? I need to see what he looks like. And I may be able to learn something from him that will help me find a way to send him back where he belongs. To send all of them back."

"To send them . . ." She shook her head. "How could you do that?"

"I believe that the people who disturbed your husband's grave are using what they stole to control his spirit. If I can find these people and return to the burying ground what was taken, he and the others might be free once more to go back where they belong."

"Yes, all right." She still sounded doubtful.

"If you would like, I can wait outside. Once the shade appears, you can invite me in. Would that be easier?"

"No, that's all right." She backed away from the door, and beckoned him inside. "Please come in."

Ethan thanked her and entered the house. Within, the dwelling was quite similar to the Rowan house, with its polished wooden floors and fine furniture. Ethan wondered if Flagg had bought his furniture from the Rowans.

"Can I get you anything, Mister . . . I'm sorry, I've forgotten your name."

"Kaille," Ethan said. "And no thank you. I'm fine."

"Would you like to wait in my husband's study?"

"Yes, of course."

She led him through the house, past the harpsichord, where Alice was picking out "Come, Follow, Follow Me" as Cecille sat beside her singing to the babe.

Once they were beyond the hearing of Alice and the others, Ethan asked, "Missus Flagg, do you remember your husband mentioning a sea captain named Nate Ramsey? Or perhaps a pair of merchants: Deron Forrs and Isaac Keller?"

She shook her head. "No. I'm afraid Bertram didn't tell me much about his work." She unlocked a door off a narrow corridor and ushered Ethan into a spacious study. "Here you are," she said with false bright-

ness. "You can wait here until night falls. Are you sure I can't have Cecille bring you something?"

"Yes, I'm sure. Thank you." Ethan surveyed the study. The air in the
room smelled stale; he didn't think it had been disturbed for months.
"If I may ask, when did your husband die?"

"It was the tenth of April."

He nodded, staring at a sheaf of papers on the writing desk against
the war wall. "Would you mind if I examined some of those documents," he asked, pointing at the desk. "It may be—"

"If you can find something that will help to rid of us of the demon
haunting our home, it will be a blessing. Look at whatever you want."

"Yes, ma'am," Ethan said. "Thank you."

She left him, closing the door behind her. Ethan crossed to the desk
and after hesitating for a few breaths, lowered himself into the chair
positioned behind it and picked up the sheaf of papers. A quick perusal
of the contents convinced him that it consisted of invoices and bills of
sale. He laid the papers aside and pulled open one of the desk drawers,
and then another. In the third, he found several ledgers. He opened one,
and began to read. In addition to the bills of sale Flagg kept, he had
also maintained a careful ledger of every transaction by date: payments
in, payments out, the names of those with whom he did business. Ethan
retrieved the other ledgers stored in the drawer and thumbed through
the pages until he found what he had sought.

In 1751, Bertram Flagg's shipyard built a pink for a merchant captain
named Nathaniel Ramsey. The *Muirenn*. Twice in subsequent years—1758
and 1760—Flagg's workers performed minor repairs on the ship. The
1760 entry was the last mention of anyone named Ramsey.

The light outside was failing and Ethan could barely see, even if he
held up the ledger to the window. There were candles set throughout
the study. Ethan glanced toward the door before pulling his knife and
cutting himself.

"*Ignis ex cruore evocatus.*" Fire, conjured from blood. Flames appeared
atop three of the candles. Reg winked into view for a moment as well,
but when Ethan paid him no heed, he faded. Ethan turned his attention back to the ledgers, thumbing through all of them a second time
to make certain he hadn't missed anything. This time, he found several

mentions of Alexander Rowan and a few of Sebastian Wise, but none of these transactions struck him as out of the ordinary. And he saw no more entries for the Ramseys. What he had found didn't tell him much, but at least he knew that Flagg, like the Rowan and Wise families, had dealings with Nate Ramsey's father.

He sat back, stretched his back, rubbed the bridge of his nose between his thumb and forefinger. Not for the first time, he considered whether he might need to be fitted with a pair of reading spectacles. No doubt Kannice would find this amusing.

Opening his eyes once more, he froze.

The ghost of Bertram Flagg stood in the middle of the study, his eyes gleaming balefully. He was in little better condition than the shade of Abigail Rowan had been, and like her he glowed bone white. His skin had darkened and stretched so that the contours of his skull were plainly visible. He wore a dark coat, waistcoat, and breeches with a light shirt and cravat. He held a cane in one leathery hand—it must have been buried with him—and he hovered just off the floor, bobbing like a bird sitting on the surface of the harbor.

The shade seemed far more agitated than Abigail's ghost had been, and Ethan felt certain that he was the object of the shade's wrath.

"*Veni ad me*," Ethan said, holding himself still. Come to me.

Uncle Reg appeared beside the desk, his glowing eyes fixed on the shade.

"Can you tell him that I'm here to speak with him, and to find out who brought him back. I meant no harm in going through his documents."

Ethan glanced up at Reg, who glared back down at him, a dour expression on his face. "It's the truth!" he said.

The corners of Reg's mouth twitched, but he turned to the shade and stared at it for several seconds. Whatever he said did little to mollify Flagg. The shade gestured wildly with his cane, at one point jabbing it so forcefully, that Ethan jerked back out of the way before remembering that the shade couldn't hurt him.

Reg looked at Ethan again and shrugged.

Ethan stood, holding his hands where Flagg's shade could see them. He opened his mouth to ask one of the many questions running through his mind, but stopped without asking any of them. When he had seen Abigail Rowan he had thought he glimpsed some faint hue in her form. Now, looking at Flagg, he was certain of it. Silvery light suffused the figure, but his face and head were tinged with a color Ethan recognized as Ramsey's aqua. So was the shade's right hand.

"Ask him if Ramsey has communicated with him in any way."

Reg stood motionless for a few seconds, then turned quickly back to Ethan and nodded once more.

His heart began to race, though at the same time his frustration grew. How did he ask a ghost who couldn't speak to tell him what another mute ghost had said?

"Is he giving them instructions?"

Reg shook his head.

"But Flagg knows that Ramsey is the one holding him here."

The old ghost nodded.

Ethan looked at the shade again. "I'm trying to help you. You have my word on that."

Flagg still looked angry, but he gave a reluctant nod, and he was using his cane for support again, rather than as a weapon, which Ethan took as a minor victory. He regarded the shade, marking once more the hint of color in his hand and head. The ghost's foot, he noticed, had no hue at all. It seemed that had been something Ramsey did entirely to grab Ethan's attention. And it had worked.

He eyed the ghost again. The head and hand. The foot.

"His chest," Ethan whispered. To Reg, he said, "Can you ask him to open his coat and shirt. I need to see his chest."

Reg scowled. Ethan had noticed a year ago, when he had Reg summon the murdered conjurer to his room above Henry's cooperage, and again in the past couple of days in dealing with the shades roaming Boston, that the old ghost was protective of the dead. Ethan thought he understood, but he also knew that Reg couldn't refuse him in this matter or any other.

"You know why," Ethan said. "I wouldn't ask it otherwise."

The old warrior's expression softened and he faced Flagg once more. After a brief pause, the shade released his cane, which remained upright, and unbuttoned his coat, his waistcoat, and finally the shirt.

When at last he pulled the shirt open to expose his chest, Ethan could not help the oath that escaped him.

On the left side of his chest, over his heart, the symbol that had been carved into the skin of every male corpse mutilated in the burying grounds—the triangle with three straight lines cutting through it— blazed like sea-green fire. Here alone, the color of Ramsey's power was not muted or diminished by the white glow of the shade. Rather it shone so brightly that it cast Ethan's shadow in stark relief on the wall behind him.

He was more convinced than ever that the shade's head and hand were what held it here in the mortal world. But he knew intuitively that this symbol controlled the spirit and turned him to Ramsey's purpose, whatever that might be.

The door to the study opened, and Missus Flagg walked in.

"Mister Kaille I believe—" She halted at the sight of her husband's shade, and drew a sharp breath. When he turned to her, his glowing chest still exposed, she cried out. "What have you done to him?" she asked in a strangled voice.

"I did nothing," Ethan said. He stepped out from behind the desk, followed by Reg, whom he assumed the woman could not see.

"This was done to his corpse at the burying ground, and I believe that those who desecrated his grave intend to use that mark as a means of controlling his actions."

"I don't understand any of this. How could they control him? What you're describing sounds like . . . like witchcraft."

He didn't correct her. "Aye, it does," he said. "You can call it that, if you wish. The powers used by the men who did this are real—you can see that for yourself. This is why they have to be stopped."

"Is he in pain?"

Ethan cast a quick look Reg's way. The old ghost shook his head.

"I don't believe he is, at least not as I think you mean it. But he does not wish to be here. He doesn't want to scare you or your children. And that, I suppose, is a kind of pain."

"You said before that there are other shades in Boston right now. Do they all bear that mark? Are they all trapped here, as Bertram is?"

He almost said yes before remembering Patience Walters, who was caught here as the others were, but who looked so different and who glowed with what he now realized was a blend of Ramsey's aqua and the color of her own powers. Was it just Patience who looked this way, or were there others? And if so, had all of those who looked as Patience did been conjurers in life?

"To be honest, ma'am, I don't yet understand all that's happening. I know that there are other shades like this one—that the cadavers mutilated at the burying grounds seem to be manifesting themselves in their old homes, while looking as they do now in their graves. But there are other shades as well." He shook his head. "I'm sorry I can't tell you more."

The shade had buttoned up his clothing. It seemed odd to think of a ghost as being modest, but Bertram Flagg had retrieved his cane and now stood by the window, gazing out into the night. Ethan had the distinct feeling that he was ashamed to look his young wife in the eye.

"I think I should go," he said. "Thank you, Missus Flagg."

"Of course," she said, eyeing her husband's shade.

"I can let myself out, ma'am."

"Thank you, Mister Kaille."

Ethan started to leave. "He won't hurt you," he said, facing her once more. "He can't, and he wouldn't want to."

She looked at him, nodded.

Ethan left the house with Reg beside him, waiting to be released. As Ethan walked, he seethed. Ramsey was playing with forces he couldn't have understood, and inflicting pain on people who had done nothing to deserve such cruelty.

"Do you have any idea how we can stop him?" Ethan asked.

Reg shook his head. Ethan could see that the ghost's rage was a match for his own.

"Would killing Ramsey do it?"

Reg faltered, nodded.

Ethan frowned. "It would, but you don't think I can kill him, do you? He's gotten too strong."

The ghost averted his bright gaze. Ethan didn't need to see him nod to know that it was true.

"Damn." He took a long breath. "Thank you for your help tonight," he said to the ghost. *"Dimitto te."* I release you.

He walked back to the Dowser, knowing that he should have gone to see the other shades that had been driven from their graves, but knowing as well that he couldn't face them. Not tonight. He wasn't sure he saw the point in going tomorrow night either. He knew what he would find: lost souls like Abigail Rowan and Bertram Flagg, families too ashamed or frightened to ask for help until it showed up at their door, and more evidence of Ramsey's power and his own inability to match it.

By the time he reached the Dowser, his legs felt leaden and his shoulders drooped with exhaustion. For a panicked instant, he thought he might be growing ill, but he knew better. He had spent the day walking from one end of the city to the other, and he had little to show for his efforts. He wasn't sick; he was dispirited. Before entering the tavern, he drew himself up and put on a brave face, lest he scare Kannice.

It was warm and loud in the great room, and even the aromas of chowder and bread couldn't mask entirely the stink of sweat that clung to the workmen drawn in by Kannice's cooking. Kannice and Kelf were so busy ladling out chowder that they didn't notice that Ethan had come in until he stepped to the bar.

"I'll get ya an ale in a minute, Ethan," the barkeep said, his words stumbling over one another.

"There's no hurry, Kelf."

"Aye," Kannice said. "And he probably won't be staying long." The words came out flat, and there was a troubled look in her eyes.

"What's happened now?" he asked, unable to keep the weariness from his voice.

"Another message has come for you," she said. "I'll get it in a moment."

"If all my letters are going to come here, I might have to start paying you more for my ales and chowder." He smiled.

Her expression didn't change.

"Who's it from, Kannice?" But already he had an inkling.

"Marielle Harper."

Of course. Marielle Harper: his first love, and once his betrothed. Ethan loved Kannice, and she knew that. But she also remembered that for a long time, even after they began to share a bed, he had mourned the end of his engagement to Elli. Kannice was not the kind to be jealous, or to tolerate jealousy in her man. But to this day, she freely admitted being jealous of Elli.

For her part, Marielle remained standoffish toward Ethan. She didn't approve of his spellmaking, and had yet to forgive him for concealing his powers from her during their brief betrothal. She had come to accept that her children, Holin and Clara, cared for him, and she grudgingly allowed him to be a small part of their lives. But she would not have sent a message to him, particularly here at Kannice's tavern, had her need not been great.

He tried to conceal his impatience to see the missive, but Kannice knew him too well. She glanced his way, her expression darkening, and muttered, "I'll get it now."

She handed another bowl to Kelf before walking to the far end of the bar and retrieving a small, folded piece of parchment from a shelf below the polished wood top.

Walking back to Ethan, she handed it to him, saying not a word. He unfolded it and saw that in fact the missive was not written in Elli's hand. He read, his blood turning colder with each line:

> Mister Kaille,
> I am writing to you on behalf of Marielle Harper, who bids
> me tell you that her son, Holin, has taken ill with the
> smallpox. The family has been removed from their home in the
> North End and is now staying at the Hospital in New
> Boston.
>
> Louise Colson

"What does it say?" Kannice asked, watching him.

He handed the missive back to her.

She scanned it, and looked back up at him. "Ethan, I'm so sorry. I didn't know . . ." She winced, canting her head to the side. "Let me get you something to eat and then you can go to them."

"Thank you, but I'm not hungry. I came back here to sit and rest." He cupped her smooth cheek in his hand. "And to see you. But it seems that's not going to be part of my evening, at least not yet."

"You will come back later, though, won't you?"

"I don't know. It will be late, if I do."

Kannice pulled a key from within her bodice and slipped the lanyard from which it hung over her head. "Here," she said, holding it out to him. "You can let yourself in, even if I've gone to sleep. But I want to see you. I want to know you're all right."

He took the key, put the lanyard around his neck, and brushed a strand of hair off her brow. "Then I suppose I'll see you later," he said, and walked out once more into the humid night air.

It was a dark and desolate walk out to Pest House Point, as the strip of land on which sat the Province Hospital was known. The streets of New Boston were largely empty, and too many of the houses in this part of the city bore red flags, which rose and fell in the light breeze, rustling softly. Between Kannice's tavern and the West Meeting House, he must have seen at least a half-dozen houses marked as quarantined. Once Ethan was past Chambers Street, walking west on Cambridge, there was little to see at all. Houses and gardens gave way to open leas, empty save for lowing cows.

Before long, the hospital loomed up ahead of him, homely and austere. A few of its windows shone dimly with inconstant candlelight, their glow reflected in the waters of the Charles River, just beyond the point. Others were dark. A murmur of voices reached him from within the building, along with the sound of crying. He wondered if Elli and Clara were among those he heard.

He approached the entrance to the hospital, but was stopped by a guard before he reached the door.

"You can't go in there," he said. "And you wouldn't want to if you could."

"Someone I know came here today. A boy. I want to speak with his mother."

The man shook his head. "You can't."

"Not even if she were to stand by her window and I were to stay out here?"

"Do you know which room they're in?"

Ethan fished in his pocket for a few pence. He held them up for the guard to see. "You could find out for me. The lad's name is Holin Harper; his mother is Marielle Harper."

The man's gaze shifted between Ethan and the coins. At last he held out a hand. Ethan dropped the coins into his palm, taking care not to let his fingers so much as brush the man's hand. The guard nodded and went inside.

Ethan waited on the path leading to the entrance, staring out across the river toward Cambridge. Mosquitos buzzed his ears, and whip-poor-wills called from over the Common. He glanced repeatedly at the door to the hospital, looking for the guard, but seeing no one. The minutes dragged on, and Ethan started to wonder if the guard had taken his coins and retreated to where Ethan couldn't reach him.

He considered knocking on the hospital door, but chose to give the guard a few minutes more. It was a large building, and no doubt there were many unwell people within.

As Ethan gazed out across the water again, something caught his eye. A flash of light reflected on the river's surface. He looked up at the sky and back at the building, but saw nothing. He assumed that he had imagined the light.

He decided that he had waited long enough and resolved to knock on the hospital door. But just as he turned away from the water, he saw it again: a glimmer of white light that danced across the surface of the river for a few seconds between reflections of candlelight, and then vanished. He turned to face the hospital, gazed back over his shoulder at the spot where the light had appeared.

And saw it again.

He looked up at the hospital and saw its source. A glowing ghostly form had appeared in one of the windows. It stood there for but a moment before moving out of sight.

Ethan knew that he shouldn't have been surprised. People died at the hospital with some frequency. That shades should be appearing here, as well, made perfect sense. But he could only imagine how the hospital's patients would respond to seeing spirits of the dead in their rooms.

"You there!" The guard stood in the doorway. "She's around back, on the second floor."

"Thank you." Ethan walked to the door as the man watched him, wary and hopeful, as if unable to decide whether Ethan meant to give him more money or force his way inside.

Ethan stopped a few paces short of the door. "How long have the shades been here?"

The guard stared at him and licked his lips. "I don't know what you're talking about."

"Aye, you do. I think that's why some rooms are darkened and others aren't. They could fill every room in the hospital, couldn't they, but they're forced to keep some of the rooms locked, because the ghosts show up every night after the sun goes down."

"That's . . ." The guard rubbed a hand over his mouth. "How'd you know?"

"I saw one in the window. And I've seen others all over the city. When did they first appear?"

"You can't speak of this to anyone," the guard said, taking a step toward him and lowering his voice. "If folks think the hospital is haunted, they won't come here, and the epidemic will spread even more quickly."

"I understand."

The guard swallowed. "It's been three nights now since we saw the first of them."

"How many are there?"

"Six, right now. But we seem to get a new one every evening."

"What do they look like?"

The guard cringed. "Demons," he said. "They look like they've come back from the grave. They're rotted, or they're not much more than bone. Except their eyes, which glow as bright as little suns." He faltered. "You say you've seen others?"

"Several," Ethan said, silently cursing Ramsey.

"What do they want?" the man asked.

"The shades? They want to go back where they belong."

Chapter
THIRTEEN

than walked around to the rear of the building and across the sloping lawn until he spotted a lone figure standing at a second-floor window, her frame silhouetted against the pale yellow glow of candles.

"Elli?" Ethan said, pitching his voice to carry.

"Ethan," she answered immediately.

There was candlelight coming from the window just to the left of hers. The window to the right was dark.

"How is he?" Ethan asked, his gaze flicking toward that darkened window. He was thankful Elli couldn't see him clearly; she would have been furious to know that she didn't have his undivided attention.

"He's resting, but he looks . . ." She shook her head. "The pox started on his chest, but it's spread to his face now, and I'm afraid—" Her voice cracked. "I'm afraid he's never going to look the same."

"The important thing is that he get better."

"Yes. Yes, you're right. Of course."

"You and Clara are well? Has there been any sign of the distemper in either of you?"

"We're fine. They made us come here because they say we might have been exposed. It could be as long as two weeks before we know for certain. I would have come anyway, but I wanted to leave Clara with the family of one of her friends. The selectmen wouldn't allow it."

Ethan wasn't surprised. "Do you need anything?" he asked.

"No. Thank you. I didn't mean for you to come. I just thought you should know where we are, in case you decided to come to the house to see the children."

"Thank you. I would have come sooner if had I known." He glanced again at the darkened window and thought he saw a faint white glow emanating from the room. But he didn't actually see a shade. "Are you comfortable?" he asked her, breaking a brief silence.

"Yes, though it's crowded in here. I don't understand why they have people in some rooms but not in others."

He wasn't sure what to say. "If you discover that you do need something—anything at all—get another message to me. I'll bring you whatever you want."

"Thank you. You were very kind to come."

He smiled. There was a time, just a few years ago, when even this small praise from her would have set his heart afire. Not anymore. "Tell Holin that I expect to see him up and about in short order."

"Yes, I will. Good night, Ethan."

"Good night."

She stepped away from the window, but Ethan lingered on the lawn, watching the window next to hers. Several times he thought he saw that faint silvery glow brighten, and he expected the shade to drift into view. But each time the light dimmed again. At last, Ethan walked around to the front of the hospital and started back toward the city, his eyes drawn to the illuminated steeple of the West Church.

He passed the houses on Cambridge Street, and as he neared Sudbury Street, he heard in the distance the cries of the night watchmen. It was midnight. Rather than returning to the Dowser, Ethan stopped along a lonely stretch of road, drew his knife, and cut himself.

"*Velamentum ex cruore evocatum.*" Concealment, conjured from blood.

He felt the spell, just as he did the others he had cast in recent days. Reg appeared before him, his bright eyes fixed on his face. But that was all. Usually when he cast a concealment spell, he felt the conjuring settle over him like a fine cool mist. Not this time.

"It didn't work, did it?" Ethan asked.

The old ghost shook his head.

Ethan cast a second time. Again the casting failed. He could hear the pounding of his own heart as he raised his knife to his arm once more. But he hesitated, the blade poised over his raw skin. No doubt Ramsey, along with every other conjurer in the city, had sensed these failed spells. The captain might not be able to discern what kind of conjurings Ethan was attempting; he might not even know that it was Ethan casting the spells. But he would know that the conjurings were the same. And Ethan guessed that he would take satisfaction in this.

Ethan was certain that whatever the captain had done to bring the shades to Boston was also making it harder for other conjurers to cast their spells. He didn't yet understand the connection, but he would eventually.

"I'm going to try this one last time," Ethan said to Reg, who still watched him.

The ghost nodded, his expression even more grim than usual.

"*Velamentum ex cruore evocatum.*" This time the pulse of power was followed an instant later by the touch of the spell on his skin.

Reg appeared to exhale.

"Let's hope I can remove the conjuring later," Ethan said. "I'd rather not be invisible for the rest of my days."

The ghost grinned.

They resumed walking and soon came to the Tyler house, a short distance south of the Dowser. Men had gathered there; several of them were already inside. Ethan could see torchlight shining from the windows.

He kept his distance, unwilling to risk exposing himself to the distemper. But he watched as two men carried the corpse out of the house. They had already wrapped her in a tarred sheet, as they did all those who died of smallpox, and now they lowered her into a plain wooden coffin. As another man nailed the lid in place, Ethan heard quiet sobs coming from his left. A white-haired man—Mr. Tyler, Ethan assumed—stood with two young women, watching the proceedings. With them was a minister in black robes and a white cravat.

Four pallbearers lifted the coffin, and with a man walking ahead of them to clear the streets, and Mrs. Tyler's family following at the rear of the procession, they set out southward along Treamount Street. Ethan walked a short distance behind them, making as little noise as possible, and feeling a bit guilty for intruding upon the private grief of Mr. Tyler and his daughters.

It soon became clear to him that they were headed to the Granary Burying Ground. On instinct, he turned to Reg, who still walked with him, and whispered, "I don't know who we might encounter in the burying ground. But just in case, *Dimitto te*." I release you.

Reg didn't look happy, but he faded from view. Ethan followed the procession through the stone gate and to an open gravesite near the center of the burying ground.

The burial itself took but a few minutes. Once the pallbearers had lowered the coffin into the ground, Mr. Tyler and his daughters walked to the edge of the grave. There they were joined by the minister, who spoke in quiet tones as the pallbearers began to shovel dirt onto the coffin.

Ethan had seen enough. He knew where Mrs. Tyler had been buried; he could keep an eye on her grave. He didn't think that he could stop Ramsey and his men from desecrating it if they chose to, not without getting himself killed. But if they managed to take control of her shade, as they had so many others, he would use Janna's sachet and spell to enter the Tyler house and speak to her. He didn't know for certain that she would be able to tell him more than had the other shades he'd encountered, but he hoped that in this case time would be on his side. She had died recently, and he hoped to confront her the night of her return to the house. Perhaps that would make some difference.

Keeping his concealment spell in place, Ethan walked back down to Tileston's Wharf. He didn't know what he expected to find, but he wanted to know what Ramsey was doing.

Upon reaching the wharf, however, Ethan halted, his gaze sweeping over the pier. The *Muirenn* was gone.

He strode toward the bollards to which it had been moored, heedless now of making noise. There was no one on the wharf, and he had nothing to fear.

Or so he thought.

As he neared the bollards, he felt the brush of a conjuring on his face, neck, and chest, as if he had walked through a spiderweb.

He knew that feeling. *Detection spell!* he had time to think.

The blow caught him full in the chest, knocking him off his feet.

He landed hard on his back, the air rushing from his lungs. He rolled over, tried to stand, but already he sensed that his vision was darkening. He collapsed to the ground again, and knew no more.

~~~

Consciousness lapped at his mind like gentle waves. The floor beneath him seemed to roll and he squeezed his eyes shut, fearing that if he opened them, his vision would spin. Sounds reached him—the familiar creak and groan of a ship—and he realized that he was asea.

"A concealment spell? A deserted wharf? You're fortunate that we found you at all." Ramsey's voice.

Ethan forced his eyes open and saw the captain and several members of his crew standing over him. They were on the deck of the *Muirenn*. Torches burned in sconces mounted on the masts. "After a few minutes of searching, some of my men were ready to leave you there, to be trampled in the morning." Ramsey squatted. "But I wouldn't do that to you, Kaille."

Ethan sat up, and found himself staring down the barrels of three flintlock pistols.

"Slowly," Ramsey warned, straightening. "They probably won't shoot you without me telling them to, but you wouldn't want to take any chances."

One of the men chuckled; the others leered at Ethan.

"A detection conjuring," Ethan said, rubbing the back of his neck. His entire body hurt. "That was quite a precaution to take when your ship wasn't even moored at the wharf anymore."

Ramsey shrugged and took a drink from a flask of wine. "Not really. It was specific to you. Anyone else could have walked onto the wharf, and they wouldn't have known I'd cast."

"Why were you so interested in me?"

"What were you doing on that dock?" This last he asked with sudden intensity, and with none of his usual sardonic humor. He glanced at the men standing with him. "Leave us, lads. Our friend isn't going anywhere, and I don't imagine he'll do anything too foolish."

The men holding pistols lowered them, and all of the sailors moved off toward the ship's stern. Ramsey extended a hand to Ethan. Ethan gripped it, and the captain pulled him to his feet. He braced his feet, enduring a moment of dizziness—a result of Ramsey's spell, no doubt. As a younger man, he had spent much of his time at sea; already he could feel himself adjusting to the gentle pitch and roll of the vessel.

"What were you doing?" Ramsey asked again.

"I had planned to spy on you."

The captain nodded and clapped him on the back. "I've always liked that about you, Kaille. Whatever else you might be, you're honest."

"How did you know to cast the detection spell?"

Ramsey laughed. "You had to come back, after what I said the last time we spoke."

"But you had left. There was nothing for me to see. I don't understand this, Ramsey."

Ramsey found an empty pewter cup on a barrel, poured some Madeira into it, and handed the cup to Ethan. "I know you don't. You're not supposed to. Soon perhaps. But you must realize, even after you've learned everything there is to know, you won't be able to stop me."

Ethan sipped the wine, eyeing him over the rim of his cup. "Then there's no danger in telling me what you intend to do."

The captain flashed a wicked grin and took another swig from the flask. "You'll have to do better than that."

"All right, how's this?" Ethan said. "I can stop you, and I will. It's not the hands and heads that are most important. I understand that now. And the mutilation of the feet—that was just something you did to draw my attention. Which means that on some level you want me to understand it all. But the key to it all lies in that symbol you carved into the chests of the cadavers."

Ramsey gazed back at him, his grin had faded, though the ghost of it remained on his lips. His eyes gleamed with torch fire.

"What does it mean? Where does that symbol come from?"

The captain tapped his temple with his forefinger. "It's one of my own. But go on. This is all very interesting."

"All right," Ethan said. He knew little else, but if he could keep Ramsey talking, he might learn something of value. And as long as they were speaking, Ramsey wouldn't kill him. Or so he hoped.

"The ghosts you've brought back are yours to control. You haven't done anything with them yet, but you have it in mind to."

Ramsey shook his head, appearing disappointed. "You're grasping now. You don't know anything at all, do you?"

He should have known better than to allow himself to be goaded, but Ramsey had a way of twisting Ethan's emotions, of turning them to his own purposes. "I know more than you think," he said. An image of a ghost appeared in his mind: Patience Walters, her form suffused with that odd green glow. "For instance," Ethan said, "I know that the ghost of a conjurer looks different from these other shades you control."

Ramsey's face fell. "What are you talking about? What conjurer?"

"The conjurer's form hadn't been mutilated," Ethan said, ignoring the questions and thinking back on what he had seen at the Walters house. "There were no signs of decay, either. Nothing to indicate that the conjurer had been dead and buried. Whatever you're doing affects conjurers differently."

"What conjurer?" Ramsey asked again, his voice rising. Several members of the *Muirenn*'s crew looked their way.

"I had thought you ignored this person's grave because it wasn't in one of the older burying grounds, where you did your dark work. It wasn't with Cotton Mather, John Sewall, and John Cotton. That was intentional, wasn't it? Violating the burying grounds where those who have persecuted conjurers are buried?" When Ramsey said nothing, he shrugged and went on. He was guessing now, still grasping at whatever came to mind. But Ramsey grew more agitated with every word he spoke, and Ethan sensed that he had stumbled upon a weakness in the captain's planning. "I wonder now if you would have intentionally disturbed any grave belonging to a conjurer. I think not. That would have made all of this much harder. Isn't that so?"

Ramsey lunged forward and grabbed Ethan by the collar. "Tell me who it was!" he demanded, his breath stinking of wine.

"I don't think I will."

All of Ramsey's men were watching them now. Several of them had come closer. Ethan knew that he was taking a risk, but right now he was helpless, which seemed the greatest risk of all. He could use the mullein he carried, but he didn't want to alert Ramsey to the fact that he had it. Mullein was valuable, a powerful herb; Ramsey would not scruple to take it from him. So he ignored the captain's question, knowing that eventually doing so would infuriate the man.

"What do the dead give you, Ramsey? And what would a dead conjurer do to complicate matters?"

"*Who. Was. It?*" Ramsey said, shouting the words. He reared back and hit Ethan in the jaw.

Ethan sprawled across the deck, tasting blood. It took a few seconds for his vision to clear, and by the time it did, Ramsey was striding toward him.

"*Tegimen ex cruore evocatum,*" Ethan said under his breath. Warding, conjured from blood.

Ramsey faltered in midstep at the pulse of power. "A warding," he said. "All that to cast a warding?"

Ethan climbed to his feet, Uncle Reg beside him.

"You know a warding doesn't help you if I decide to have my men shoot you and dump your body in the harbor."

"Or if you have them cut off my head and hand and carve that symbol into my chest."

"Just so."

"I don't think you're going to do those things," Ethan said, hoping he sounded confident.

"Who was the conjurer, Kaille?"

"Why are you so eager to know?"

The captain didn't answer.

"I'm not going to tell you," Ethan said, "because I don't want you desecrating the grave and mutilating the body. I don't want this person's family to suffer as other Boston families are suffering."

Ramsey slid his knife from its sheath on his belt. "I can make you tell me."

"You can try."

The captain stilled, like a wolf when it spots prey. "What are you going to do? Even if you could match my conjuring power—which you can't, not anymore—you would also have to overpower my crew. I think we both know that's not going to happen."

"You're right," Ethan said. "But I'm still not going to tell you."

"Even knowing that I intend to torture you?"

"Aye," Ethan said, his heart starting to labor. "I'll not trade my safety for the soul of a friend."

"You're scared," Ramsey said. "I can tell."

"That changes nothing."

Ramsey regarded him through narrowed eyes. A moment passed, and another. He sheathed his blade once more. "I'll find out," he said. "I sense that this person died recently. And you told me that the body isn't at Copp's Hill, or the Granary, or King's Chapel. That was something else that I did just for you, by the way. Only desecrating graves in burying grounds where men like Cotton Mather are buried. I'm glad you noticed; I would have been disappointed if you hadn't." He shrugged. "Anyway, that means this conjurer must be in the Common Ground. I'll find the grave."

Realizing that Ramsey wouldn't torture him after all, Ethan felt something in his chest loosen, even as he cursed himself for revealing as much as he had about Patience.

"You and I could be great friends, Kaille," Ramsey said, still watching him. "You're honest, you have some courage, you're handy with a spell. From what I gather, you spent a good deal of time at sea as a younger man. What do you say? I could use another mate to help me sail the *Muirenn*, particularly one who can cast."

Ethan almost laughed away the offer. But a quick glance at the captain's face told him that would be a mistake. Regardless of what had passed between them this day, and in their last encounter, Ethan had a feeling that his proposal was genuine. "It's been a long time since I took orders from anyone," he said, choosing his words with care. "Being a thieftaker may not seem like much, but it does allow me to be master of my own fate. I wouldn't want to give that up."

The captain nodded, the smile on his face turning brittle. "I figured you would say as much," he said. He gave a piercing whistle. Two men scurried over to them. "Prepare the pinnace. Mister Kaille will be returning to Boston now."

"Aye, Captain," said one of the men.

They moved to the starboard ratlines and swung themselves over the rail.

"I can't guarantee your safety once you leave this ship," Ramsey said, gazing back toward the city. "You don't want to be part of my crew. I understand that. But you also don't want to get in my way." He looked at Ethan. "I'll kill you if I have to."

Ethan had been threatened before, more times than he cared to count, by toughs and overconfident thieves, as well as by Sephira Pryce. But this threat, from this obsessed and unbalanced conjurer, struck him as different, as more chilling. Even Sephira, who was as dangerous a rival as he could imagine, often seemed to admonish him out of pique or wounded pride. But Ramsey spoke of killing him with calm assurance. Ethan heard no boast in the words, and he knew that Ramsey didn't speak for effect. Whatever his true abilities as a conjurer, he believed he could overpower Ethan at will, and he seemed perfectly willing to do so.

"I've been asked to inquire into the desecrations at King's Chapel," Ethan said, "and to recover that which was taken. I have a job to do."

"You had a job to do last time as well," Ramsey said testily. "You were supposed to keep Forrs and Keller alive. You didn't. You should know better than to make promises you can't keep."

Ethan proffered a hand, rather than continue to argue the point. "Thank you for your hospitality, Captain. Whatever our disagreements, I have always thought the *Muirenn* a fine ship, with an admirable crew."

It was, Ethan knew, as fair a compliment as he could offer to a ship's captain.

Ramsey hesitated before responding, but then he shook Ethan's hand and muttered, "Thank you."

Ethan handed him the cup of wine. "Permission to leave the ship."

"Granted."

Ethan walked to the rail.

"Kaille."

He turned toward the captain again, had time to note the gleaming blade in Ramsey's hand, and the welling of blood on his forearm.

"Pugnus ex cruore evocatus," the captain said. Fist, conjured from blood. Power pulsed; the ship shuddered with it, magnified as it was by the water beneath them. A stooped, glowing figure appeared beside Ramsey.

And an invisible blow to Ethan's gut doubled him over, stole his breath.

"It seems your warding didn't work after all. *Ignis ex cruore evocatus.*" Fire, conjured from blood. This conjuring thrummed as the first one had.

Ethan's right shirt sleeve burst into flames, searing the skin on his arm, his shoulder, his neck. He dropped to the deck and rolled back and forth until he managed to extinguish the fire. Lying there, panting, he heard Ramsey take a step toward him.

"From what I've heard in recent days," the captain said, "I gather that some conjurers in Boston are finding it difficult to cast their spells. Or rather, are having trouble making them work. I hadn't understood all I heard, but now I see that it's true. How else do we explain the fact that an otherwise competent conjurer, one who I saw ward himself, should be so utterly vulnerable to simple conjurings like these? *Discuti ex cruore evocatum.*" Shatter, conjured from blood.

Ethan felt the pulse, heard the snap of bone. Pain exploded in his left arm, tearing a cry from his throat. He cradled his arm to his chest. He still had mullein in his pocket, as well as Janna's sachet, but he couldn't be sure the next warding he tried would work any better than his first, and he wasn't sure what more Ramsey would do to him if he sensed that Ethan was trying to conjure again.

"Did you recognize that last one?" Ramsey asked. "You used it against me the last time we met. It's not very pleasant, is it?" The captain squatted beside him. "You can't fight me, Kaille," he said, in the same tone he might use to discuss cod runs off the New England shores. "And you should know better than to defy me when I ask you a question. I've half a mind to kill you where you lie and throw you overboard. But I'm going to enjoy destroying you slowly, and watching your desperate attempts to stop me from following through on my plans. You stopped being my equal as a conjurer long, long ago. Soon, I'll have rendered you completely defenseless, and there isn't a damn thing you can do to prevent it." He started to straighten, but stopped himself. "Oh, and the next time you try to flatter me by complimenting my ship and crew, I'll snap your neck. You were a navy boy for less than a year, and you weren't on the *Ruby Blade* for more than a week before you mutinied. You're not qualified to judge my ship or her men."

Ramsey stood. Ethan saw his blade flash in the torchlight. "*Impedi respirationem ex cruore evocatum.*" Stop breathing, conjured from blood.

The sudden pressure on Ethan's chest made him forget the agony in his arm. He tried to inhale, but couldn't. It felt as though the full weight of the *Muirenn* had fallen on top of him, pinning him to the deck, stilling his lungs.

Ramsey gazed down at him, a benign smile on his lips. He cut himself again and held out his forearm for Ethan to see. "Here's blood for you. You can end the spell if you'd like. It's as simple as speaking the Latin. Or is it? What if your conjuring doesn't work? I'm not going to cut myself again. You have but one chance to live. Do you trust yourself to cast the spell that would save your life, or do you need me to do it?"

Ethan's lungs burned. He knew he was beginning to panic, but he couldn't help himself. His body had gone rigid; he clawed at the wood of the deck with taloned hands.

"Aye, I suppose you're right," Ramsey said, regarding his bleeding arm. "It's my responsibility, isn't it?" He sighed like an impatient child. "Very well. *Fini evocationem ex cruore evocatum.*" End conjuring, conjured from blood.

Ethan inhaled deeply, and knew a moment of blessed relief as a breath rushed into his lungs. He closed his eyes, gulping greedily, savoring the cool touch of the harbor air on the back of his throat.

"Get him off my ship," Ramsey said. He sounded disgusted.

Chapter
FOURTEEN

wo sailors walked to where Ethan lay and dragged him to his feet, making no effort to be gentle with his broken arm. He gritted his teeth and tried once more to cradle the arm against his body, though this did him little good. One of the men swung himself nimbly over the rail. The other man lifted Ethan and practically tossed him to the first man. Together, the two sailors half carried him down the rope ladder to the pinnace waiting below.

As they reached the small boat, Ramsey appeared above them at the rail. Ethan flinched at the sight of him, expecting to be attacked with yet another conjuring.

"Take him wherever he wants to go," the captain told the men.

"Aye, Captain."

To Ethan, Ramsey said, "Remember what I told you. It begins in earnest now, and I can't be bothered to worry about any one person."

Ethan wanted to ask him what he meant. What was to begin? But he was too weary and in too much pain to speak. Besides, he knew better than to expect an answer.

Ramsey grinned again, and vanished from view.

"Where to?" one of the men asked him.

"The Town Dock," Ethan said, the words scraped from his throat. It was the shore point closest to the Dowser, and still he wasn't certain he could walk that short distance.

He had little notion of the time, but he thought that it must be only a few hours before dawn.

The water was calm, and the breeze light. Ramsey's men had him at the dock in less than a quarter hour, though it seemed to take much longer. The men lifted him out of the boat and rolled him onto the wharf, before pushing off and rowing back toward their ship.

Ethan climbed to his feet, his movements slow and stiff. He staggered with his first few steps, but righted himself and continued on to the Dowser. He didn't have the strength to go out of his way and so walked right past Murray's Barracks. There were few soldiers on the street at this hour, but a pair of them stopped him and demanded to know what he was doing walking the city so late. Upon seeing the condition he was in, their bearing changed. One of the men even offered to find the regiment's surgeon.

"Thank you," Ethan said, and meant it. "I'm on my way to see a friend who is a surgeon."

They let him go, and Ethan walked the rest of the way to the Dowser without incident. He let himself into the tavern, locked the door, and collapsed into the first chair he found, the leg scraping on the tavern floor.

He pulled out his knife and having little choice, cut his broken arm. He dabbed the blood onto his skin, just over the break, and said, "*Remedium ex cruore evocatum.*" Healing, conjured from blood.

He felt the hum of power in the floor and walls, and was aware of Reg's glow beside him. But while the blood vanished, the pain in his arm remained unabated. He didn't feel the bone knitting itself back together, either.

"Damn it!" he muttered under his breath.

Footsteps overhead told him that he had awakened Kannice, and he cursed himself for this as well. He cut his arm a second time, spoke the spell again. Nothing.

"Ethan?"

"Aye, it's me."

Blood welled from yet another cut. He rubbed it gently on the injury, repeated the spell, and watched it disappear. No relief, no healing.

Kannice stepped into the great room, holding a candle.

"Are you—?"

He slashed at his arm, heedless of the pain. Kannice winced. Blood dripped onto his breeches. *"Remedium ex cruore evocatum!"* he said, shouting the words. Healing, conjured from blood!

It was like he was a boy again, new to his power and unable to rely on his conjurings. Except that after a lifetime of casting spells, he had come to depend on them, to regard them as his greatest strength, the one thing that defined who and what he was. He couldn't give up conjuring now, not with Ramsey poised to strike at the city and at him.

He raised the blade again.

"Ethan, no!" Kannice said, leaping forward, and grabbing both his blade arm and the arm he intended to cut.

He gasped.

"What?" she said, recoiling. "What did I do?"

"Nothing. It's—" He pointed at his left arm with the tip of his blade. "This arm is broken."

She covered her mouth with a shaking hand. He saw that there were tears on her face. "I'm sorry," she said, staring at his wounded arm. "I didn't know."

He shook his head, gazing at her, his chest rising and falling.

She raised her eyes to his. "What's happening, Ethan? What is all this?"

"I can't conjure, not even to heal myself."

"Why not?"

He started to say that he didn't know, but that wasn't true. "Nate Ramsey is back," he said.

She frowned. "Ramsey," she repeated.

It had been a long time, and his last encounter with the captain had coincided with the very beginning of their love affair. But still, she surprised him.

"The sea captain. The one who killed those two merchants."

"Aye," Ethan said.

"He was a conjurer, too. I remember you telling me about him."

"That's right."

"What does he have to do with your ability to conjure?"

"It's not just mine," Ethan said. "Gavin Black told me that he can't conjure either. And I expect others are having the same problem."

"But why would Ramsey make it impossible to conjure? Wouldn't he be hurting himself as much as you?"

"One would think so," Ethan said. "But he can conjure as well as ever—better actually. It's the rest of us who are struggling to cast."

"I don't like the sound of that." She looked him over, taking in the burns on his bared right arm, the bruise on his face from where Ramsey hit him. "He did all of this to you?"

"Aye."

"You should tell Sephira. She'll be so jealous that she'll take care of him for you."

It was so unexpected that he couldn't help but laugh out loud. "That's better than any idea I've had."

Her smile didn't linger for long. "If you can't heal yourself, we'll have to get you to a surgeon."

He nodded, glanced at the knife in his hand. "All right. First, I'm going to try once more."

Kannice said nothing, but crossed her arms over her chest. As uncomfortable as she was speaking of his spellmaking, she was, he knew, even more unsettled by watching him conjure. Still, she didn't turn away as he cut himself and put blood on his wounded arm.

He took a breath. *"Remedium ex cruore evocatum."*

The conjuring thrummed, and this time the effect was immediate. He sucked air through his teeth as the pain increased at the first touch of his healing power. After a few seconds, though, the pain decreased. He could feel the bone mending.

"Did it work?" Kannice asked.

"Aye, it's working now. It takes some time, but the spell did what it was supposed to."

"Why would it not work one moment and then work perfectly the next?"

It was a good question: one more for which he had no sure answer. "I would presume that whatever Ramsey is doing isn't complete yet. Before long it will be, but for now he's still putting the pieces in place."

"What pieces?" she asked.

He looked up from his arm, meeting her gaze again. "I'm trying to work that out. It has to do with ghosts and mutilated corpses."

Kannice blanched. "I wish you hadn't told me that."

"I'm sorry." He ended his healing spell, probed his arm gently with his fingers. "It's sore still, but the bone is mended." He looked at the burns on his right arm. "Let's see if I can heal these, as well."

It took two castings before the healing worked, but soon, the pain of the burns had begun to subside.

"What do ghosts and cadavers have to do with conjuring?" Kannice asked, breaking a brief silence.

"I thought you didn't want to talk about those things."

She shrugged. "Explain it to me."

"I'm not sure I can."

"When you cast, a ghost appears. Isn't that right?"

"Aye," Ethan said, glancing at Reg. "He's here right now."

"So, ghosts are part of your spellmaking."

Ethan nodded, comprehension dawning on him. Kannice's understanding of conjurings was crude, but essentially she was correct. The power for spells existed at the boundary between the living world and the realm of the dead. In order to access that power, every conjurer needed a ghost like Reg: a spectral guide who could travel through that boundary, between the two realms.

He turned to Reg, recalling their exchange from the night when the old warrior spoke with the shade of Patience Walters.

"You told me that something—some conjuring—had prevented Patience from moving on to the realm of the dead. Do you remember that?"

The old ghost nodded.

"Are you talking to your ghost?" Kannice asked, sounding frightened. "I didn't know you could do that."

"I do it more often than I care to admit." To Reg he said, "Could the same conjuring that is keeping Patience here also be blocking my spells?"

Reg nodded again.

"Could that be what the ghosts are for? Are they being held here to keep our conjurings from working, to make it so that only Ramsey can conjure?"

The warrior didn't answer right off. He appeared to weigh the question. When at last he did nod, he did so with some hesitation; he remained uncertain.

"What did he say?" Kannice asked.

"He thinks it's possible, but I don't think he's sure." *He may never be.* This last, Ethan kept to himself.

"If you were to do the things Ramsey is doing, and your ghost didn't approve, could he defy you, keep you from conjuring?"

"No," Ethan said. "I have done things he didn't condone." He held up his hand, forestalling Kannice's next question. "I'd rather not say what. But while he's made his disapproval clear, he has never kept me from conjuring. I honestly don't believe he can. Or that Ramsey's ghost can stop him, if that's what you had in mind."

"It is." She took Ethan's hand. "What does Ramsey want, Ethan?"

"I don't know," he said. "Beyond wanting to be powerful and to hurt me, I'm not sure that he knows."

"He does," she said, with a certainty he didn't share. "No one goes to such lengths without a purpose."

He took a breath, his free hand wandering to his chest. He wasn't sure he would ever forget the feeling of not being able to breathe, of being utterly at the mercy of a man he knew to be mad. "He's not sane," he said, his voice low. "His moods ebb and flow like the tide. He can seem perfectly reasonable, even friendly. And a heartbeat later, he's threatening murder and using his power to shatter bones. At least Sephira is predictable. She's driven by greed and malice and vanity. But Ramsey . . ."

What does he want?

Kannice was right. There had to be something.

"It'll be morning soon," she said, tugging gently at his hand. "You need some sleep."

"I can't sleep."

She stood, pulled his hand with greater insistence. "You're going to try."

Ethan knew better than to argue with her when she was right. He stood, groaned at the stiffness in his back and legs.

"You honestly enjoy your work?" she said. "And you tell me that Ramsey isn't sane?"

He smiled. She tried to lead him to the stairs, but he held his ground, forcing her to face him again. "Thank you," he said.

"For what?"

"For listening. For asking questions that make me think in ways I wouldn't otherwise. For taking care of me."

She kissed him, her lips soft and warm against his. "You're welcome," she whispered. "Now, come along. I'm tired."

"Yes, ma'am."

Fingers entwined, they started up the stairs. She eyed his burned clothes and shook her head. "Honestly, Ethan: I've never met a man who goes through shirts the way you do."

"It wasn't my idea to light my sleeve on fire."

"No, I don't imagine."

They reached her room, and Kannice helped Ethan into her bed. When he was settled, she kissed his brow and smoothed his hair, the way she might have for a little boy.

Despite his protestations to the contrary, he fell almost immediately into a deep dreamless slumber.

When he woke to a warm room and a half-empty bed, sunlight was seeping around the window shutters and voices were drifting up from the street below.

Ethan pulled a spare shirt from the corner of Kannice's wardrobe, where he kept a few changes of clothes, then dressed and went down to the Dowser's great room.

Uniformed regulars sat at several of the tables, eating chowder and drinking ales. They ignored him as he crossed to the bar. Kannice watched the men, her mouth set in a hard line. She seemed calmer, though, than she had the last time the soldiers were here. Kelf stood at the far end of the bar, drying glasses and watching the men as well.

"You slept," Kannice said, concern in her eyes as she searched his face.

"Aye. Thank you. What's the hour?"

"Close to midday. Are you hungry?"

He opened his mouth to say that he had too much to do to eat. But he realized that he was famished, and also that he wasn't sure that he could do anything before the sun went down. The shades couldn't be seen by day, and he doubted that Ramsey would disturb the burying grounds with the sun shining overhead.

"Yes," he said. "Very."

"I'll get it," Kelf said before Kannice could answer. He tossed his rag on the bar, gave the soldiers a final glance, and walked back into the kitchen.

He came back out a moment later with a full bowl of chowder and some bread.

"There ya go," he said.

"My thanks, Kelf."

The barman filled a tankard for him, and placed it beside the bowl.

He ate quickly, and didn't argue when Kelf refilled his bowl. But he did insist on paying Kannice for his food and drink.

Kelf went back to drying glasses, but Kannice leaned on the bar across from Ethan, her chin in her hand.

"How are you feeling?" she asked.

"My arm, you mean?" he said, keeping his voice low. When she nodded, he said, "Still sore, but better."

"Where will you—"

She stopped, staring toward the door, which had opened, allowing in a glare of sunlight. A frail figure entered the tavern, and paused at the door to take in her surroundings.

"Janna?" Ethan said, stepping away from the bar.

She limped toward him, scowling. "Kaille," she said, in a voice that accused him of being responsible for all her troubles.

"What are you doing here? Why are you limping like that?"

"You and your damn questions. I'm limpin' like this because I'm old, and I'm here because I'm lookin' for you."

He pulled out a chair for her at the nearest table and helped her to it. Kannice joined them at the table.

"This is Janna?" she asked, smiling at the woman.

"That's right," Janna said, regarding her with a wary eye. "Who are you?"

"I'm Kannice Lester. I own the Dowsing Rod. Miss Windcatcher, it is such an honor to meet you. Ethan has talked to me about you for years. I feel like I'm meeting royalty."

Whether or not Kannice knew it, she had said the perfect thing.

Janna beamed at her. "Well, aren't you the sweetest thing." Janna faced Ethan. "This your woman?"

"Aye," Ethan said.

"That's what I thought. What on earth is she doin' with you?"

"Can I get you something to eat, Miss Windcatcher?"

Janna hesitated.

"It's on me, Janna," Ethan said.

She smiled again. "Well, in that case, your stew smells fine."

"I'll get you some right away."

"And a glass of Madeira," Ethan said. Lowering his voice, he added, "Watered just a little bit."

Kannice nodded and went back to the bar. Ethan sat across from Janna, who was surveying her surroundings.

"This is a nice place," she said with grudging admiration.

"It was her husband's once," Ethan said. "From what I've heard it wasn't much when he ran it. He died of smallpox in sixty-one and she took over, made it more respectable."

Janna looked around for a moment more before settling her gaze on Ethan. "I'm guessin' you know why I'm here."

"I think I do," he said. "You tried a spell and it didn't work?"

"I tried several. I tried to send an illusion spell to talk to you, but I couldn't even get an elemental conjurin' to work. That ain't happened to me since I was a girl."

"I saw Gavin early yesterday. The same thing has happened to him."

"I figured as much. So, what did you do?"

"Well, I told him that I would try—"

"No," Janna said, leaning forward. "I mean what did you do to mess up my conjurin'?"

"Here you go, Miss Windcatcher," Kannice said, bringing a steaming bowl of chowder to Janna. Kelf lumbered behind her, carrying what Ethan assumed was a cup of Madeira.

"Thank you," Janna said, a smile brightening her face once more.

Kannice must have noticed Ethan's expression, because she led Kelf away from the table saying, "We'll be by the bar if you need anything else."

For his part, Ethan could only gape at Janna, his mouth hanging open.

"Whatever you did," Janna went on, her voice dropping, "you better fix it, and soon."

"You think I did this?" Ethan said, knowing he sounded like a fool, but unable to think of anything else to say.

"Who else would it be?"

"This arm was broken last night, Janna," he said, pointing to his left arm, struggling to keep his voice low so that the regulars wouldn't hear. "And the other one had burns from the wrist to the shoulder. It took me a half-dozen castings to heal myself because I couldn't get the spells to work. And you want to blame this on me?"

She looked down at her chowder. "I'm sorry. I just assumed . . ."

"Do you really think of me as being that careless or stupid or evil that I would do something to take away your power to conjure? For that matter, to you think I'm strong enough to do such a thing?"

"I think you're stronger than you know, Kaille." She looked up again. "But I know you're not stupid or careless, and I know there ain't an evil bone in your body. I'm sorry."

Ethan nodded, still stung by her accusation. "We've had to apologize to each other a lot in the past few days."

"I was thinkin' that," she said. "I'll be more careful."

"So will I." He nodded toward her bowl. "How do you like your chowder?"

She picked up her spoon and tasted it. Her eyes widened. "That's good," she said. "A woman who looks like that and cooks like this? You should marry her before she comes to her senses and kicks you out."

Ethan grinned, but then turned serious once more. "Did you know Nathaniel Ramsey?" he asked her.

"Which one?"

"Both, I suppose."

She nodded, taking another spoonful of Kannice's stew. "The father was a friend. I always liked him. He would come to see me when he put in to port. Sometimes he'd buy an ale or a meal. Sometimes he'd buy herbs from me. One time he brought me a great big shell he'd found in the islands." Her smile this time was wistful. "Told me it was a piece of my home. I still have it. He was a good conjurer. Not the most powerful I ever met, but reliable."

"What about the son?"

"I liked him, too, but I only met him a few times. The last time was right after his father died. He come to tell me that his papa used to say nice things about me. He didn't stay long—seemed lost in a way, if you know what I mean. I haven't seen him since."

"Well," Ethan said, "he's back. And he's the one who's behind whatever is happening to our conjurings. He's also responsible for the grave desecrations we talked about the last time I visited you at the Fat Spider." He leaned in closer to her. "Last night, Kannice and I were talking about this. When we conjure, our ghosts give us access to the power between the realms of the living and the dead. There are shades all over Boston. The corpses Ramsey mutilated are now appearing as shades in their old homes. Could those ghosts be keeping us from casting our spells?"

"Maybe," she said. "Might be they could keep our ghosts from that power you talked about. That's the one way I can think they would do it."

"Of course," Ethan said. "That makes a good deal of sense."

"But why would he do it?" she asked. "He needs to conjure, too, doesn't he?"

"Yes, but he's controlling the ghosts. Do you remember that symbol I showed you?"

"Of course I do. Carving runes into corpses isn't anythin' I'm likely to forget."

"Right. I think those symbols allow Ramsey to bend the shades to his will. And I also think that the shades recognize Ramsey's spectral guide, and allow him to do as he pleases. Ramsey's spells work just the way they're intended. He made that much clear to me last night."

"Why is he so angry with you?"

Ethan recounted for Janna his encounter with the captain back in 1763. "I believe he's been making inquiries about me ever since. He seems to know a lot about me."

"Including what that maimed foot of yours looks like."

"Exactly."

She shook her head, and took a sip of wine. "You're gonna need help before all of this is through. You know that."

Ethan thought of Mariz. "Aye, I know it."

"So you tell me what you need me to do, and I'll be there."

He reached over and patted her hand. "Thank you, Janna."

She glared at him. "You're humorin' me. Don't. I might be old, but I can conjure better than you, and better than Ramsey, too. You need me."

"Before this is over, I may need every conjurer in Boston."

"You intendin' to kill him?" Janna asked.

Ethan faltered. "If I have to."

"So you're willin' to spend those souls when the time comes."

He frowned. "I'm not sure I understand."

"The souls: those shades you been seein'." When his expression didn't change, she placed her spoon on the table. "Every time a conjurer summons the spirit of someone who's dead, he puts that soul at risk. If the conjurer dies before releasin' the spirit, the soul is lost forever. No heaven, if that's what you believe. No spirit to summon another time. The soul's just gone. If you kill Ramsey while he still controls those poor folk, you'll be makin' it so them souls are gone for good."

"You're sure of this?" Ethan asked.

Janna glowered.

"Of course you are. My apologies for asking."

"If you want to save the souls, you have to get Ramsey to release them before you kill him. And that ain't gonna be easy."

Ethan rubbed a hand over his face. He hadn't thought that this matter with the captain could be any more difficult than it was. He'd been wrong. "No," he said, "it's not."

"Like I told you, Kaille: You need me."

"Aye, I do. And when the time comes to fight him, I'll make certain that you're there."

"Good." She picked up the spoon again. "Now go away. Let me eat this fine food, before I have to walk back home."

"Aye, all right," he said and stood.

"You used that sachet yet?" Janna asked, before he could walk away.

"No, not yet."

"Don't," she said. "If your spells ain't workin' you can't risk it. If you go in that house where the woman died of the pox, you won't know if the spell worked or failed until it's too late. You understand me?"

A chill ran through his body. "Aye. Thank you, Janna."

He joined Kannice and Kelf at the bar.

"How long have you known her?" Kelf asked, the words a quick jumble.

"A long time," Ethan said.

"I've heard folks say that she's mad—think she's a witch, and seems proud of it."

Ethan merely nodded, taking care to avoid Kannice's gaze. "I've heard that, too."

"What will you do now?" Kannice asked him.

"I'm not sure. Until nightfall, I really can't . . ." He trailed off. "Damn," he whispered. "I have to go," he said. "I don't know when I'll be back."

Kannice's mouth twitched: an attempt at a smile. "I know better than to tell you to have a care, but I don't like this business."

"Neither do I. And I will." He gave her hand a squeeze and returned to Janna's table, squatting down beside the old woman's chair so that he could look her in the eye. "Did you feel any spells last night or this morning?" he asked her, voice lowered again.

"Several last night and a couple this morning," she said. "I assumed you were castin', though the ones this morning came from your place, not from here."

Ethan shook his head, inwardly cursing himself once more. "No," he said. "They came from the waterfront. Thank you, Janna."

Ethan left the tavern for the Common Burying Ground. What Janna had told him about the souls of the summoned dead made it more imperative than ever that he keep Ramsey from desecrating Patience's grave. He thought about casting a finding spell to locate the captain, but he had little confidence that it would work. Upon reaching the burying ground he walked its perimeter once, before searching a section of the cemetery a good distance away from where Patience had been buried. After a few minutes he found what he sought: the grave of a woman who had died within the last few months—March, to be precise. He positioned himself by the grave, and pulled out his blade.

He didn't like the idea of fooling Ramsey into disturbing the grave of an innocent, but as much as he feared for Patience's soul, he also dreaded what might happen if the captain managed to add the shade of a conjurer to his army of ghosts. And he was convinced that Ramsey was abroad in the city, walking freely under the protection of a concealment spell, confident that any finding spell Ethan attempted would fail.

Ethan remained in the burying ground for the better part of an hour, wondering if he was wasting his time. At last, another thought came to him. He left the Common Burying Ground and walked the short distance to the Granary. This burying ground looked different in sunlight than it had the previous night, but he had little trouble locating once more the gravesite of Mrs. Tyler. And as he did, he thought he heard quick footfalls.

"Ramsey," he said, his voice carrying over the breeze and rustle of leaves.

No response.

Ethan drew his knife once more. "Looking for another corpse?" he said. "Another shade for your collection?"

As sure as he had been that the captain was near, he was still surprised by the pulse of power, which came from but a few feet away.

Suddenly, Ramsey was there, the sun shining on his tanned face and dark, untamed hair.

"You're all healed," he said. "I suppose that means you have a bit of power left yet."

"A bit," Ethan said.

Ramsey strolled to where Ethan stood and looked down at the newly covered grave. "Was she a friend of yours? A conjurer, perhaps?" Before Ethan could answer, he shook his head. "Forgive me; I forgot. Your friend is in the Common Burying Ground. I've already been there."

Ethan schooled his features.

"You were looking for me?" Ramsey asked.

"I thought we might speak a bit more. Perhaps we can find some accommodation that would allow you to get whatever it is you want, and allow me to offer some solace to the families being haunted by your shades."

"There can be no accommodation."

"But surely—"

"No! I warned you last night, Kaille. I owe you nothing now, and we both know that your spells aren't reliable enough to fight me." Ramsey grinned. "How many healing spells did it take you to repair that arm? Four? Five? You took a great and foolish risk coming here to-day. I suppose there's something admirable in that, and I'm willing to forgive a moment of folly. But my . . ." His smile deepened. "My *patience* wears thin. I would suggest you leave."

Ethan's blade hand itched. The incantations for a thousand different attack spells, each more painful than the last, flashed through his mind. But as Ramsey well knew, he didn't trust his conjuring enough to insti-gate a battle of conjurings. If any one of his castings failed, Ramsey would kill him.

The captain appeared to read the fury in his eyes, and also the un-certainty. He laughed. "It's ironic, isn't it? So many people spend their whole lives ignorant of the power we wield. They go about their affairs, seeking out a surgeon to mend their burns and broken bones, and strik-ing flints to kindle a fire. And they think nothing of it. But we—those of us who are accustomed to using our spells to accomplish similar aims—we grow so dependent on those powers that when they fail us, we feel helpless. Just as you do now."

"What I find ironic," Ethan said, his hands trembling with rage, "is that you think I lack confidence in my spellmaking, and you see that as my greatest weakness right now. Whereas I *know* that yours is your confidence, your hubris. It will be your downfall in the end."

"Maybe," Ramsey said, sounding unfazed as he started away. "But I doubt very much that you'll live long enough to see that end."

Once Ramsey was gone, and Ethan was sure that the captain would not double back and follow him, he hurried to the Walters home. This was his fault. He had said too much to Ramsey the night before, and now the captain knew who Patience was and where she was buried. Ethan owed it to her, and to Darcy and Ruth, to do all he could to protect her from Ramsey's power.

Darcy probably would not be at home—he often worked in the market at Faneuil Hall—but Ruth would be.

He was sweating and limping by the time he reached the small home, but he wasted no time approaching the door and knocking. Ruth opened the door. She held the babe in her arms, and her face looked even paler and more pinched than it had the last time Ethan saw her.

"Ethan," she said, sounding surprised.

"Forgive me for disturbing you, Ruth. But I need to see Patience again."

"But she doesn't come until nightfall."

"I think I can summon her, and I believe I have the best chance of succeeding if I do it here."

"What's happened?" she asked, shifting the babe to her other arm.

"It's nothing. Just a question I forgot to ask the other night."

She nodded and stepped aside so that he could enter. Once he was inside she closed the door and sat in a rocking chair near a window. "I'll wait out here," she said.

"Of course."

Before he could leave the small common room, she said, "You know, as frightened as I am of Mother's shade, I'm more scared by far of not knowing what all this means and what might happen next."

He exhaled, faced her again. "I apologize for being less than honest with you," he said. "There is a man, a conjurer, who is using spells to control the shades of the recently dead. As far as I know, he has yet to control Patience. But I said something to him—something foolish—and now he knows of her, both that she died not long ago, and that she was a conjurer. I believe he means to control her, too. I wish to warn her, and to see if somehow we can thwart his plans."

"How does he control them?"

"Ruth—"

"He mutilates the bodies. Doesn't he?" Her eyes were so filled with fear and despair that it made his chest ache. "I overheard some of what you and Darcy discussed that day you came."

"Yes, that's right," Ethan said. "I don't know if I can prevent it, but this is my fault, and I have to try."

"I don't think Darcy would blame you, nor would Patience. But I understand."

He held her gaze for another moment before making his way back to Patience's bedroom. Once there, he called in Latin for Uncle Reg.

"I know you don't like it when I summon the dead," Ethan said. "But in this case I have to. You know why?"

Reg nodded.

Ethan pulled out the pouch of mullein and removed nine leaves, the same number he had used the year before when he cast similar spells. He hoped that the conjuring would work; he didn't wish to waste so much of the herb. He also knew that this spell wouldn't be quite the same as those he cast previously to summon conjurers. Usually he had to summon them from the realm of the dead. But Patience had yet to reach that realm. In theory, at least, this spell should have been easier.

"Are you ready?" Ethan asked.

Again, the ghost nodded.

"*Provoco te, Patience Walters, ex verbasco evocatum.*" I summon thee, Patience Walters, conjured from mullein.

The pulse of power was like the pealing of some great bell. It shook the house; Ethan felt the hum of it in his chest, and knew that Ramsey would feel it as well.

"Let him," Ethan muttered.

He looked to Reg for some sign that the casting had worked, and inhaled sharply. Patience had come. She stood beside the old warrior, still glowing with that same greenish color. She didn't appear to be angry, as Ethan had feared she might. But her expression was grim, her eyes bright and fixed on him.

"Forgive me," he said to the shade. "I wouldn't have disturbed you without cause." He glanced at Reg. "Does she understand me?"

The warrior nodded once more.

Ethan started to tell her of the burying ground desecrations and the number of shades already haunting homes throughout the city, but he hadn't gotten far before the shade raised a hand to stop him and nodded.

"She knows already?" Ethan asked Reg.

Another nod. *Yes.*

Ethan wasn't sure whether to be alarmed or reassured. "The man responsible is a conjurer named Ramsey. He and I share some history, and without meaning to, I let him know that you died recently, and that you were a conjurer. I'm afraid . . . I think he means to disturb your grave and add you to his legion of shades. I'm so sorry, Patience. It was careless of me."

She shook her head: a gesture of absolution.

"I want to know if there is some way you can protect yourself, to keep him from controlling you."

It took a moment for his words to reach her; it seemed he was speaking to her across a great distance. But at last the shade frowned, and gave a small shrug that was so like the shrugs Patience gave in life it brought a smile to Ethan's lips.

"I miss you, Patience."

A pause, and a smile in return.

"I believe it's the symbol that he cuts into the cadavers that gives him control over the shades," Ethan said. "But I don't know how it works, or what kind of conjuring to use to overcome his power."

He shook his head, realizing that this wasn't doing any good, and that he had disturbed the shade of his friend for no reason. But his thoughts were churning. When he spoke of the symbol with Ramsey, the captain had tapped a finger on his temple and said, "It's one of my own."

Could that mean the symbol itself had no inherent power, that its potency lay in whatever meaning Ramsey assigned to it? If so, that meant that no countermanding symbol existed. No doubt that was why Ramsey had chosen a rune of his own design. Ethan felt himself sag. He still didn't know what the captain sought to accomplish, but already he sensed that there was nothing he could do to stop him. Ignorance and helplessness: they made for a demoralizing combination.

"I'm sorry, Patience," he said to the shade. "I wanted you to know that Ramsey would be coming for you, and I thought you should know that it's my fault. I'll do everything I can to stop him." He started to say more, but stopped himself, realizing he had nothing else to offer her. He would do his best, but he wondered if she knew as he did how woefully inadequate his best might prove to be.

She nodded to him again. If she was afraid, she didn't show it.

"Thank you," Ethan said to Reg. *"Dimitto vos ambos."* I release you both.

Both ghosts faded, melting into the daylight that lit the room. Ethan returned to the common room, his legs heavy. He felt a pulse of power, followed by a second. Both of them seemed to come from the waterfront.

"Did she come to you?" Ruth asked.

"Aye. I'm not sure it did much good. But I spoke to her." He searched for the right words.

More spells made the house tremble, though of course Ruth showed no sign of feeling anything. A part of him was desperate to be away, to learn what Ramsey had done now. But even if he learned all there was to know, he probably couldn't stop the man, and saving Patience from his control was more important than fighting another losing battle.

"Ruth, I don't know how to stop this conjurer. But I'm certain he intends to desecrate Patience's grave, and I want to prevent that, even if it means . . ." He shook his head, unsure of exactly what he wanted to say.

"Darcy and I both trust you, Ethan, just as Mother did. We know that you would never do anything to harm her. So, do what you must."

"Thank you."

He bade her good day, and left the house, walking back toward the burying ground, though with little urgency. Ramsey could conceal himself with a spell, but he couldn't violate the gravesite in the middle of the day without drawing notice. He would wait until nightfall, which gave Ethan a few hours. To do what?

With what Ruth had just said to him, he had permission to remove Patience's body from its grave. He could hide her somewhere, make it impossible for Ramsey to mutilate the corpse. He thought that by now he ran little risk of contracting the illness that had killed her, though he couldn't be certain. But he could not allow her to fall under Ramsey's thrall. It was a daunting notion, but he had few other options. And he knew just the person to help him.

Diver lived on Pudding Lane, in the middle of Cornhill. The street had been renamed Devonshire, but Ethan still referred to it by its old name, as did most people he knew. Diver's room sat above a bakery in a brick building constructed after the great fire of 1760, when much of Cornhill was destroyed.

These days, when not working, his friend spent most of his time at Deborah's room on Pierce's Alley, which was also in Cornhill. But after the argument Ethan had witnessed in the Dowser a few nights before, he expected that he would find Diver on Pudding Lane.

He was right.

His friend appeared somewhat disappointed when he opened the door and saw him standing on the landing. He looked past Ethan down the stairs and along the length of the lane.

"Expecting someone else?" Ethan asked.

Diver ran a hand through his black curls. Ethan wasn't sure he had ever seen Diver look more morose, not even on the many occasions when his schemes to make a bit of coin failed.

"I haven't talked to her since that night in the Dowser," he said. "I've been by her place, and she's never there. I even left her a note." He gazed down at the lane again. "I think she's gone."

"She's not gone, Diver. She's angry with you, and she's making certain that you know it. Elli once did the same thing to me."

"That's supposed to cheer me up?"

"Aye. This was early on, long before the *Ruby Blade*. She forgave me eventually."

"Really?" Diver asked.

"Really. You just have to be patient, and when finally she deigns to speak to you again, you have to apologize and tell her that it was all your fault."

"But I'm not sure it was. All I did was tell her that I—"

"Diver, do you want to be right, or do you want her back?"

He weighed the choice for all of two seconds. "I see your point."

"Good," Ethan said. "Let me in. We have other things to discuss."

Diver stepped aside and Ethan walked into the room.

"Close the door," he said.

Diver closed it and dropped himself into a chair. If any man in Boston could be cheered up by robbing a grave, it was Ethan's friend.

"I need your help," Ethan said. "I have to do something that's neither legal nor pleasant, and I can't do it alone."

A smile stole over Diver's face. "How much are you getting paid?"

"Nothing at all. I'm doing it for the congregation of King's Chapel."

Diver raised an eyebrow. "So it's illegal, it's unpleasant, *and* there's no money in it for either of us."

"Right. Will you help me?"

"I can hardly refuse. What will we be doing?"

"Digging up a grave, removing the body, and finding a place to hide it."

His friend blinked. "Are you serious?"

"Aye."

"You're mad. You can't walk into a burying ground, dig up a grave, and pull up the corpse. Even I'm not that much a fool."

Ethan considered this. "You're right. We'll need help from someone else, as well." He walked back to the door and pulled it open. "Come along then."

"I'm not going anywhere until you tell me what this is about."

"I'll tell you, Diver. I swear it. But we have to get this done before sundown, so I need to explain as we walk."

Still Diver sat, eyeing him. At last he pushed himself up out of the chair. "I must be mad, too."

Ethan grinned.

They walked south to Water Street and turned right toward Marlborough. As they walked, Ethan explained to Diver all that had happened in the past several days: the grave desecrations, the appearance of the shades, and his encounters with Ramsey. Diver remembered little of Ethan's last encounter with the captain, and so he had to describe those events as well. He hadn't yet finished when they reached King's Chapel.

"What are we doing here?" Diver asked, gazing up at the stark façade of the sanctuary.

"As you said, we can't walk into a burying ground and simply dig up a grave. Not alone, anyway. But if we have a minister with us, looking on, making it seem that we're doing the Lord's work, no one will give it a second thought."

"Your friend," Diver said, smiling. "Pell."

"Aye, Pell. Why don't you wait out here?"

Ethan entered the churchyard and the chapel itself. Caner stood at the pulpit. Hearing the door open, he looked up from the great Bible on its wooden stand, marking his place with a finger.

"Who is that?" he asked, squinting.

"Ethan Kaille, reverend sir."

"Mister Kaille!" Caner said. Ethan thought that the rector had never sounded so pleased to see him. "Do you have tidings for us?"

"None that are good, reverend sir, and nothing that's certain. I came to ask if I might borrow Mister Pell for a short while. I require his help."

"May I ask what for?" Caner had stepped down from the pulpit and was walking toward Ethan.

"I think it best that I tell you as little as possible."

"And I would prefer to keep Trevor out of harm's way. I'm afraid I must refuse to let him go with you."

"Reverend, sir, please understand. I am trying to prevent the desecration of more graves, and the mutilation of more corpses."

"Here at our chapel?"

Ethan hesitated. "No. The body in question is buried elsewhere. But surely you wouldn't wish such foul trespass on any soul, regardless of where the unfortunate lies."

Caner's mouth turned down, but he said, "He's outside with the sexton."

"Thank you, Reverend, sir. I'll do my utmost to keep him safe."

"See that you do."

Ethan left the sanctuary before the rector could change his mind, and went around to the back of the chapel. There he found Pell standing over Mr. Thomson, who was working in one of the disturbed graves.

"Ethan!" Pell said upon spotting him. "Do you bring news?"

"I'm afraid not. I've come because I need your help."

Pell quirked an eyebrow. "Even better."

"You might be less enthusiastic when you hear what I require of you. Mister Thomson," he said to the sexton, "might we borrow a pair of spades?"

"Spades? What for?" He didn't wait for Ethan to reply. "Never mind. I don't care to know. Take this one." He handed Ethan the spade he had been using, and climbed out of the grave. "Mister Pell, you know where the other one is kept. Bring them back when you're done."

"My thanks," Ethan said.

Pell led Ethan to a small hut set back in the farthest recesses of the churchyard. There they found the other spade.

"What is this about, Ethan?"

"We need to dig up a cadaver in order to keep the body from being mutilated."

"I don't understand."

"I'll explain along the way."

They walked around to the front of the chapel, where Diver still waited for them.

"Don't we need a third spade?" Pell asked.

"You won't be digging," Ethan said. "You'll be standing by the gravesite, making it seem that we're not doing anything wrong."

A faint smile curved Pell's lips. "I see."

Diver and Pell greeted each other—they had met before on a few occasions—and the three of them marched through the city streets to the Common Burying Ground, and the grave of Patience Walters.

"She was a conjurer?" Pell asked, as they stood over the grave.

Diver toed the fresh dirt, looking pale.

"Aye," Ethan said. "I don't know what Ramsey has in mind, but I'm certain that I don't want him having control over the shade of a spell-maker."

Pell glanced at the sun, which was already sinking toward the western horizon. "Then I'd suggest you start digging."

Ethan shared a look with Diver, hoping that it would reassure his friend. They both began to dig.

The air was warm, and what little breeze there was helped not at all. Within a few minutes, Ethan's hands began to burn. He knew he would have blisters before long; it had been too many years since he had toiled in this way. But despite all this, he felt good. At last he was doing something that Ramsey could neither anticipate nor prevent.

A few people walked past as they worked, but having Pell with them served its purpose. No one questioned them.

Ethan paused to remove his waistcoat and resumed his labors. His shirt was soaked through, as was Diver's. By the time Diver's spade struck wood, Ethan was breathing hard. He could almost hear Kannice telling him that he was too old for this sort of thing.

They cleared the dirt away from the coffin and paused to rest. Diver leaned both his arms on the handle of his spade. Ethan gazed down at the coffin, sweat dripping from his brow. The faint stench of rot surrounded them, not yet overpowering, but promising to be once they disturbed the coffin.

"Now what?" Diver asked, wrinkling his nose. "Do you want to take the coffin, or leave it and just take her body?"

"I don't like the idea of carrying a dead body through the city streets," Pell said. "Especially one that smells as badly as this one. Even I can't protect you from the sort of attention that would draw."

"I could conceal the body with a spell," Ethan said. "And me along with it. I might even be able to mask the smell. No one would know we had it. Not that I relish the idea, but leaving the empty coffin here for Ramsey to find does have some appeal."

Diver checked the position of the sun. "If we take the coffin, what will we do with it?"

"That's a good question," Pell said. "I don't think the rector would want it on chapel grounds, and we can't bury it again just anywhere."

Ethan nodded, but his thoughts were elsewhere. *It's one of my own.* Perhaps he had been thinking of this the wrong way. Maybe the fact that he knew of no countermanding symbol for the one Ramsey had created didn't matter at all. Maybe it made his work easier rather than harder.

"What if the symbol isn't important at all?" he said.

Diver and Pell shared a look.

"But you said the symbol enabled Ramsey to control the shades," Pell said. He kept his voice low and shrank back as he spoke, seeming to fear Ethan's reaction.

"Aye, it does. What I mean is, what if the form of the symbol doesn't matter as much as whatever spell Ramsey casts on it? In other words, it's possible that the importance of the symbol lies not in how it looks, but rather in what Ramsey has done with it."

"I'm not sure I follow," Diver said. "I've never understood all that you do with your spells and such. And I don't see how that would make a difference as to where we take the body."

Ethan wiped a hand across his damp forehead. "It might make no difference at all. Or it might mean that we wouldn't have to move the body anywhere."

"I'm lost as well," Pell said. "Now you're saying we don't have to move the body? Does that mean you did all that work for nothing?"

"Not at all. But I have another idea that might protect Patience from Ramsey's spells, without alerting him to the fact that we've been here, or that we've taken steps to thwart his plans."

"And this has to do with the symbols?" Pell asked.

"Aye. Ramsey's symbol is what enables him to control the shades. From what he told me, I know that the symbol itself has no inherent power, he made it up himself. It's not an ancient rune that raises the dead or any such thing. He carved it into the corpses as a way of placing his mark, and therefore his power, on the cadavers."

Pell's face paled.

Diver, though, still appeared confused. "So . . . ?"

"So, what if I were to do the same thing? I could place a symbol on her, too. Something Ramsey wouldn't find that would enable me to guard her from his conjurings."

"Do you know how to do that?" Pell asked, his features sharp in the late afternoon light.

"I'd be inventing the conjuring; I've never done this before, or anything remotely like it. But I have an idea of how I might word the spell." He didn't mention that he couldn't be sure if any conjuring he attempted would work, or that he wouldn't know for certain one way or another until after Ramsey had desecrated the grave and tried to add Patience to his army of shades.

Diver regarded Ethan the way he might a fiend. "You want to open this coffin and carve a mark into her body?"

"I don't want to do anything of the sort!" Ethan said. "I don't want to be here, digging up the grave of a friend, and I certainly don't want to be guilty of the same foul deeds as Ramsey. But neither do I wish to see the shade of my friend being used as a marionette!" *Nor do I wish to see her soul lost forever.* This he kept to himself. He paused, exhaled. He hadn't meant to respond with quite so much heat. When he went on, it was in a calmer tone. "I think I can do this, and thus deny him access to the ghost of a conjurer. Despite the horror of what I'm contemplating, I don't feel that I have much of a choice."

Ruth had said that they trusted him, and had given him permission to do what was necessary. He hoped that she and Darcy would someday forgive him for this.

A hint of color had returned to Pell's face. "Ramsey won't expect it."

"No, he won't. And that's the best reason for doing it." Ethan looked at Diver. "If you can help me prise the lid off the coffin, I can do the rest."

His friend nodded. They both placed the tips of their spades under the edge of the lid—Ethan at the head, Diver at the foot—and pushed down on the handles. With a shriek of iron on wood, the lid rose.

Instantly the air around them turned sickeningly foul. Pell spun away from the grave, covering his mouth and nose with both hands. Diver threw his spade onto the grass and scrambled out of the hole.

Ethan's eyes watered, and he had to clamp his teeth together to keep from being ill.

"You said that you know a spell to mask the smell?" Pell said, his voice muffled.

"Aye." He pulled out his knife and cut his arm. *"Madesce nidorem ex cruore evocatum."* Dampen odor, conjured from blood.

Ethan felt the spell hum in the earth, and regretted casting it. Ramsey would feel it. He might even guess its origin. Worse, the spell had no effect. Reg stood beside him, barely visible in the daylight. Ethan looked his way; the ghost wore a scowl, his bright eyes trained on the disturbed grave.

"It didn't work."

"Obviously," Diver said. "Try it again."

"I can't. The risk is too great. I'll get this done and we can put the lid back in place."

He lifted the lid the rest of the way off the coffin, doing his best to breathe through his mouth. Not that it helped much.

Patience's corpse was not as far gone in decay as others he had seen in recent days, which actually made this worse. Her skin was mottled, blotchy, her body distended.

He hesitated to touch her, not only because he dreaded what he was about to do, but also because he didn't know where to place his mark, or what mark to use.

"Get on with it, Ethan," Diver said from several paces away.

Right. Steeling himself, he worked the corpse free of the burial cloth. Then he loosened the ties of her mantua and rolled the body onto its side so that he could reach her back. With his knife still in hand, he cut a symbol into her skin that was both similar to Ramsey's and different: an inverted triangle with a line from each leg converging at the center of the top piece.

He didn't wish to use blood for this conjuring; he didn't like the idea of using blood spells on the dead. But he also didn't think that mullein would be strong enough.

Mulling the decision, it occurred to him that he had a third choice: Janna's sachet.

He pulled the gathered herbs from his pocket and held the bundle in the palm of his hand.

"Tegi hunc corpus et spiritum contra magias, sit immune ab aliena aucto-ritate, ex herbis et signo meo evocatum." Protect this corpse and its spirit

from magick, keep it free from the influence of others, conjured in herbs and this symbol.

The thrum of power from this spell seemed to make the earth tremble. Pell, who had conjuring blood in his veins and so could feel the conjuring as Ethan did, gaped at him. Ethan stared at his empty hand where Janna's sachet had been, marveling at the potency of her concoction.

"Do you know if it worked?" Ethan asked Uncle Reg.

The ghost opened his hands.

"What does that mean?" Pell asked.

"It means he doesn't know."

"Who doesn't know what?" Diver asked, looking from Ethan to the young minister.

"My spectral guide doesn't know if the spell worked. We won't know until Ramsey comes and desecrates the grave." *We might not even know then.*

Ethan rolled the corpse back onto her back, retied her gown, fitted the burial cloth around her as well as he could, and put the coffin lid back in place, taking care to line up the nails with the holes they had been in. "Diver, see if you can find a rock."

It took him a minute or two, but soon Diver had found a rock that was about the size of his fist. He tossed it to Ethan, who wrapped it in his waistcoat and used it to hammer the lid down until it sat square and was fastened tight to the coffin sides once more.

He climbed out of the grave and retrieved his spade. Diver grabbed his as well, and together they shoveled dirt back onto the coffin. When they had finished, Ethan smoothed the earth as much as possible, trying to make it appear that the site had not been disturbed since Patience's burial. At last, he picked up his knife, which he had left on the ground when he picked up his spade, and wiped the blade on the grass. He hoped he wouldn't have to conjure with blood until he had a chance to wash the knife properly.

The sun sat on the horizon, a great orange ball, and a cool wind, the first in days, had freshened from the east.

"I'm grateful to both of you. I couldn't have done this alone."

"I pray that it works," Pell said.

Diver nodded. "I do, too."

Pell walked toward the burying ground gate.

Diver lingered, however, looking uncertain. "I didn't mean anything before. I just didn't expect that you would . . . You surprised me, that's all."

"It's all right, Diver. I'm sorry I got angry. To be honest, I was afraid of what I intended to do. I shouldn't have spoken to you the way I did."

"Well," Diver said, "buy me an ale and all will be forgiven."

They followed Pell, and Ethan put his waistcoat back on. As they reached the gate, he glanced back toward the gravesite. A fine, pale mist had settled over the grass and grave markers, looking ghostly in the gloaming. Ethan shuddered.

Chapter
SIXTEEN

The three men walked back to King's Chapel and returned the spades to the churchyard hut. After Pell bade Ethan
and Diver good night and went into the chapel, the two friends
made their way to the Dowser. Ethan washed the blade of his knife at a
pump along the edge of Sudbury Street before entering the tavern and
buying Diver an ale and a plate of oysters.

They took seats near the back of the tavern. Ethan sipped an ale of
his own, but he had left his appetite in the Common Burying Ground.
Diver didn't appear to notice. He ate his oysters, drank his ale, and
bought himself seconds of both.

Kannice had been in back when they walked in, but she saw them
now and joined them at their table. She eyed Ethan as she sat.

"You don't look well. Are you feeling all right?"

"I'm fine. I had to do something earlier today that I hope never to do
again. I'm still recovering."

"What was it?"

He shook his head. "Truly, Kannice, I don't even wish to speak of it.
Perhaps I'll tell you eventually, but not tonight."

She cast a dark look Diver's way.

"It wasn't his fault," Ethan said. "I forced him into it, not the other
way around."

She continued to glare at Diver, her lips pressed thin. Ethan thought
she might find a way to blame his friend anyway. But she stood and

draped her towel over her shoulder. "I'll leave you." She scanned their table. "You're not eating?"

Ethan shook his head. "I can't. Not yet."

"Are you sure you're well?"

"Aye."

He saw the doubt in her eyes, but he couldn't bring himself to say more. The truth was, he felt ashamed of what he had done and feared her reaction.

She returned to the bar, but she eschewed any banter with other customers. He could tell that she was worried about him, or angry with him, or some blend of the two.

"What are you going to do now?" Diver asked, talking around the oyster he had just popped in his mouth.

"I'll be heading back to the burying grounds in another few minutes. I expect Ramsey will be there, too, and I want to see what he does."

"To Patience, you mean?"

"To Patience, and to Missus Tyler. I believe he's still gathering more shades to his cause."

"You've been involved in some dark business over the years, Ethan, but this is the worst. I never thought I'd say this, but maybe Kannice is right: Maybe it's time you found another line of work."

"Maybe it is."

"We could start a business together, you and I. I don't know what we'd do, but we work pretty well together, and—"

"Leave it, Diver. It might be a good idea, but it's not a decision I'm likely to make this evening."

"Right. Sorry."

Ethan drained his ale. His stomach felt hollow and sour; eating something probably would have been a good idea. Instead he pushed back from the table and stood.

"I have to go," he said. "Again, my thanks for what you did today. I know it was . . ." He shook his head. "Unspeakable. I'm grateful."

Diver shrugged. "Of course. Anytime you need help, you know where to find me."

Ethan smiled, laid a hand on the younger man's shoulder. He walked by the bar without stopping, but he tipped his hat to Kannice as he passed.

Once on the street, he attempted a concealment spell. He had to cast three times before it worked, which essentially defeated the purpose of the spell. Ramsey would know what he had done and would be watching for any sign of him. He dismissed Uncle Reg, and alone navigated the streets to the Common.

He went first to the Common Burying Ground, knowing that in a choice between the shades of Missus Tyler and Patience Walters, the latter was the greater prize by far.

Concealed as he was, he could position himself anywhere in the burying ground, but he chose to keep his distance. Ramsey would have men with him, and—damn the man—could rely on his spells. Ethan hoped to watch and learn; he had no interest in another confrontation.

He stood in a far corner of the cemetery, thinking that over the past few days he had spent enough time in burying grounds to last a lifetime. He chuckled to himself at the irony.

Silver moonlight shone down on the grave markers, casting long shadows across the grass. The cool wind still blew, and somewhere behind him an owl hooted, low and resonant. But otherwise he saw and heard nothing.

He began to wonder if perhaps the pulses from his concealment spells had convinced Ramsey to delay his return to the burying grounds. And as this thought came to him, he felt a powerful conjuring hum in the ground. He drew his knife and pushed up his sleeve, expecting to feel a finding spell flow around his legs. But none came.

He hadn't yet cut himself for a warding, and now he wondered if the spell had been directed at him at all. It hadn't come from close by. In fact, it had seemed to originate some distance away; and it hadn't come from the waterfront either. He closed his eyes, trying to recall precisely what he felt. With his eyes still closed, he turned until he was facing the direction whence the spell had come.

Opening his eyes, he found himself gazing almost directly northward. He could see in the distance the spire of the Old Meeting House, and far beyond the North Church.

Copp's Hill. Ramsey must have been in the burying ground.

He set out for the North End, cursing his limp, walking as swiftly as it would allow, and trying to calculate the most direct route that

would still allow him to skirt the barracks of General Mackay's soldiers.

He followed School Street into the heart of Cornhill, turned north
at Marlborough, and continued onto King Street, intending to keep close
to the waterfront, and thus as far from the regulars as possible. But as he
turned on Merchant's Row, he felt a second pulse of power, every bit as
powerful as the first. He halted, puzzled and uncertain. This spell seemed
to come from some distance behind him. Not far; it had been closer
than the first spell. Ethan didn't think it possible that Ramsey could
have cast both spells.

Yet, if he had to guess, he would have placed this conjuring in the
area around King's Chapel, or perhaps the Granary. He didn't know
what to do. He could continue on to Copp's Hill, but he wondered if he
would find anyone there. He could also backtrack to one of the closer
burying grounds. Again, though, he didn't know if this would prove
fruitless. Who had cast these spells?

"Veni ad me." Come to me.

Reg appeared in front of him, gleaming in the dark lane.

"Those pulses of power: Do you know where they came from?"

Reg nodded.

"The first was at Copp's Hill, isn't that right?"

Again, a nod.

"And the second was at King's Chapel?"

Yes.

"Do you know who cast them?"

No.

"Could it have been Ramsey at Copp's Hill and one of his—?" He
broke off.

Reg was shaking his head again, and had held up one finger.

"They were cast by the same conjurer?"

Yes.

"But how is that possible? I didn't linger long in the Common Burying
Ground after I felt the first casting, and I walked this far as fast as I could.
I know that others can move faster than I do, but not that much faster."

Reg stared back at him, his gleaming gaze boring into Ethan's, and
he again held up that one finger.

"I have to assume that it's Ramsey. Can you tell where he is? Has he found some way to move himself with a conjuring?"

The old warrior shrugged. He looked back over his shoulder toward the North End, then stared past Ethan in the direction of King's Chapel. After a moment he shook his head.

"There's one other possibility," Ethan said. "Perhaps he can conjure in one location and have the spell manifest itself in another."

The ghost's frown deepened.

"I know. If he can do that there's no telling what sort of mischief he might cause. But that would explain—"

A third conjuring made the cobblestones beneath Ethan's feet hum. Reg's eyes widened; once again he gazed past Ethan toward the Common.

"If the second spell came from King's Chapel, that one was cast at the Granary."

Reg's nod this time was emphatic.

"That's where he is, isn't it? He's in the burying ground there."

The ghost nodded again. He pointed in that direction, clenched his fists and bent his arms, flexing his muscles, if a spirit could be said to have them.

"He's strong. Am I to assume that he's growing stronger still?"

When Reg nodded this time, there was an apology in his eyes, and perhaps a hint of fear as well.

"All right," Ethan said. "My thanks. *Dimitto te.*" I release you.

Once Reg had vanished, Ethan strode back toward the Granary Burying Ground. His concealment spell remained in place. He considered casting a warding as well, but he couldn't be certain it would work. He knew, though, that if he cast it, he would alert Ramsey to his location. The captain might guess that Ethan was trying to find him.

He retraced the path he had followed so recently, and soon came to the stone gate of the cemetery. He had feared that Ramsey might be concealed as well, and that it might take a finding spell to locate the captain. He needn't have worried. It seemed Ramsey no longer feared being found. Or maybe he knew that he couldn't conceal all of those he had with him, and so didn't bother trying.

Whatever Ramsey's thinking, Ethan spotted the captain as soon as he entered the burying ground. How could he not?

Ramsey stood beside a gravesite; from what Ethan could see, it hadn't been disturbed. He had his arms raised, and the old bent ghost who served as his spectral guide stood next to him. Or Ethan thought he did; it was hard to be certain, for Ramsey was surrounded by a retinue of glowing shades, one more gruesome than the next. Ethan thought he recognized Abigail Rowan and Bertram Flagg in their ranks, and he took some solace in not being able to spot Patience. But there were dozens of them, far more than he could account for just by counting the number of desecrated graves he had seen in the burying grounds.

The shades moved little, and made not a sound. They resembled the chorus from some twisted Greek drama: witnessing all, but doing nothing themselves. Their collective glow seemed to illuminate the grounds; Ramsey's face was alight with it. His eyes were closed, his expression exultant.

Ethan crept closer, trying to hear what the captain was saying. But before he was near enough to make out the conjurer's incantation, another pulse of power rumbled in the ground, thunderous and puissant. One more radiant figure appeared within the circle of shades. This one glowed with a color Ethan had not seen before. It was green, but unlike the sickly shade that Ethan had seen on Patience's ghost, this was the green of life, of young leaves and spring grass.

He could see that this was the shade of an older man, not bent like Ramsey's ghost or even as grizzled as Uncle Reg, but older than both Ethan and the captain. He wore dark breeches and a light shirt, a captain's jacket and a tricorn hat.

Ethan gasped audibly. He thought that Ramsey might have heard, though in the next moment, the captain said something else that Ethan couldn't hear and seemed once more absorbed in his conjuring.

But Ethan's mind reeled. *What does Ramsey want?* That was the question Kannice had put to him, the question he had struggled to answer. And here was the answer, so stark, so achingly simple, so breathtaking in its horror and audacity, that Ethan had failed even to consider it.

He wanted his father to live once more. And while it appeared that on this night the captain had done no more than summon the ghost of Nathaniel Ramsey the elder, Ethan feared he might well have the power to achieve his aim. If he could do that, might he also bring back others who were less benign? And to what degree would the reanimated dead be his to control, rather than free beings? Ethan couldn't say which he feared more: a legion of the awakened dead under Ramsey's power, or newly animated corpses wandering the world of the living without anyone controlling them. Both prospects terrified him.

Several of the silvery shades who had surrounded Ramsey from the beginning reached out toward the ghost of the conjurer's father—Ethan knew not why. But at a sharp word from the captain, they snatched back their glowing hands.

Ethan heard Ramsey laugh.

"They want to touch him, Kaille!" he called. "They know that he will soon be alive, and they wish to be carried back with him to this realm. Should I grant them their hearts' desire?"

Ethan did not answer, but instead began to creep back toward the burying ground gate. He didn't wish to confront Ramsey here, alone; he needed time to consider what he had seen. Surely his father's return was not Ramsey's sole ambition, but it might well be the one that would allow Ethan to learn all that he needed to defeat the man.

First, though, he had to get away.

"Find him," Ramsey said.

The shades turned as one and began to fan out across the burying ground, a glimmering wave breaking over grave markers and grass. Ethan didn't know what they could do to him. He wanted to think that they remained too insubstantial to do him any harm, but he wasn't willing to risk his life on that hope. He hastened toward the gate, repeatedly glancing back at the shades. They glided like buzzards—far faster than he could walk.

Still, he managed to reach the gate and the unpaved road beyond, before the ghosts caught up with him. He hurried to School Street, intending to take shelter in King's Chapel if necessary.

But the shades halted at the boundary of the burying ground, lingering there briefly before drifting back toward Ramsey and the ghost of his father.

"Soon, Kaille!" Ethan heard the captain shout. "You can't escape them forever! You can't escape *me* forever!"

He should have returned to his room, and locked and warded the door. His hands shook and his heart was racing like that of an over-worked horse. In all his years as a conjurer and a thieftaker, never before had he been stalked by an army of shades. He didn't wish to repeat the experience any time soon. But neither was he ready to surrender this night to Ramsey. He had an idea, but he couldn't act on it until he was certain that the captain wouldn't find him out.

So once again he returned to the Common Burying Ground. He kept his distance from Patience's grave, and he positioned himself near the Frog Lane entrance to the cemetery, so that he would have an easy path of escape if he needed it. And there he waited. He felt the thrum of another conjuring, followed by a second. He had to resist the urge to return to the Granary and see what Ramsey was doing. He held his blade ready, but as before, he didn't trust himself to conjure, even for a warding.

Sooner than he had expected, his persistence was rewarded. Alone for now, unaccompanied by his shades, moonlight shining on his uncov-ered head, the captain sauntered into the burying ground and made his way to the grave of Patience Walters. There, he waited, leaning against a nearby grave marker, staring up at the stars. Occasionally, he glanced around, at one point staring straight at Ethan, his gaze lingering for so long that Ethan began to wonder if perhaps his concealment spell had failed.

Only when he heard voices approaching from behind did he under-stand. Ramsey's men were approaching the burying ground from the waterfront, bearing spades and shovels, speaking in hushed tones. Ethan sidled out of their way and watched as they walked past him and into the cemetery.

He knew that they had come to violate Patience's grave, and knew as well that he could do nothing to stop them. He was all too aware of his own powerlessness. He couldn't escape the feeling that he had betrayed Patience, had abandoned her to this monster, without knowing for certain that the one precaution he had taken would work. She deserved better.

But though he could do nothing here, he believed he could strike a blow against the captain elsewhere. When he was convinced that Ramsey and his men would be occupied for some time, he slipped away and hurried back to his room.

Once there, he locked the door and barred it with a spell, which he cast three times, just to be safe. He lit several candles, unwilling to do in the dark what he had in mind.

When the room was light enough, he summoned Reg.

"I need to speak with Ramsey's father," he said. "Another summoning."

The old warrior didn't appear pleased, but he made no effort to dissuade him. Ethan wasn't entirely certain that he could summon the shade of the elder Ramsey, but he didn't believe that the son would make of his father's ghost another foot soldier in his army of spirits. He wanted his father beside him, and he would never assume that he needed to control the old captain's shade to keep it there.

Ethan removed nine leaves of mullein from his pouch, noting once more how quickly he was depleting the supply he had bought from Janna. His pouch was more than half empty.

Holding the leaves in his hand, he said in a clear voice, "*Provoco te, Nathaniel Ramsey, ex regno mortuorum, ex verbasco evocatum.*" I summon thee, Nathaniel Ramsey, from the realm of the dead, conjured from mullein.

The leaves vanished from his palm. His conjuring shook the building to its foundation, and a form suffused with soft green light appeared in the middle of the room.

Standing so near to the shade of Nathaniel Ramsey, Ethan could see what he had missed earlier in the burying ground: the son bore a striking resemblance to the father. He couldn't see the color of the elder Ramsey's eyes; they glimmered too brightly. But in the curve of the nose, the shape of the mouth, the tapering of the chin, he saw Nate Ramsey. Older, yes, and perhaps sadder. But it was the same face.

"I apologize for compelling you," Ethan said to the ghost. "I wouldn't have called you here without cause."

Ramsey regarded him through narrowed eyes, his chin raised as in defiance. Ethan saw something of the son's hauteur in the father's expression. It occurred to him that summoning the spirit might well have been a mistake.

"Your son is awakening shades all over the city. He has desecrated graves, mutilated corpses. You know this, don't you?"

The shade answered with a slow nod.

"Has he done all this because he wishes to bring you back? Is that his sole purpose?"

Ramsey looked away, first gazing toward Reg, and then looking at something Ethan couldn't see. At last he shook his head. Something in his manner gave Ethan a shred of hope.

"You don't approve of what he's doing, do you?"

No.

"Do you want to come back? Did you ask to be awakened?"

No. The response was more pointed this time.

"What is it he wants, Captain Ramsey?"

The shade tapped a finger to his own chest.

"Aye, he wants you to live again. I understand that. But you indicated that there was more to his scheming. What else is he trying to do?"

Ramsey's features hardened.

"You don't trust me," Ethan said. "You shouldn't. I could claim to be a friend to your son, but the truth is I'm a thieftaker who has been hired to prevent the desecration of more graves, and to recover that which your son has taken from the bodies he's mutilated. He and I met once before: He killed two merchants who had hired me to protect them. They were men you knew, men who treated you poorly and drove you to take your own life. Deron Forrs and Isaac Keller."

The shade glowered, and his ghostly hand strayed to the pistol holstered on his belt.

"You have every right to despise me. So does your son, for that matter. But what he's doing is wrong. You know this; I can see you do. And I need your help to stop him. This will not end well for him."

The shade shook his head and pointed a finger at Ethan. *It won't end well for you.*

"Probably not. But that changes nothing. You've already told me that you don't wish to come back. You prefer to rest. Your son wants you to live once more, but you must know that it's not that simple, that bringing back the dead will have unintended consequences. Did Nate even ask you if you want this? Or did he assume that you did?"

The shade's gaze slid away.

"At least you know that he's acting out of love for you. The other shades don't have even that. He has disturbed their rest, made them slaves to his will, for no other reason than because he can. Surely you see the injustice of that."

The ghost's anger appeared to have sluiced away, leaving him troubled and forlorn.

"What is he trying to do?" Ethan asked. A thought came to him. "I've assumed that the difficulty I'm having casting spells is incidental to his ultimate aim. But it's not, is it?"

The ghost fixed his eyes on Ethan again.

"That's what he wants: he seeks to render the rest of us powerless, and thus to make himself the lone conjurer in our world."

It was madness, and yet so utterly logical that once he put words to it he felt certain that he was right. The shade did not deny it. Ethan hoped that he would shake his head, communicate in some way that while his son was ruthless and cunning, his ambitions did not run so deep. But he continued to stare at Ethan, offering no response.

"Can he do it?" Ethan asked.

Ramsey's shade opened his hands and shrugged.

Ethan turned to Reg. "Can he?"

The old warrior nodded.

"Damn. Is he close to succeeding? I've struggled with other spells, but I had no trouble summoning Patience and now the captain."

Reg pointed to himself and to the shade of Nathaniel Ramsey. He opened his arms wide.

"There are shades everywhere," Ethan said. When Reg nodded, he said, "And that's why the summonings have worked. Of all the conjuring I could do, calling shades to me is the easiest right now. Because of Ramsey." At last he was beginning to make sense of all that had happened to him in recent days. "My other spells still won't work reliably."

Reg nodded.

Ethan turned back to Ramsey's shade. "Again I ask you, what is his purpose? If he can stand unopposed, with no other conjurers able to stop him, what will he do with such power?"

The shade made a small gesture with his hand; Ethan wasn't sure what he intended it to signify. Before the old captain could do more, he stiffened, his eyes growing wide. He spun toward the door.

And even as he did, the door exploded inward, the hinges twisting, the wooden planks snapping as if they were made of twigs. Ethan was thrown back. He tumbled over his bed and crashed into the wall behind it. He narrowly missed the window, which shattered, shards of glass raining down onto him.

Dazed, his back and shoulders and head aching, he raised himself up and saw Nate Ramsey standing in the doorway. The captain had his fists clenched; his face was contorted in a snarl.

"You want to know what I would do?" the man said. "Whatever the hell I want!"

Chapter
SEVENTEEN

amsey——"

"Release my father this instant, or I swear I'll burn to the ground every house within three streets of here."

Ethan climbed to his feet, felt a trickle of blood on his temple. He didn't wish to endanger Henry's shop or the other homes and businesses nearby. But he knew from what Janna had told him that Ramsey couldn't risk killing him, not if he intended to bring back his father. He hoped that Ramsey knew this as well. "I don't think you will. I think you understand that if you kill me, your father's spirit will be lost to you."

The younger Ramsey glared at him, hatred in his eyes, his knife held ready. The shade of the old captain spared Ethan not a glance, but kept his gleaming green eyes on his son. Eventually, Nate shifted his gaze to his father's ghost, his expression softening, his rage giving way to pain.

Taking this opportunity, Ethan chanted a spell in his head. *Tegimen ex verbasco evocatum.* Warding, conjured from mullein. He felt the pulse of the spell, but he had no idea if it had worked.

At the first rumble of the conjuring, however, Ramsey seemed to remember where he was. He slashed his blade across his exposed forearm.

"Exure ex cruore evocatum!" Burn, conjured from blood.

The pain—sudden, needle-sharp—tore a cry from Ethan's throat. He clutched his arm, saw blisters rising on his skin. So much for his warding.

"How dare you summon the spirit of my father! Release him now!"

With his good hand, Ethan pulled his knife from the sheath on his belt.

Ramsey glanced at the blade and shook his head. "You've learned nothing! You're like a moth singeing its wings on a candle flame over and over again. Your warding failed, Kaille. So will whatever spell you're considering. You cannot fight me. I've told you this before, and still you try."

"Of course I try. The alternative is surrender, and that I won't do."

"No, the alternative is failure, and it's already overtaken you." He cut himself again. "*Discuti ex cruore evocatum.*" Shatter, conjured from blood.

The conjuring hummed, bone snapped, and Ethan's bad leg gave way beneath him, the agony threatening to overwhelm him.

"Let my father go!" Ramsey said, bellowing the words and taking a step toward him.

Ethan gritted his teeth and closed his eyes. He would have liked to set the man's hair and clothes on fire, even if it meant burning his room and Henry's shop to the ground. Or better yet, he wanted to break every bone in Ramsey's body. But he knew that his conjurings would fail, and the attempts themselves would provoke the captain to hurt him more. He knew as well that he could no more kill Ramsey than the captain could kill him. Ethan held the father's soul; Ramsey held the souls of dozens, including, perhaps, that of Patience Walters. It was as if they each held a pistol aimed at the other's heart. They could threaten, they could hurt one another. But neither dared fire the killing shot.

Still, it galled Ethan that he could not even protect himself from the captain's assaults. The last time he had felt this impotent, this defenseless, he had been a prisoner. And yet, it seemed that Ramsey was not yet done sounding the depths of Ethan's despair.

"You know that you failed as well to save your friend." He lowered himself into a chair, watching his father's ghost, perhaps deciding that Ethan could not harm the shade in any meaningful way. "I felt your conjuring. I know what you did, and yet I still managed to dig her up and take what I needed. She's mine now, just like the others. Except we both know that she's nothing like the rest. She was a conjurer in life, and so her shade has access to powers that the others can't even comprehend.

She will lead them, and I will command her. And you can do nothing to stop me."

It was too much. Foolish though he might have been, Ethan refused to relent. Most conjurers would have warded themselves before coming to attack one of their kind, but Ramsey was so convinced of his own superiority that Ethan thought it possible he had neglected to take that precaution. If he could manage to cast a spell, he could hurt the captain and perhaps drive him off. At the very least, he could keep Ramsey from hurting him again. But what spell? Was it possible that a more obscure conjuring, one the captain could not anticipate, would have a better chance of succeeding?

He bit down on the inside of his cheek, drawing blood. *"Corpus alligare ex cruore evocatum!"* Bind body, conjured from blood!

The spell thrummed. Uncle Reg turned to Ramsey, as eager as Ethan to see if the spell had worked.

Ramsey no longer looked so smug; instead his face was a rictus of anger and frustration. But though Ethan could see the muscles in his neck and arms straining, he moved not at all. His fingers still gripped his knife, but he could do nothing with it.

Ethan struggled to get up and balance himself on one leg. He drew his knife and cut his arm. Catching the welling blood on the flat of his blade, he rubbed it on the skin over his broken bone.

"Remedium ex cruore evocatum." Healing, conjured from blood.

The first spell didn't work, but he cast it a second time, and the bone began to knit itself back together. Initially, the pain increased, and he ground his teeth together. Soon, though, the anguish began to abate. After a few minutes, his leg was strong enough that it could bear some of his weight.

"It seems I have more spells left in me than you thought," Ethan said.

Ramsey stared daggers at him.

"I understand wanting your father back, Ramsey. You may not believe me, but it's true. There isn't a day that goes by when I don't wish I could see my mother one more time. I lost her while I was in prison. It's not the same, I know. She wasn't hounded to her death the way your father was. If she had been . . . well, I would want vengeance, too. But

my point is this: As much as you want him to live once more, you have
to know that whatever you bring back from the realm of the dead won't
be him. It will be dark and unnatural and beyond even your control."

The captain closed his eyes. It was probably the one way the man
could think to block out Ethan's words.

Or so Ethan thought.

Ethan felt a spell growl in the floor and walls of his home.

"What are you doing?"

Ramsey didn't move. But an instant later, a shade appeared in the
room. It was no one Ethan recognized, but he could tell that it was one
of the ghosts Ramsey had awakened in recent days. It glowed as white
as winter mist and it shuffled toward Ethan wearing a man's breeches
and jacket, its face decayed and ghoulish, its leathery hands hanging at
its sides.

Ethan sensed a second spell, and another shade materialized beside
the first. Ramsey bared his teeth in his own skeletal grin, though he
didn't appear capable of any other movement.

Two more spells pulsed, one right after the other. Two more shades
joined the others.

"That was a good conjuring, Kaille. Better than I thought you could
cast, it's true. But as you can see, I have powers that go far deeper than
even you can imagine."

Ramsey rocked his head from side to side. He hadn't yet regained motion in his hands or feet, but Ethan guessed that he would soon enough.

"Thank you for the use of the mullein, by the way," Ramsey said.

Ethan saw him bite down on his own cheek, as Ethan had done moments before. The next spell was more powerful than the previous ones
had been. Another pair of ghosts winked into view. Their comrades had
forced Ethan to the back corner of his room. He straightened now, refusing to be cowed by the shades.

He reached out, allowing his hand to pass through the head of the
nearest ghost. And yanked it back with a gasp. The touch of the fiend
was bitingly cold, and left his skin blue.

"I wouldn't do that again, if I were you," Ramsey said. He pushed
himself up out of the chair, swayed but didn't fall. He slowly curled and
straightened his fingers.

Ethan didn't understand how the captain could have overcome the binding spell so soon. Whatever Ramsey had done to enhance his power seemed also to make him less vulnerable to the spells of others.

"Hold," Ramsey said.

The shades halted their shambling advance.

He knew that the captain meant to attack again, and so he cut his forearm with a flick of his blade and cast first. *"Ignis ex cruore evocatus."* Fire, conjured from blood.

The conjuring thrummed, but no flames appeared.

"A coincidence," Ramsey said. "I had been thinking of the same spell." He cut himself, and murmured the conjuring.

A swirling ball of fire burst from Ramsey's hand, soared across the room and through the insubstantial body of one of the shades, and hammered into Ethan's chest. The force of the blow lifted Ethan off his feet and sent him sprawling into the wall once more, his shirt and waistcoat ablaze.

He flailed at the flames, and rolled from side to side until he had put them out. The smell of singed hair and burnt flesh hung in the air. Burns throbbed on Ethan's chest, arms, and hands. He felt like he had been run over by a horse and carriage.

Ramsey walked to where he lay, the shades parting to let him pass.

"It seems to me that we've done this before. I've already shattered a bone in your leg, so I believe the next spell I cast is supposed to keep you from breathing. Is that how you remember it?" He tipped his head to the side, his brow furrowing. "Or we could try something new. I could burn the building, or just destroy it. No one would be the wiser." He glanced around, an expression of distaste on his face. "They'd blame inferior workmanship, and who could argue? They would never guess that it was a conjuring that did the damage."

Ramsey's knife flashed again.

"Strangula ex cruore evocatum." Strangle, conjured from blood.

Invisible hands squeezed Ethan's neck, choking him, crushing his throat.

"You won't kill me," Ethan said, croaking the words. "You won't do that to your father."

"Don't be so sure," Ramsey said. "I believe I can reach my father anywhere. My power runs that deep. Still, if you release him, I may spare you. And just so you know, your longing for Mommy is nothing like the suffering he and I have endured. I should kill you for your presumption."

Ethan grabbed at his neck, trying to prise away fingers that weren't there.

Dormite ex verbasco evocatum! He screamed in his mind. Slumber, conjured from mullein! He didn't know how many leaves he used. He didn't care. And it didn't seem to matter. For though the conjuring made the floor tremble, it had no effect on Ramsey.

"I don't know what that was," the captain said, enjoying himself far too much. "But it didn't work."

Spots of light clouded Ethan's vision. The room seemed to be spinning and darkening. He clawed at his throat again, but he could tell that his hands weren't working as he wanted them to. He didn't think Ramsey would go so far as to kill him, but his certainty was fading.

Yet another conjuring shook the building. Ramsey turned, still grinning.

"I'm afraid you're no better than he is."

A second man spoke in Latin. Ethan recognized the voice, but couldn't put a name to it. His thoughts were fragmented, incoherent. But he sensed the hum of one more spell, and he saw Ramsey stagger as from a blow. The captain raised a hand to his temple. It came away bloody.

Fini evocationem ex cruore evocatum! Ethan cried in his mind. End conjuring, conjured from blood!

The blood vanished from Ramsey's hand, and the building hummed again. Ethan breathed in, exhaled. The pressure on his throat was gone.

"I can kill you just as easily as I can kill him," Ramsey said. "Easier, since you haven't summoned a shade." He glared at Mariz, who stood in the doorway, fresh blood running down his arm, his bloodied blade held in his other hand.

Ethan forced himself up onto his knees and crawled to retrieve his blade.

"I think you will find that more difficult than you imagine," Mariz said. He looked past Ramsey to Ethan.

"All right, Kaille?"

Ethan nodded, cut his arm.

Several of Ramsey's shades were advancing on Ethan again. Others had turned their attention to Mariz.

"*Remedium ex cruore evocatum,*" Ethan said. Healing, conjured from blood. He directed the conjuring at Ramsey's leg, hoping to use his healing spell to shatter the bone from within. But the spell failed, drawing a laugh from Ramsey. Another conjuring pulsed in the floor. Ethan didn't know what kind of spell it was, but he saw the blood vanish from Mariz's arm. Again, though, nothing happened.

Mariz and Ethan shared a look.

"You're persistent," Ramsey said. "I'll give you both credit for that. But you see now how futile this is. I will not be stopped."

Iubeo, Nathaniel Ramsey, te mea iussa facere ex verbasco evocatum, Ethan chanted silently, caring not at all how many leaves he used. I command you, Nathaniel Ramsey, do my bidding, conjured in mullein.

The shade of Ramsey's father stepped directly in front of Ethan, forcing the other shades, including those advancing on Mariz, to stop in their tracks. Ramsey's ghost stared hard at Ethan, his brow bunched.

"I know that you don't approve," Ethan said to the glowing figure. "This is your chance to stop him."

Nate Ramsey's face reddened, and he leveled a rigid finger at Ethan's heart. "My father is not yours to command!"

"Apparently he is."

The shade turned to face his son.

"Release him!" Ramsey roared, his gaze sliding away from that of his father.

"Call back your shades."

Ethan cut himself again. "*Tegimen ex cruore evocatum.*" Warding, conjured from blood. At the touch of power, Reg faced Ethan, their eyes meeting. Ethan wasn't sure why, but this one time he sensed that his spell had worked. Perhaps by drawing the attention of the ghosts, Ramsey had left the boundary between the living and the dead unguarded, allowing Ethan access to the power there.

The shades watched both Ramseys; Ethan sensed that they were awaiting commands from one of them or the other.

Nate Ramsey hacked at his arm and muttered a spell Ethan couldn't hear. He felt the conjuring and was nearly knocked off his feet by the force of whatever the captain had thrown at him. But his warding held.

"Damn you!" Ramsey said, shouting the words. "Let him go!"

"Get out of here," Ethan said. "When you and your shades are gone, I'll release him. And not before."

"I can kill you where you stand!"

"I believe you just tried that. It didn't work. And it's fortunate for you that it failed. Or to be more precise, it's fortunate for your father."

Ethan heard a loud click. Mariz had pulled out a pistol and now held it full-cocked and aimed at Ramsey.

"Nigel's," he said for Ethan's benefit.

"I can destroy that weapon with any number of spells," Ramsey said, sounding like a boastful child.

"And I can blow a hole in your head before the Latin crosses your lips." Mariz shifted his gaze to Ethan. "Indeed, I feel compelled to ask why I should not do this, regardless of whether he casts."

"Because he's leaving now," Ethan said. He gestured at Ramsey's shades. "And because I'm not ready to condemn all of these souls to oblivion."

"I can bring this entire building down," Ramsey said. "I can kill both of you."

"Is that truly a risk you wish to take?" Ethan asked.

The spirit of Ramsey the elder had not moved since turning to look at his son, but he stepped forward now, shaking his head. He pointed toward the door with a glowing hand.

Ramsey held his father's gaze for several seconds. No being in the room moved or made a sound, until at last the captain broke eye contact with the shade of his father.

"You have one night's reprieve, Kaille. That's all you've accomplished here."

Ethan kept his silence.

The corner of Ramsey's mouth quirked upward in a bitter smile. And as it did, the shades he had summoned vanished. With their departure, the room dimmed.

Mariz sidled away from the door, keeping his eyes on Ramsey and his pistol aimed at the captain's head.

"You've made an enemy tonight," Ramsey said to him. "You shouldn't have come here, and"—he jerked a thumb in Ethan's direction—"you shouldn't have cast your lot with him."

When Mariz didn't answer either, Ramsey laughed. "Fools," he said. An instant later, his expression hardened once more. "You will release him as soon as I'm gone. I'll know if you don't. And for every second he is forced to linger here, I'll prolong by an hour your final torment. You'll endure pain beyond your darkest imaginings."

"When you're on your ship, and not before."

The look Ramsey gave him could have flayed the flesh from his bones. The captain cast one last glance at his father, and left the room. Ethan listened for his steps on the wooden stairway leading down to the narrow alley below.

Mariz started to speak, but Ethan raised a hand, silencing him. When Ethan no longer heard Ramsey's footsteps he walked past Mariz and onto the landing outside his door. He caught a glimpse of the captain turning the corner onto Cooper's Alley; Ramsey did not appear to see him.

Still he waited, listening, watchful. Mariz joined him on the landing.

"We should not have let him go."

Ethan leaned his arms on the wooden railing and took several slow, deep breaths. There was little left of his shirt and waistcoat save charred tatters, and the cool night air felt good on his burns and his blistered arm. The bruises on his back and shoulders throbbed. "Killing him might have been easier. It's what he would have done in my position. But I was hired to protect the souls he has bound to his service, to win their freedom if I can. Reverend Caner might not understand that he hired me to do this, but he did. I can't kill him yet." He glanced at Mariz, offering a wan smile. "I don't suppose Sephira would have handled things this way."

"Not at all. She would have killed him without hesitation. He continues to destroy the goods of merchants she is paid to protect. There were two more incidents today. Not fires this time; instead spells that ground items to dust. The *senhora* wants him dead. I do not want her to know that you and I have met without her knowledge. I do not want her to know that I was here. Otherwise, I would have killed him despite your wishes."

Ethan shrugged, and glanced toward his doorway. The shade of Nathaniel Ramsey stood on the threshold, with Reg at his shoulder, watching the ghost's every move.

"Before this is over, it may come to that," Ethan said. "But I wasn't ready to make such a choice tonight."

"The *senhora* would say that you have delayed what is inevitable, and you have put other lives at risk. It is a dangerous choice."

Ethan could think of nothing to say. Mariz was right: Sephira would see the matter just that way. He wondered if his refusal to do so was a weakness. Sephira would have said it was; so might Ramsey, though it was his life Ethan had spared.

"You need healing," Mariz said.

"How did you know to come?" Ethan asked, ignoring his comment for the moment.

"I sensed the spells—his and yours. The more I felt, the more concerned I grew."

"I'm grateful to you."

Mariz inclined his head, acknowledging Ethan's thanks. "Your injuries?"

"The burns are the worst of it. But I can heal myself."

"You may have to. I do not know if my spells will work. But allow me to try."

Mariz cut himself, put blood on Ethan's burns, and cast a healing spell. The first conjuring failed, but not the second, and for several minutes Mariz and Ethan did not speak.

Another spell thrummed, and an image of Ramsey materialized before them, hanging in midair. "I'm on the *Muirenn*, Kaille," the vision said. "Release him."

Ethan nodded. To the two ghosts—Reg and the elder Ramsey—he said, "*Dimitto vos ambos.*" I release you both. He watched the old captain, but the shade refused to return his gaze, even as he faded into the night.

Mariz finished the healing conjuring a short while after. He removed his spectacles and rubbed the bridge of his nose with his thumb and forefinger.

"My thanks," Ethan said. "I assume that this squares things between us."

"Squares things?" Mariz repeated with a frown. He replaced his spectacles.

"Makes us even. I saved your life last year, you saved mine tonight. You don't owe me your friendship anymore."

Mariz chuckled and shook his head. "Your mind works strangely, Kaille. Friendship is not owed, it is given. That is something that the *senhora* would have said. I thought you and she were most dissimilar; perhaps I was mistaken, and you are more alike than you seem."

That stung.

"No," Ethan said, "we're not. Forgive me. It's been a long and difficult night. I'm grateful to you, and I would like very much to go on being your friend."

"Then you shall." Mariz sheathed his knife. "But you are right: It has been a long night, and the *senhora* expects me to be at her home early in the morning. Good night."

"Good night, Mariz. Again, I'm grateful to you."

The man flashed a quick grin and descended the stairs. As the click of his boots on the cobblestone street receded, Ethan heard someone else call his name.

"Henry," Ethan said under his breath. He went back into his room, threw on a shirt—one that was whole—and buttoned it as he hurried down the stairs.

Henry lived in a small, one-room house behind the cooperage. He stood in his doorway, peering out into the night and holding a candle in one hand and a hammer in the other. Shelly stood next to him, her ears pricked up. When she saw Ethan, she wagged her tail and bounded forward.

The cooper wore a loose nightshirt, and his hair stuck up at odd angles. Ethan assumed he had been asleep and would want an explanation. Ethan wasn't sure what to tell him. He prided himself on being a good tenant; he usually paid his rent on time, he took good care of his room, and for the most part he made little noise. But he had been late with June's rent, and tonight he had not only wakened Henry from a sound sleep, he had also broken his door and window. It didn't matter that Ramsey was responsible for the actual damage; it was Ethan's fault.

And on top of everything else, he needed to explain what had happened without revealing to the cooper that he was a conjurer.

"I'm sorry to have woken you, Henry," Ethan said, scratching Shelly behind the ears, not yet able to look the man in the eye.

"I'm not worried about that. Are you all right?"

Ethan stood and walked to where the cooper waited. "Aye, thank you. I'm fine."

"It didn't thound very good," Henry said, lisping. He stared up at the broken window. "It sounded like a fight."

"I'll pay you for the window, Henry. And for the other damage, too."

"What other damage?"

Ethan glanced down at Shelly, who had followed him and was nudging his hand with her snout. "The door is broken."

The cooper's eyebrows went up. "I put that door on there myself. It was solid. That must have been some strong magicking."

Ethan was sure that his jaw dropped to the ground. He gaped at Henry, eyes so wide they hurt. The cooper couldn't have surprised him more if he had cast a spell of his own. It occurred to him that Henry could have seen that floating image of Ramsey from this vantage point.

"Aye, it was," Ethan said, trying to mask his astonishment. "This inquiry I'm working on now—there's a . . . a witch who's causing all sorts of mischief. As their kind always do."

Henry chuckled at that, exposing the gap in his teeth. " 'As their kind do'? Come now, Ethan. I might not be as smart as some folk, but I'm not a fool."

Ethan stared at him for another moment before starting to laugh himself. "No, Henry. You're not a fool at all. You might be the smartest man I've ever met." He rubbed a hand over his mouth. "How long have you known?"

"That you're a speller?" He said it like "thpeller" and Ethan laughed again. "Oh, I guess I've known for six or seven years now."

"Why didn't you say anything?"

The cooper shrugged. "It wasn't any of my business. And you always were trying to hide it from me, so I figured you were ashamed of it or something."

"No. I was afraid you wouldn't approve. A lot of people think con-jurers are witches, and I figured you wouldn't want me living here if you knew the truth."

"You're welcome to live here as long as you want, Ethan. I don't care about the rest. I always figured it would be handy to have a speller around. I would have asked you to do stuff for me, if I hadn't been sure that it would make you feel bad."

"I'll cast for you any time, Henry." He chuckled and shook his head again. For years he had congratulated himself on keeping his secret from the cooper despite living over the man's shop. Now it turned out that he had done a poor job of hiding his abilities, while Henry had been superb at keeping the truth from Ethan. "All right," he said, still tickled, "I have to sleep. This has been quite a day." He put out a hand, which Henry gripped. "Thank you, Henry."

"For what?"

"For being a good friend. I'll help you with the repairs, and I'll pay you back for all the cost."

"Sure, all right," Henry said. "Just be careful, though. That speller who broke your door—he sounds dangerous."

Ethan couldn't argue.

EIGHTEEN

If there was a bright side to having his window shattered and his door broken into pieces, it was that Ramsey had returned to Boston in midsummer, rather than in the dead of winter. With the breeze that flowed through his room, Ethan actually enjoyed the most comfortable night's sleep he'd had in several weeks. The new day, however, brought complications. He didn't wish to leave his room unattended with no door in place. He possessed few valuables, but with Ramsey loose in the city, and Sephira a constant menace, he preferred to know that what little he had was safe.

Henry had work to do and couldn't watch his room all day, and though Shelly might have guarded his door for a time, Ethan feared that the first thief with a tasty piece of mutton or fowl would have little trouble slipping past her.

He had never cast a detection spell, but he had fallen victim to more than his share. He decided that the time had come to use one himself. After considering the matter for but a moment, he elected to cast two; he could easily imagine Diver or Pell coming to his room, seeing that the door had been destroyed, and rushing in out of concern for Ethan's well-being. He didn't wish to subject them to an incapacitating spell. Thus, his first casting would rely on an illusion spell, an image of himself that would warn away those who approached his door. A second conjuring would deal with anyone who ignored his warning and entered the room.

He didn't know how to create a spell that he himself would not trigger, so he hoped that upon seeing the damaged doorway, he would remember to remove the conjuring. He also thought that he should warn Henry about the spells, lest the cooper take it upon himself to begin the repairs on his own.

These were difficult conjurings; each had to be constructed in two parts, one to create the detection web, and the second to set in place the spell that the breaking of the web would trigger. He worked on the spells for the better part of an hour, figuring out the exact wording and then casting the spells in the correct order. Even after he finished, he could not be entirely sure that the spells had worked.

Without any other means of determining if they had, Ethan had no choice but to disrupt one of the detection webs himself. The first several times he did this nothing happened. Finally, on his fourth try, the spell took hold. He cast the second spell—the sleep spell—four times, hoping that at least one of them would work. He dared not test this one. When at last he was done, his arm was raw and tender.

His next task was far more serious. He needed to speak with Ramsey again, and he guessed that doing so would be next to impossible. But his memory of the captain's illusion conjuring the night before gave him an idea. He removed his last leaves of mullein from the pouch— six of them in all—and held them in the palm of his hand.

"*Videre et audire, per mea imagine, ex verbasco evocatum.*" Sight and hearing, through my illusion, conjured from mullein.

He felt this conjuring in the wood of the stairway landing, and knew that Ramsey would feel it, too. In this one instance, that mattered not at all. Ethan closed his eyes and pictured in his mind the deck of the *Muirenn*, which he assumed he would find once more at Tileston's Wharf. Within just a few seconds, he knew that the illusion of himself had materialized on the ship, for the vision he had summoned from memory gave way to a view that included members of Ramsey's crew. He heard their voices, knew that they fell silent at the sight of him.

"I wish to speak with your captain," he made the image say.

The men gave no indication that they were alarmed by Ethan's conjuring; clearly they were used to spells.

After a few seconds one of the men said, "What if he don't wish to speak with you?"

He and his friends laughed.

"He can tell me so himself. But I want to hear it in his words, not yours. And I don't imagine he would want you making that choice for him."

The sailor sobered. He whispered something to one of his comrades, who went belowdecks.

Moments later Ramsey emerged onto the deck with the second sailor in tow.

"What the hell do you want?" he asked. He surveyed his ship and the wharf before returning his glower to Ethan's conjured image.

"I want to speak with you," Ethan said through the illusion. "Not like this. Face-to-face. I'm asking for your permission to approach your vessel."

"What is it you think we have to say to each other? You're alive because you dared summon the shade of my father, and because your friend happened to arrive when he did. He still lives because he managed to produce his pistol while I was occupied with you. We're at war, you and I. And our next battle will be our last. I promise you that."

"Fine, Ramsey. We're at war. Grant me a truce for one last parley."

Ethan was certain that Ramsey would refuse and demand he remove the conjured image of himself from his ship. But he didn't, at least not right away. "To what end?" he asked after some time. "What are you playing at?"

"I'm not playing. I'm trying to save lives: yours, mine, and those of anyone unfortunate enough to wind up between us when next we meet. And I'm trying to save the souls of the dead you have disturbed. I have a proposal for you."

"I'm listening."

"I should never have said what I did about your intent to bring back your father. That is your choice and his. It's no business of mine. As I told you, I understood why you want him alive again."

The look in Ramsey's eyes had turned flinty. "Is there a point to this?"

"Use the power you've gathered to bring him back. If you need me to help you do it, I will."

"What kind of help can you offer?"

"I don't know," Ethan admitted. He was growing weary. Illusion spells were not difficult, but speaking, hearing, and seeing through the image of himself made the conjuring that much more taxing. He couldn't maintain the spell indefinitely, and he was all too aware of how little time he had to convince Ramsey of his sincerity. "I assume that bringing the dead back fully to the living world takes a good deal of power. I'm offering to let you use what power I possess to that end."

"In exchange for what?"

"Once your father is back, you release the shades, return that which you stole from the graves, and leave Boston."

The captain laughed. "You don't ask for much, do you?"

"You'd have your father back. Between your last visit to Boston and what you've done in the past few days, you've avenged him. Forrs and Keller are dead. The families of Alexander Rowan and Bertram Flagg have been terrified by the shades of their dead. You even managed to desecrate the three burying grounds in this city where the men responsible for the persecution of Salem's 'witches' are interred. You've done well, Ramsey."

The captain's grin appeared genuine.

"You have nothing more to prove," Ethan said, pressing the small advantage he seemed to have gained. "Let us bring back your father, and the two of you can set sail again. You can leave behind the tragedies inflicted upon you by this town."

Ramsey narrowed his eyes. "Why would you help me?"

Ethan saw no point in denying the truth. "Because I fear you and the damage you could do here. Because I enjoy being a conjurer, and don't want to have my power taken from me. Because even if I manage to kill you, I'll be dooming the souls that you control. And because, as you have said before, if we had first met under different circumstances we might well have become friends."

"How do you know that I won't accept your aid, and then refuse to uphold my end of our bargain?"

"I don't. I'm offering you my trust. Mariz could have killed you last night. I told him not to. I'm hoping that small mercy might have earned me a modicum of goodwill."

Ramsey regarded the conjured image of Ethan. On the wooden stairway above Henry's cooperage, Ethan held his breath.

"You're an odd man, Kaille. You're stubborn to a fault, and your devotion to duty is foolhardy, at best. And yet, you can also be quite pragmatic, and even compassionate. I don't know if that last is a weakness or an asset, but in this case it serves you well." He hesitated for another few seconds before nodding. "Very well. I'll accept your help, and when my father and I are together, we'll sail."

"You'll forswear further acts of vengeance?"

"To be away from this city? With my father? Aye."

Ethan smiled, and knew that his image mirrored his relief. "Good."

"When do you wish to do this?" Ramsey asked.

"I'll make my way down to the wharf shortly," Ethan said. "If all goes as it should, you'll be putting out to sea by this evening."

"Very well."

Ethan allowed the conjuring to end. Opening his eyes, he endured a wave of dizziness, and braced himself on the wooden railing outside his door.

Once he had his bearings again, he descended the stairs and walked out to Milk Street. He didn't wish to keep Ramsey waiting, but he also knew better than to place all his faith in the captain's word. Rather than face the man with no way to conjure except through blood spells, he hastened to Janna's tavern, walking so quickly that his bad leg, which was still tender from having been broken by Ramsey the previous night, soon ached even more than usual.

Still, he begrudged every minute, knowing that Ramsey would already be questioning the choice he had made.

Upon reaching the Fat Spider, Ethan entered and crossed to Janna's bar.

"Kaille," she said, her tone sour. "What you want now?"

"I just need to buy more mullein from you, Janna." He placed three shillings on the polished wood.

"That's all?" She sounded suspicious. "No questions?"

Previously, she had offered to help him, but Ethan didn't wish to put her life in peril if he didn't absolutely have to.

"Not right now," he said. "I'm in a bit of a hurry."

She nodded, her lower lip protruding. "Well, all right then." She took the money and walked into her back room. "You know any more 'bout what's happenin' to our spells?" she called to him.

"I've learned a few things. In another day or two, I should have answers for you." He could have told her more. Lord knew that with all she had told him over the years, he owed her as many answers as she wanted. But he didn't wish to risk any additional delays.

After what seemed like an eternity, she emerged once more, carrying a pouch filled near to overflowing with the herb. "Here you go," she said. "You went through that last bit awfully fast. You don't need to use a lot. Not that I mind the sales."

Ethan forced a smile, and had to keep himself from saying that if Ramsey hadn't been using his mullein as well, and if he hadn't needed to speak with so many dead conjurers, his last purchase would have lasted longer.

"My thanks, Janna," he said instead, already crossing to the door. "I'll come back soon, and tell you everything I can about the conjurings."

"You do that," she said.

Back on the street once more, Ethan half walked, half ran to the waterfront. He felt safer now that he had a pouch full of mullein, and as he hurried through the streets, he considered casting a warding spell, just as a precaution. Ramsey would feel it, though, and Ethan couldn't be sure that his conjuring would be effective. He decided not to try.

The closer he got to the wharves, the heavier the scent of brine in the air, and the louder the cries of circling gulls. For the first time in several days, Ethan thought that he might be on the verge of helping the families of the King's Chapel congregation.

Until he felt the first pulse of power tremble in the cobblestone street. This first conjuring was followed an instant later by two more in quick succession. Ethan bolted for the wharf. A pistol shot rang out across the waterfront. He heard shouting.

When he reached the dock, he found a pitched battle under way. In the shadow of the *Muirenn*, Sephira and her men fought hand-to-hand against Ramsey's crew. Sephira and her toughs were outnumbered nearly two to one, but Ethan could tell from a single glance that hers were the more skilled fighters. Already a few of Ramsey's men had fallen back, all of them bleeding from what appeared to be knife wounds, several of them needing support from their fellow sailors.

Ramsey stood on the deck of his ship, one hand gripping the rail, the other a blade. Blood flowed from a fresh cut on his forearm. Mariz stood apart from the fighting, also bleeding, also with his knife at the ready. Sephira fought with the grace and lethal efficiency Ethan remembered from past encounters with her. As he watched, she dispatched one of her foes with a vicious arcing kick that caught the hapless sailor square on the jaw. She leaped toward the other man fighting her, but he fell back. Seeing this, she rushed to join Nap, who was being harried by three men.

Ethan didn't know what to do. He had paused at the top of the wharf, but he ran forward now, shouting for Sephira to stop fighting. No one heeded him, though Ramsey looked his way, his face white with rage.

Ethan called Sephira's name again.

"Get out of here, Ethan!" she answered, even as she slashed at another sailor with her knife. Blood blossomed from the man's side, just above his waist. He staggered, backpedaled several steps. "This doesn't concern you!"

"It does! You're doing more damage than you know! If you could have waited a few hours, Ramsey might have been gone! Perhaps none of this would have been necessary!"

"I don't want him gone! I want him dead!"

"You can't kill him!"

She flashed a cruel, brilliant smile. "Watch me!"

"There are souls at stake, Sephira!"

She fought on, ignoring him. Ethan should have known that she would be beyond reason; she lived for this sort of combat.

"Ramsey!" Ethan said, spinning to face the captain. But whatever plea he might have made died on his lips. Sephira's assault had enraged the captain, and worse, it appeared to have convinced him that Ethan's proposal a short while before had been a ruse.

"I didn't know she would do this!" Ethan hollered.

Ramsey's expression didn't change.

One of Ramsey's crew broke off from another fight and confronted Ethan, a knife in one hand and a loop of rope in the other. Reluctantly, Ethan dropped into a fighting crouch and pulled his blade free. The man rushed him, his assault awkward and obvious. Ethan evaded him with ease and swiped at the man's blade arm with his knife.

He missed, and the sailor lashed out with the rope, nearly snaring Ethan's blade hand.

The sailor lunged for him a second time. Ethan parried with his knife and kicked out, catching the man in the gut. He fell back with a grunt, but kept his feet. Ethan closed the distance between them with one quick stride. He feinted with his knife and landed a punch with his left hand. Blood flowed from the sailor's nose.

Pressing his advantage, Ethan hacked at the man with his knife. It was a haphazard attack; Ethan knew it immediately. The sailor eluded him and captured Ethan's wrist in the rope. He gave the loop a hard twist, trapping Ethan's arm. And he drew back his knife, as to plunge it into Ethan's chest.

"*Incide ex cruore evocatum!*" Slash, conjured from blood!

Perhaps it was desperation, the urgency with which he conjured. Perhaps Ramsey was occupied with the battle unfolding before him, and so gave little thought to disrupting his spells. Whatever the reason, Ethan's conjuring did what he needed it to. Power thrummed, the blood on the sailor's face vanished, and the rope holding Ethan's blade arm fell away, all in the span of a single heartbeat. Ethan thrust out his knife to block the sailor's blow; his blade buried itself to the hilt in the man's forearm. The sailor howled; his knife flew from his fingers and clattered across the dirt fill of the wharf. Ethan yanked his knife free as the man dropped to his knees, clutching his bleeding arm to his belly.

Ethan turned away from him. Not much had changed. A few more of Ramsey's men had fallen back, and one of Sephira's men had re-treated several paces, a bloody wound on his shoulder.

"Ramsey, call back your men!"

"I will not!"

Ethan looked to Sephira. "End this now! Please, before it's too late!"

"I intend to."

"That's not what I mean, Sephira!"

She opened her mouth to answer. But as she did, another sailor loomed behind her, a knife raised to strike. Ethan had no idea where he had come from; he seemed to appear from nowhere, like one of Ramsey's shades.

Ethan didn't even have time to shout a warning. The knife started to descend in a blurred, silvery arc.

A shot rang out, deafening, its report echoing among the ware-houses and ships. The sailor's arm stopped; his knife slipped from his fingers. His eyes widened, and rolled back in his head. Sephira turned. A bloodstain spread over the sailor's side under his blade arm. He coughed once, blood spurting from his mouth, and fell forward. If Sephira hadn't stepped out of the way, he would have fallen onto her. As it was, his blood splattered her shirt and waistcoat.

Ethan could hear the man's wet, labored breathing—slow, desperate gasps, each weaker than the last.

Nigel stood a short distance away, his pistol held steady, a cloud of gray smoke surrounding him like a halo. He appeared to be as sur-prised as anyone by what he had done. He looked at his weapon, before lifting his gaze to Sephira. The other fights had stopped. Everyone stared at the fallen sailor.

"*No!*"

There was something tortured and unearthly in that cry, as if it had been torn from Ramsey's throat by a taloned hand.

A conjuring pulsed; the blood on Ramsey's arm disappeared. And an instant later Nigel's body flew backward as if smote by some giant unseen fist. He rolled several times across the wharf, finally coming to rest in a crumpled, dusty heap.

"Nigel!" Even as the name crossed Sephira's lips she lunged for an-other sailor, her blade flashing again, her lovely features contorted with anguish and hatred.

Ethan cut his arm and cast a fire spell, so that a wall of flame erupted just in front of her. She staggered back, as did the man she had been fighting. Ramsey's men still battled with the rest of Sephira's toughs, and the captain had cut his arm once more. Ethan feared that he would kill the rest of them with his next conjuring.

He didn't dare take the time to pull out the pouch of mullein; he merely cast his spell, hoping he would be quicker than Ramsey. "*Provoco te, Nathaniel Ramsey, ex regno mortuorum, ex verbasco evocatum.*" I summon thee, Nathaniel Ramsey, from the realm of the dead, conjured from mullein.

The ghost of the old captain appeared beside him, pale green in the glare of day. Ramsey screamed Ethan's name, but he didn't cast a spell. Ethan didn't know if the captain feared for his father's soul, or didn't wish for the spirit to see what he might do next. Really, he didn't care. He had hoped to keep Ramsey from doing more damage, and he had accomplished that much. For the moment.

"This ends now!" Ethan said, pitching his voice to carry. "Sephira, Ramsey, call back your men."

"Stay out of this, Ethan!"

He had never heard Sephira's voice sound like this—forlorn, enraged, quaking with emotion.

He faced her, shaking his head. "I can't. Call them back, or I'll use a spell to stop them."

She glared at him, her eyes red-rimmed. But after a moment she shouted for Nap, Gordon, and the others to fall back. Ramsey called to his men as well, although his venomous gaze never left Ethan and the ghost of his father.

Sephira turned on her heel and hurried to where Nigel lay. When she reached him, she dropped to her knees by his side. Nap, Mariz, Afton, Gordon, and Sephira's other men joined her a few seconds after, as did Ethan, who was trailed by Uncle Reg and the ghost of Nathaniel Ramsey.

Nigel lay utterly still, his eyes open, sightless, fixed on the hazy blue sky. A strand of yellow hair fell across his face, and a trickle of blood ran from his nose.

"Nigel," Sephira said, a whisper this time.

She stood, took a step toward Ramsey's ship. Ethan planted himself in front of her and took hold of both her arms. There was murder in her eyes, and something else Ethan had never thought to see: a welling of tears.

"Out of my way," she said, her voice thick.

Ethan didn't release her. "No. He'll kill you, Sephira. He'll kill every one of your men."

"No, I'm going to kill him." She said this softly, but then bellowed at Ramsey, "I'm going to kill you, you conjuring bastard!"

"By all means try, Miss Pryce," Ramsey said, his voice taut.

Other members of Ramsey's crew had gathered around the man shot by Nigel. One of them called to their captain that the man was dead. The sailors turned as one to glare at Sephira and the others, including Ethan.

They were moments away from renewing their battle, and who knew how many more men would die before they were done?

"What's going on here?"

Ethan knew that voice. Looking past Sephira, he saw Sheriff Stephen Greenleaf stride onto the wharf with half a dozen armed regulars in tow. He and the sheriff had never liked each other, mostly, in Ethan's estimation, because Greenleaf was determined to see Ethan hanged as a witch, or at the very least thrown in gaol for whatever offense the sheriff could concoct. But this one time, Ethan could not have been more pleased to see him.

He was an imposing man: tall, broad-shouldered, with a prominent hook nose and pale, piercing eyes. Though Ethan had often questioned his principles and on occasion his competence as well, he never doubted that Greenleaf was a formidable presence. Upon seeing him, Ramsey's crew retreated toward the *Muirenn*, pausing to help their wounded shipmates. They left the dead man, stepping around the blood that had pooled by the body.

"Kaille," Greenleaf said. "I should have known that I'd find you in the middle of his nonsense. What is—?" He stopped, his mouth dropping open at the sight of Nathaniel Ramsey's ghost. "What in God's name—?"

"It's the shade of a dead man, Sheriff," Ethan said. "Haven't you heard? Boston is full of them right now."

Greenleaf took a step back. "You did this! You and your damned witchery! Make it go away!"

"I can't," Ethan said, leaving it for the sheriff to work out what he meant.

"Where did it come from?"

"I don't know. Heaven? Hell? You tell me."

"You're playing games now." His gaze darted toward Ramsey's ship. "What is this all about? Who are those men?"

"That's the crew of the *Muirenn*."

Greenleaf narrowed his eyes. "Why is that name so familiar?"

"The ship belongs to Nate Ramsey."

"Ramsey!" he said. "Ramsey's back?"

"Aye. This is the shade of his father."

"He killed my man, Sheriff," Sephira said. "I want him arrested."

"And who killed that man there?" Greenleaf asked, pointing at the fallen sailor, even as he cast another nervous glance at the ghost.

"Nigel did," Ethan said.

"I see. And what was your role in all of this?"

"He had nothing to do with any of it," Sephira said, before Ethan could answer. "He tried to warn me away from here."

Ethan couldn't have been more shocked if she had declared her love for him.

Greenleaf seemed to be thinking along similar lines. His tone when next he spoke was a good deal more subdued. "Very well. Miss Pryce, it might be best if you leave for now. I give you my word that justice will be done. Kaille can tell me what happened, and if I have questions, I'll call on you at your home."

Sephira nodded but cast a dark, lingering look at the ship. "I won't leave Nigel here," she said. "My men will carry him up to my carriage."

"Yes, ma'am," the sheriff said.

Ethan and sheriff backed away as Sephira's toughs arranged themselves around Nigel's corpse and lifted the yellow-haired man. Mariz, who was far smaller than the others, kept out of their way. He caught Ethan's eye, his expression grim.

Ethan thought he knew what the conjurer was thinking, for the thought was in his mind, too. If Ethan had allowed Mariz to kill Ramsey the night before, Nigel would still be alive, as would Ramsey's sailor. Mariz said nothing, of course. Even if he was cruel enough to give voice to the words, he wouldn't have wanted Sephira to know that he had helped Ethan fight off Ramsey.

"How long has Ramsey been back?" Greenleaf asked, as he and Ethan watched them carry Nigel's body back up to Flounder Lane.

"It's been several days now."

"And you didn't think it important to inform me? The last time the fiend set foot in my city, two men died. Men of means." He glanced Ethan's way. "Men you were hired to protect."

"I remember." Ethan tried to keep his voice level, though at that moment he needed no reminders of Ramsey's past crimes, or of his own repeated failures to keep the captain from killing.

"Are you working with him?"

"No." The denial crossed Ethan's lips before he could even consider the question. He wasn't working with Ramsey to any nefarious end, as Greenleaf's question was meant to imply. But he had come to Tileston's Wharf intending to help Ramsey bring his father back from the realm of the dead. It had been a devil's bargain, an idea shaped by fear and wishful thinking. And more, he knew that if Ramsey had been an ordinary criminal, one who had committed murders during their last encounter and had desecrated more than two dozen graves in the past week, he wouldn't have given a thought to helping him. Was he willing to aid Ramsey simply to keep the captain from doing more harm, or was he also helping him because they were both conjurers? No doubt Greenleaf would believe the latter.

The sheriff watched him, seeming to read Ethan's thoughts. "You say no, but there's doubt in your eyes. What have you done, Kaille?"

"I've done nothing. If anything, I've done too little." He related to the sheriff much of what had happened in recent days: the grave robberies, his confrontations with Ramsey, his encounters with the many shades. And, with some reluctance, he also shared with Greenleaf his belief that Ramsey was making himself more powerful and at the same time denying other conjurers access to their power. He knew that the sheriff would take this as proof that he himself could conjure, though he took great care to admit no such thing. He said nothing about Mariz, or about his battle with Ramsey the previous night.

"Why did Caner hire you? Why wouldn't he have come to me first? Is it that he knows what you are, and therefore assumed that you would be able to commune with whatever demons and shades Ramsey unleashed?"

"I believe it was Mister Pell who encouraged the rector to seek my help. Pell is a friend and he has faith in my skills as a thieftaker, as well as in my discretion."

"I see," Greenleaf said, sounding smug. "So your friend thought he would throw a little coin your way."

Ethan bristled. "I refused to let them pay me, Sheriff. I'm conducting this inquiry at my own expense."

Greenleaf seemed disappointed by this. "Well, what brought you here today? And why were Miss Pryce and her men here?"

"I came hoping I could convince Ramsey to leave Boston. He is engaged in one pursuit which is both legal and harmless to the rest of us, and I told him I would help him with that if he would set sail, never to return. But when I reached the wharf, Sephira and the others were already here, and they were fighting with Ramsey's crew. Sephira is protecting merchants who refuse to abide by the non-importation agreement, and Ramsey has been harassing those merchants. I believe Sephira hoped to impress upon him the dangers of pitting himself against her."

"I've heard of incidents at several warehouses. Miss Pryce has been working for non-compliant merchants?"

"Aye, although I doubt she wants that known too widely."

"And Ramsey has been working with your friends, the Sons of Liberty."

"They're hardly my friends."

"You've worked with Adams in the past," Greenleaf said. "I know you have."

Arguing with the man was pointless. "I don't believe Ramsey has been working with anyone. He has his own aims, and he cares for nothing else."

The sheriff regarded Ethan with manifest mistrust. At last he said, "So Miss Pryce came here to stop him. And instead, Nigel was killed."

Ethan took a long breath. *Nigel is dead.* "Aye."

"How did he die?"

"I believe Ramsey used a spell against him."

Greenleaf scowled. "You believe . . . Damn you, Kaille! You know he did! Why do you protect him?"

"I'm not protecting him. But anytime I speak to you of conjurers, you assume that I'm conspiring with them and you accuse me of being a witch. And I will not swing for Ramsey's crimes!"

"Of course you won't," the sheriff said, the words laden with irony. "Would I be correct in assuming that you also won't tell me more about this 'harmless and legal' pursuit with which you intended to help the good captain?"

Ethan glared at him, but could say nothing without either lying outright, or admitting that he was a conjurer.

"Do you also refuse to tell me where this ghost came from?"

Still Ethan held his tongue.

Greenleaf smirked. "I thought as much. And you wonder why I remain suspicious of you." He strode toward the *Muirenn*, the regulars just behind him. "Come along. It's time I had a word with Nate Ramsey, and I want you there with me."

"He's dangerous, Sheriff," Ethan said, hurrying to keep up with him, Reg and the shade of Ramsey's father following. "More so now than he was when he took his revenge on Keller and Forrs."

Greenleaf didn't slow. "So I gather. A man who can go up against Sephira Pryce and prevail is not to be trifled with." He flashed a malicious grin. "But I've got a witch with me, so I ought to be safe."

amsey still stood at the rail of his vessel, his arms crossed over his chest, the wind stirring his hair. He stared down at Greenleaf and Ethan, marking their approach. When they reached the base of the *Muirenn*'s gangplank, he said, "The two of you. I won't have soldiers on my ship." Before Ethan or the sheriff could respond, he turned away.

Greenleaf and Ethan shared a look.

"Stay here," the sheriff said to the regulars. To Ethan he said, "After you." He indicated the plank with an open hand, and backed out of the way of Captain Ramsey's ghost.

Ethan started up the incline. He thought of the knife on his belt and the pouch of mullein in his pocket. It was too late for him to cast a warding spell. Whether he cut himself or drew leaves from the pouch, the sheriff would see, and even if he managed to cast without drawing Greenleaf's notice, Ramsey would sense the conjuring. He felt vulnerable, weak. His only protection was the ghost following him up to the ship. He wondered if Greenleaf had brought a pistol.

At the top of the plank, Ethan hopped onto the deck and found himself facing eight members of Ramsey's crew, who had arranged themselves in a semicircle. All of them held knives, although with Ramsey standing behind them, fresh blood on his forearm, Ethan wasn't sure their weapons were necessary.

A few seconds later, Greenleaf joined him on the deck. He eyed the men briefly before pulling a pistol from his coat pocket.

"You should put that away, Sheriff," Ramsey said. "Someone could get hurt."

"Tell your men to stand down."

Ramsey's eyes found Ethan's and a mordant smile crossed his lips.

"Very well," he said. "If that will make you feel better." To the sailors he said, "Leave us."

Most of the men moved to the stern. A few lingered; one of them had blood on his shirt: from his fallen comrade, no doubt.

"It's all right," Ramsey said. "They won't be staying long."

The last men joined the others at the rear of the ship.

"I thought you and I had an understanding, Kaille," Ramsey said.

"We do."

The captain shook his head. "We did. That ended once Pryce showed up with your friend and attacked my ship."

"What friend?" Greenleaf asked. "Who's he talking about, Kaille?"

Ethan kept his gaze on the captain. "Mariz, the bespectacled man who works for Sephira."

"Since when are you friends with Sephira's boys?"

"We're not . . . It's not worth explaining right now."

Ramsey's eyebrows went up. "I see. The truth is, Sheriff, this Mariz is a speller, just as I am, and just as Kaille is. But our friend here is too shy to say as much aloud."

It was a measure of how much the sheriff hated and feared Ramsey that he wasted not even a moment to gloat over this tidbit.

"It doesn't matter," he said. "Captain Ramsey, you are under arrest for the murder of Nigel Billings."

"Am I? Tell me: Who saw me kill this man?"

"Sephira Pryce did," Greenleaf said. "She is a respected and admired personage in our city, and she told me herself that you had done the deed."

"I don't doubt that she did. But what did she see, exactly?"

Greenleaf faltered. "Well . . . what did you see, Kaille?"

"I'll tell you what I saw," the captain said before Ethan could answer.

"I saw Pryce's man shoot my bosun dead. That's right: Two men died today. Where's the justice for me and my crew?"

When Greenleaf didn't respond, Ramsey nodded. "I thought as much. So after he shot Stip, I saw Pryce's man go tumbling across the wharf, and then lie still. It was almost like God himself reached down and gave us the justice you won't offer."

The sheriff recoiled. "You dare claim it was God who killed him?"

"You dare to accuse me," Ramsey said with a shrug. "Yet you have no more or less proof than I."

Greenleaf rounded on Ethan. "You saw what happened! Say something!"

"Aye," Ramsey said, drawing out the word. "Tell us what you saw, Kaille. And spare no detail."

What could Ethan say? *I saw precisely the same thing Ramsey saw, but I also felt the spell he cast to kill Nigel.* He might as well have tied his own noose and handed the rope to Greenleaf.

He looked the sheriff in the eye. "As he said, two men died today. And from all I saw, Captain Ramsey and Sephira Pryce bear equal blame for both deaths. We need to get this ship and her crew away from Boston, or there will be more bloodshed. I'm certain of that."

"That's not good enough, damn it!" Greenleaf said, growling the words. He faced Ramsey again, his pistol aimed at the captain's heart. "You're under arrest, I say. I'll sort out the details later. If nothing else, I'll see you hanged for the murders of Deron Forrs and Isaac Keller."

Ramsey's laugh was dry and mirthless. Ethan reached for his blade.

"Don't do it, Kaille," the captain said, still staring at Greenleaf.

"Sheriff, you need to leave," Ethan said. "Right now."

"The hell I—"

"Sheriff, please."

"I want him to stay," Ramsey said.

Greenleaf looked from one of them to the other. "You are working together. Why else would he want me to leave while you stay?"

The captain laughed. "You really are a fool, aren't you? You understand nothing. Kaille knows that I can kill both of you with a thought. He believes he's safe because he has summoned the ghost of my father. He may be right. But you? I have nothing to fear from killing you."

"Don't do it, Ramsey!" Ethan said. "Let him go. If you kill him, every soldier in this city will come for you." *And if they kill you, the souls you control will be lost.*

"I'm not afraid of the king's men. I'm not afraid of any of you." He eyed the ghost of his father. "My father's spirit is the only thing keeping you alive right now. You betrayed me, Kaille. That wasn't smart. And now one of my men is dead."

"I had nothing to do with what happened here today. Ask the sheriff: Sephira and I despise each other. If she wasn't trying to kill you, she'd probably be trying to kill me. We don't work together."

For several seconds, Ramsey held himself still. Ethan felt a pulse of power and saw the captain's ancient spectral guide appear on the deck, faint and insubstantial in the sunlight.

The sheriff let out a sharp cry and jerked his hand back. His pistol fell to the deck and discharged, the report drawing the stares of Ramsey's men. The shot hit the base of the rail near the ship's prow, gouging the wood.

"I want you both off of my ship right now."

"Ramsey—"

"Go, Kaille, before I do something more than burn the sheriff's hand. I don't want your help, and I don't trust you. I'd kill you both now, but . . ." The captain eyed his father's ghost and then Greenleaf. "Well, let's just say that it would complicate matters." He flashed a smile. "Besides, before the end, I want you to see how powerful I've grown."

Before the end . . . Ethan suppressed a shudder at the threat in those words. Still, he held the man's gaze before turning to Greenleaf.

"Come along, Sheriff. There's nothing more to be done here."

Greenleaf stared at the captain, but Ethan could see that his confidence had evaporated. He looked frightened as he bent to retrieve his pistol. He hesitated with his hand mere inches from the weapon, and finally snatched it up and shoved it back into his pocket.

Ethan led him to the gangplank, and they both left the ship.

"He used witchery against me!" Greenleaf said, as they reached the wharf once more. "He made my pistol . . . One moment it was normal, and the next it was too hot for me to hold."

Ethan kept walking. Reg and the ghost watched him, expectant, their eyes glowing, but Ethan wasn't yet ready to dismiss the one advantage he had over Ramsey.

"He didn't do anything," the sheriff said. "I thought he would have to wave his hands around in all manner, or speak some sort of magicking nonsense. But he did nothing. It just happened."

Ethan thought it likely that Ramsey had drawn blood by biting the inside of his cheek, or perhaps he had used some of the mullein Ethan carried. But he didn't respond.

"This is your fault, Kaille."

He halted, turned. "My fault?"

Greenleaf and the regulars caught up with him.

"That's right. You let him get away all those years ago. At the time you said yourself that you had made a mess of things, and you were right. Now he's back and you need to clean up your mess."

They had reached the street. Ethan halted and faced the sheriff, a denial on his tongue. But he clamped his mouth shut. As much as he hated to admit it, Greenleaf was right, even more than he knew. Six years ago, Ethan had failed to protect Forrs and Keller, and last night he had failed to rid the world of Nate Ramsey. This was his fault as much as anyone's.

"All right," he said. "That's what I'll do."

Greenleaf looked surprised, but he recovered quickly and nodded. "Do what you have to. I know you're a witch; I don't give a damn. Not right now. Do you understand what I'm saying?"

"Aye."

"Good. Tell me when he's been dealt with."

Greenleaf started away.

"What if I fail again?" Ethan called after him.

"I'll find another of your kind to help me." The sheriff looked back at him. "It sounds as though Miss Pryce might know someone."

Right. Mariz wouldn't be happy about that. If their new friendship survived this week, it would be nothing short of miraculous.

Then again, if Ethan himself survived, that would be something of a miracle in and of itself. He was at a loss as to how to combat Ramsey's growing power, particularly when his own spells were so unreliable.

It occurred to him that as long as he considered this a battle between himself and Ramsey, he could not prevail. Ramsey had gathered a
force of shades who were working on his behalf, albeit against their will.
Ethan needed allies as well. A year before, Ethan pitted himself against
what he thought was the most powerful conjurer he had ever encountered.
In the end, it turned out to be two conjurers who had learned to cast as
one and thus combine their might. What if he could do the same?

It seemed that every conjurer in the city was having trouble casting
spells. But perhaps if several of them worked together they could be
both stronger and more certain that their conjurings would work.

For the second time that day, Ethan walked to the Fat Spider, only
dismissing Reg and Ramsey's ghost when he reached the tavern.

"What are you doin' back here?" Janna demanded as soon as he entered her tavern. "You can't be out o' mullein already."

"No, I'm not. I need your help, Janna."

"My help," she repeated. "I thought we were through with you comin' in here an' asking me questions an' offerin' nothin' in return."

"I'm not here for information. I'm here to ask you if you'll help me
fight Nate Ramsey."

She straightened, her face like stone. "I already told you I would. Do
you know how to make our spells work?"

Ethan shook his head. "Not yet. But I was thinking that if we com-
bined our spells, cast them together, we might have a better chance."

"I ain't never done that."

"Neither have I. But last year, when those men died aboard the
Graystone, that was how the sisters Osborne made their conjurings so
powerful. I know it can be done."

"Then we'll find a way," Janna said. "Have you talked to ole Black
yet?"

"No. I came to you first."

"Well, it sounds like we'll need him, too."

"Aye, we will. And also Mariz."

"Who is that?" she asked, though Ethan thought that she already
knew.

"He works for Sephira."

"That's what I thought! Did you get hit on the head or somethin'? You want to fight Ramsey with one of Pryce's men on our side? You might as well put your knife to your throat!"

"If it was anyone else I would agree with you. But Mariz is different. I trust him. He's already saved my life once, and now he has more reasons than most to hate Ramsey."

"Why? What's happened?"

Ethan told her about the battle at the wharf and his subsequent confrontation with Ramsey and the sheriff.

She didn't look happy, but aside from those few moments in the Dowser, when Kannice was doting on her and Ethan was buying her chowder, he couldn't remember the last time she had.

"Well, I suppose that this once havin' Pryce and her boys on our side might help."

"I'm going to speak with Gavin next," Ethan said, already starting toward the door. "I don't know yet what we're going to do, or when. But I'll let you know as soon as I can." He paused, looking back at her. She was tiny and frail; her dark skin seemed to be stretched thin over the bones of her face. He had no doubts about her skill as a conjurer, but he couldn't helping thinking that he was making a mistake asking her to fight this battle with him.

"I know what you're thinkin'," she said, meeting his gaze and raising her chin defiantly. "I'm old. I ain't as strong as I once was, and I wake up some mornin's thinkin' that a good wind could blow me over. But there ain't no one else in this city knows magicking like I do. There ain't no one else who can help you as much as I can."

"I believe that. You've been a good friend to me over the years, Janna."

"No, I haven't. I'm mean as a snake, and you know it. But that's just my way. It don't mean that I don't . . ." She gave a vague wave of her hand. "You know."

"I do. And I don't want something to happen to you because of anything that I ask you to do."

"Ramsey didn't start this because of you. Boy's got darkness in his soul. It ain't your fault. We can let him win, or we can fight him an' get our conjurin's back. You know which I choose. Now, go see ole Black."

"Yes, ma'am."

She grinned at that.

Ethan left her and walked back toward Hillier's Lane. He could have saved himself some walking by going to Black first, before he visited Janna. But if Janna had refused him, Gavin would have, too. And Ethan needed Janna's knowledge of spellmaking to make all of this work.

Gavin's house on Hillier's Lane, which stood but a stone's throw from the Dowsing Rod, was one of the older homes on the street. Its clapboard siding had been weathered to a pale gray by nearly one hundred winters and more storms than Ethan could count.

Gavin had once told him that the house was first built for his great-grandfather, who had also been a sea captain, and who had given up the sea after losing his arm in a whaling accident. The house had been passed down to Gavin, who leased it during his years at sea, and finally returned to it when he sold his ship.

Ethan knocked on the door, waited, knocked again, and was beginning to wonder if he should look for the old man elsewhere when at last the door opened.

Gavin blinked against the daylight. His clothes were rumpled, and his white hair was in tangles.

"Ethan," he said, his surprise apparent.

"Did I wake you?"

"Aye." He tried to smooth his hair. "It's been thirteen years since I gave up sailing, and still I don't sleep well on land. I catch what sleep I can, regardless of the time." He fixed a smile on his face and gestured for Ethan to enter the house. "Come in."

Ethan stepped past him. He had been in the house only a few times before, and not for some time. It hadn't changed much in the intervening years. It was sparsely furnished and in need of fresh paint.

"Can I offer you some wine?"

"No, thank you. I'm sorry to disturb you, Gavin, but I need your help."

"My help?" Gavin said. He sat in a threadbare chair beside an empty hearth, and indicated a second chair for Ethan. "You're the thieftaker. What help could you need from an old man?"

Ethan lowered himself into the other chair. "It's related to what we talked about in the street the other day: the trouble you were having with your conjurings."

Gavin averted his gaze. "How can my inability to conjure help you?"

"In all your years at sea, did you know a merchant captain named Nathaniel Ramsey?"

"Of course. He was a friend, a good man."

"Did you know his son?"

"Aye. I haven't seen Nate in years, but as a lad he spent some time on my ship. His father felt that he should have experience sailing under more than a single captain."

Ethan sat forward. "So you know him well."

"I'm not sure I'd say that. It's been years since last we spoke. And after Nathaniel's death . . . Nate changed."

Ethan didn't need for Gavin to elaborate. "He's back in Boston; his ship is moored at Tileston's Wharf. It's he who is responsible for the grave robberies I mentioned. He's using the shades of the dead to strengthen his own conjurings and deny the rest of us access to the power we need to cast."

Gavin looked stricken. "Nate's doing all of that?"

"I'm afraid so. He's also trying to bring back his father from the dead."

"Good God, no! He has to understand: it won't be Nathaniel. It would be something else, something twisted, dark, more wraith than man."

"He's not thinking clearly, Gavin. I believe he's more than a little insane. Brilliant and powerful, but mad. I've tried to reason with him, and I had hoped that I could get him to leave Boston, even if it meant helping him raise his father. But he believes that I've wronged him, and he seeks to avenge himself upon me, regardless of the pain it brings to others."

"I'm sorry to hear it," Gavin said. "But I don't see what I can do."

"Janna and I intend to fight him. I'm going to enlist another speller I know, and I hoped that you—"

"No." Gavin stood and began to pace the room. "I have no power, Ethan. I'm old and weak and I can't help you."

"Working together, we might be able to cast more reliably, and we might enhance our power, as well."

The old man shook his head, still pacing. "No. I can't do it."

Ethan frowned and watched him in silence. "I wish I'd known that you knew him so well," he said at last. "You might have reached him where others couldn't."

Gavin halted, stared at him. "Are you asking me to talk to him?"

"No. I think it's too late for that."

"Nate and I don't know each other well, at least not anymore," Gavin went on, as if he hadn't heard. He shook his head again and resumed his pacing. "I'm afraid of what he's become. The last time I saw him I sensed the seeds of that madness you speak of now. It frightened me. And I think that he harbors resentment toward me, too. I didn't do enough for his father at the end. That's what he said, and I suppose it's true."

"Are you sure you won't help us fight him?"

"I'm sorry, Ethan. There was a time when I thought myself brave. I might have stood with you then."

"But your spellmaking—"

"I can live the rest of my days without conjuring. But I'm not ready to die."

Ethan eyed him for a few seconds more. He and Gavin had never been close friends; he spent far less time with the old captain than with Janna. But he had expected more from this encounter.

Gavin had walked to a window that overlooked the lane, and stood gazing out at the street.

"I'll go," Ethan said, getting to his feet.

"You're disappointed in me."

He stepped to the door and pulled it open. "It's not my place to be disappointed in you. I was asking you to risk your life; you're well within your rights to refuse. We've known each other for a long time, Gavin. This changes nothing between us."

Gavin faced him, a pained smile on his wan features. "Thank you, Ethan."

Ethan left him and struck out southward again. As difficult as his conversation with Gavin had been, his next task promised to be even worse. He needed to enlist Mariz's help, and that meant he had to face Sephira.

ordon stood outside Sephira's house, hands in his pockets, his massive shoulders hunched. His homely face was slack, his eyes fixed on something Ethan couldn't see. He seemed not to notice Ethan as he approached the house along the street. But when Ethan started up the path to Sephira's door, the man straightened and puffed out his chest. A scowl settled on his face, but it wasn't the menacing expression Ethan was accustomed to. He sensed that more than anything else, Gordon resented the intrusion.

Ethan drew his knife, flipped it over and handed it hilt-first to the man. "I'd like to speak with Sephira," he said, his voice low.

Gordon pocketed the knife. "Wait here."

The tough lumbered into the house. Ethan surveyed the grounds of Sephira's estate. Her gardens were in full bloom; yellow finches flitted in nearby branches, singing boldly; a soft wind stirred the leaves and bent the grasses on her lawn. It was too bright a day for all that had happened, and for what promised to come.

"She'll see you."

Ethan turned. Gordon held the door open for him. He nodded and entered the house.

Sephira sat in the common room just off the entryway, in a large arm chair near the hearth. Nap, Mariz, Afton, and several of her other toughs were seated with her. The room was silent save for the rustle of lace window curtains and the strains of birdsong.

"Did Greenleaf arrest him?" Sephira asked, before Ethan could say a word.

"No. Frankly, I think he and I were fortunate to get away with our lives."

She gave no indication of being surprised or angry. "Mariz tells me that he's very powerful, and that he's found some way to weaken the rest of your kind. Is that true?"

"Aye."

"So, what are you going to do about it?"

"I'm going to fight him," Ethan said. "But I need Mariz's help."

"You'll have help from all of us."

"Sephira—"

"He killed him," she said, her voice shaking. "He didn't raise a hand or say any of the things you say when you use your witchery. He just killed him, with nothing more than a thought."

"I know."

"You've threatened me before," she said. "You've threatened all of us. I suppose you've had cause. And you've said to me that if you wanted to you could snap my neck or tear apart this house or burn all of my men to ash. And though I've seen you do your magicking, all this time I dismissed those threats as mere talk." She looked up, her blue eyes meeting his. "But you really could have done it. Not until today did I realize that for all these years, you've kept your witchery in check."

He chanced a small smile. "You haven't always made it easy."

"No, I haven't. And I'm not saying that I intend to start. But I . . . I respect your forbearance."

"Thank you."

"Ramsey, on the other hand, has ensured his own death. No one who kills one of my men goes unpunished. I don't care what it takes; I will see this man dead, and I will spit upon his grave."

Nap and the others watched, avid, alert. Ethan could see her rage mirrored in their eyes. He had long assumed that Sephira's toughs were little more than well-paid mercenaries who remained in her employ because there were no better opportunities in the city for men of their particular talents. He realized now that he did Sephira and them a disservice. Whatever he might have thought of her, Nap, Afton, Gordon and the others loved her as soldiers do a trusted commander. He was sure that Nigel had as well. Alone among her men, Mariz held himself apart. Perhaps he hadn't been with her long enough to feel the same loyalty and affection. Or maybe because he was a conjurer he remained wary of his companions and they of him. But Ethan didn't doubt that if Sephira ordered her men back to the wharf, they would follow her, even if it meant their deaths.

"What I was going to say," Ethan began again, "is that Mariz can help me far more than the rest of you. In fact, you being there might make matters more difficult."

"That's too bad," she said. "We're going to be there."

"If Mariz and I—"

"Can you fight off Ramsey's crew and also fight him?"

Ethan glanced at Mariz, who stared back at him, his expression revealing little. "Probably not," he said to Sephira.

"I figured as much. So stop arguing with me, and tell me what it is you intend to do."

"Right now there are three of us: Mariz, Janna Windcatcher, and me—"

"Windcatcher," Sephira said. "You mean the daft old African woman who owns that hovel out on the Neck?"

"That's right. She's not daft, and she's as skilled a conjurer as we have here in Boston."

Sephira pressed her lips thin, her brow knitting. But she gestured for him to go on.

"I'm hoping that the three of us can combine our conjurings, so that our spells are stronger and more apt to work."

She watched him, plainly expecting him to say more. When he didn't, her expression turned even more skeptical. "That's it? That's your plan?"

"There is not much planning that can be done, *Senhora*," Mariz said. "Ramsey is more powerful than we are. He will be expecting us to attack his ship again. Surprising him will be most difficult. But if what Kaille has in mind can work, that itself might be a surprise."

"Have you ever used your witchery like that before?" Sephira asked, looking from Ethan to Mariz. "Can this be done?"

"It's how Caleb Osborne's daughters killed the men aboard the *Graystone*," Ethan said. "It's how they almost killed Mariz."

"We would speak our incantations at the same time?" Mariz asked.

"Aye. But I believe there's more to it than that. I'm hoping that Janna can help us figure out what else is involved. She told me that she's never done it either, but her knowledge of conjuring runs deep."

"I am curious as to whether our spectral guides can help us with this. If they work together it may be that speaking the spells simultaneously will be enough."

Ethan nodded, remembering his violent encounter with the Osborne family. At one point, after Diver had been shot, the sisters cast a powerful healing spell to save his life. He could still picture their two ghosts standing together, one yellow, the other red, their hands clasped, so that their entwined fingers glowed orange. "I believe you're right," he said. "That might well be the key to making this work."

Sephira's brow had creased again. She regarded Mariz and Ethan the way a jealous lover might her beloved and a rival.

"Mariz and I need to speak with Janna," Ethan said, eager now to be on his way. "I want to see if we can cast this way."

"Why don't you go get Windcatcher and bring her back here," Sephira said. "The three of you can figure this out together."

In spite of everything, Ethan laughed.

"Did I say something funny?" Sephira asked, biting off her words.

"Forgive me. It's just that Janna would sooner swim with sharks than set foot in your home."

He saw her bristle.

"What have I done to her?"

"You don't know?" Ethan asked, incredulous. For years, Janna had made clear to him that she hated Sephira with a fiery passion; Ethan had always assumed that theirs was an ancient feud. Was it possible that whatever slight Janna remembered with such passion had escaped Sephira's notice?

"I barely know who she is."

Ethan shook his head. "This is a matter for another time. For now, it will be quicker if Mariz and I can go to her tavern and speak with her there."

Sephira glowered. He was sure that she would refuse. But it seemed that her desire for vengeance outweighed her discomfort at having Ethan and her pet conjurer work together.

"Yes, all right," she said. "When you've figured out how to work your witchery come back here and we'll go to the wharf."

"We will."

Ethan turned to Mariz, who nodded. Together they crossed to the door and left the house.

Once they were on Summer Street and some distance from Sephira's home, Mariz said, "She has been slow to trust me. This will make matters worse."

"I'm sorry for that."

The conjurer shrugged. "It cannot be helped."

They walked some distance without speaking.

"This woman, she is African?"

Ethan nodded. "That's right."

"And she is free?"

"Not only that, she owns a tavern."

"I thought that Africans in your country could not own property."

"A small number do. Janna is . . . Well, there's no one else like her. I don't know a lot about her past, but from what I've pieced together it seems that as a young girl she was rescued at sea and taken in by a man of means. Eventually they fell in love. They never married of course, but I believe that he provided for her and made certain she would never want for anything." Ethan paused. "And now she's a marriage smith."

Mariz gave him a puzzled look. "A what?"

"She casts love spells, and she makes little effort to hide her spell-making ability. She also sells items you might find useful—herbs, oils; things of that sort."

"I do not think you should be telling me this," Mariz said, a thread of laughter in his voice.

"Perhaps not. If you buy something from her, don't use it against me."

"That is for the *senhora* to decide."

They reached the Fat Spider a short time later, and let themselves in. Two patrons sat at a table near the door, but otherwise the great room was empty.

Janna stood at the bar, drying glasses. Seeing Ethan and Mariz, she scowled. "Who is this?" she asked, lifting her chin to point it at Mariz.

"This is the man I told you about," Ethan said.

"Pryce's conjurer."

"That's right."

Mariz walked to the bar and sketched a small bow. "I am pleased to make your acquaintance, Miss Windcatcher. Kaille has told me that there is no one in Boston who knows more about conjuring than you."

Ethan suppressed a grin. With Kannice and Mariz falling over themselves to be nice to Janna, it wouldn't be long before she expected him to do the same thing. Of course, if he did, she might be more forthcoming with information.

Janna's expression had softened, though only a little. "Why you workin' for that woman, anyway?" she asked.

Mariz opened his hands. "Why do you serve food to the people in your tavern? She pays me."

Ethan didn't expect Janna to be satisfied with this answer, but she shrugged, nodded, and faced Ethan again. "What about ole Black?"

He shook his head. "Gavin won't be joining us."

Janna didn't appear surprised. "All right," she said. "So how're we gonna do this? I've done a lot of conjurin' in my time, but I ain't never conjured with one other speller before, much less two."

"Mariz has had some thoughts on the matter," Ethan said. "He thinks that the first step might be bringing together our guides and letting them know what it is we wish to do. Based on what I saw last year during my encounter with Caleb Osborne's daughters, I believe he may be right."

Again she nodded. "All right, you two," she called to the men at the nearby table. "Time to be on your way. I have to close for a while."

"But we haven't finished," one of the men said.

"Here are your shillings back," Ethan said, crossing to them and handing each a coin. "Your next meal is at my expense."

The men exchanged looks, but then stood with a scrape of chair legs on the wooden floor, and left the tavern.

Janna followed them to the door and locked it before looking Ethan's way again. "You didn't have to do that. They're regulars; they woulda come back anyway."

"I'm sure they would have. But we don't have time for arguments right now."

Without waiting for her response, Ethan whispered *"Veni ad me."* Come to me.

Reg appeared beside him, glowing bright russet in the dim light of the tavern.

He heard Mariz and Janna summon their spectral guides as well and with a faint thrum of power, two more gleaming figures joined Ethan's ghost. One, an aged African woman, shining pale blue, surveyed the great room, her gaze lingering on Reg and on the other glowing figure. She stood straight-backed and proud, her arms crossed over her chest. The second ghost was the same young man Ethan had seen a few days before. He wore Renaissance clothing, his glow a warm ecru.

"We need to be able to conjure together," Ethan said to Reg, "the way Hester and Molly Osborne did. Conjuring alone, our power won't be enough to defeat Ramsey, but perhaps it will if we can combine our strength. Do you understand what I'm asking of you?"

Reg nodded and turned to the other two ghosts, both of whom hesitated.

Mariz spoke in Portuguese to his ghost, who also nodded once and faced Reg.

"Talk to them," Janna said to her guide. "There's no harm in talkin'."

The blue figure replied with a scowl that was so much like a face Janna might have made, Ethan nearly laughed. But she joined the other two ghosts, and for some time the three figures huddled together. They made not a sound, but Ethan could tell from their aspects and their gestures that they were deep in discussion.

When at last they had finished, Reg faced Ethan once more and gave a single decisive nod.

"All right," Janna said. "What now?"

"Now, I think we try a spell."

Mariz pulled out his blade, but Ethan gave a shake of his head.

"We'll cast with mullein first."

"Why?" Janna glared at him. "You tryin' to protect me, Kaille? You think I'm too old to be spillin' blood for my conjurin's?"

Ethan felt his cheeks color. The truth was he had been thinking just that, and had suggested mullein for her benefit.

"We're gonna need blood to fight Ramsey, ain't we?"

"Aye."

"Then we use blood now." She retrieved a knife from her bar and held it up.

Ethan drew his own blade and pushed up his sleeve.

"What is the spell?" Mariz asked.

"A wind," Ethan said. He glanced Janna's way. "Conjured from blood."

The three of them cut themselves and recited the spell: "*Provoca ventum ex cruore evocatum.*" Summon wind, conjured from blood.

Ethan felt the pulses of power—three of them, separate, though in such quick succession that they were very nearly simultaneous—and knew that they had cast the spell incorrectly. Moreover, none of the conjurings worked; no wind rose in the tavern.

Janna's mouth twisted, like that of a child puzzling over a difficult bit of arithmetic. Mariz watched Ethan.

For his part, Ethan was thinking once more of the Osborne sisters, of how similar all their gestures and actions had been. The spells they recited together had sounded as rehearsed as the repertoire of professional musicians.

"We should be standing together," he said. "Side by side. And our guides should clasp hands."

All of them repositioned themselves.

"What else?" Mariz asked.

"It should all be done precisely. Our cuts should be the same length, the same depth, and simultaneous. And we need to speak the spell as one, at exactly the same time." He turned to Janna. "How do you say it?"

She recited the Latin for him.

"Again," Ethan said.

Janna spoke the spell a second time.

Looking at Mariz, Ethan said, "Can you repeat it the same way?"

"I believe so, yes."

Ethan placed his knife against his skin. "Let's try the spell again."

They cut themselves and spoke the conjuring. But though Ethan could hear that they were more in unison than they had been on their first attempt, he also knew that once again they had failed. He felt three distinct thrums of power, and while a wind did rise, it was no more forceful than a wind he could have summoned on his own.

"That was my fault," Mariz said. "I was too slow with the second half of the spell. Let us try it once more."

"Is that all right with you, Janna?" Ethan asked, eyeing her.

"I don't know," she said, her voice quavering. "I's feelin' a bit faint."

"Are you? Because we can—"

"No, I'm not!" she snapped at him. "Stop treatin' me like some frail old woman!"

Mariz laughed; after a moment Ethan did as well.

Janna tried to look cross, but after a few seconds, she grinned, too. "I ain't that old," she said, the smile lingering. "And I'm a lot stronger than I look."

"All right," Ethan said. "Consider me properly chastened."

He raised his knife once more. Janna and Mariz did the same.

"*Provoca ventum ex cruore evocatum,*" they said as one.

There could be no mistaking the powerful rumble of the spell as it shook the walls of Janna's tavern. Once more a wind rose, this time building into a gale that rattled the door and overturned several tables and chairs.

Mariz was smiling, looking amazed; even Janna beamed.

Ethan raised his knife. "We need to release this wind," he shouted over the howl, "before it tears the Spider apart."

Janna nodded.

They cut themselves, and said together, "*Dimitte ventum ex cruore evocatum.*" Release wind, conjured from blood.

Another pulse rumbled beneath their feet, and the gale died away.

"Well, I'll be," Janna said. "I didn't think we could do this, Kaille. I'm impressed."

"As am I."

He and Mariz righted the tables and chairs.

"Ramsey will have felt those conjurings," Mariz said in a low voice as they worked. "He will be ready."

"Aye, he will," Ethan said. "Perhaps he'll even think twice about facing us."

Mariz did not answer.

"You disagree?"

"I think you are too eager to avoid a fight. That can be an admirable trait, but it is not always appropriate."

Ethan picked up a chair and set it down smartly before looking the man in the eye. "And today it got Nigel killed."

"Nigel's death was not your fault. I would never claim otherwise."

"Would Sephira, if she knew of the choice I made last night?"

"She will not learn of it."

"That's not what I asked."

Mariz faltered. "Yes," he finally said. "I believe she would."

Ethan felt certain that he was right.

"What do we do now?" Janna asked.

Both men turned.

"We go to Tileston's Wharf," Ethan said. "And we talk to Ramsey."

Janna raised an eyebrow. "We talk to him? What if he don't want to talk?"

"Then we cast, just as we have here. But understand, he still controls an army of shades, innocents whose souls he holds in the palm of his hand. If he dies, they're lost."

Mariz and Janna shared a look.

"Kaille—" Janna began.

"I know what you're going to say. But if there's any chance we can save them, I'm going to try."

"All right," she said. "Let's be goin'."

"First, we have to go to the *senhora*'s house," Mariz said.

Janna's eyes narrowed. "What's he talkin' about?" she asked, but Ethan could tell that she already understood.

"He's talking about Sephira. She and her men will be coming with us to the dock."

"And when were you plannin' to tell me that?" Janna asked, fists on her hips.

"At the very last minute, if possible." Ethan assayed a smile.

Janna's expression didn't change.

"We need her, Miss Windcatcher," Mariz said. "Ramsey will have his crew to protect him. We need the *senhora* and her men to help us past them."

"Fine," she said, spitting the word. To Ethan she added pointedly, "You and I will talk later."

Before anyone could say more, Ethan felt the rumble of a spell, distant but powerful.

"Ramsey?" Mariz asked.

The pulse of a second conjuring vibrated in the floor and walls.

"That's strong magick," Janna said. "Must be Ramsey."

Ethan agreed. "We need to go."

They left the Fat Spider, pausing so that Janna could lock the door, and set out for Sephira's estate. Their ghosts remained with them. The conjurers said little as they walked, though they felt one more spell. Ethan thought that the spells were coming from near the waterfront, and though he wasn't certain, he noticed that Janna and Mariz both gazed toward the harbor. When they reached Sephira's estate, Mariz went up the path and entered the house, while Ethan and Janna waited in the lane. Janna eyed the house, her lips pursed. Her blue spectral guide stood with her, also looking up at the house. Reg, Ethan noticed, was watching Janna's ghost,

"This is where she lives?" Janna asked at length.

"Aye."

"Sure is big."

"It is."

"You ever been inside?"

"Aye," Ethan said. "It's nice. Nicer than she deserves."

Janna chuckled. "So why are you workin' with her now?"

"Because I can't beat Ramsey on my own, and she hates him even more than she hates me." He took a long breath, his throat tightening. "Ramsey killed one of her men today. She doesn't know it, but Mariz and I could have killed Ramsey last night. I elected to spare his life, and so Sephira's man is dead."

Janna shook her head. "Life don't always work that way. Sure, if you'd killed Ramsey, he couldn't have killed Sephira's boy. But you don't know what would have happened to him later today or tomorrow or the next day. We can all take blame for one thing or another. Don't make it harder on yourself than it needs to be. You spared a man's life. What he does with his life after, that ain't your responsibility."

Ethan nodded.

Before either of them could say more, the door to the house opened and Sephira's men—at least ten of them—filed out, followed by the Empress herself.

Upon spotting Ethan and Janna, Sephira hesitated for an instant. Lifting her chin, she walked past her men to the street, where she halted, facing Janna.

"Miss Windcatcher," she said.

Janna looked her up and down. "Pryce."

"Have you and I had dealings before?"

"Not directly. But once, a long time ago. A man offered me a lot o' coin to get a girl to like him, and before he could pay me, you did somethin' to him. I don't know what. But I know it was you, and I know that I never saw him or his money again."

"What was his name?"

"Don't know that either," Janna said, still sounding guarded. "For today it don't matter."

Sephira nodded, glancing at Ethan. "You're right. It doesn't. You're ready?" she asked of Ethan.

"Aye. Let's be going."

They set out toward the waterfront, Nap, Gordon, and Afton walking ahead of them, followed by Ethan and Janna, Mariz and Sephira. The rest of Sephira's toughs followed.

As they neared the center of the South End, and the streets grew more crowded, people stopped to stare at their odd procession. For most people, seeing Sephira was an occasion to be remembered. But the sight of her in such strange company—with all of her men, as well as a wizened African woman—would be something people spoke of for days to come.

"You handled that well," Ethan said to Janna, keeping his voice low.

"What? Pryce?" She waved a hand, dismissing the compliment. "I'm just bein' practical. You've seen her house. It ain't smart business to stay mad at a woman who's livin' like that."

Even under these circumstances, Ethan couldn't help but smile. He wondered if Janna wasn't being more clever about her animosity for Sephira than Ethan had been over the years.

As they drew near to the wharves, these other thoughts fled his mind. By returning to the wharf with Sephira, Ethan had all but declared himself at war with Ramsey. On the other hand, the captain himself had done as much in their most recent encounter.

Sephira's men—at least those walking behind him—had been talking among themselves as they walked through the city lanes, but as the wharves loomed before them, the men fell silent. Ethan sensed Sephira's tension as well.

Mariz glanced back at him, and they drew their blades at the same time. Ethan looked at Janna. She already had her knife in hand.

They reached Tileston's Wharf and walked toward the spot where the *Muirenn* had been moored earlier in the day. Halfway out, Ethan halted.

"Where did he go?" Sephira asked. She turned to Ethan. "*Where did he go?*"

Ethan shook his head. He had no idea. All he knew was that Ramsey's ship had vanished.

TWENTY-ONE

want answers, Ethan!"

He stared hard at Sephira. "I have none for you. When I left the wharf this morning, he was here. I expected that he still would be, just as you did."

"Is it possible that he left Boston?" Mariz asked. "He must have known that the *senhora* would be coming for him, and he might have guessed that you and I would work together to destroy him. Perhaps he fled."

Ethan shook his head. "That doesn't sound like Ramsey to me. He wanted to fight me. He believes that he can destroy all of us, and he's eager to prove to us and to himself that he's right."

"One of us can try a findin' spell," Janna said. "Or we can do it together if we have to."

"He will expect that," Mariz said.

Janna shrugged. "So? He knew that we'd come lookin' for him; that's why he ain't here. He's already thinkin' ahead of us. We might as well play his game and find him."

Mariz turned to Ethan, a question in his eyes.

"I'm afraid she's right," Ethan said. "If he's still in Boston, I want to know where. We'll give away our position with the spell, but as Janna says, he already knows where we are. On the other hand, I don't think we have to cast this spell together—I'd rather he didn't know we've mastered that particular skill."

Ethan cut his arm. *"Locus magi ex cruore evocatus."* Location of conjurer, conjured from blood.

The spell hummed in the ground, but otherwise Ethan felt nothing. He glanced at Reg, who merely shrugged. Ethan tried the spell twice more, with the same result.

"We may need to conjure together after all," he said.

"Whatever you intend to do, do it quickly!" Sephira said. "For all we know he's gone already!"

The way she said it, one might have thought this would be the worst thing that could have happened. Ethan thought otherwise.

Mariz stepped closer to Ethan, as did Janna. They raised their blades.

"Ethan!"

He turned with the others. A gray-haired man strode toward them, a hitch in his step.

"Gavin?"

Janna sidled closer to Ethan. "I thought you said he wasn't comin'."

"That's what he told me."

The old captain walked to where they waited, his cheeks red, his face damp with sweat. He was breathing hard, leading Ethan to wonder how far he had walked.

"Good day, Janna," he said.

"Black."

A frown crossed the man's face as he glanced at Sephira and her toughs, but he turned his attention back to Ethan.

"I've just come from Nate Ramsey's ship."

Ethan and Janna shared a look.

"Where?" Ethan asked.

"He's moored at Drake's Wharf."

Drake's Wharf was located near the top of the North End, between Hunt and White's Shipyard and the Charlestown Ferry. It was just about as far from their present location as a ship in Boston could be.

"I don't understand. He's been here on Tileston's Wharf for days. Why now would he choose to go to Drake's Wharf, of all places?"

"I don't know," Gavin said.

"The question I have," Janna said, regarding Gavin with manifest distrust, "is what were you doin' with him in the first place?"

Gavin's face turned an even deeper shade of crimson. "After Ethan talked to me, I felt awful—like a coward. So I put my fears aside and I came here." He looked at Ethan. "This is where you told me he was. And sure enough, there he was on his father's old ship, looking so much like Nathaniel had as a younger man that it broke my heart."

"You spoke to him?" Ethan asked.

Gavin nodded. "He welcomed me aboard the *Muirenn.* His crew looked like they were readying the ship to leave, but I went up to talk to him, to ask him about the things you told me, Ethan. About the graves and my . . . well, the trouble I've been having with my spells. And he said all of it was true. I couldn't believe it. He just admitted everything."

"What did he say, Gavin?" Ethan asked. "What were his exact words?"

Gavin screwed up his face, trying to remember. "He said that he needed the ghosts to bring back his father, and also to make the rest of us weak. He said, 'The weaker you get, the stronger I am. The shades see to that.' I wasn't sure what he meant, but it sounded a lot like what you told me he was doing."

"What else?"

"Well, I tried to talk him out of it, of course. I told him that his father wouldn't approve of what he was doing, and I tried to remind him of the times he and I had spent together, when he was a lad. But he barely heard me. And before I knew it, Ramsey's crew had the ship's sweeps out, and we were leaving the wharf. I got scared and told him that I wanted to go back, and he laughed at me. So, I pulled out my knife, and I tried a spell."

Ethan narrowed his eyes. "What kind of spell?"

"I wanted to hurt him. I tried to set him on fire. I did it twice and both times the spell failed. Ramsey and his men laughed at me. And then Ramsey cast a spell of his own." Gavin rubbed his jaw. "It felt like someone punched me right here. I blacked out, and the next thing I knew, we were at Drake's Wharf, and two of Ramsey's men were carrying me off the ship."

"So all three spells were cast while you were on the water?" Ethan asked.

"Aye."

"Those were the conjurings we felt," Mariz said. "They were powerful because they were cast on water."

"He wants you to go there, Ethan," Gavin said. "He's waiting for you. That was the other thing he said: He wants to destroy you and use your shade to complete his mastery of the realm where our power dwells. And he wants to avenge himself upon you for using the shade of his father against him. He said that, too. If you go there, you'll be helping him. You'll be walking into an ambush."

Ethan shrugged. "I never expected to surprise him."

"You're going anyway?"

"Aye. You've done us a great service, Gavin. And we owe you our thanks for trying to reason with Ramsey. But we have to face him. He's not going to leave Boston of his own accord, and none of us is safe so long as he remains here."

The old man took a long breath. "I should come with you."

"That's not necessary."

"I know. But if something happens to one of you, and I'm not there, I'll never forgive myself. I'm not brave. We both know that. But I need to do this."

Ethan's gaze strayed to Janna. She nodded, but Ethan saw some reluctance in her dark eyes.

"All right." He marked the position of the sun, which had already begun its descent across the western sky. "We've learned to conjure together, to combine our power. We don't have time to teach you. I want to face Ramsey during the day, when he can't call up his army of shades. So you'll watch us and learn, or you'll have to conjure on your own and hope that some of your spells work."

"That's fine," Gavin said.

"Does this mean we're ready to go?" Sephira asked, sounding a bit like a bored child.

"Aye." Ethan stepped closer to her. "You and your men need to take the fight to Ramsey's crew. Leave the captain himself to us. You can't beat him with blades and bullets."

"Why, Ethan, one might almost think you were worried about me."

Ethan didn't so much as quirk a corner of his mouth. "I don't want him dead, at least not until he has released the shades he controls."

"That doesn't matter to me."

"It matters to me. I'm serious, Sephira."

She didn't flinch under his gaze; her eyes were like chips of ice. "So am I."

"Fight the crew," he said again. "Let us handle Ramsey."

Sephira said nothing, but at last she gave a single curt nod.

They returned to the street and began the long march to the North End. Once more, Nap, Gordon, and Afton led the way, followed by Sephira, Ethan and the other conjurers, and the rest of Sephira's toughs. As they walked, Ethan felt several new conjurings thrum in the cobblestones, one after another.

"What do you suppose he is doing?" Mariz asked after the fourth or fifth pulse.

"If I was in his position, and I knew that we were coming, I would cast detection spells, and I would tie each one to a different sort of attack."

"I would do something similar. We should ward ourselves, and we should walk at the fore."

"I agree," Ethan said. He called for Nap and the others to halt.

"What now?" Sephira demanded.

"Ramsey is casting spells," Mariz said. "We need to ward ourselves, and then we will lead the rest of you there."

"Can you ward all of us?" Sephira asked.

"I believe we can." Sephira's man turned to Ethan and Janna. *"Tegimen, omnibus nostrum, ex cruore evocatum."* Warding, all of us, conjured from blood. "That would be the wording, correct?"

Ethan deferred to Janna, who nodded. "Sounds right to me."

They positioned themselves shoulder-to-shoulder, and waited as their spectral guides joined hands.

"Now," Ethan said. They cut themselves and chanted the spell. Their power growled in the street, an answer to Ramsey's conjurings.

"Do you think it worked?" Mariz asked.

"I hope it did. I don't want to cast it again, lest we make it too clear to Ramsey what we've done. Let's go." Ethan strode past Sephira, Nap, and the others, and led them on through the streets. Mariz caught up with him a moment later. When Ethan glanced back, he saw that Janna and Gavin were just behind them.

By now they were in the North End; Copp's Hill loomed before them, the late-afternoon sunlight giving a golden cast to the rooftops of the houses. They walked around the base of the hill on the western side, following Princes Street to Ferry Way, and approaching Drake's Wharf from the south.

As they came to the ferry dock, Ethan felt the brush of a conjuring on his face.

"Spell!" he had time to say.

He tensed, as did Mariz beside him. But no attack came. Instead, Ethan heard a high-pitched keening, like the cry of some wild beast.

"I guess he knows which direction we'll be coming from," Ethan said.

Mariz said nothing. Ethan tightened his grip on his knife.

With his next step, he felt the web of a second detection spell. This time he had no chance to shout a warning. The triggered conjuring slammed into them like a giant hammer, lifting Ethan off his feet so that he flew backward and landed hard on his shoulder. Mariz landed beside him and let out a low groan.

Ethan climbed to his feet and hurried to Janna's side. She lay on the cobblestone, wincing and gripping her arm.

"How bad is it?" Ethan asked.

"Not as bad as it would have been without that wardin'," she said. "That was a blade spell. I could taste it in the magick."

She sat up, rubbed her arm again, and stood. Mariz helped Gavin up. He appeared to be no worse off than Janna. From what Ethan could see, it seemed that Sephira and her men were more surprised than hurt, although they too had been knocked to the ground. If Janna was right—if that had been a blade spell—all of them were fortunate to be alive. If their warding hadn't withstood the assault, they would have been sliced in half.

"That wasn't the last of his spells," Ethan said, drawing the gazes of all of them. "I felt at least six conjurings as we walked here. Assuming that he set detection spells on both sides of the wharf, there could still be another one waiting for us."

"Will your warding hold against another spell?" Sephira asked.

Ethan shrugged. "I hope so."

She rolled her eyes.

They resumed their advance on the wharf, walking with more care this time. Ethan braced himself for the next assault, knowing that this would do him little good.

He was right.

The touch of the third detection spell felt much like the first two. But this time the pulse of power was far stronger, and the conjuring was directed not at them, but at the cobbled lane beneath their feet.

The street bucked like an untamed horse, and a fissure opened down its center. Once more, all of them were thrown to the ground, like a child's dolls strewn across a bedroom floor. At least one of Sephira's men disappeared into the chasm Ramsey's spell had opened.

Gavin lay writhing on the street, clutching his arm to his belly. Janna was slow to get up, but once more she seemed to have escaped serious injury.

To Ethan's relief, Afton and Gordon managed to pull Sephira's man out of the street. And though this third fellow had bloody scrapes on his face and arms, he was able to stand on his own.

"I've had just about enough of this, Ethan," Sephira said, standing and brushing herself off.

"Well, I'll be sure to tell Ramsey as much."

"I believe that was the last of the detection spells," Mariz said. He pointed. They were but a few steps from the edge of Drake's Wharf.

Ethan walked to the pier, knowing that the others would follow him. The *Muirenn* was moored at the base of the wharf, near the street, the ropes holding it to the iron cleats creaking as the ship shifted in the gentle swells of the harbor. He saw no one on board, but still as he approached the vessel he kept his knife poised over his arm.

"Kaille."

He turned at the sound of the voice, which was thin and ghostly. A glowing figure stood near the entrance to a large warehouse. It was dressed in a man's suit, but its face was so desiccated that Ethan couldn't have said for certain if it had been a man or a woman. He assumed that it was an illusion, conjured by Ramsey.

"He's in here," the figure said, gesturing toward the doorway with a skeletal hand.

It didn't wait for his response, but instead turned and shambled into the building.

"Charming," Sephira muttered.

Gavin planted himself in front of Ethan. "Don't go in there. It's not too late for us to leave."

"I've already told you, unless Ramsey is willing to leave Boston, never to return, I have no choice. I won't cede my conjuring power to him, nor will I allow him to torture the families of Boston's dead."

"He'll kill you. He'll kill all of us."

"I expect he'll try. But if you want to leave, Gavin, you should. None of us will think any less of you."

Gavin's gaze wandered over their company, coming to rest at last on Janna. "No," he said. "I won't leave you now."

"Very well."

"I don't relish the idea of stepping into a trap," Sephira said. "Can you set fire to the warehouse and force them out?"

Ethan considered this. "Aye. That's a fine idea." To Mariz and Janna he said, "A fire spell."

The conjurers faced the warehouse, their ghosts beside them, clasping hands once more. They cut themselves and recited in unison, *"Ignis ex cruore evocatus."* Fire, conjured from blood.

Even as Ethan felt the spell humming in his bones, as if he himself were a musical instrument, it occurred to him that this couldn't work, that it was too easy, too expected. He saw flames erupt from the warehouse walls and roof, and then saw them leap, just as abruptly, from the building back toward where they were standing.

For a single horrifying moment, he feared that their warding would fail; it was intended to block the conjurings of others, but might have no effect on their own spells. He felt the heat of those conjured flames on his face, his neck, his hands, and he threw up an arm to shield himself. Mariz and Janna did the same.

The force of the spell hit them an instant after the heat, pounding them like an ocean breaker and leaving them sprawled across the wharf.

Mercifully, none of them was burned, but this time Janna was slow to stir, and when Mariz joined Ethan at her side, he was limping.

"I've had just about enough of this shit," Janna said, as Ethan helped her sit up.

Sephira walked to them, slapping the dust and dirt off of her waist-coat. "What in God's name was that?"

"I would guess that Ramsey warded the warehouse," Ethan said.

"And that possibility never entered your mind?"

"Not soon enough, no."

Gavin sat a few feet away, appearing dazed.

"Maybe he's right," Ethan said to Mariz. "Maybe this isn't a fight we can win."

"I am more inclined to think that you were right when you said that this is not a fight we can avoid."

"I didn't come all this way to turn back now," Janna said, a snarl in her voice. "So help me up, and let's get in there."

Ethan and Mariz helped her to her feet and retrieved her knife, which she had dropped.

To Sephira, Ethan said, "I don't know what other wardings he has in place. Your pistols may not work against him or his men."

"What about our knives?"

"I don't know. These are uncharted waters for me. Ramsey is cunning, he's powerful, and he's girded for a war."

She nodded, thin-lipped. "We'll do what we can with his men. You just find a way to kill him." She looked at Nap and her other men, before facing Ethan again. "We're ready."

Ethan wiped his sweaty palm on his breeches, gripped the hilt of his blade, and led them through the doorway into the warehouse.

The building was mostly empty, save for piles of wooden pallets, barrels, and crates. The captain stood at the far end of the structure, leaning against the wall, a knife in hand. His men were arrayed loosely before him in clusters of three and four. Ethan had no doubt that they had been expecting this confrontation, and were ready for a battle. But he had expected more elaborate preparations; either Ramsey had been careless, or he remained supremely confident. Ethan would have wagered every coin he had on the latter.

Seeing them, Ramsey straightened. "At last. I take it you're done trying to burn down the building?"

His men positioned themselves in a broad arc. As in previous encounters, they were armed with knives and lengths of rope.

Ramsey walked forward, stepping between two of his men and halting a short distance from where Ethan stood. "I'm so glad to see that you survived my detection spells. I would have been disappointed if you hadn't, but of course I couldn't be sure. Your spellmaking doesn't strike me as being particularly reliable."

"Our spells are working well enough," Ethan said. "You might consider that before doing anything rash."

Ramsey's gaze flicked to Mariz and to Janna. "I'm sorry to see you here, Miss Windcatcher. I always liked you. You shouldn't have allowed Kaille to involve you in this matter."

"Nobody talks me into anythin', Nate. You know that about me. You're tryin' to take away my livelihood. You thought I'd let you do that?"

"So," the captain said, his glare settling on Ethan once more. "You've managed to combine your power and conjure as one. And you think that will be enough to defeat me?"

"I think it should be enough to convince you that you can't win. Take your ship and leave Boston, as you and I discussed. This doesn't have to end badly for any of us."

"I will admit that I'm impressed," Ramsey went on, ignoring Ethan's plea. "Blending your conjurings; that's high spellmaking, Kaille. Obviously you've warded yourselves, which affords you some small protection. But this sort of magicking limits you so. Your sole hope in all of this was your numbers: three conjurers against one. If each of you could conjure on your own, I might have cause to fear you. But you can't, can you?"

Ethan looked over at Gavin, who stood beside Janna, and who still appeared to be in a haze.

"We're four conjurers," Ethan said.

A grin split the captain's face. "No, you're really not." And turning to Gavin, he said, "Now."

The glazed look in Gavin's eyes didn't change. But he raised his knife—Ethan thought he intended to cut himself and cast a spell. Instead, he spun with more speed than a man of his age should have possessed, and hacked at Janna with the blade.

Ethan had no time to shout a warning. Janna's eyes widened, and she managed to retreat half a step before the old man's weapon found her. Her movement, however slight, saved her life. Gavin buried the blade to its hilt in her flesh, but it caught her high on her chest, closer to her left shoulder than to her heart.

She cried out. Blood gushed from the wound as she fell to the floor.

Gavin managed to wrench his knife free, drawing a gasp from Janna. He raised the weapon to strike again, but before he could Mariz launched himself at the man, tackling him around the waist. Gavin's knife skittered across the warehouse floor. The old man made a croaking sound and struggled frantically to break free of Mariz's grasp. Mariz reared back and hit him once, twice. Gavin went limp, blood seeping from his nose.

Ethan knelt beside Janna, whose face was contorted in a grimace.

"I'm all right," she said, her teeth gritted, a hand pressed to the bloody wound. "Keep your eyes on Ramsey."

Ethan stood again, the hand holding his knife white-knuckled. "A control spell," he said.

Ramsey shrugged. "Not very imaginative, I know. But I expected you would be warded against my conjurings, and I thought that if one of you died, it might disrupt your plans just a bit."

Ethan held his tongue, but Ramsey's words offered him a ray of hope. If he wanted Janna dead, he must have feared their blended conjurings more than he was willing to admit.

"Did he do everything I told him to?" the captain asked. He glanced at Gavin's prone form, a faint smile on his lips. "Did he tell you that he tried to use conjurings against me, that we laughed at him, that he told me my da would be so disappointed in me?" He looked up, meeting Ethan's gaze. "Did he beg you not to come here, because he knew it was a trap?"

"Can we kill him now, please?" Janna asked. "My chest hurts, and I'm sick to death of listenin' to his nonsense."

Ethan and Mariz cut themselves; Janna had enough blood on her shoulder for several conjurings. Their ghosts clasped hands.

"*Dormite,*" Ethan said. Slumber. "Now."

"*Dormite ex cruore evocatum,*" they said together. Slumber, conjured from blood.

The power of their spell seemed to shake the building to its foundations. Ramsey staggered, as from a blow. He squeezed his eyes shut, forced them open again. "How did you . . ." He staggered a second time, his eyes growing heavy.

And then he laughed. "Sorry. Just having a bit of fun. Admit it, Kaille. For just a instant you thought it had worked."

Ethan didn't respond. Janna stared daggers at the captain.

"Enough," Sephira said. She pulled a pistol from her jacket pocket and in one fluid motion leveled it at Ramsey's chest and fired, the report deafening within the warehouse walls.

Ramsey didn't flinch. And by the time the echo of the gunshot had died away, the lead ball from her pistol was on the floor at the captain's feet. He picked it up, holding it in the palm of his hand.

"It's still warm," he said. He fixed Sephira with a murderous glare. "That was a mistake. After watching your man kill my bosun, did you think that I wouldn't protect myself from your weapons?" He cut his forearm; blood welled from the wound, only to vanish a second later.

Whatever spell he intended for Sephira, he didn't speak it aloud. She grunted at its impact, tumbled to the floor. But nothing else happened to her, and a moment later she was on her feet again.

"You warded them as well," Ramsey said, his voice flat. "How clever of you. It seems I need reinforcements." He cut himself a second time. "*Veni ad me ex regno mortuorum ex cruore evocatum.*" Come to me from the realm of the dead, conjured from blood.

The spell thundered, as powerful as any spell Ethan had ever felt. A shade appeared beside Ramsey and was joined a heartbeat later by two more. Four shades winked into view to Sephira's left, and another three appeared behind them. In mere seconds, they were surrounded by more than a dozen ghosts, and more continued to join them. All of them looked like the decomposed cadavers Ethan had seen at the burying grounds; he could almost smell the fetor of their decay.

He cast a quick glance over his shoulder toward the open door. The sun had not yet set; there was still plenty of daylight.

"That's right, Kaille. I can summon them during the day now. Thanks to my new closest friend, I can do just about anything with them that I want." He gazed past Ethan, triumphant. "Ah, here she is now. The new captain of my army of wraiths."

Ethan turned and felt his body sag. Standing before him, glowing a sickly shade of green, stood the ghost of Patience Walters.

*D*on't let them get too close if you can help it," Ethan said in a raised voice. "They are brutally cold to the touch, perhaps even fatally so if they were reach into your chest or your head."

The shades began to advance on them, their movements slow, unsteady, but inexorable. Now Ethan understood why Ramsey had wanted this confrontation here in the warehouse rather than aboard the *Muirenn*. With so many shades on the ship, the captain's crew would have been in as much peril as Ethan and his companions.

"How do we stop them?" Sephira asked.

"I don't know that we can."

"Sure we can," Janna said. "We stop him, we stop them."

Ramsey chuckled at that.

More shades were still appearing; there had to be close to three dozen of them now. Ethan backed away from one of them and wound up beside Sephira.

"Start with the crew," he said under his breath. "Ramsey will want to protect them. You and your men will be safe from the shades as long as you're fighting. Mariz, Janna and I will stay here. We're the ones Ramsey wants. You go fight."

"Gladly," she said. She put her fingers in her mouth, whistled sharply, and made a small crisp motion with her hand.

Nap barked an order that Ethan couldn't make out, and Sephira's men leapt forward, dodging the shades, and throwing themselves at Ramsey's crew.

Abruptly all was tumult. Sailors confronted toughs. Knife blades flashed; fists connected with flesh and bone with raw, echoing cracks.

Ethan and Mariz helped Janna to her feet; Ethan held on to her so that she wouldn't fall again.

"A binding spell," Mariz whispered. "Now."

He and Ethan cut themselves again; Janna's wound was still oozing blood, so she didn't bother.

"*Corpus alligare ex cruore evocatum.*" Bind body, conjured from blood.

Ramsey frowned at the thrum of power, but once it had passed, he raised a hand and wriggled his fingers. "I don't think that worked. You should try something more like this."

He swiped his blade across his arm. "*Vola ex cruore evocatum.*" Fly, conjured from blood.

One of the wooden barrels surged toward them. Ethan and Mariz dropped to the floor, dragging Janna down with them. The barrel soared over their heads with an audible whoosh, crashed into the far wall, and shattered.

Already, Ramsey had more blood on his arm. He cast the same spell a second time, and several crates leaped from their piles, arced across the warehouse, and rained down on them. Ethan and Mariz shielded Janna with their bodies, and so were battered by the containers.

His back and shoulders aching, Ethan could see that the shades were converging on where they lay. And he knew that Ramsey would have no trouble keeping them occupied until the ghosts reached them.

He heard a low moan. Gavin was waking up. The old man struggled to his feet and lurched to where his blade had fallen.

"Ah, Gavin," Ramsey said. "Care to finish what you started?"

Gavin bent and picked up the knife, reeling as he straightened once more. But instead of attacking Ethan and the others, he advanced on Ramsey, his blade raised.

"Gavin, no!"

"You used a control spell on me, you whelp!" Gavin said, ignoring Ethan's plea.

"Yes, I did. It was as easy as this."

He cut himself again. *"Obsequere meae voluntati ex cruore evocatum."* Submit to my will, conjured from blood.

Control conjurings usually demanded stronger sources; years before, Ethan had fought a conjurer who used killing spells to cast them. But Ramsey had deepened his power to the point where he could cast them with blood.

On the other hand, the warding Ethan had cast still offered Gavin some protection. If not for the earlier control spell, that might have been enough to protect him. But Gavin remained partially under the captain's thrall, and so this new spell ensnared him again.

"Put down your knife," Ramsey said.

Gavin hesitated, his blade hand trembling.

"I said put it down!"

Beads of sweat broke out on the old man's brow, but the knife slipped from his fingers.

"Now . . ." Ramsey glanced around and pointed to a shade just a few strides from where Gavin stood. She was hideous; the skin on her face was putrified and pitted. Her dress was stained through from her rotting body. "Embrace her."

"No!" Ethan shouted.

Ramsey's blade flashed. *"Vola ex cruore evocatum."*

More crates soared toward them. Ethan had no choice but to protect Janna and shield his head and neck from the containers.

Peering out at Gavin as the crates rained down on him, Ethan saw the man face the shade. His entire body appeared to be quaking; Ethan thought that he was fighting Ramsey's control spell. He didn't take a step forward, but the ghostly form continued to drift toward him. She held her arms open, a leering grin on her gruesome visage.

"Embrace her!" Ramsey shouted again.

Gavin's arms began to open, slowly, as if they were being prised apart. He squeezed his eyes shut, tears coursing down his cheeks.

The last of the crates tumbled over Ethan's back, and he jumped to his feet.

But by then the shade had reached Gavin. At her first touch, the old man screamed, his head thrown back, his face a mask of agony. The shade enveloped him in her grasp, cutting short Gavin's howl. His trembling ceased. The shade seemed to pass through him, and when she had cleared the back of his body, Gavin fell forward, as rigid as an iron post. He made no effort to protect himself as he fell. Ethan guessed that he was dead before he hit the ground.

Reaching Gavin at last, Ethan found him frigid to the touch. He turned him over. The man's face remained twisted from his final moments of torment. The sweat on his brow had turned to ice.

"Kaille!" Mariz called.

He and Janna were standing again, but the other shades continued to converge on them. If Ethan didn't return to them now, he might not be able to at all. They would be unable to conjure together.

With a last glance down at Gavin, Ethan hurried back to the other conjurers. Patience's ghost was but a short distance from them. He stared keenly at her, hoping that he might see some hint of recognition in her gleaming eyes, some sign that Ramsey's control over her was less than absolute. But she barely noticed him; she gave no sign that she knew him for the friend he had been to her when she lived.

"What spell do you wanna try now?" Janna asked, her voice low. "Not that it's gonna work." Her eyes met Ethan's. "He's too strong, Kaille."

"Aye, I am," Ramsey said. "And when all of you are dead, you and Gavin will join Patience among my army of shades. With the ghosts of five conjurers under my control, I'll be able to do whatever I want. No other conjurers will be able to stand against me, and no spells will be beyond my abilities." He smiled. "I'd enlist Gavin in my cause now, but as you know, the process is rather involved, and I doubt you'd grant me the opportunity."

"What spell?" Janna asked again, with more urgency.

You should try something like this, Ramsey had said when he threw the first barrel at them. And he was right. Spells aimed at Ramsey wouldn't work; he was warded. Sephira's bullet hadn't harmed him, which meant that barrels and crates might not even work. But something similar to Ramsey's third detection spell could.

"The floor," Ethan mouthed silently.

Comprehension crept over Janna's face.

The three of them cut themselves. "*Aperi hiatum ex cruore evocatum.*" Open chasm, conjured from blood.

The rumble of their spell was swallowed by the rending of wood and stone as the floor and ground beneath Ramsey's feet split open. The captain tried to leap to safety, but this once Ethan, Janna, and Mariz had caught him unawares, and the opening had formed too quickly. He teetered at the edge before falling in.

The opening was not deep, and the harbor lay beneath the warehouse and the wharf; the fall wouldn't kill him. But Ethan hoped it would give them time to cast a second spell that would.

"Now close it!" Mariz said. "We can crush him, or drown him."

"No!" Ethan shook his head. "Patience and the others! I don't want them lost!"

"They're lost already!" Janna said. "This is our one chance. He has to die, Kaille. There's no other way."

Ethan stared at her, his heart laboring. Had it been anyone else, he would have argued further. He had sworn that he would do all he could to help those whose graves had been violated. He had promised Ruth and Darcy that he would not allow any harm to come to Patience. But after watching what he had done to Gavin, he knew that there could be no reasoning with the man. Janna was right: This might well be their only chance to finish him.

"Very well," he whispered, the words like shards of glass in his mouth.

They cut themselves again. *"Occlude hiatum ex cruore evocatum."* Close chasm, conjured from blood.

Their spell pulsed, and the gap in the middle of the warehouse began to close, like a wound healing under a spellmaker's touch.

Sephira and her men continued to battle Ramsey's crew, but Ethan could see that the sailors were falling back. Even the shades had halted their advance. Without Ramsey to guide them—

Before Ethan could finish the thought, the building's floor, which had almost mended itself, exploded. Ethan and his companions were tossed back and slammed to the ground. Splintered wood and jagged pieces of fill and rock rained down on them, and a cloud of dust billowed through the warehouse.

Ethan pushed himself to his feet. Through the haze of debris, he saw a blood-streaked arm emerge from the crater that had formed in the warehouse floor. A moment later a leg hooked itself over the lip of the hole.

Ethan stumbled to where Janna lay and tried to rouse her. There was a gash on her temple, and the wound on her chest had started to bleed again. She was covered with dust and splinters. He could see that she still breathed, but she didn't stir. A short distance away, Mariz sat up and felt around for his spectacles. Finding them, he pushed them onto the bridge of his nose and looked around.

When he spotted Ethan and Janna, he asked, "Is she dead?"

"No. But I can't wake her."

A ragged cheer went up from Ramsey's crew. Ethan knew why before he looked.

Ramsey stood beside the pit from which he had emerged, his fists clenched, his clothes soaked and ragged. An instant later, the blood vanished from his arm. Fire shot up out of the floor all around Ethan, the blaze building until it towered over his head. Flames licked at Janna as well. He pulled her away from the nearest of them, though in truth, the circle of fire was so tight that he couldn't do much to protect her. The heat from the flames was almost unbearable.

"Kaille!" Mariz called.

"We're all right. For now at least."

"I cannot move," Mariz said. "There is fire all around me."

Of course. If they couldn't see each other, they couldn't conjure together and Ramsey would have nothing to fear from them. Ethan had actually allowed himself to believe that they had defeated the captain. He'd been a fool.

And yet, as bad as circumstances seemed, an instant later they grew far worse.

He saw movement out of the corner of his eye; a variation in the circle of flame within which he was trapped. An insubstantial hand. Then an arm. And soon the form of a shade had shuffled through the fire, seemingly unaffected by the heat. It advanced on him and on Janna, who still had not woken.

"Kaille!" Mariz called.

"I know!"

He wasn't sure how to fight the wraith; he knew only that he couldn't allow it to touch him or Janna, and that they couldn't avoid the shade for long in this hellish prison.

Knowing he had no choice, he dropped to one knee and gathered Janna in his arms. Standing again, he pulled her close to him, took a deep breath, and rushed at the wall of fire.

It was more dense than he had expected. He could feel the blaze searing his skin; he knew that his clothes and hair were burning. But he couldn't stop, and he couldn't go back. It took him no more than a second to clear the flames, but it felt like far longer, and upon emerging from the fire, he had to spin away from another shade that loomed just in front of him.

He stumbled, fell. Janna slipped from his arms. Her dress was on fire; so was his shirt. He batted at the flames on Janna until they were out, and threw himself to the ground and rolled. When at last he was no longer burning, he stopped and lay still on his back, his eyes closed, his chest rising and falling, his heart racing.

"I can do that again any time I choose," Ramsey said.

Ethan forced himself up.

Mariz burst through the wall of fire to Ethan's left, rolled, and jumped to his feet, his shirt sleeve charred and smoking, but no longer ablaze.

Moments later a shade slipped through the same fire. Looking behind him, Ethan saw that the ghost that had menaced him had also emerged from within the flames. Other shades were closing on them as well, including that of Patience.

"How do you wish to die, Kaille?" Ramsey asked. "Burning? Freezing? Something in between?"

Mariz cut his forearm and looked expectantly at Ethan. Ethan cut himself as well.

"We'll die fighting you," Ethan said.

"Bravely said. But those are empty words, and we all know it."

Ethan had one more weapon at his disposal. He had thought of using it sooner, but had not wanted to enrage Ramsey further and thus place Janna in even more danger. Now, though, he had little choice.

"A summoning," Ethan whispered to Mariz, staring hard at him. "Do you understand?"

Mariz's eyes widened. "But I don't know the name."

"He's his namesake."

The conjurer nodded.

Together they said, *"Provocamus te, Nathaniel Ramsey, ex regno mortuo-rum, ex cruore evocatum."* We summon thee, Nathaniel Ramsey, from the realm of the dead, conjured in blood.

Ethan had always used mullein for such summoning spells, believ-ing that it was safer to use a protective herb than blood in dealing with the dead. They hadn't that luxury this time, and Ethan could no longer concern himself with what was or wasn't safe.

The spell thrummed and Nathaniel Ramsey appeared before them. He glanced at Ethan, but then turned, seeming to know that his son was there.

The other shades halted. The younger Ramsey paled.

"I told you never to do this again!" he said, death in his voice.

"Aye," Ethan said. "I don't much care. I won't release him. If you want to kill me, you'll have to do it with your father's spirit watching, knowing that you're dooming him as well."

"Can't you fight him?" Ramsey asked his father, desperation in his voice. He pointed at Uncle Reg. "Can't you do something to his ghost?" He clenched his fists again. "I'm doing this for you!" he shouted. "You'll be with me soon! Alive again!"

The shade stared back at his son briefly before turning and walking to where Gavin's body lay. He stood over the dead man, shaking his head.

"He betrayed you at the end," Ramsey said. There was a plea in his voice. "He could have helped you; he could have saved you. But he didn't."

The shade gave no indication that he had heard.

Ramsey cut his arm. *"Interfice eos ex cruore evocatum!"* he said. Kill them, conjured from blood!

The other shades jerked into motion and began to converge on them once more. Mariz sidled closer to him.

"Another spell, Kaille. Quickly!"

The shades moved slowly, but they were near enough now that in just a few seconds they could kill the conjurers much as the other wraith had killed Gavin. But that, Ethan realized, was not their purpose. They were converging not only on Ethan and Mariz, but also on Uncle Reg and Mariz's ghost. If the shades could destroy them, Ethan and Mariz would be robbed of their powers, and the ghost of Nathaniel Ramsey would be released from their summons.

Ethan said nothing, but turned to Patience's ghost. She would be one of the first shades to reach them. Ramsey had cast a spell to make them appear, and had cast again just now to order them back into motion. Did the symbol he had carved in the cadavers require a spell in order to work? And if so, was it possible that the spell Ethan had carved into Patience's body worked the same way?

"Now, Kaille!" Mariz said, his voice rising.

What would the wording be? How had he cast that initial spell? The Latin, roughly translated, had said, *Protect this corpse and its spirit from magick, keep it free from the influence of others, conjured in herbs and this symbol.* So a spell now . . .

Ethan slashed at his arm. "There's no time to teach you," he said. "We just have to hope that I can conjure on my own this one time."

Mariz cut his arm too, and held it out just beside Ethan's. "I do not know what you are doing, but perhaps this will help."

Ethan nodded. *"Tega hunc spiritum contra alienam auctoritatem, ex cruore nostro et signo meo evocatum."* Protect this spirit from the influence of others, conjured from our blood and my symbol.

The spell pealed like a church bell and wiped the blood from their forearms. But still the shades closed in on them. One reached out a translucent hand and touched Ethan's neck. He gasped, jerked away.

"That didn't seem to help you very much, Kaille!" Ramsey called.

Ethan cut himself again, thinking that perhaps he had time to try the spell one last time.

But before he could speak the incantation, the shade of Patience Walters halted. Her eyes changed; they didn't grow dimmer or brighter, but they seemed to focus once more. She could see him.

"Patience?" Ethan whispered.

She hesitated, nodded. She raised a hand, and the other shades halted their advance.

"What are you doing?" Ramsey demanded. "I told you to kill them!"

Patience gestured for the other shades to back away, and almost immediately they began to do so.

Ramsey dragged his blade across his arm and shouted out the same killing command he had given seconds before. The conjuring hummed in the floor and walls, but the shades didn't obey him.

"What have you done, Kaille?"

"They're not yours to control anymore."

"Of course they are! My symbol is on them! They can't refuse me!"

"They have a new captain. You said so yourself."

"And she's marked as mine, just like the rest!"

"I marked her before you did. And my symbol keeps her free."

Ramsey's mouth fell open. "Impossible!" he said, breathing the word. "I would have seen it!"

"Would you, Ramsey? Did you really look at her, or did you merely defile her grave, mutilate her corpse, and claim her as your own?"

The captain said nothing.

Ethan still had blood on his arm. *"Ignis ex cruore evocatus!"* Fire, conjured from blood!

Ramsey staggered as from a blow, and nearly toppled back into the hole in the floor from which he had climbed. But his warding still held. He retreated to the other side of the pit, and cut his arm, even as Ethan and Mariz cut theirs again.

Sephira and her men still fought the crew of the *Muirenn*. Several men lay on the floor; some of them bled, others appeared to have broken limbs. Several weren't moving at all; Ethan couldn't tell if they were dead or unconscious. The fight still seemed to be going Sephira's way.

Ethan faced Patience. "Don't let the shades kill anyone," he said. "But don't let Ramsey out of here, either. If he escapes he'll find a way to control you again, and I'm not sure I can save you a second time."

She nodded and turned away from him, encompassing the other ghosts in her gaze. Seconds later, the shades began to fan out across the warehouse floor. Ramsey backed away from them, his eyes wide as they darted from one decayed visage to another.

One of the shades broke away from the others, and moved to Ramsey's side: the ghost of Nathaniel Ramsey. The others, including Patience, stopped.

"If you release them, Ramsey, I'll release your father. We still have to end this, one way or another, but he doesn't have to watch it all."

"All right," the captain said. "I'll send them away. You do the same."

"No. I'm not talking about making your shades disappear for a while. I want you to release them. Use a conjuring to end your mastery of that symbol you carved into them, and tell what's left of your crew to unload from your ship the body parts you stole."

Ramsey shook his head. "I won't do that."

"Then your father will watch you die. Patience."

The shade looked back at him.

Ethan nodded once, and the shades resumed their advance. Ramsey backed away, his father keeping pace with him.

"I don't like this, Ethan," Sephira called, eyeing the shades.

There didn't appear to be a back door to the warehouse, something Ethan hadn't noticed before. And neither Sephira and her men nor the crew of the *Muirenn* could reach the front of the building without passing uncomfortably close to the wraiths.

"Help them," Ethan said to Mariz. "I'll stay with Ramsey."

Mariz nodded and ran to join Sephira.

"Just you and me now, eh?" Ramsey asked, smiling but looking pale. "Good. That's what I've wanted all along."

Power thrummed and the building shook. Mariz had broken a large hole in the side of the building. Sephira and her men streamed out into the gloaming, as did most of Ramsey's crew. Both sides helped up some of the men who lay on the floor. But others they left. It seemed that both Sephira and Ramsey had lost more men this day.

"Captain?" one of them called, lingering beside the gap in the wall.

"Go!" Ramsey said.

"Tell him to return the body parts, Ramsey. Let me send your father away."

"I won't."

The sailor watched them for another moment before leaving the building. Mariz stared after the man, then turned and walked back toward Ethan and Ramsey, cutting his arm again as he did.

"I thought you were going to fight me alone, Kaille? Are you that afraid of me?"

"Your problem, Ramsey, is that you hate me so much you've allowed that hatred to consume you. I'm trying to bring peace to the shades you've awakened, and to the families of the dead. That's why I'm here. And if I have to enlist a hundred conjurers to help me defeat you, that's what I'll do. You don't control these souls anymore. I can kill you if I want. No one will be lost. I'm offering you one last chance to surrender and live."

The shades had the captain surrounded now, though they kept their distance. He was in no imminent danger from them, but he was very much trapped.

"You think you've beaten me," he said. "You think that without the shades, I'm just another conjurer, like you and your friend here. You're wrong. I'm still stronger than both of you, and I will never surrender to you."

He raised his arm, which still was still bloody. "*Vola ex cruore evocatum.*"

Ethan ducked out of instinct, but the barrel that flew from the far wall didn't move in his direction. Instead, it soared toward Janna.

"*Subsiste!*" Ramsey said as it reached her. Stop!

And it did. The barrel remained suspended perhaps ten feet above Janna's motionless form.

"If I die, it falls on her," Ramsey said. "At the first word of Latin you speak, it falls on her. If you go near her or come closer to me, or if even one of those shades moves a finger, she dies." He grinned. "Your move, Kaille."

Chapter
Twenty-three

The barrel revolved slowly, but it did not otherwise move. And neither did Janna.

"Now, release my father."

Ramsey might as well have had a pistol aimed at Ethan's head, full-cocked and ready to fire.

"I swear, I'll kill her if you don't."

"No, he will not," Mariz said before Ethan could answer. "She is all he has. If he kills her, we kill him, and this is over. He will not spend his one advantage for the benefit of his father's ghost. He is afraid to die; I can see it in his eyes. He will keep Janna alive until he is free of this place. In the end, that is all he cares about."

Ramsey sliced his forearm again. *"Discuti ex cruore evocatum!"* Shatter, conjured from blood!

Mariz fell back, as if he had been punched in the jaw. But immediately he climbed to his feet once more. The warding the three of them had cast had proven more durable and more powerful than any warding Ethan had ever cast on his own. Without it, Ramsey would have killed all of them by now. And though he hadn't managed to kill Mariz, it didn't escape Ethan's notice that he could cast spells while also holding that barrel over Janna. He might have been desperate and outnumbered, but he remained dangerously powerful.

"I do not think he liked what I had to say. Perhaps there was too much truth to it, yes?"

"Another word out of you, and I swear I'll kill her!"

The shade of Ramsey's father had been watching all of this, and now he left Ramsey's side.

"Father, where are you going?"

They shade didn't falter, but walked to where Patience stood, turned, and took his place next to her, his arms crossed over his chest as he glowered at his son.

"Don't you understand?" Ramsey said. "I'm doing this for you! I'm going to bring you back, and together we'll be able to cast any spell, avenge every wrong!"

Ethan lowered his gaze. He couldn't allow to Ramsey to leave this place as long as he still had the means to control the shades, and he was prepared to kill the captain if he had to. But just then, he couldn't bear the pain he saw in Ramsey's eyes.

"They're our enemies," Ramsey said, his voice dropping almost to a whisper. "You may not see it, but that's all right. I know what they are, and I'll fight them, even if you won't."

"I can let him go, Ramsey," Ethan said, speaking softly. "Do what I've asked of you, and he won't have to see any more of this."

"Stop!" Ramsey shouted, the word echoing through the building. "Don't say another word, or I really will kill her! I need . . . Just don't say another word!"

"*Discuti ex cruore evocatum.*" Shatter, conjured from blood.

The voice and the spell came from behind them, and was followed an instant after by a violent rending of wood. Scraps of the suspended barrel scattered over the floor of the warehouse, and the metal stays, twisted nearly beyond recognition, fell with a loud clatter.

"Those shouldn't be hangin' in the air like that," Janna said, sitting up. "A person could get hurt." She stood, tottered, but kept her feet and walked unsteadily to join Ethan and Mariz. "If you need me, I can conjure more."

"We don't need to conjure as one anymore," Ethan said, keeping his gaze fixed on Ramsey. "But we might need a spell or two before this is over."

"Fine," Ramsey said. "I'll release them, and you can let my father go."

"And the body parts you stole?"

"I'll use an illusion spell now to tell my crew to unload them. If you don't believe me, use an illusion spell of your own to watch."

"Do not trust him, Kaille," Mariz said. "Even now, he tries to deceive us."

Janna nodded, her eyes on the captain. "I agree."

In recent days, Ethan had been too trusting, too willing to believe that he could reason with Ramsey. He wasn't about to make the same mistake. Ramsey had lost control of the shades; he could not escape unless he first rid himself of his ghosts. He was prepared to fight to the death, and he didn't want his father to bear witness to whatever end awaited him.

Ethan understood this. But from the outset of this ordeal, his first goal had been to win the freedom of the dead, so that they could rest once more. He couldn't waste this opportunity.

"All right," Ethan said. "I'll cast with you. Once I see you give the order to your men, I'll release your father."

Janna gripped his arm. "Kaille, no!"

"We cannot let you do this," Mariz said.

"You have to! As long as he has those body parts, he can do this again. He can keep all of us from conjuring."

Mariz shook his head. "Not if he is dead. Order the shades to kill him, just as he did to your friend, Gavin. Then this will be over."

Hearing this, the shade of Nathaniel Ramsey drew a knife from his belt, and lunged at Patience, seeking to stab her through the heart. Ethan didn't know what damage one shade could do to another, but Patience leaped back out of Nathaniel's reach. The other shades scattered, as frightened as she of the old captain's wrath.

And perhaps sensing that this was his one chance to get away, Ramsey cut himself again. *"Ignis ex cruore evocatus!"* Fire, conjured from blood!

A great ball of flame, seething and swirling, the color of a setting sun, burst from his hand, soared upward and crashed into the warehouse ceiling. The flames spread as if fueled by oil, and smoke began to fill the building.

Ramsey sprinted toward the hole in the wall through which Sephira and the others had escaped.

Ethan slashed his forearm. *"Pugnus ex cruore evocatus!"* Fist, conjured from blood!

He needed only to knock the captain off balance, and this spell did.

Ethan's conjured fist struck Ramsey in the back and sent him sprawling onto the floor, his arms splayed.

Nathaniel Ramsey's shade still had his knife out, and was stalking Patience's ghost. Ethan thought that if he managed to destroy her, it might well return control of the other shades to Ramsey.

He cut himself again. *"Dimitto te, Nathaniel Ramsey, ex cruore evocatum."* I release you, Nathaniel Ramsey, conjured from blood.

He didn't usually use blood when dismissing spirits, but he feared that Captain Ramsey would resist a less powerful dismissal. As it was, at the thrum of power, the shade whirled toward Ethan, eyes blazing, and started in his direction. But the ghost had already started to fade; he was gone well before he reached Ethan.

Patience marshaled the other shades once more. Ramsey was back on his feet, but Mariz blocked his path to the opening in the wall. Janna and Ethan both stood between the captain and the door.

"You can't win, Ramsey," Ethan said, walking toward him.

"I don't have to win. All I need to do is not lose."

He backed away from Mariz, and at the same time carved another wound in his arm, which was already livid from all the spells he had cast.

He spoke a second fire spell, throwing the flame at another section of the ceiling. His knife flashed again, and he set the nearest wall ablaze. Twice more he cut himself and cast fire spells. The warehouse was fully engulfed now; flames roared, and black smoke filled the building, making Ethan's eyes and throat burn. The heat was intensifying. The ceiling groaned; it would collapse before long.

And still Ramsey cast more spells.

"You'll kill us all!" Ethan shouted at him.

"If I have to!"

"I can't let you leave, Ramsey! Not unless you get your men to unload the body parts."

"You do what you have to, Kaille. I'll do the same."

He cut himself yet again.

Before he could cast, Ethan spoke a spell of his own: a shatter spell that he hoped would break Ramsey's arm and incapacitate him. But though his spell hammered at the captain, it didn't fell him or break a bone, or keep him from conjuring another mass of flame, which he sent spiraling upward into the ceiling and through. Burning pieces of wood pelted down onto them all.

Janna coughed, clutching at her chest.

"Get her out of here, Mariz!"

"I don't need—" Another fit of coughing cut off her objections.

"Patience!" Ethan called.

The shade faced him, her expression pained. She seemed to know before he spoke what he would say. She had been a gentle soul in life; now he would ask her to kill.

"He can't be allowed to leave. Do you understand?"

She nodded.

"*Dimitto omnes eorum ex cruore evocatos!*" Ramsey said, his conjuring interrupted by a paroxysm of coughing of his own. I release all of them, conjured from blood!

Ethan felt the spell, but the shades remained. It seemed that when the captain lost control of them, he also lost his ability to send them away.

Mariz and Janna had almost reached the door. Ethan had no desire to die in this inferno, but he had to be sure that Ramsey didn't find a way out.

In that instant, though, with an unearthly growl and a shower of sparks and blackened, fiery wood, the center of the roof gave way. Another part of the roof nearer to where Ethan stood did the same. He heard Mariz and Janna calling his name, but he couldn't see them, and he had no clear path to either the door or the gap.

Ramsey had cut his arm again and turned toward the nearest wall.

"*Discuti ex cruore evocatum!*" he shouted over the roar of the fire. Shatter, conjured from blood.

"Ramsey, no!"

No doubt he was trying to break the wall, to forge a path to safety. Instead, he brought down what was left of the ceiling, as well as the nearest walls. Ethan jumped back, stumbled over a fallen beam, which was blackened and still aflame, and fell, nearly landing on a pile of burning timber. Still, he saw Ramsey go down, saw fiery debris come down on top of him. He shouted the captain's name, but heard no response.

Another section of wall caved in. Ethan scrambled to his feet. He couldn't see much, and he could barely breathe. He felt the pulse of a spell and wondered if it had come from Ramsey, struggling to get free, or Mariz, trying to reach him.

He turned a quick circle, saw nothing but flame and charred wood. And Patience, beckoning to him. He ran toward her, and realized that she might well have saved his life. There was a path, barely; he could see no way through that wouldn't leave him burned. But if he remained where he was, he was a dead man.

He cut his arm. *"Tegimen contra ignem ex cruore evocatum."* Protection from fire, conjured from blood.

Though he felt the spell, he had no idea if it would work; he had never attempted such a conjuring. He pulled off his waistcoat, and wrapped it around his right arm. And with one last deep breath, he sprinted into the narrow gap Patience's shade had pointed out to him.

Before he had taken more than a half dozen steps, he was convinced that he had made a grave mistake. He no longer could find the path he had spotted mere moments before. He could hardly see for the bitter smoke; his eyes stung and tears coursed down his cheeks. Heat clawed at him, searing every bit of exposed skin. He used his wrapped arm to bat aside burning planks that got in his way, but it seemed that flame and smoldering wood were everywhere.

I'm going to die here.

Every breath scorched his throat, his lungs. Still he fought on, but his heart labored in his chest, as much from grief as from fear.

Pushing through what had become a wall of burning wood, he abruptly found himself at the edge of the inferno. He stumbled into the open, cool air a balm on his face and neck, his hands and arms. He managed one more step and collapsed.

Strong hands grabbed hold of his arms and dragged him on, until the crackling of wood and the hissing of flames were lost to the soft lapping of waves at timbers. Ethan opened his eyes just as Nap and Gordon set him down beside Janna.

He croaked a "Thank you." Neither man said a word.

"You need healing," Janna said. She looked at him more closely. "At least I thought you would."

"I cast a protection spell to guard me from the flames. I didn't think it worked. I felt like I was on fire."

"You're bright red. But there's no blisterin' and no blackened skin." She glanced up at his head and grinned. "Your hair didn't even get singed. That's some good conjurin', Kaille."

"Thanks," Ethan said, looking back toward the burning warehouse. "Do you think he's still in there?"

"Ramsey?"

"Aye."

"I didn't see him come out, and his men are still watchin' for him. I think he's dead. I hope he is."

Ethan nodded, though he didn't actually believe that Ramsey had died. Not yet. As long as Patience's shade and the ghosts of the others lingered in the warehouse, Ramsey still lived, since his conjurings had awakened them. He watched the burning building for signs of the shades, but he couldn't see for the smoke and flames. He knew only that Patience had still been there seconds before.

Men—laborers and sailors—had formed lines leading from the edge of the wharf to the burning warehouse, and were passing buckets of water to those nearest the flames. The building itself was too far gone to save, but there were warehouses on either side of it that needed to be protected. Ethan knew that he should get up and help douse the fire, but he couldn't bring himself to move.

"You just rest," Janna said, seeming to read his thoughts. "You've done enough."

Sephira's men, including Mariz, had joined the effort, as had several of Ramsey's crew. It was odd to see them working together, so soon after they had been pummeling one another.

"I shoulda known that man would come around here eventually."

Ethan twisted to follow the direction of Janna's gaze. Sheriff Greenleaf had reached the wharf and was striding in their direction, a scornful look on his face. Several men of the watch walked behind him. Ethan knew that he would be searching for someone to blame for the fire and the additional deaths; without Ramsey here, the sheriff would lay on him responsibility for all that had happened.

"What did you do now, Kaille?" Greenleaf called while still several yards away. The man was predictable.

"I fought Ramsey," Ethan said, making no effort to get up. "And I barely escaped the warehouse when he set it on fire."

"You look none the worse for wear."

"I was fortunate."

"Aye," the sheriff said, his voice cold. "It seems to me that you're always fortunate. Some would call that coincidence. Others might credit your bonny luck to something darker."

Ethan said nothing, but continued to stare up at the man.

"Where's Ramsey?" the sheriff asked after some time.

Ethan pointed at the fire. "He's in there."

"He's dead?"

"I didn't say that."

"But surely if he's . . ." Comprehension darkened Greenleaf's face. He shook his head. "Damn you and your kind."

"If it wasn't for our kind, you woulda had to fight Ramsey yourself," Janna said, her scowl no less intimidating than the sheriff's. "How do you think that woulda gone?"

"Janna . . ." Ethan said, his voice low.

The sheriff stared down his nose at her. "You should watch yourself, woman. You keep saying things like that, and you may wind up with a noose around your neck."

Her smile was so pleasant one might have thought they were discussing the sunset. "I ain't never seen a rope that would hold me or a man brave enough to try to put one around my neck. And I sure don't see one now."

Even in the failing light, Ethan could tell that Greenleaf's cheeks had reddened.

But the way the sheriff glowered at Ethan, one might have thought that he had spoken and not Janna. "Don't leave," he said. To the men of the watch, he added, "Make sure he doesn't go anywhere." He stalked off toward Sephira.

"You shouldn't goad him like that," Ethan said, his voice low.

"Why not? He ain't gonna hang an old woman, and even if he tried, it wouldn't work."

"No, but he might hang me."

"That wouldn't work, either, now would it? Sometimes it seems like you forget you're a speller."

Ethan had to laugh.

Janna watched the sheriff and Sephira. "What do you suppose they're talkin' about?"

"I'm sure Greenleaf is looking for some way to blame me for all of this. And if Sephira is feeling less than charitable, she might just help him."

"I don't think so. I'm a good judge of people's character, and I think you can trust her."

Ethan almost laughed again. Yesterday she had hated Sephira more than anyone in the world. From the way she was talking now, one might have thought that they were old friends.

"I should have asked before, Janna. Do you need healing?"

She shook her head. "Mariz took care of me. I just need rest."

Rest sounded good.

Greenleaf continued to talk to Sephira, though he looked less happy with every word she said. When he made his way back to where Ethan and Janna were sitting, he appeared so forlorn it warmed Ethan's heart.

"You're free to go," he said. "Both of you." He leveled a finger at Ethan. "But I want to see you back here tomorrow. This is still your mess, and I'm going to have more questions for you before long."

"I'll come back in the morning," Ethan said.

He climbed to his feet, his muscles sore, his legs leaden. He had escaped the warehouse without serious burns, but he had been hammered by Ramsey's spells again and again. He felt bruised, beaten.

Before he could walk away, Greenleaf said, "He couldn't really be alive, could he?" He nodded toward the warehouse, which still burned. The flames had died down, but the embers glowed balefully in the twilight. "Look at that. If he was trapped in there, he would have to be dead. Even a witch can be burned." He faced Ethan. After a brief silence, he said, "I want an answer, Kaille."

"I don't have one."

"Could you have survived a fire like that?"

"No. But I'm not a witch." And with that, Ethan turned from him and began the long walk back to the Dowser.

Chapter
TWENTY-FOUR

Stepping into the Dowsing Rod was like returning home after a years-long voyage. Ethan was so relieved to be back in the tavern that his legs almost gave out beneath him before he reached the bar. Too late, he realized that while he had come through the fire relatively unscathed, his clothes had not. His waistcoat had been burned beyond hope of mending, and he had left it at the wharf. His shirt was blackened on the sleeves and stained everywhere else, and his breeches looked no better.

Before he could leave the tavern, Kannice spotted him and came out from behind the bar, concern etched on her face.

"You've looked better," she said, taking his hand.

"Aye. I've felt better as well."

She pulled him toward an empty table, at the same time signaling to Kelf.

"Ale and chowder; that's what you need."

He should have been famished; he couldn't remember his last meal. But all he wanted to do was sleep. He kept his mouth shut, though; Kannice had decided that he needed to eat, and so eat he would.

As he sat, she winced at something on the side of his face—a burn or bruise no doubt.

"This business with Ramsey—"

"Is over," he said, hoping it was true.

"It is?"

"I think so. There was a fire at Drake's Wharf. No one saw Ramsey come out."

He didn't go so far as to say that the captain was dead, and she didn't ask.

"God forgive me for saying this, but I'm glad."

"That's a common sentiment." He paused, as Kelf arrived with an ale and a bowl of fish stew.

"Anything else, Ethan?" he asked, the words running together.

"No, Kelf. My thanks."

He began to eat, and found that he was ravenous after all. Just as Kannice had known he would be. "Gavin is dead," he said between mouthfuls.

"The old sea captain? The one who could conjure?"

"Aye."

"I'm sorry, Ethan. I know he was a friend."

"Ramsey controlled him with a spell. Gavin lured us to the wharf, and tried to kill Janna."

"Is she all right?"

"She'll be fine." He smiled. "She's stronger than all of us."

Kannice leaned down and kissed his cheek. "I'm not sure I believe that, but I'm glad she's well." She touched her lips to his, and he returned the kiss hungrily. "You'll be staying the night?" she asked.

"I'd like that."

She straightened. "Good. Eat up." She flashed a coy grin. "I want to be sure you have your strength."

It was a late night.

❦

Upon waking the following morning, Ethan found that he had slept far longer than he intended. Kannice had already left her bedroom; he could hear her moving around in the great room, and could smell bacon and fresh bread.

He swung out of bed, inhaling through his teeth with a sharp hiss at the ache of his abused muscles. Gingerly, he pulled clean, unburnt clothes from Kannice's wardrobe and dressed. Every movement hurt. His hat was gone, he realized, lost in the warehouse fire. He checked to be sure that he still had his knife and his pouch of mullein, and left the room.

As he neared the stairway that led down to the tavern, he heard voices from below: Kannice's, and a second that he recognized as that of Sheriff Greenleaf.

". . . Need to speak with him now!" the sheriff was saying, his voice rising.

"And I've already told you that he's sleeping."

"I'm here," he said, descending the stairs. "What do you need, Sheriff?"

Greenleaf seemed to be alone, though even on his own he could still be intimidating. Kannice, however, didn't appear to be the least bit frightened.

"We've been searching the warehouse, or what's left of it. I want you to accompany me to the wharf, and answer a few questions."

Ethan could tell that Kannice didn't like this idea. Neither did he, but he doubted that he had much choice.

"Of course," he said.

"And your breakfast?" she asked, with an arch glance at the sheriff.

"That will have to wait," Ethan said. "I'll be back before long."

Greenleaf looked like he might challenge this last, but he kept his silence and gestured for Ethan to lead him out the door.

Once they were on the street, Greenleaf started toward the North End, his strides so long, Ethan struggled to keep up with him.

"Did you find Ramsey's body?" Ethan asked, after a lengthy silence.

The sheriff, eyed him sidelong, but didn't answer.

"You don't know, do you?"

"His ship's gone," Greenleaf said.

Ethan faltered. "Damn."

"Before they left the wharf, his crew unloaded a gruesome cargo."

"Body parts."

"Aye."

"Skulls and hands."

"You know a good deal for a man who just woke a short while ago."

"I told you about the grave desecrations, and the shades Ramsey awakened. He stole those body parts so that he could bend the spirits to his will. If he left them, he has relinquished his control over the dead."

"Or his men, recognizing that since Ramsey was killed they had no need to keep such foul bounty aboard the vessel, rid themselves of it before putting out to sea."

"Tell me what you found in the warehouse."

"When we get there," Greenleaf said.

They covered the remaining distance in silence. It was another clear, hot day. Already Ethan's shirt was damp with sweat, and his bad leg was hurting. They were still on Princes Street, some distance from the wharf, when Ethan caught the scent of smoke riding the soft harbor breeze.

As Drake's Wharf came into view, Ethan saw that little remained of the warehouse. There were piles of charred rubble, and several human forms covered with burlap, but nothing remained of the walls. The adjacent buildings had mostly been spared, though the exterior walls of both were damaged.

"How many dead?"

"Six. Miss Pryce lost two men, but we don't know who the others were."

"One was Gavin Black," Ethan said.

Greenleaf's eyebrows went up. "Captain Black?"

"Aye."

"Some claimed that he was a speller."

"Is that so?"

Greenleaf rolled his eyes. "Was he working with Ramsey?"

Ethan didn't wish to explain the control spells Ramsey had used, but neither did he wish to lie outright to the man, no matter how obscure the truth might have been. All he said was "Ramsey killed him."

"So, that leaves three. One of them could have been Ramsey."

"That's possible."

"Spit it out, Kaille. Why don't you think that Ramsey is dead?"

"I haven't said that I don't."

"No, but you seem unwilling to admit that he might be. What are you keeping from me?"

Ethan sighed. Despite sleeping away half the morning, he remained

weary, and he found few things in his life more tiresome than his un-
ceasing verbal jousts with the good sheriff.

"I'm not keeping anything from you. You found six dead, and we've
accounted for three. Much of my memory of what happened yesterday
evening is clouded, but it seems to me that Ramsey's crew lost at least
as many men as Sephira did, perhaps more. In which case Ramsey
might not be one of those last three."

"I see. And the gruesome cargo his crew left on the wharf?"

Ethan dared not respond to this question with as much candor.
"That's harder to explain," he said, with intentional ambiguity. "It may
well mean that Ramsey is gone, and his men want nothing more to do
with his black arts. We can only hope."

Greenleaf's eyes narrowed. "You think he's still out there."

"I think he might be, yes. And wouldn't you prefer that I believe he's
alive, and thus remain vigilant, rather than assume he's dead and let
down my guard?"

"Aye," the sheriff said. "That I would."

"Is there anything else, Sheriff?"

"No. As you say, I'll be expecting you to keep watch, and to let me
know if you find Ramsey, or even hear rumors of him. This is still your
mess, Kaille, and I'll hold you responsible until I see the man's corpse."

Ethan left him at Drake's Wharf, and thought of going to see Alexander Rowan. He had asked Ethan to keep him apprised of the inquiry,
and had hinted at offering Ethan a bit of coin for his trouble. On the
one hand, Ethan was not yet certain that the inquiry was over, and even
if it was, he remained convinced of what he had said to Reverend Caner
the day it began: This was a dark business, and he didn't think anyone
should profit from it. On the other hand, he had ruined several shirts
and a couple of waistcoats in the past several days. He would have welcomed a few pounds. He resolved to seek out Mr. Rowan in another day
or two, when the emotions of the past week were not quite so raw.

Instead, he walked west along Ferry Way to the Water Mill and the
Mill Dam. In the heat, with the level of water down because of the lack
of rain, the pond smelled especially rank. But the dam itself was deserted, and Ethan welcomed the solitude. Halfway across, he stopped
and cast an illusion spell using the water as a source. It was a simple

conjuring. He sent an image of himself into his room over Henry's cooperage, and was able to see through its eyes the disarray left by his
battle with Ramsey: the shattered door and broken window. Shelly sat
on the stairway landing outside the doorway. She whined at the sight of
Ethan's conjuring and stood, baring her teeth. Dogs, he had noticed
before, responded this way to illusion spells, as well as to spectral
guides.

"It's all right, Shelly," Ethan said through the image he had summoned. "It's just me."

The dog gave a tentative wag of her tail.

Ethan allowed the conjuring to end, and opened his eyes to the
bright glare of the summer sun. A simple conjuring: just the sort of
spell that Ramsey's control of the shades had made impossible a single
day before. Perhaps the captain *was* dead.

Reg stood beside him, ghostly pale in the sunlight.

"I can conjure," Ethan said. "Does that mean that the boundary
between the living world and the realm of the dead is whole again?"

The old warrior nodded.

"Is Ramsey dead?"

A shrug.

"Right. Very well. My thanks for all you've done the past few days."

The ghost offered a small bow and vanished.

Ethan finished crossing the dam into New Boston, and followed
Leveret's Street down to Lynde, where sat the Walters house. At his
knock on the door, Ruth opened the door, her son in her arms.

"Ethan!" she said, smiling. "Darcy," she called into the house. "It's
Ethan."

She waved him inside, and Darcy joined them in the common room.

"Whatever you did worked," he said, gripping Ethan's hand. "We're
grateful to you."

"She wasn't here last night?" Ethan asked.

Ruth shook her head. She still looked drawn, but she was smiling
again; Ethan couldn't remember the last time he had seen her look so at
ease.

"I'm glad," he said. "I hope that she remains at rest now, as she deserves."

"We feel that we should pay you for your time," Ruth said.

"No, thank you."

"Will you at least sup with us?"

"I'd like that. In a day or two perhaps."

Ruth nodded, and as she did, Benjamin began to fuss. "He's hungry, and ready to nap. I'll take him to our room. Thank you again, Ethan." With a last glance at her husband, she retreated to the back of the house.

"What *did* you do?" Darcy asked, once he and Ethan were alone.

"I prefer not to speak of it. What matters is, I managed to shield her from the influence of another conjurer, and in the end her shade actually saved my life. To be honest, as glad as I am for your sake and Ruth's that she's gone, I had almost hoped to see her again, so that I could thank her. I suppose I'll have to thank you, instead."

"You were a good friend to her in life, Ethan. And whatever you had to do to bring peace to her spirit, I can't thank you enough."

"You're welcome." Ethan returned to the door, but after stepping outside, he turned to Darcy once more. "If by some chance she comes back, you'll let me know, won't you?"

Darcy frowned. "Do you think that's possible?"

"I don't know," Ethan said with a shrug. "Probably not. Forget that I mentioned it."

He started to walk away.

"You'll join us for supper one night?"

"Absolutely. Send a message to me at the Dowser."

Rather than heading back to the tavern or to his room in the South End, Ethan followed Cambridge Street out to Pest House Point, and the Province Hospital. He knew better than to think that he would be allowed to enter the building to see Holin, Elli, and Clara, but he hoped that he could get word of the boy's condition.

As he approached the hospital, he saw no less a personage than Dr. Joseph Warren emerging from its front entrance.

Ethan hailed him, at first drawing a puzzled look. As Ethan drew nearer, recognition lit the doctor's face.

"Mister Kaille," Warren said. "The thieftaker who doesn't wish to ally himself with the cause of liberty."

"Aye, Doctor. I'm flattered that you remember."

Ethan was still several strides away from the stairs leading to the door, but Warren held up a hand to stop him.

"I wouldn't come closer than that, sir."

Ethan slowed, then halted.

"What brings you out here, Mister Kaille?"

"A friend of mine was taken with smallpox a few days ago. I wish to know how he's faring."

"You know you can't go inside."

"Aye, but perhaps you know of him."

"Perhaps. His name?"

"Holin Harper. A young man of nineteen years."

"Ah, yes!" Warren said. "He's doing well, and as of yet, neither his mother nor his sister has taken ill."

"So, you expect him to recover?" Ethan asked. He felt a loosening in his chest; he hadn't realized how much he feared for the lad until those fears were put to rest.

"Yes, I do."

"Will he be scarred?"

Warren's expression clouded. "That I can't say, although in most cases there is some scarring."

"Of course. Thank you, Doctor."

Ethan started to turn away, but after a moment's pause, faced Warren once more.

"Did you notice anything different in the hospital last night?" Ethan asked.

Warren stared back at him and took one step closer. "What do you mean?"

"I think you know." Ethan kept his voice just loud enough for Warren to hear. "For several nights, this building was populated by shades. I'm wondering if last night was different."

"How do you know of this?" Warren asked.

"You already know the answer to that, Doctor," Ethan said, lowering his voice further. "Mister Adams has told you that I'm a conjurer. I was asked by Reverend Henry Caner to look into a matter involving desecrated graves and, it turned out, restless spirits. And when Holin was first taken ill, I came here, and saw the shades myself."

"Reverend Caner also knows that you're a . . . What did you call yourself? A conjurer?"

"Aye, Reverend Caner has some inkling of my abilities, but he also knows that I have never used my powers for evil purposes, and so he . . . he tolerates my presence here in the city."

"I see. To answer your question, yes, last night was different. For the first time in nearly a week, we saw none of the demons at all."

"I'm glad," Ethan said. "And I dare to hope that you won't encounter them again."

"I'm pleased to hear that. I know that my colleagues here will be as well."

Ethan raised a hand in farewell, and turned away.

"We could use your talents in our struggle for liberty, thieftaker. I hope that you'll consider joining us."

Ethan didn't answer, but he glanced back at the doctor and nodded once before beginning the lengthy walk to the central part of the city. Perhaps he would join them eventually. But for now he was too weary to contemplate such a thing.

He next paid a visit to King's Chapel, where he informed Mr. Pell and Reverend Caner of Ramsey's disappearance, and the discovery of the missing body parts.

"That last we had already learned," Caner told him. "Mister Thomson has already begun the grisly task of restoring the graves to their previous condition."

"Graves were desecrated in other burying grounds," Ethan said.

Pell nodded. "We know. We'll see to it that everything that was taken is returned."

"We're indebted to you, Mister Kaille," Caner said. "I know that you refused once to let us pay you, but I would offer again."

"My thanks, reverend sir, but I have no intention of changing my mind in this regard."

"Very well." Caner proffered a hand. "I suppose my gratitude will have to do instead."

Ethan shook his hand, and allowed Pell to escort him from the chapel.

Once they were outside, the young minister said, "You spoke of Ramsey disappearing. Others indicated he was dead."

"Aye. There's some dispute about that."

Pell eyed him, his youthful face pale and grave. "There's no dispute. You're convinced that he's alive, and I'm inclined to believe you."

Ethan gazed out over the churchyard, squinting against the sun. "I could be wrong."

"I don't think so. But I have to ask, if Ramsey yet lived, wouldn't he still wish to control the shades he set loose upon the city?"

"In other words, why would he have his crew give back all that he stole from the burying grounds?"

"Aye," Pell said.

"I haven't an answer. It may be that his crew prevailed upon him to give up this particular fight. Or he may have feared that I would summon the ghost of his father once again. He didn't like it when I did that; not at all. And I think he knows that I would have pursued the matter if he didn't return all that he stole. He may believe that he's bought for himself a bit of time." Ethan shrugged. "He may well be right."

"But you think he'll be back."

Ethan faced his friend. "Like I said, I could be wrong about all of this. I've spent the last several days watching over my shoulder, expecting at every turn to see Ramsey coming after me. Chances are, he really is gone. I came close to dying in that fire yesterday, and I wasn't buried under half the building, the way Ramsey was."

Pell seemed to weigh this. "Well," he said. "He's gone for now."

"Aye, he is. And good riddance."

From the chapel, Ethan walked out along the Neck to the Fat Spider so that he could look in on Janna.

He found her sitting at a table, a shawl around her shoulders and a cup of watered Madeira in front of her. She greeted him with a wan smile and waved him over to the chair next to hers.

"I'm tired today," she said. "If you want some wine, you can get it yourself."

"No, thank you. I just wanted to see how you're healing."

She pulled her shawl tighter. "I heal just fine."

They sat for some time, not speaking, until at last Janna said, "Ole Black used to come around here every now and then, just to eat a bit and talk about his conjurin' days. I'll miss that."

"I'll miss him, too. We didn't spend much time in each other's company, but he was a good man and a reliable friend." He stood. "I'll come see you again soon, Janna."

"All right."

He walked to the door, but paused with his hand on the lever. "Do you think Ramsey is dead?"

"Do you?" she asked.

Ethan looked back at her. "I'm almost certain that he's not."

She didn't appear surprised. "My spells are workin' again."

"Mine are, too. And the shades are gone. So, maybe I'm wrong."

"Maybe. Just the same, you watch yourself. If he's alive still, he'll be comin' back for you."

Ethan nodded and left her, making his way to Cooper's Alley and Henry's cooperage. He found the cooper planing a new door for his room, and spent the rest of day helping Henry with repairs. When they were done, Ethan was able to lock his room again, which he did before returning to the Dowser to spend the night with Kannice.

Chapter
TWENTY-FIVE

hey buried Nigel the next morning in the Common
Burying Ground. Ethan reached the gravesite just as a minister
he didn't recognize began to speak. More people had come to
the burial than Ethan would have expected. In addition to Sephira,
Mariz, Nap, Gordon, and Pryce's other toughs, he saw Greenleaf and
several men of the watch, Dunc, and a number of people he didn't recognize, including a young woman with two small, yellow-haired children. The woman and her children wept openly. Ethan had never
stopped to consider that Nigel might have a wife and family. He felt
like an idiot, and wondered if he should leave before too many people
saw him there.

But even as the thought came, Sephira spotted him, her gaze lingering on him for the span of a heartbeat before returning to the minister.
She didn't send Nap or the others to chase him off, and he took this as
leave to remain.

The service lasted but a few minutes. Sephira's men lowered a large,
simple coffin into the grave, and took turns throwing handfuls of dirt
over it. Sephira said something to Mariz, who walked around the grave
and approached Ethan.

"The *senhora* invites you to take part in the interment," he said.

Ethan hesitated.

"It is all right, Kaille. None of us blames you for this."

"Thank you," Ethan said.

He followed Mariz to the gravesite and joined the line of mourners. When it was his turn, he bent, took a handful of earth in his hand, and tossed it onto the coffin, which was already mostly covered.

"Good-bye, Yellow-hair," he whispered. He moved out of the way of the next person in line, and wound up next to Nap, who glanced at him and nodded a greeting.

When the last of the mourners had his turn, a pair of laborers, who until now had kept their distance, walked to the grave and began in earnest to fill it in.

Sephira approached Ethan.

"It was kind of you to come," she said, with uncharacteristic sincerity.

"It was kind of you to let me stay."

She shrugged, allowing her gaze to wander. She looked even lovelier than usual, dressed entirely in black, her curls hanging loose over her shoulders. Her eyes were dry, but he had never seen her so pale.

"He had a family?" Ethan asked.

Sephira nodded. "That surprises you."

"Very much. And I feel like a fool because of it."

"Well, good. Nigel always enjoyed making you feel like a fool."

She grinned, as did Ethan.

"I'm sure he did," he said. They fell into a brief, awkward silence. "I should go."

"I lost two other men to Ramsey and his crew," she said, before he could walk away.

"I know. I'm sorry for that."

"Sheriff Greenleaf tells me that you think he's still alive."

"I think it's possible."

"If I meet him again, I'll kill him on sight."

"With my blessing," Ethan said.

She nodded. "Good. As long as we understand each other."

"We do in this."

Her expression hardened. "Meaning what?"

"Meaning that I still plan to work for the wealthiest clients I can find, and there's not much you can do to stop me."

He saw a familiar gleam in her eyes. "That," she said, "is a conversation for another day."

❧❦❧

It was a short walk back to the Dowser, but Ethan covered the distance slowly, his gaze fixed on the sparkling waters of the harbor. Several ships approached Boston's wharves on sweeps, while others, their sails unfurled, carved across the water's surface, heading out to sea. He spotted an eagle circling above, and his heart stopped for just an instant. A memory flashed through his mind: the eagle Ramsey had conjured to lead him out to the *Muirenn* before their reunion on Tileston's Wharf a few days earlier.

This eagle, though, was real. He heard it cry out, saw it dive at a gull to steal a fish that the second bird carried in its beak.

Ethan breathed again.

"Where are you, Ramsey?" he said, whispering the words to the wind.

The eagle called again, grasping its pilfered meal in its talons.

Ethan walked on to the Dowsing Rod, trying to shake off his fears. For now, he knew, the captain was gone. He might be back before long. But for today—for the time being—he could rest easy.

Upon reaching the tavern, he found it empty, save for three laborers who stood at the bar, drinking ale and eating oysters. Kelf winked a greeting. Kannice came out from behind the bar and walked with him to a back table.

Resting on the table was a new tricorn hat.

"For me?" he asked.

"Unless you think it would look better on me."

"I'm sure it would. How did you know that I'd lost the old one?"

"You've been wearing the same damned hat just about every day since we met. Don't you think I would notice when you stopped wearing it?"

He tried it on, though he knew that Kannice would have found one that fit him perfectly. She had.

"How does it look?"

Kannice tilted her head to the side, regarding him with a critical eye. "Clean," she said at last. "Mercifully clean."

"I'm sure," he said, laughing. "Thank you. I feel badly that I don't have anything for you."

She smiled. "There are remedies for that."

"You do remember that I haven't yet earned anything for this most recent job."

"Aye, but you will. You said that Mister Rowan intends to pay you. And I also remember that before helping Reverend Caner you worked for Andrew Ellis."

"That I did. Very well, my lady," he said, offering her his arm. "What shall it be? A bauble? A new kerchief?"

She shook her head. "A sweet."

Ethan raised an eyebrow. "A sweet?"

"Aye. I've had my fill of chowder and oysters and ale. I want some sort of confection, and I know just the place to get it."

"Very well. Lead on."

She pulled him toward the door. They passed Kelf, who shook his head and gave a basso chuckle, and then they were on the street, basking in the warmth and the sunlight, confident that for at least one more day, the skies over Boston would remain clear.

Still, as they strolled arm in arm toward Faneuil Hall, Ethan couldn't help but glance toward the harbor, his eyes scanning the sunlit waters for one small, well-tended merchant ship.

Historical Note

As I have mentioned in previous historical notes, my goal in writing historical fantasy is to blend, as seamlessly as possible, my fantastical and fictional elements with the actual historical events that form the backdrop for my stories. The Thieftaker books begin with two significant historical conceits: that thieftakers were active in the American colonies, and that there were conjurers casting spells in pre-Revolutionary Boston. Neither of these things is true. So it may seem odd that I would make such a great effort to get my history right when the conceptual underpinnings of the series have no basis in fact. To which I can simply say, yes, I'm rather odd. . . .

Setting aside thieftakers and conjurers, the historical elements of this novel are largely accurate. During the late spring and summer of 1769, Boston suffered through what turned out to be a relatively mild outbreak of smallpox. Many of those afflicted were relocated to the hospital in New Boston—the so-called Pest House. Boston's selectmen did, in fact, hire men to guard the houses of those who came down with the disease but refused to leave their homes. And the bodies of those who died from the disease were treated as described in this book after the death of Mrs. Tyler. (Mrs. Tyler, by the way, was actually one of Boston's smallpox fatalities that summer, and the names of the men hired to guard houses, as well as their wages, are also taken from real events.) Nearly all of the information about smallpox and the city's response to the outbreak comes from the minutes of the town selectmen's 1769 meetings.

HISTORICAL NOTE

For more information on the scholarly and primary sources I have used for this and other Thieftaker books and stories—along with a good deal of other information—please visit my website: www.dbjackson-author.com.

Acknowledgments

Once again, I have many people to thank for their help on this novel. Dr. John C. Willis, professor of United States history at Sewanee, the University of the South, helped me with the history and offered encouragement and support. Dr. Christopher M. McDonough, professor of classical languages at Sewanee, once again translated the spells cast by Ethan, Ramsey, Janna, and Mariz, proving that Latin really can be fun. Dr. Robert D. Hughes, professor of systematic theology at the School of Theology of the University of the South, offered me guidance on writing about the Anglican Church and its offices.

As always, I wish to thank the Norman B. Leventhal Map Center at the Boston Public Library, in particular Catherine T. Wood, the center's office manager, for allowing us to use the map of Boston that appears at the front of the book.

Any mistakes that remain despite the best efforts of all these very smart people are entirely my own.

Without my agent, Lucienne Diver, Ethan and his stories would still be merely ideas floating around in my head. I am grateful to her for her professionalism, her friendship, and her insightful editorial feedback on this novel. I also wish to thank Deirdre Knight, Jia Giles, and the other great people at the Knight Agency.

This novel has had several editors working on it and shepherding it through the production process: Many thanks to James Frenkel, Stacy Hague-Hill, and Marco Palmieri. I'm also deeply grateful to Tom

ACKNOWLEDGMENTS

Doherty, Irene Gallo and her staff, Cassie Ammerman, Leah Withers, and all the wonderful people at Tor Books. I also wish to thank my friend Terry McGarry for copyediting the book.

Deepest thanks to my colleagues at the Magical Words blogsite (www.magicalwords.net): Faith Hunter, Misty Massey, John Hartness, James Tuck, Carrie Ryan, Mindy Klasky, and Diana Pharaoh Francis. And special thanks to the readers of the Magical Words blog, who critiqued the first several paragraphs of this book and steered me toward a more effective and concise opening. Many thanks as well to C. E. Murphy, Charles Coleman Finlay, Kat Richardson, Blake Charlton, Kate Elliott, Eric Flint, Mary Robinette Kowal, Alethea Kontis, Stephen Leigh, Lynn Flewelling, Joshua Palmatier, A. J. Hartley, Stuart Jaffe, Edmund Schubert, Kalayna Price, and Patricia Bray, all of whom have contributed to this series in one way or another through e-mails, online exchanges, and the occasional conversation over beers.

Finally, I am more grateful than I can say to my wife and daughters, who keep me smiling and constantly remind me that there are more important things in life than outlines, revisions, and books sales.

D. B. JACKSON is the award-winning author of fifteen fantasy novels, many short stories, and the occasional media tie-in. His books have been translated into more than a dozen languages. He has a master's degree and Ph.D. in U.S. history, which have come in handy as he has written the Thieftaker novels and short stories. He and his family live in the mountains of Appalachia.

Visit him at www.dbjackson-author.com.